Des Wilson is well known in Britain as a journalist, campaigner on social issues, and politician.

He was born in New Zealand in 1941 and travelled to London in 1960 to become a journalist. He eventually became a columnist on the *Guardian* and *The Observer* and a contributor to *The Times*, the *Independent*, the *Spectator*, the *New Statesman*, and for two years deputy editor of the *Illustrated London News*. He has written a number of campaigning books and also for Sphere BATTLE FOR POWER, the story of the Liberal-SDP Alliance 1987 General Election campaign.

As a campaigner he has been director of Shelter, the National Campaign for the Homeless, chairman of Friends of the Earth, chairman of the CLEAR campaign for lead-free petrol, chairman of the Campaign for Freedom of Information, and director of Citizen Action. He was President of the Liberal Party in 1986–87.

Des Wilson now lives in Brighton. This is his first novel.

COSTA DEL SOL

by

Des Wilson

SPHERE BOOKS LIMITED

A Sphere Book

First published in Great Britain in 1990 by
Macdonald & Co (Publishers) Ltd,
London & Sydney

This edition also published in 1990 by Sphere Books Ltd

Printed and bound in Great Britain by
Cox & Wyman Ltd, Reading

ISBN 0–7474–0648–0

A Division of
Macdonald & Co (Publishers) Ltd
Orbit House
1 New Fetter Lane
London EC4A 1AR

A member of Maxwell Macmillan Pergamon Publishing Corporation

In memory of
my Father
and with love to
my Mother,

Mr and Mrs A.H. Wilson,
New Zealand

Acknowledgements

All the poetry in this book is that of Federico Garcia Lorca, translations by Carlos Bauer (Poem of the Deep Song and Ode to Walt Whitman & other poems, City Lights Books, 1987 and 1988).

In addition to my own travels in Andalusia I owe a particular debt to many contributors to the splendid LOOKOUT magazine, and to David Baird's 'Inside Andalusia' (a LOOKOUT publication), John Hooper's 'The Spaniards' (Penguin), Julian A. Pitt-River's 'The People of the Sierra' (University of Chicago Press), and Jan Morris's 'Spain' (Penguin).

I owe special thanks to my wife Jane for limitless encouragement; to friends who kindly read and commented upon the manuscript ... Perrott Phillips, Marcel Berlins and Geoffrey Wansell; to Paul Wilson who helped out in an emergency; and above all to Barbara Boote, my generous and supportive publisher.

Through the high passes
two gentlemen are strolling

(New
  sky.
  Blue
  sky !)

. . . two gentlemen are strolling
who before were hunters

(Old sky.
  Gold sky !)

. . . two gentlemen are strolling
who before were . . .

(Night.)

Prologue

His was an old man's face. A peasant's face. Andalusia itself, especially this mountainous region, the Serrania de Ronda, was etched upon it. Its relentless summer heat in the colour. Its poverty and injustice in ravine-like lines across the coarse skin. Its dignity and secrets in the calm, enigmatic eyes. Occasionally there was a grimace as the mule stumbled on the rocky ground and jarred his barely-protected bones, but for much of the slow journey from the high walls of Ronda across the *finca*-covered plain and over the hills towards his lonely *cortijo* many kilometres away, it was a face as unmoving as it was rough, a mirror-image of the land itself.

Until now.

Now, as he tugged on the rope around the mule's scrawny neck, drawing it to a halt, his eyes widened with surprise, then narrowed in a mixture of suspicion and contempt.

The stranger blocking his path was in his mid-thirties, tall, slim, with hair so sun-bleached that it was almost white. He was dressed immaculately in an expensive lightweight grey suit, a burgundy-red shirt, and a grey

1

tie that accentuated cold grey eyes. On the streets of Malaga or Seville he would have been one of many, just another banker or lawyer, but, standing on this stony mountain path so rarely used that it was almost indistinguishable from the surrounding terrain, he looked singularly out of place, his appearance in total contrast to that of the man he faced.

It was less an encounter between generations, between affluence and poverty, between urban and rural man, than it was a confrontation between centuries and cultures.

'*Hola*, old man.'

There was no answer. The mule and his once-more expressionless rider were now so still that, in silhouette on the hilltop, they looked as if they had been sculpted out of the landscape. As in a way they had been, for both animal and man had been conceived and born in the *sierras*; they had for years survived the hot summer days and the bitterly cold winter nights because of their ability to blend into and live off these hills and valleys. This was why, according to local legend, the man had avoided capture. Some said for being a *guerrillero* in the civil war. Others said for being a smuggler, a *contrabandista*. Still others, for being a *bandido*. It was even said that at various times he had been all three. To these stories the old man would slowly shake his head, perhaps with the hint of a twinkle in those tranquil brown eyes. If he had not been captured, he would say, it was because he had not been hunted. He was, he would claim, just a peasant ... at times a charcoal burner, a whitewash maker, a breeder of pigs, a shepherd, and now a hunter of rabbits to sell in the restaurants of Ronda.

Whatever the truth of the legend, this last was a fact. The few who had seen him hunt said he knew a rabbit was there before he could see it, that his senses were so tuned to these *sierras* that he could creep close enough to

2

his targets to almost catch them by the ears. This, they said, accounted for his high strike rate, the few wasted pellets, and the regular score of 100 or more rabbits that would be hung in straw baskets on either side of the mule as he travelled once a week to Ronda, where within hours they appeared on the menu, usually cooked in garlic – *conejo al ajillo*. This, too, was why he was known as El Conejero – the Rabbit Man.

If he now wondered how the stranger could appear from nowhere looking so clean and cool when he must have had to climb and hike for several hours from the road to this isolated place, he showed no sign of it.

But then hadn't his one old friend, Miguel, on whose stone floor he had slept only last night after they had been gently and good-heartedly evicted from their customary corner of the bar in Ronda ... hadn't Miguel challenged him many times: 'Señor Conejo ... Mr Rabbit ... when do you show what you think in that peasant head of yours? When do you ever smile? When do you show anger? Or surprise? When does your face change ... when does it show you're alive ... except at *la corrida de toros*? Only then it is alive. Or do you also smile when you confront your *conejo*?' Always the old man's only answer had been to call for another bottle of red wine, his face as impassive as it was at this meeting on the mountain path.

'I came to see whether you've changed your mind,' the stranger now said in crude but comprehensible Spanish.

The rider slowly, almost imperceptibly, shook his head.

'Oh, come on, old man.' The stranger was pleading, but with ill-disguised exasperation. 'Why must you live like this? Look at you – you're decrepit, you've damn-near had it. Soon you won't be able to climb on that mule. Soon you won't be able to see the rabbits, won't be

3

able to hit them with that old gun of yours. Then what? Where will you get the money to buy your food, your vino? Take the money, old man – you can forget all this, live your last days well, make your *cortijo* warm in the winter, or live in Ronda, or even on the coast. Make sense, old man.'

The rider's only response was to tug at the rope, and then to use it to flick the mule around the neck. It remained rooted to the spot. Even when he gave it a gentle kick he was mutinously ignored. But these were old adversaries, rider and mule, and the second kick was less gentle, the third a painful warning that the familiar ritual had gone far enough. The mule mournfully inched forward towards the younger man, who was forced to step aside.

'This is your last chance, old man, Rabbit Man. Don't be a fool. Take the money. Live your last days well.'

As he passed, the rider looked briefly down into the stranger's face. At last he spoke.

'*Adiós,*' he said.

With that, the mule and his master picked their way between the rocks, down into a gully, then up to the brow of another hill. There they paused while the old rider looked down into a magnificent, barely-accessible valley, his eyes ranging across the cork and cypress trees to its green meadows and its dramatic-looking ravine, then on to a small cluster of orange and lemon trees surrounding a lonely white stone farmhouse, *el cortijo*. His gaze took in the little crops of yellow sunflowers, a golden pasture of bloom, the herbs growing wild on the hillside, lavender, sage and thyme, and then the bare red and brown hills rising, one after another, beyond the valley itself.

If his friend Miguel had been there then, at this moment on top of this hill, he would have seen for the second time that day an uncharacteristic change of

4

expression in the old man's eyes. But this was not a hardening into suspicion – this was a softening. He was nearly home, both reassured by the familiar and peaceful scene below and relieved that he would soon be able to drag his leathery bottom from the esparto and straw saddle on the mule's bony back and exercise his stiff and aching legs.

Eager to be there, he nudged the mule onwards and downwards. There was no resistance now. The animal was also responding to the draw of the valley. Resentful and stubborn it could be, but, contrary to the rider's many slanders upon its name, the mule was not stupid; the sooner it got to the *cortijo* the sooner it would be relieved of its human burden.

Instead of taking the obvious detour to the right at the foot of the hill to avoid the ravine, they cut across the grass-covered floor of the valley to where this fissure in its floor was bridged by a few logs and planks tied together with thick rope. Men as brave as matadors would have blanched at the thought of crossing the ravine this way, but the old man and his mule approached it without fear. This was their own bridge. Their short-cut to home, food and sleep. They could have traversed it blindfolded.

The ravine was only five metres wide. They were halfway over the makeshift bridge before the old man was conscious of being followed. There was a sound, and then stunning pain as a sharp rock hit the back of his head. The shock of the blow caused him to jerk the rope round the mule's neck and it stumbled to the left, its front legs beginning to crumple under it. Desperately he tried to drag it back to its feet and to the right. For a few seconds it appeared as if the animal was regaining its balance but then, fatally, its rider concentrated all of his strength on one last pull. It had the opposite effect. The mule's legs slid from under it and, together, animal and

5

rider toppled sideways and tumbled into the crevasse.

The mule fell with an awful, panic-stricken, honking wail, a sound so full of terror that rabbits in their grassy hiding places froze in fear.

The man fell without a sound. Possibly panic had stilled his ancient heart. Probably he was just as stoic in the face of death as he had been in life.

For a few moments all was silent and unmoving. It was as if even the mountains themselves were shocked by the drama that had been played out within their hidden valley. Then the blond stranger stepped from the shade of a tree above the ravine and descended carefully to its edge.

On reaching it he lit a cigarette and, it being his last match, carelessly tossed the empty book into the chasm at his feet.

For several minutes he looked down, trying to discern any movement. Then he untied the rope around the logs and planks and one by one hurled them onto the bodies far below.

The nearby *cortijo* looked as if it had been abandoned for years. The stranger guessed it probably had been before the old man moved in, confident of being undisturbed by an absentee landlord. Beside the stone hut was a crudely-made wooden lean-to, a shady resting place for the mule, shared with a few tired-looking hens. Part of the *cortijo* wall was blackened; clearly the old man had for most of the year heated water for his coffee or cooked his rabbit stew over an open fire. There was no door, but a heavy hand-woven wool curtain kept out the light and the heat of the sun. The focal point of the one room was another fireplace, a big grey-stone one, ashes still in the grate. It was surrounded by sticks and logs and in front of it was an old rocking chair. To the left of the fireplace there were a table and two chairs, a number of pots and pans and some cutlery on a wooden bench, and two old rifles propped up in a corner. To the right, but near to the fireplace for warmth, there was a pile of bedding on the clay floor. Rabbit skins hung from the beams in the ceiling.

The smell of the skins, no doubt redolent of home and good hunting to the old man, caused the stranger to recoil in shock, but, grimacing in disgust, he began thoroughly to search the meagre furniture and possessions.

Onto the table he put every piece of paper he could find. There weren't many. He studied each carefully but whatever he was seeking was not there.

Frustrated, he tossed the last item onto the pile and went over every inch of the hut a second time. His only fresh discovery was a dirty, torn envelope containing some photographs, most of them years old and badly faded, but one or two more recent, and one a striking colour picture of a beautiful, dark-haired girl, aged about twelve, in traditional Andalusian costume, taken, judging by the background, at a fair.

Finally, satisfied that the object of his search wasn't to be found, he left, too intent on removing his tie and gasping for clean air to immediately feel the impact of the mid-afternoon sun.

After a few minutes he took the path back to the top of the hill from where, sweating now, he looked down on the same peaceful and desolate scene the old man had surveyed less than an hour earlier.

Just as he was about to turn away, a movement caught his eye.

He stared intently into the valley. There it was again, near to where the bridge had been. Definitely a movement.

Was there a witness to the old man's death?

He waited for a few tense minutes and then, at last, he saw what it was.

A rabbit.

He smiled, grimly.

No-one's going to kill you, he thought. There's no Rabbit Man now ... there'll be no *conejo* on the menu in Ronda for a while.

He turned away and began to walk west towards the road he had left some four hours back, the road that would return him to Ronda, to San Pedro de Alcantera ... to the Costa del Sol.

Chapter One

SUNDAY, MARCH 18, 1990

The white and red-orange Air Europe plane began its descent above the hills surrounding Malaga, swept on over the shimmering Mediterranean, and then swung in a leisurely semi-circle across the sea to land on the bumpy single runway beside the Rock of Gibraltar some 130 kilometres further south.

At the front of the plane the Club Class steward sighed with relief. It had been a miserable journey. He liked his work and flattered himself he was convivial company, but the only two passengers in his small section, both men, travelling separately and oblivious of each other in their self-absorption, had been indifferent to his hospitality, each only toying with the smoked salmon and scarcely touching his champagne. He could have been catering for a funeral.

As the plane came to a stop a few yards from the small terminal building, one of the men, the distinguished-looking, expensively-dressed one, picked up a

9

black leather briefcase and moved swiftly, impatiently to the exit.

The other, unshaven, untidy-looking, hesitated before slowly unfastening his seat belt and gathering together his belongings.

Bill Sheedy's problem was that he couldn't decide what to do about the red-haired girl sitting a few rows back in Economy.

For the whole of the flight he had been absorbed by the dilemma.

Or by what he perceived as a dilemma.

For once, Sheedy, calm, easy-going, imperturbable, rational Sheedy, was not thinking clearly, shaken by the sudden surfacing of half-forgotten desires and unfamiliar doubts ... all caused by the girl with red hair.

There were, he convinced himself, just two options. To consolidate their friendship as it was, close, good-humoured, trusting, but platonic. Or to risk jeopardising it by, in effect, raising the stakes and seeking to become her lover.

Now, as they walked across the tarmac, he felt her softly take his arm.

'Hey, Sheedy,' she said, 'thanks for the bubbly.'

Embarrassed that his office had booked him Club Class when she was flying Economy, he had asked the Chief Steward to take her some Moet and Chandon.

'That's OK,' he said, 'I wish you'd let me change places. Then you could have had the slippers and hot towels too.'

'Only old men like you wander round in public in slippers. I prefer to show off my toes.' She lifted a shapely leg and wriggled a foot at him, her brightly-painted toenails glinting in the sun.

He laughed. Now he was back in her company, her warm smile and her relaxed confidence in their friendship were already making his confusion and uncertainties seem foolish. He felt better. Maybe he could handle this thing – whichever way it went.

'Come on,' he said to her, 'let's get our bags and hit the road. Tonight you're going to have your first *gambas pil pil* and *conejo al ajillo*. If the garlic doesn't knock you out, the Rioja will.'

Sheedy's only half-noticed fellow passenger, Sir Brian Cruickshank, unencumbered by luggage, had already waved his UK passport at immigration, passed by the one sleepy customs officer, and was climbing into the chauffeur-driven, olive-green Rolls Royce that had been waiting outside the terminal, conspicuous alongside a score or more of tiny, weary-looking hire cars.

Cruickshank, too, had spent the journey tormented by unaccustomed doubts.

He, too, was now reminding himself to keep a sense of perspective, but with less success than Sheedy, probably because his problem loomed larger. His project – the Spanish project that would seal his business career, consolidate his wealth, change his whole way of life – appeared to be in jeopardy, and all because of the insane act of one man.

'Is Mr Canning waiting at the yacht?' he asked the chauffeur.

'Yes, Sir Brian.'

'Good.'

But there was no pleasure in his voice, only controlled anger. He sat back and, as he had done on the plane, gloomily reviewed the options.

He, too, had concluded that there were only two courses of action, but in his case both were unpalatable.

Whatever he chose to do, the fun had gone out of the thing.

And for that the man he was travelling to see would not be forgiven.

11

*

How much more straight-forward life had been just four hours earlier. Her flight from New York had been delayed and Sheedy had settled himself at one end of a semi-circular bar in the departure lounge at Gatwick's South Terminal. Untypically, he had ordered a gin and tonic. He didn't usually drink before noon but he was counting on the chilled gin to give him a bit of a lift after a sleepless night and, judging by the way the alcohol hit the spot, it had been a good move.

He didn't mind the delay. He liked the slightly manic atmosphere of airports and amused himself by inventing stories about the other travellers – who they were, where they were going and why. Even now he was chuckling to himself as in his imagination he sent them off as eloping lovers to Mexico, smugglers to Marseilles or spies to Moscow.

A big fair-haired man, Sheedy was just over six feet tall and of what he liked to describe as 'comfortable build', (i.e. by no means disguising a love of food and drink), and a 'variable' forty-seven, (meaning that he could, when rested and relaxed, get away with being nearer forty, while after a bad night he could appear to be in his early fifties).

His face was his strength, reflecting warmth and humour and encouraging trust. People found it easy to talk to him, quickly took to him. As a reporter he got half his stories that way. His blue eyes were the outstanding feature: they were watchful and perceptive but – and this was the giveaway – they were kind. In his days as a managing editor he had been a hopeless disciplinarian of the younger staff members.

And yet he could also be tough and obstinate. There were scores of victims of his investigative reporting to testify that he had been fearless and relentless in pursuit of stories they would have preferred unpublished. Employers and even colleagues and friends could also find him discomfortingly stubborn. Sheedy was not a 'yes man'. He was an uncompromising searcher for truth, a reporter of the old school, raised on a small local paper in Connecticut to believe journalism was about public service as well as private gain. He had arrived in New York with a reputation for getting his stories right and for striving to make the power of the media work for those who had most need of it, the disadvantaged and exploited.

After several years as a top City Desk reporter, his life was threatened by a crime syndicate he was investigating. The newspaper took it seriously and, over-ruling his objections, transferred him to the Foreign Desk to get him out of the country for a while. As he good-humouredly complained at the time, this gesture of concern would have been more gratifying if they hadn't then sent him into the holocaust called Vietnam, from where he became famous for his distinctive coverage of the war. Refusing to get by on the hand-outs and the carefully-arranged front-line trips organised by the army's PR men, Sheedy was one of the first to reveal the unique horrors of that conflict and to tell of its de-humanising effect on US servicemen as well as on the Vietnamese.

This didn't make him popular in Washington or with the jingoistic brigade but his fellow journalists recognised the risks he was taking and the truth he was telling. To them he returned a hero in his own right.

But he also returned to a wife who had become sick and so, abandoning reporting, he elected to work as a sub-editor on a Manhattan tabloid so that he could be within reach in an emergency. Soon he became the paper's news editor, then its managing editor.

Sheedy didn't talk much about the war. When the

subject was raised he would become withdrawn, the shadow crossing his usually good-humoured face suggesting he had been permanently saddened by what he had seen. But, apart from that, he did like to gossip and reminisce and sort out the world's problems with other reporters over a few drinks.

He was uncomfortable with the new breed of hungry young hustlers who were cutting each other's throats in the competitive world of modern American journalism with no apparent desire to make friends with colleagues.

After a few years working uneasily, albeit well paid, on the tabloid, he had, to his surprise, made it to the upper levels of the best-seller list and earned half a million dollars from a book on American involvement in South-east Asia. Its publication coincided with the death of his wife and was followed by a deep desire to leave New York, to change his life and surroundings. He travelled extensively and ended up in Spain where he invested his royalties in a villa on the Costa del Sol. From there he now produced and presented a weekly thirty-minute investigative programme for a television company broadcasting from neighbouring Gibraltar.

As he publicised the high pressure tactics of time-share salesmen, exposed drug smuggling, waged war on corrupt officials and greedy developers, raised embarrassing questions about the shooting in Gilbraltar of IRA suspects by the SAS, and was one of the first to report the Barlow Clowes financial scandal, he became, to his relatively small Costa del Sol, mainly English expatriates, a bit of a celebrity. 'Good old Bill – he'll show them'. But to Sheedy it was no big deal. He was just doing the only thing he knew how, and the rest of the time he was engrossed in his love affair with Spain ... devoting his plentiful spare time to exploring the ancient cities and white towns (the *pueblos*), enjoying the food and wine, and, in particular, researching a book he hoped to write on the Andalusia of Federico Garcia Lorca, the poet who was murdered during the civil war.

Sheedy attributed his fascination with Lorca to their shared love for Andalusia, but friends wondered whether the American, so profoundly affected by the loss of his wife, was actually identifying with Lorca's own preoccupation with death. Why else would he, late at night, when the wine had turned to whisky, endlessly recite the more plaintive of Lorca's laments to whoever would listen?

But now, on this morning in the departure lounge at Gatwick, while he was considering whether or not he should have a second gin and tonic, there arose the danger that the primacy of his love for Andalusia and its martyred poet could be contested by another. One more challenging. One he had believed, maybe even hoped, he had experienced for the only time.

The possibility had, of course, existed ever since he got Kate's letter.

Hi, Sheedy, it had said. *Guess who's coming to Spain? Right, me. How about a bed for a few days? The floor will do. I'm flying into Gatwick on the 18th of March and then directly on to Gibraltar. Can you drop me a line and tell me how to find you? Can't wait to see you, you old grouch. Love Kate.*

He had replied that he would be in London that weekend and would fly down with her and had been looking forward to seeing her the way you look forward to good-humoured company, news of old friends, and the chance to share new discoveries.

But that was all.

Sheedy hadn't loved a woman, hadn't wanted to, since Jan died after suffering a devastating form of cancer. They had been childhood sweethearts in Connecticut, had attended the same college, and had married the weekend before they both began work, he as a junior reporter on the local newspaper and she as a librarian at the local school. From then on nothing stood a chance of coming between them. Not even learning they were fated to be childless. Not even his two-year absence in Vietnam (from where he wrote a letter every night, fifteen or twenty sometimes arriving at the same time thanks to the vagaries of the post). Not even his being deposited on their doorstep in a pool of his own blood after pressing his research into crime too far.

But no-one, he believed, who had spent night after night lying awake tormented by the tears of the woman he loved while she endured such pain that she ended her life pleading for death, no-one would want to expose himself to that kind of love a second time. Or to the overpowering sense of impotence in the face of her suffering.

So he hadn't loved or wanted to love since.

Anyway, apart from occasional attacks of anguish when he was alone late at night, attacks repelled by bottles of Scotch imported weekly from Gibraltar, life was good. He was answerable to no-one and there wasn't time to get lonely; he had, as always, accumulated good friends, and there was plenty to do. There had been nights of warmth from time to time, usually after a few drinks, usually more an intimate cuddle than a passionate coupling, but they had been followed by crippling, albeit irrational, feelings of guilt, and he was increasingly content to go home alone. No woman, he had decided, was going to turn up with enough desire and determination to clamber over all the barriers he had erected to protect that part of him that was forever Jan's.

Until that morning at Gatwick, when a woman's voice asked him whether he always sat in bars laughing to himself, and he turned round to look into a face that caused such a crashing and crumbling of psychological blocks that you could almost hear them hitting the ground.

She was in her late twenties, with red hair, fresh face and freckles, and green eyes that challenged and laughed at Sheedy at the same time.

Reflecting on it later, he realised the possibility had always been there. She had been his special protegée on the paper, an exceptionally talented photographer, the one he could never get angry with, the one whose early career he had guided as if she were his daughter. He had always been ... what's the word? ... fond? ... yes, fond of her, indulgent of her enthusiasm and her excesses, proud of her talent.

But now, possibly because there had been building up within him a stockpile of unacknowledged need, maybe because she had a head start in his affections over any other candidate, or even just because the girl internee had become a beautiful and vibrant young woman, but most likely because of all of this and more, *fond*, inadequate word at the best of times, no longer seemed enough.

He had been expecting an old friend with whom he was comfortable. That hadn't changed. Yet at the same time she had become a stranger, one he found instantly desirable.

'Hi, Sheedy, you old tyrant,' she said, 'bit early for the booze isn't it?'

'For Christ's sake, Kate, I was giving up on you. You look terrific ... I always said you would make a hell of a woman.'

'I was a woman when you said it, Sheedy. You were too busy bullying reporters to notice.'

'I was never a bully.'

'OK, I know. Anyway, how are things?' For the first time the laughter left her eyes as she searched his face, ready to disbelieve what she heard.

17

But he told her he was in good shape and, compared with the sad, haunted figure he had been when she last saw him, at Jan's funeral, he looked it.

'I hear you're a big shot TV man down there.'

'Hardly. It's a small station. Gibraltar would fit into Central Park. My stuff's mainly aimed at the Costa del Sol, at the English living down there, probably only a few of them. Still, it's fun and maybe useful. But what's really terrific is Spain. I love it. You'll love it.' He squeezed her arm. 'Anyway, it's good to see you. What made you decide to come?'

'It was ... well, a last-minute decision.' She went quiet.

He looked at her thoughtfully. 'There's been a problem, hasn't there?'

'Damn it, you know me too well, Bill.' Her face clouded over. 'I guess when I tell you what happened you'll say I'm just running away. Fact is, I've had a rough time. I had a big story that went badly wrong. I'll tell you all about it later, but what mattered was that either the picture editor or I had to take the blame, and there was no way he was going to let it be him.'

'Creep.'

'It's worse than that, Bill. You expect people to betray colleagues these days. Well, some of them, you know how damn competitive it is in New York. But we were ... well, we were lovers too. I just couldn't believe it when he set me up to take the blame for a mistake that was really his.' She paused, biting her lip at the memory. 'I guess I was ready to get out of the paper anyway, it's got more and more gross recently; but after the way he behaved I simply couldn't bear to go to work and even see him at his desk. So I went in at the peak of the day, you know, when all the copy's piled up on the news and picture desks, and picked up his cigarette and set fire to the lot and while he was running round in circles

18

screaming for a fire extinguisher, I told him he was a double-crossing, heartless asshole ... and then I walked out.'

'Holy shit.' Sheedy was angry and amused at the same time, but most of all he was relieved. It was hardly a major disaster. She would get over it. It was mostly her pride that was hurt. And she was free and she was no-one's and that was a minor miracle that suddenly mattered to him a lot.

'But why Spain?'

'No particular reason.' She evaded his eyes, then feeling his sceptical gaze, she laughed. 'Oh hell, I might as well say it ... because you were there. I figured you could help me sort it out. I guess I needed old Sheedy's shoulder one more time.'

For a moment they just looked at each other, affectionately. Then he said 'I'm glad. I can't tell you how much', and he asked about her plans.

'Bill, I don't have any. I need a break. I figured I would get some sun and do some water-skiing, then maybe I'll research a few photo-features for a while; with Expo and the Olympic Games coming up in '92 there should be no trouble selling them.'

'Terrific. That's all we hacks in Spain need. A competitor.'

They laughed and then she suddenly slipped off the bar stool and came closer to hug him.

For a moment he buried his face in her soft hair. He couldn't believe what he was feeling, didn't trust himself to speak.

Fortunately he was saved by a flashing red light on the departure board. The plane was boarding.

If he were honest with himself, and he usually was, he was more than a little relieved they were not sitting together, so unsettling was her physical presence and so confused were his feelings.

'Christ,' he thought as he absent-mindedly toyed with his drink, 'I want her.'

But did he *want* to want her? What about Jan?

Sometimes when he needed to kill the ache inside him by forcing his feelings of loss and loneliness to the surface, he would deliberately revive her memory so vividly that he would be reduced to tears. He attempted this now, almost as if he were summoning her to protect her interests. But it didn't happen like the other times, at least not like the worst times, the times at night that caused him to flee his bed and reach for the bottle. This wasn't the Jan who came back to him out of the dark, crying in pain and clutching him and begging him to help her die. This was Jan smiling, teasing, the ever-encouraging, ever-supportive Jan he had almost forgotten. And then, for the first time since he watched the life fade from her eyes, he knew there was no need for guilt. 'Go for it, Sheedy,' she used to say when he was weighing a project in the balance. He could almost hear her saying it now, and he felt ashamed. How unfair he had been to her to try to make his life a mausoleum of memories, instead of living it as it came.

She would have understood his need.

She would have wanted him to love someone.

And she would have been glad about Kate ... especially Kate.

But Kate? Why should she want him? She was at least twenty years younger. A few hours with her and, age apart, all sorts of differences and incompatibilities would surely emerge.

He remembered how she had looked, walking in front of him to the plane. She was about five feet nine, tall for a girl. (Damn it, why did he keep thinking of her as a girl? He'd have to watch that.) She was wearing a white track suit, comfortable for travelling, soft-looking and close-fitting, and she walked with the grace of an athlete.

When she had turned to smile and tease him about travelling 'with the nobs' while she had to slum it 'with the peasants', and then laughed when he offered to swap and told him age must come before beauty, her face had looked so young and fresh that he suddenly felt absurdly silly in his middle age and embarrassed by his crumpled suit and unshaven appearance.

Really, the whole thing was ridiculous. She saw him as a father figure, not a possible lover. She had come to him for refuge, not excitement. And even if he could persuade her to love him, did he have the right? She should be building a life with a younger man, not with him.

On the other hand, some women preferred older men. And he didn't feel that old. In fact, he didn't feel old at all. Maybe he needed to lose some weight, but, he lied to himself, that wasn't impossible.

Now, as he was leaving the plane, he came up with a kind of a plan. She had come for a shoulder to lean on, and his would be there. But he'd be damned if he'd be cast as an avuncular, or father, figure. He would try to be a friend as she would be a friend, care-free and full of fun.

And he would buy time by taking a few days off work; they would spend a few days driving in the mountains.

They would go to Granada, Cordoba, Ronda, maybe even Seville.

That way she wouldn't be meeting the lusty, suntanned young animals at the beach wearing the flimsy pouches that passed for swimming trunks these days ... at least, not meeting them until things became clearer. Sheedy felt in no shape for that kind of competition.

Back in Economy, Kate, weary of travelling after the all-night flight from New York, and made even more sleepy by the champagne, had dozed for an hour or so and

21

daydreamed about Spain for the remainder of the journey, untroubled by the questions that were worrying Sheedy. She was, of course, much more in tune with her feelings than he was. She was more fed-up than heart-broken by the betrayal she had experienced in New York. Irrespective of that she needed a change and a good time after seven tough years building a career and fighting to get what she knew were good pictures into a bad paper. A combination of Sheedy and Spain were just what she needed to get her act together.

And she had known he would be pleased to see her. He may not have loved her as she had loved him, but he was a good and caring friend.

And, boy, she *had* loved him. From the first day she had come onto the paper as an internee, straight from college in her home city of Boston, she had liked and respected him and, as she thrived on the attention he gave her, she had fallen hopelessly in love with him (hopeless, she realised, in every sense, because everyone knew how close he was to his wife). His opinion became all that mattered. When he praised one of her pictures she would walk forty blocks home because she was on too much of a high to sit still; when he found fault, or when, under pressure, he used someone else's picture or worse an agency picture, without even a consoling word, she would cry all the way home in a taxi. When he called out at the end of the day 'anyone for the bar?' she would be the first to move. The happiest hours of her life had been spent sitting in smoke-filled bars with the small group of veteran reporters from their own paper and the rival *New York Times* who congregated around Sheedy to gossip about papers and New York and the Mets and the Jets and the world generally. If she was a good news photographer, and she was, she owed it as much to the encouragement of that group as she did from her experience on the paper.

She knew Sheedy hadn't known how she felt, had just been responding to her ambition and enthusiasm. In fact, after his wife became ill he hadn't known much about anything. She was sad when he left, and working on the paper never seemed the same – but life had gone on. She had got a place on the Upper West Side and worked hard to build her now considerable reputation as a photographer. She had survived three or four affairs – at least two of them good while they lasted – before the latest disaster.

As she thought of him now, in his seat up ahead, she realised what a surprising reunion it had been. Maybe she had expected to meet an emotional wreck, or a much older man. What she had not expected was a Sheedy who looked remarkably the same as he had before Jan became ill, as good-humoured and trustworthy as ever, but fitter and burnt brown by the sun.

She was surprised, too, how moved she was to be back in his company. She had come to believe over the years that hers had been a classic case of hero worship, that she had just been fortunate to have a decent boss who believed in encouraging youth. But now they were together once more, away from the paper and New York, each free of emotional entanglements and he no longer her boss and mentor, she felt a re-awakening of the old deeper feelings. It had, after all, been more than hero worship; this was a good man, and an attractive one too.

Just the same, there was for her none of the inner turmoil Sheedy was experiencing. On the contrary, any doubts she had entertained about landing herself on Sheedy had dissolved.

Kate was in a mood to take life and Sheedy as they came. Friends. Housemates for a while. Maybe colleagues if there was some work they could do together.

And, what the hell ... if there was only one bed and he wanted to wrap her up in his arms and keep her warm, that would be OK with her too.

While Bill Sheedy and Kate Callaghan were climbing into his battered but still powerful late seventies' sports car and setting off for the Costa del Sol, the green Rolls Royce was already leaving the dusty Spanish border town of La Linea and turning onto the crowded and hazardous main highway to Malaga.

In the back Sir Brian Cruickshank, former permanent secretary at the Treasury, now chairman of a number of city companies, including the fast-rising Anglo-Spanish Investors Ltd, was recalling for the umpteenth time the telephone call that had ruined his weekend.

He had on Friday been in his penthouse office in one of the new skyscrapers towering over the City in London. At six o'clock his senior secretary had entered with the day's letters for signature and a list of the following week's engagements. Once he had approved them and given a few additional instructions, the door was closed, and he had poured himself a single Scotch into a crystal glass full of ice, added water, and then settled himself with the drink and a cigar in a soft leather rocking chair at the window and meditated while looking out at the lights of the city and their reflection in the Thames. It was a well-established routine. He called it his 'special hour'.

Cruickshank had been experiencing a difficult patch. The economy had been depressed and the past couple of years had been awkward ones for the Thatcher administration. It had appeared to lose its sense of direction, while Labour, increasingly disciplined and moderate-looking, had been consistently ahead in the opinion polls. The City was jittery and as a result unreliable. A

24

number of his subsidiary companies were in trouble, suffering from a combination of high interest rates and wary investors. Only this morning he had chaired the board meeting of one that would have to be sold at a considerable loss.

And now this welcome pause at the end of the week, this hour of peace to review his affairs, was being disturbed. Expecting no calls of importance and assuming his secretary had temporarily taken leave of her senses, he answered with an asperity that made his displeasure only too clear. His temper was not improved by the identity of the caller. Jason Canning, his young American project coordinator in Spain, was efficient; Cruickshank couldn't fault him there. The problem was his manner, and in particular his attitude to Cruickshank. For some reason the Englishman couldn't understand, he always felt as if Canning was amused by him ... that he, Cruickshank, was the subject of some private joke. This he was not accustomed to and didn't like.

'Jason, I presume you're impatient to tell me our problem with the old man has been overcome?'

'In a manner of speaking, Sir Brian, but I'm afraid not the easy way.' It was said with a casual, slightly-mocking drawl that grated on Cruickshank's nerves. 'He wouldn't even talk about it. It was hopeless. No matter what I offered him, he just didn't want to know.'

'What do you mean, didn't want to know? Offer him more.' If, as he suspected, Canning had a sneer on his face, Cruickshank's tone was calculated to wipe it off. 'Are you really telling me you can't out-negotiate a peasant, Jason? Look, you're trying to beat him down a few pesetas while every day's delay is costing millions. Stop toying with the man and make him an offer he can't refuse. I don't care how much he wants, it can't be that much compared with what's at stake.'

'Sir Brian, that's not necessary or possible. The old man's no longer around to negotiate.' The American paused for a moment, then added without emotion, 'He's dead.'

Cruickshank sat forward in his chair, surprised, but also unable to repress feelings of relief. 'Dead! What do you mean, dead? When? How?'

'He had an accident . . . well, a sort of accident. In any case, he's out of the way now . . . I'm already investigating the next steps we should take.'

There was a lengthy silence while Cruickshank, relief giving way to apprehension, slowly reviewed every word Canning had said.

Then, anxious to be convinced he had misunderstood, for surely he *had* misunderstood, he carefully asked: 'Jason, what do you mean by "*a sort* of accident"?'

'He fell down a ravine.'

'Fell?'

'Well, if he's ever found it'll look like a fall. No-one'll even bother to climb down and get him. He's just an old man who fell down a ravine. No-one's likely to think he was helped on his way, let alone trace it to you.'

'*Me!*'

He couldn't believe what he was hearing.

'*Trace it to me!* For Christ's sake, why should they trace it to me? It's not any of my doing.'

He couldn't remember standing, but he was on his feet. Lowering his voice, he said 'Jason, if I understand you correctly, and I hope I do not, if you're responsible for this . . . this man's death . . . you must be mad.'

The voice at the other end remained cool. 'Look, he was old and worn out. He was going to die soon anyway. In the meantime, as you say, he was costing us a fortune every day. Now we can get the project moving. It was the only way.'

Carrying the phone, Cruickshank walked to the

window and looked out, as if seeking reassurance in the familiarity and the solidity of the City, its lights glittering in the dusk.

He was only starting to believe what he had heard.

Canning must be a psychopath.

He had killed the old man.

The project and he, Cruickshank, could be linked to it.

He believed in being tough, yes, even ruthless when it came to business, it was the only way, it's what he was paid for, but this . . . this was crazy. Disaster.

It was also incredible. He was a highly reputable City figure at the head of an equally respectable group of companies. How could he be involved in the sordid killing of a complete nonentity somewhere in Spain? Surely the answer was that he couldn't. He must be reading more into Canning's words than was justified. Or maybe the American was up to some game of his own, trying to unsettle Cruickshank.

Distrusting the lack of privacy provided by the phone and needing to see the American's face as they talked, he curtailed the conversation. 'Jason, I'm still hoping I misunderstand you. But I don't like what I hear. I'm coming down.' He quickly reviewed his weekend plans. 'On Sunday. I'll be down on Sunday.'

'There's no need for panic, Sir Brian . . .'

'I'll decide that. You stay on the yacht until I get there. Don't move. Do you understand?'

There was a sullen acknowledgement and a click as the phone was put down.

Quickly he dialled the number of his outer office and, struggling to appear composed, summoned his senior secretary. 'Miss Chambers, I need to go to Spain on the earliest available flight on Sunday, coming back Monday. Please organise it and re-arrange all meetings planned before Tuesday. Ask Green to pick me up at

Gibraltar and tell Hobbs that I'll be going directly to the yacht and then later to the villa.'

He paused, looking at a series of clocks above the mantlepiece showing the time in the world's financial capitals. 'And see if you can get Mr Jordan in New York before he goes for lunch.'

As his secretary, accustomed to sudden changes of plan, calmly left the room, Cruickshank went to the desk to pick up the Scotch and cigar, but instead of returning to the window he walked to the far end of the room and stood before a huge model of the Spanish project.

Breath-taking in its originality and size, it was to be constructed in and around hills and valleys south and inland from Marbella, between San Pedro de Alcantara and Estapona, and was intended to be a recreational resort so expansive and exclusive that even Sotogrande, further south, would be over-shadowed by comparison.

Despite the fact that every penny he possessed, huge sums he was borrowing, and the money of a number of other investors was at stake, Cruickshank had complete confidence in what had become known as 'the Spanish project', and never failed to feel excited and proud when, before leaving in the evening, he had one last look at his model. It was to be the achievement of his business life. It would not only make him and the other investors a huge sum of money, but it would allow him to live in Spain for much of the year in luxury and with considerable influence. (Cruickshank suffered occasionally from arthritis, so far not seriously, but he was advised by his doctor that, as he became older, he should avoid as much of the English winters as possible.) Also the project would remain after him as a monument to his daring and imagination and leadership. Just as the vision of Jose Banus would forever be commemorated by the Puerto Banus marina, so would he, Cruickshank, be forever remembered as the creator of his village, as yet un-named, on the Costa del Sol.

Just a glance at the model usually made him feel better, no matter how bad the day had been.

But tonight it was not so.

His heart was pounding, his mind reeling.

How could it have happened? The peasant had been a damn nuisance but somehow the problem would have been overcome. Now the man was dead, and, unless Canning had been exaggerating his part in it (and Cruickshank feared not), he had not died accidentally, but been deliberately killed. Murdered! There was no other word.

Not by Cruickshank, not at his command, but in his name. And no matter what he chose to do about it, whether it was cleared up or covered up, it would cast a shadow over the project ... possibly over his whole life.

Cruickshank was in his early-fifties, tall and lean, his fair hair thinning. His half-moon spectacles made him look more like a senior academic than a businessman, but his rather severe features changed the moment he smiled; it was generally acknowledged that the humour that entered his face, the hint of mischief in the twinkle in his eyes, were genuine, the key to his charm. The possessor of a brilliant analytical mind, he had been a high-flier in the civil service from the start and after reaching the top at an exceptionally early age had found himself hankering for the chance to match his skills with others in a more competitive and less secure world. On reaching fifty he made an impressively easy transition from Whitehall mandarin to top financier, picking up directorships and then chairmanships almost at will. This had enabled him to develop a luxurious lifestyle that he shamelessly enjoyed and which he had shown no desire to share by re-marrying after a discreet divorce some years earlier. Employing his knighthood and diplomatic skills to the best possible advantage, he had been a particularly effective operator in the United States, attracting an unusually high percentage of American investors in a number of his companies, and especially in the Spanish project. It was Theodore Jordan, by far the biggest, the most financially committed of those investors, who now came on the line.

Cruickshank came straight to the point. Canning had been Jordan's nominee and he now wanted to know more about him.

There was a pause and then, thought Cruickshank, a too-careful edge to the responding voice. 'Of course. But what's the problem?'

'I'm afraid that must wait until we meet. It's not a matter we can discuss on the phone. When do you next plan to be in London?'

'Well, there are a number of things I could usefully do there. I could fly over on Concorde on Monday.'

Again there was a careful edge to the voice that Cruickshank found disconcerting.

He suggested dinner on Monday night and, after completing the call, poured another Scotch, re-lit the neglected cigar, and went back to the rocking chair in the window.

There he sat for a very long time looking disconsolately out into the night.

Chapter Two

Bill Sheedy's villa was one of a Spanish-style cluster built round a swimming pool in a spacious garden of grass and sub-tropical flowers on a hill about three kilometres from the *costa* on the Ronda road. It offered spectacular views of the mountains further inland and, from the balconies at the front, of the bustling town of San Pedro and the sea beyond it.

It had taken just over an hour to drive from Gibraltar. Sheedy, who had produced a much-praised television programme on the suicidal driving and notoriously high accident rate on the N340, the main coastal road stretching the length of Andalusia, from Cadiz in the west to Almeria in the east, had been content to concentrate on the traffic, leaving Kate to chat about old friends and about her plans for swimming and sun-bathing, water-skiing and wind-surfing. Now, as he accelerated up the hill to the villa, he suppressed a sudden, heart-thumping vision of her lying topless on the beach, and at last interrupted her happy monologue.

'Hold on a minute, Callaghan, just cool it. If you think I'm going to let you become like the rest of the unadventurous, unimaginative fun-lovers on the costa, forget it. You're going to start by seeing the real Spain so that you get your priorities right. I'll give you one day by the pool and then we're heading for the hills.'

She laughed and told him he was no longer the boss. Really she was pleased. But could he spare the time?

'No problem. I've recorded a programme for this week so I have a few days. It's time I had a break and, anyway, I owe it to Spain to stick with you ... an un-controlled Callaghan on the loose is more than the place deserves.'

Then, as they rounded a bend, he pointed to the villas on the hillside 100 yards above the road. 'Well, there it is. Welcome to Spain.'

'Bill, it looks great. I can't wait to get into all this. Spanish Señoritas step aside, Callaghan's on her way.'

He grinned at her enthusiasm but he guessed how she felt. He had only been away a couple of days but as always his spirits were lifted on his return by the bright light and by the colour and warmth of the place. And, as she walked around the villa, exclaiming with delight at the roomy, two-level lounge with its big stone fireplace and uninterrupted view to the sea, and again as Sheedy took her into a bedroom suite with an equally spectacu-lar view, he felt buoyed up by her pleasure. 'I'm giving you my room,' he said. 'I can look at the view any time; you should have it while you're here.'

She dropped her bag and, wrapping her arms round him, she kissed him on the cheek and buried her face in his chest.

'Bill, what can I say ... I'm just so grateful ... that you're you, and that you live in this place, and that I can be with you for a while.'

Touched and suspecting she was near to tears, a condition he put down to exhaustion as much as emotion, he quickly lifted her off her feet, sat her on the

32

bed, and walked out of the room, saying he was going to make some coffee.

'Once you've unpacked I suggest you have a siesta,' he called back to her. 'You must be whacked.'

By the time he returned with the coffee she was already asleep, stretched out on top of the bed in her track suit, her face half-hidden by a swirl of red-gold curls. He reached out and gently moved the hair aside and stood for a few moments absorbed by her beauty.

Then he quietly drew the curtains and left her alone, retiring to the smaller suite where he showered and shaved and, after dressing in light-blue trousers and a dark-blue sleeveless shirt, slipped out of the villa and drove to San Pedro to buy fish and other ingredients for a *paella*, all the time thinking about her and what he would like them to do together.

Even the old men who sit and drink coffee and cognac outside La Antartida bar at the top of San Pedro's main shopping strip commented to each other 'Señor Bill *hoy mucho sonreia*' ...

... Señor Bill smiles a lot today.

Puerto Banus is just a few kilometres up the *costa* from San Pedro, about halfway between San Pedro and Marbella's 'golden mile' of Arab banks and palaces and the exclusive hideaways and playgrounds of the rich. Usually referred to by the cosmopolitan residents of this part of the Costa del Sol as 'the port', Puerto Banus had grown since the sixties into one of the biggest marinas on any of the costas, with hundreds of yachts surrounded by scores of bars, boutiques, restaurants and nightclubs. The most expensive restaurants are on the front, just a few feet from the water's edge – places like the Don Leone, Los Bandidos, Antonio's, Silk's, and La Bodega del Puerta. Above and behind them, white-washed buildings have risen higher and higher, like man-made

33

cliffs overhanging the harbour. Neon lights and arrows point the way down alley-ways or up mysterious, enticing stairways to bars and night clubs tucked away at every level, out of sight of the casual passerby ... to Bobby's and Shirlee's, to Rumours and Alexander's, to Joe's and Capone's, and to many more.

Puerto Banus is a mix of class and tack, of quality and rip-off, of the gracefully and the tastelessly rich. Most people just come to look and fantasise. These dreamers and the voyeurs of the wealthy pour in every day, the middle-aged to promenade up and down the rows of yachts, exclaiming at their size and opulence, and the younger set to lounge in their best gear outside the Salduba Pub or Sinatra's Bar and throw glances at each other ... and dream of accidentally finding themselves next to a wealthy yacht-owner who just happened to be lonely and single.

The more sophisticated or wealthy who frequent the port usually do so only because they own, rent, or are guests on a yacht too big to be moored anywhere else. The biggest are at the western end of the marina. Some are more like small ships, two or three storeys high, their impressive size matched by the luxury of their spacious bars and lounges, dining rooms and bedroom suites. These yachts are worth many millions, some of them literally hundreds of millions of dollars.

One of them this spring was *La Gaviota*, The Seagull, dark-blue, sleek, breath-takingly luxurious, with its interior rooms on two levels, and a swimming pool on its main sun deck. It had been purchased in 1989 by Anglo-Spanish Investors Ltd. Apart from appearing as an increasingly valuable asset on its balance sheet, the yacht was used by the company for entertaining investors and useful contacts, and for both the leisure and the business headquarters in Spain of its directors, especially the chairman, Sir Brian. (He also owned a well-guarded and equally-luxurious villa on the beach near San Pedro. This – and, some suspected, the yacht too – was mortgaged to the hilt to help finance the Spanish project.)

It was to this small ship that the Rolls Royce now glided from Gibraltar, its owner temporarily distracted from his problems, as he always was on this journey, by close inspection of the tidal wave of concrete sweeping up the costa all the way to Malaga. This was the downside of the Costa del Sol. Developers, unchecked by proper planning controls until it was too late, had turned a once wild and beautiful coastline into one almost uninterrupted line of buildings extending from San Roque, just north of Gibraltar, to Nerja, an hour's drive beyond Malaga. Some of them were attractive, in the Spanish style, but many were hideous blocks of flats and hotels. Fifty years back the English writer Laurie Lee had hiked up the coast and written of a 'beautiful but exhausted shore, seemingly forgotten by the world'. At that time, wrote Lee, 'you could have bought the whole coast for a shilling'. Now the strip of land between the sea and the main highway was so over-exploited and badly-developed that those who could afford the prices were buying land and building their villas further inland.

Inspecting all this usually raised Cruickshank's spirits. He became more convinced every time that he had come up with the right idea and captured the right piece of land at the right time. Thinking this now, he momentarily experienced the old excitement but, just before the car reached the Nueva Andalusia complex opposite Puerto Banus, it passed the turn-off to a small unpaved road. Emerging from it onto a dirt track skirting the main highway, oblivious to the heavy traffic, like a survivor of centuries-old Spain stubbornly resisting the passing of time, was an old man, bent almost double over the neck of his mule, obviously on the way home after working from dawn to dusk at one of the *fincas* nestling in the foothills. Cruickshank felt as if a cold hand had reached out to clutch his heart; this was probably how the other old man had looked, the one it seemed Canning had killed.

Back came the memory of the phone call and with it the anger.

Why, in God's name, had Canning done it?

How much was he, Cruickshank, responsible?

He desperately tried to recall his orders; had there been any words of his that Canning could have mis-interpreted, taking them as a hint that he had wanted this to happen? He couldn't believe it was so. The idea of harming the peasant had never entered his head. No, there had been no misunderstanding. If Canning had done this thing, he had done it on his own initiative.

As the Rolls turned into Puerto Banus he decided what to do. He would record his interview with Canning, obtain a clear account of what happened, and, if it was as Cruickshank feared, he would take the tape to the police. The publicity would hurt him and it wouldn't help the project either, but surely his open and honest handling of the affair would earn respect. He would not be an accomplice to murder, he would be its exposer; he would not be part-killer of the old man, he would be his avenger.

Trying hard to look his usual commanding self, he walked quickly up the gangplank of the yacht, barely acknowledging the salutes of the crew members at the top. His butler, Hobbs, was waiting with Jason Canning on the deck. He nodded coldly to the latter and told him to report to the library in thirty minutes.

The library could have been in an English country house. It was book-lined, and furnished with thick dark-brown carpets, red leather armchairs and a beautiful antique desk. Cruickshank asked the butler for a Scotch on the rocks, told him to keep the Rolls standing by, and asked not to be disturbed for half an hour, when he would like Canning to join him. They, too, were not to be disturbed.

Left on his own, he took from his desk the small cassette recorder he sometimes used to record complicated negotiations, inserted a brand-new tape, tested that it was operating properly, and placed it under a magazine close to but out of reach of the armchair by the drinks cabinet.

Satisfied that all was ready he slowly reclined in his own chair, a replica of the rocking chair in his London office, and sipping the Scotch, carefully rehearsed the questions he would need to ask.

Twenty minutes later Canning entered, his cool demeanour and the customary hint of a mocking smile causing Cruickshank to clench his fists under the table to hide his anger.

He waved him to the chair near the hidden cassette recorder, but didn't offer him a drink. 'Jason, I want you to tell me exactly what happened to the old man.'

The younger man slipped casually into the armchair and lit a cigarette.

'I found him in a bar just outside Ronda a couple of weeks back. I offered him three million pesetas. He just shook his head. So I offered five million, then seven and a half. As I told you on the phone, it was hopeless. He wouldn't discuss it. I don't think he knew what seven and a half million pesetas was or what he could do with it. So I spelt it out to him at some length, then, just in case he was cleverer than I imagined, I went up to ten million and even hinted there could be more. I told him I would come back in a week. And I left.'

'Who saw you together?'

'Only the barman and he took no notice. He'll never remember we were there.'

Cruickshank looked coldly sceptical. 'Go on.'

'Yesterday morning I went back, but this time I cut across the hills near to where he lives. There was no-one within miles. I swear no-one saw us. I tried to persuade him, but he wouldn't even talk. He was either incredibly stupid or bloody-mindedly contemptuous, I couldn't tell ... he was kind of impassive. I tell you, we were going to get nowhere.'

He paused, as if this was all that needed saying.

Once more Cruickshank felt the chill hand on his heart. Canning clearly believed that, in the circumstances he described, murdering the old man was an unexceptional measure, that it was the logical, inevitable outcome of his failed negotiations, so customary a way of dealing with business that it was hardly worth discussing.

Who the hell was this man?

How could Jordan have chosen him?

Controlling himself with difficulty, he demanded to hear the rest.

'Well, there's this ravine near his hut. He was crossing some kind of bridge, just a few bits of wood. If that was his way of going home it was only a matter of time before he fell off it ... all I did was help a little.'

'How?'

'I hit him on the back of the head with a stone. He and the mule fell off. And that's it. No-one saw it. And if he's found, if anyone actually goes down there, any cut or bruise from the stone will just look like it was caused by the fall. No bullet hole, no knife wound. No-one could ever prove it wasn't an accident.'

So there it was.

There was no longer any doubt.

Cruickshank's indignation swelled. His voice rising, he exclaimed 'But it wasn't an accident, Jason. You killed him. Don't you understand that whether you covered up the crime or not is hardly the point? You, Jason, are a murderer. What on earth makes you think that I, the company, or anyone else involved in the project can countenance such criminal behaviour? Who or what do you think we are? The Mafia? You must be mad, Jason. I'm afraid we can't allow it in our name, we can't pretend it didn't happen, we can't protect you.'

The younger man looked undisturbed.

'You don't *need* to protect me, Sir Brian. I told you, it will be written off as an accident.'

'I don't think you understand, Jason. You will be exposed because I intend to do it. I may play hard but I am not abandoning the rules of the human race I belong to. I have my duty as a citizen and I intend to carry it out.'

'Isn't that a bit pompous in the circumstances? It could be argued that I was acting for you. You told me to do what was necessary to get a deal.'

'Necessary within the usual confines, Canning,' Cruickshank raged. 'You have gone beyond them, far beyond them – for God's sake, man, are you so amoral that you really believe that an instruction to do what is "necessary" in business means killing anyone who gets in your way?'

The young man rose to his feet. 'This is getting us nowhere. I did what I had to do, what you needed done, what I believed to be implied in your orders. I should forget it if I were you, because if it comes out, and only you could make it known, I'll simply say I was acting on your explicit orders – to kill the man – and, as that won't be a legal defence for me, people will have no reason not to believe it.'

Now the older man rose too, 'I'm afraid that's not so, Canning.' He pressed a buzzer under the desk top and the butler appeared. 'Hobbs, I want you to take this cassette' (he took the recorder from under the magazine, removed the cassette and handed it to the butler) 'and give it to Green. Ask two of the crew to wait with him at the Rolls until I get there. I want it protected.'

As the butler left, Cruickshank, now in front of his desk, leaned back upon it and, with increasing confidence that he had handled the matter rather well, with decreasing fear that the project was endangered, looked down at the other almost triumphantly. 'I'm going to the police in Marbella with the recording of our conversation, Canning. I intend the Spanish authorities to see that I have as much respect for the law as they have.

'As for you,' he added, feeling magnanimous in his moment of mastery, 'you will not in the meantime be detained on the yacht. What you do before they come looking for you is up to you.'

To his surprise the younger man's only move was to casually sit down in the red leather chair and light another cigarette.

'Canning, do you understand what is happening?'

'Oh, I do, Sir Brian, I'm afraid it's you who do not.'

For the third time that evening Cruickshank felt a warning chill. The man's confidence was unreal. There was something the American knew that Cruickshank didn't.

'Sir Brian, I most strongly advise you that before you go anywhere with that tape you speak to Mr Jordan.'

Cruickshank's disquiet grew. He remembered the cautious edge to Jordan's voice when they had spoken the previous night.

Still he tried to remain calm, to keep control of the confrontation. 'I hope you are not suggesting that Mr Jordan is the kind of man to condone murder, Canning, because I have more confidence in him than that.'

'*Ring him,* Sir Brian.' This time there was an authority, an insistence about the younger man's voice that added considerably to Cruickshank's fears.

'I assure you Canning that this will make no difference, but on the other hand it can only help me to have Mr Jordan's endorsement of my action.' He picked up the phone and, after checking with the butler that Green had the cassette safe, told him to get Jordan on the phone.

For some minutes they sat in near silence, Cruickshank quietly drumming his fingers on the desk, Canning smoking his cigarette. Then the phone rang.

'Mr Jordan? I'm sorry to disturb you once more and even more sorry to have to deal with this matter by phone. I assume your line is secure?'

Jordan, as he had always done, imitated the formality of the Englishman. 'That cannot be guaranteed, Sir Brian, but in any case I strongly advise you to leave the matter until we meet in London. I am assuming, of course, that it concerns the task of tidying up we entrusted to Mr Canning and that I believe he has satisfactorily undertaken?'

'Tidying up?' There was the icy hand on his heart again; this time Cruickshank thought it was going to freeze it altogether. 'Am I to understand that you're aware of *all* the measures Canning has taken?'

'Mr Canning has our full confidence, Sir Brian, as I intended to convey when we met on Monday.'

Cruickshank could hardly believe his ears.

The Americans *knew* what Canning had done.

Condoned it.

Goddamn it, *they seemed pleased with it.*

'Mr Jordan, I'm sorry to hear that,' he said. 'It would be a pity to lose your input.' Then, choosing his words carefully, for he had no idea who could listen in, he said 'I must tell you, however, that there are norms of behaviour I insist on adhering to.'

'Sir Brian, I have authorised Canning to tell you a little more about our involvement in the project. You can be assured he speaks with my authority. I suspect that once you have heard him you will choose to reserve your options until we meet in London. Goodbye.'

Cruickshank was left holding the now-dead receiver in his hand, his face taut and white, his mind struggling to grasp the fact that he was losing control of the situation, that perhaps he had never been in control.

Now it was Canning who rose from his chair, walked to the drinks cabinet and poured himself a Scotch, re-filling Cruickshank's glass at the same time.

'Sir Brian, I have no wish to fall out with you. I and my employers in the States are more than happy for you to remain the top man on the project. Your qualities are appreciated. But you need to know that you no longer own it. You'll recall that when you set up Anglo-Spanish Investors as the company to develop the project you put together forty per cent of the money, Mr Jordan and his partners provided thirty-five per cent of it, and the other twenty-five per cent you spread around in such a way that it was unlikely anyone but you would ever be in charge. Well, it's not been easy, thanks to your caution and skill, and it's taken time, but we have purchased another sixteen per cent. We own it now. Naturally we had to pay a lot, both for the shares and the discretion of the previous owners. Hence an even greater sense of urgency than yours to get the project moving.'

Cruickshank sank back into his rocking chair, his hand shaking too much to pick up the Scotch.

Greater urgency?

How could anyone have pushed the project harder and faster than he? Except by some sort of extreme behaviour. And what could be more extreme than murder?

Seemingly from a distance he heard a voice and realised Canning hadn't finished. 'Now, of course you could pull out. But why? This remains your project, your

42

idea. And it's your name everyone associates with it. Are you really going to let the unfortunate affair of one crazy, stubborn old man who would have died soon anyway, cause you to lose all this – the yacht, the villa, the company, your good name?'

Cruickshank's mind was in turmoil, trying to grasp all the implications. Jordan and his company had come highly recommended by merchant banks of standing on both sides of the Atlantic, and had been thoroughly checked out. They were investors in scores of highly-respectable businesses. He had personally conducted the meetings with them, both in New York and London. He had believed them to be a real find. And so far they had behaved impeccably.

Who really were they?

He had made a sarcastic remark about the Mafia earlier, but could that really be the answer? Were Jordan and the company using the project to launder the profits from organised crime? And even if they were, why did they need overall ownership? Surely their ends were satisfactorily served as investors without the notoriety and responsibility of running it.

Then there were the other investors. He had selected them carefully, spread the shares so that it would be almost impossible for anyone to reach them all without him knowing. Yet that's what Canning was claiming.

Reminding himself of his own stature, his good standing in both the UK and with the Spanish author-ities, he desperately tried to fight back: 'Canning, I may lose some money and even the project altogether, but I will not be, I cannot be associated with this ... this criminality. To cover up for you would make me an accessory to murder. I will not have it. I'm taking the cassette to the police. And,' he said, his hopes rising as he saw a way out, 'my guess is that the permission to develop will be withdrawn if you and your associates remain in control. You'll end up begging to sell back to me.'

Canning rose and walked across to the desk, leaning over so that his face was close to Cruickshank's.

'Sir Brian, I've tried to make this easy for you, but you're missing the point. Your cassette is worthless. Green and almost the whole crew were chosen and employed by me, acting on behalf of my New York employers. They may be on the Anglo-Spanish Investors payroll but their loyalty is to us. You have no evidence that the man's death was other than an accident – we have your cassette now – and if you make such a charge it will be denied. It won't stick. You will be portrayed as a desperate man deprived of power and seeking to discredit those who stripped you of it. You have only two choices, you can destroy yourself, at least as far as the project is concerned, or you can forget this thing and life can go on as it did before. The project will be built, you will preside over it, everyone'll be happy.'

Cruickshank was hardly aware of the other leaving. He sat motionless until he was disturbed by a discreet knock on the door. It was the butler. For a moment Cruickshank looked at him suspiciously, then relaxed. Hobbs, at least, was his man.

'The Rolls is blocking the walkway, sir, and we've been asked to move it. Green wishes to know your intentions.'

For a moment he remained still, then, slowly, dejectedly, he looked up. 'Tell Green I won't be needing it tonight. I'll sleep on the yacht.'

As the Butler was closing the door he called him back. 'Oh, Hobbs . . .'

'Sir?'

'Tell Green to give the tape to Mr Canning. He's kindly offered to deal with the matter.'

As the door closed, he switched off all the lights save

44

for a small one at the desk, poured himself another Scotch, lit a cigar, and allowed the rocking chair to tilt back. Sitting in the semi-darkness he made a tremendous effort to calm himself, to set his analytical skills to work, reviewing every detail, considering every facet of the problem. From the top drawer of the desk he took a piece of paper and, as he liked to do, listed the key points.

One, Jordan and his associates now controlled the project. Why they needed to do so was not clear, but hopefully the motive was just greed.

Two, the Americans were clearly happy to have him as front man and probably would continue to let him call the shots. However, for him to continue was to take advantage of, and thus share complicity for, the murder.

Three, he could expose the murder, but what would that achieve? While there was probably inadequate evidence to convict Canning, it would undoubtedly lead to the project being stopped. Thus he would gain nothing and lose everything.

Four, there was one thing he would achieve by going to the police – he would retain his self-respect. Also, people would believe him even if Canning could not be convicted, and his reputation for integrity would be seen to be justified, even enhanced. This meant a lot to him. Like others of his kind, Cruickshank was more than capable of rationalising his ruthless moments, of squaring his conscience with the inequities and injustices that were necessary if people, relatively few people, were to acquire and keep power and wealth. This was life, all part and parcel of the human condition. There were strong and there were weak, there were winners and there were losers, and the mark of intelligence and decency was not to naively combat that reality but to accept and enjoy its rewards while showing compassion and generosity to its victims. If there were any incon-

45

sistencies between his self-image and the effects of his activities and decisions he was oblivious to them; he genuinely believed himself to be a man of honour and genuinely cared about setting and maintaining what he believed to be high standards of behaviour.

But now a new thought struck him and once more he felt the cold hand on his heart ... if he did appear to be ready to reveal all and damage Jordan and his associates and the project, *what would they do to him?* If they would kill a peasant because they couldn't be bothered to take the time to solve the problem another way, would they stop short of arranging another accident, this time for him?

He went to the port-hole and, drawing the curtain, looked out. Usually there was one crew member at the gang plank throughout the night. Tonight there were three.

Cruickshank shivered.

Who had tripled the guard?

And why?

For a moment it all seemed too unreal.

His life in danger?

No, this couldn't be happening. He was letting his imagination run away with him.

He picked up the phone, intending to ask the reason for the increased guard, but as it began to ring he put it down.

At least for the moment he felt better not knowing.

As he turned from the window his eye caught the small replica of the model on a table in the far corner of the study. He walked over and switched on the lamp beside it. Despite himself, he experienced a moment of elation. It was magnificent in its conception, it would be one of the most pleasurable places to live anywhere in the world. And on a hill overlooking it was to be his villa, from where, retired in a few years time, he had intended to reign, sovereign over all he surveyed, President of the Community, host, he had imagined, to some of the world's richest and most powerful, for who would be able to resist invitations to rest and relax in such surroundings and with such facilities? Yes, Cruickshank was a man of intelligence and integrity but he was not short of ego, or of appetite for the good things of life; he had intended to enjoy every minute of his last two or three decades.

So he came to the last of the questions on his sheet of paper: *Were his integrity and this ambition not reconcilable? Did he really have to abandon the dream?*

Whatever he did, he couldn't bring the old man back. If he stayed with the project he could surely prevent any further excesses; he would be able to exact that guarantee as a reasonable price for his silence and continued involvement. This, he rationalised, would make him a protector of all involved, the remaining small investors, the workers, the local people, and ultimately the project's members and residents. It was not a dishonourable objective.

For nearly ten minutes he stood looking at the model then, switching off the lamp, returned to his rocking chair and another Scotch. There he stayed until the early hours, slowly and wretchedly considering a question that twenty-four hours earlier he would never have believed could possibly arise.

Was he capable of reconciling himself to murder?

It was dark now, and the Costa del Sol had become a glittering ribbon of lights. From his balcony on the hill Sheedy showed Kate the sparkling strip that was the golden mile and the bright cluster that was Puerto Banus.

They were drinking the Veuve Cliquot champagne she had bought duty-free at Kennedy Airport and were standing close together.

47

Behind them in the main room a log fire was crackling in the hearth, more for atmosphere than warmth, for they had decided to stay at the villa and dine on salad and the *paella* that Sheedy promised her was his speciality, the best, he said, in Andalusia.

Kate was wearing a gypsy-style red and white blouse and tight white jeans that exposed her figure to best advantage, and was effervescent in her enthusiasm for all things Spanish she had so far encountered – not least the villa, the view, and the warmth of the evening. Sheedy was both immensely happy in her company and at the same time tense, unsettled by an almost uncontrollable urge to take her in his arms, to run his fingers through her hair, down her back and over her shapely bottom; and yet afraid that even a fractional revelation of his desires and feelings could spoil the moment.

A sizzling from the open kitchen at one end of the room warned them that the *paella* was ready and they went in. Proudly he carried to the table the *paellera*, the two-handled steel pan piled high with rice and rabbit, prawns and mussels and *calamares*, all spiced with red peppers, garlic, and herbs.

She had watched him prepare it earlier, first cleaning the mussels and steaming them till they were open. Then peeling and cooking the prawns and cutting up the rabbit that he said he preferred to chicken. Then heating olive oil in the pan together with a couple of cloves of garlic and some bay leaf, and browning the rabbit in the same pan. She marvelled at the way he could chat while at the same time heating some ingredients, onion and peppers and rings of squid, and then removing them from the pan while sautéing others, feeding in saffron, peppercorn, paprika, and, of course, rice, then gradually bringing back each ingredient to add to the dish until the whole *paella* slowly cooked on a low heat.

Now, while it cooled for a few minutes, he tossed the

salad, opened a bottle of Rioja and served her with a flourish of Spanish that she took to mean 'eat well'.

And she did. They both did, happy to reserve conversation until the first pangs of hunger were quelled. Then she asked him about his plans for the next few days.

'Well, I figure you'll be jet-lagged tomorrow so I propose you spend it by the pool while I clear up some work, and maybe we'll go up to Benahavis in the evening. I've got friends there and we can have dinner at one of the restaurants, maybe Las Faroles, or Rufino's.'

'Where's Benahavis?'

'Not far. Three kilometres west of San Pedro, then seven kilometres up into the hills beyond Atalaya Park *campo de golf.* You'll be amazed. It's a small white village, yet it had sixteen restaurants at the last count. Maybe more now. There's a new one every time I go there. The whole village has become one big restaurant.'

'How did it get like that?'

'Well, when I first saw it back in the late sixties there was, I think, only one, but gradually as first it, and then others, became popular and made money, the families opened more until virtually everyone in the village either works in a restaurant or in a business related to it.

'Anyway, in a day or two I reckon we should start with Granada and the Alhambra. From there we can go on a quick introductory trip to Cordoba, then across to Ronda. I know there's a corrida on Sunday, not one of the tawdry bullfights they turn on for the tourists on the costa but the real thing. I reckon we can spend two or three days in Ronda and thereabouts and then it'll be safe to let you onto the beaches of the costa.'

'How kind,' she responded with good-humoured irony. 'Tell me about the corrida, how do you know we'll get in? Do you book tickets?'

'Ah ha, that's where Miguel comes in.'

Then he told her how one time when he was in Ronda

he ended up late at night in the corner of a bar with two ageing bullfight aficionados, a captain in the *Guardia Civil* and a hunter from the Serrania de Ronda, the mountainous country around the town. Sheedy had quizzed them on bullfighting and on life in the *sierras* until they were all too drunk to continue, and they had arranged to go to the following day's corrida together. Despite the improbability of them remembering, let alone all making it to the same place, it had worked out and since then they had met in the bar the night before each corrida and gone to the *plaza de toros* together the next day.

For reasons it was best not to enquire, the policeman, Miguel, appeared to have an endless supply of tickets, said Sheedy, so there would be no difficulty getting in.

'You'll love them. They're real characters, complete opposites, Miguel fat and the Rabbit Man skinny, Miguel gregarious and jolly, the Rabbit Man more inclined to melancholy, Miguel opinionated, the Rabbit Man introverted. They look a bit like a Spanish Laurel and Hardy. But what they don't know about the *sierras*, no-one does.'

'But why call him the Rabbit Man?'

'Ah, the Rabbit Man, El Conejero. I should warn you, he smells a bit. He spends all his time shooting and skinning and transporting rabbits on his mule, selling them to the restaurants in Ronda.'

'What's his real name?'

'I don't know. Even Miguel calls him Señor Conejo, Mr Rabbit.'

She screwed up her nose in mock horror. 'Holy cow ... or should I say rabbit?'

They laughed and drank more wine and he read her some Federico Garcia Lorca until the fire died out and, the jet-lag taking its toll, she became sleepy, eventually dozing off, her head coming to rest on his shoulder.

For nearly an hour he sat still, happy to feel her warmth and listen to her breathing, proud of her trust.

He remembered how Jan and he had often ended an evening like this, she falling asleep in front of the television, he content for a while to be her pillow. Miraculously, this time the memory was painless.

Finally he manoeuvered himself free and picked her up and carried her into her room. As he did so she woke. 'Where are you taking me, Sheedy?' she asked sleepily.

'To bed.'

'With you?'

With super-human restraint he softly replied, 'Not tonight.'

'Oh . . . pity.' Then, once more, she fell asleep.

He lay her down on the bed and pulled the covers over her. Then he kissed her on the top of her head and said 'Thanks for saying that' and quickly left.

That night Sheedy dreamt of Jan once more. She was on the roof garden of their flat in New York, her arms full of flowers she was planting in boxes. She was smiling, but he knew she was dying and he was sad. Then she was dropping the flowers, throwing her arms round him, telling him that it was all right, not to grieve.

He woke up with tears running down his face.

It was, of course, not the first time, but this time was different.

This time he felt no need for solace from a bottle.

This time he didn't feel alone.

Chapter Three

FRIDAY, MARCH 23

On the journey from the costa to Granada and Cordoba and then back south to Ronda, Kate came to understand why the writer Jan Morris had described Andalusia as *sol y sombra* – 'sun on one side of the street, shadow on the other'. She saw and photographed the contrasts. Widows, short, bent, broad-bummed, who still wore only black. The communal tap, in many *pueblos* still the sole source of water. Donkeys, still for many the only means of transport. But also a people adjusting to the world *'as seen on TV'*, to cars and motorbikes, to the disco in places where only a few years back courtship took place via a grilled window of the *pueblo* home, the young *caballero* standing in the street, his señorita discreetly protected by thick white walls and watchful parents.

She photographed, too, the physical contrasts, the rugged scenery that changed from valley to valley, so that every bend on every mountain road produced its own surprise.

Sheedy talked to her of the Spaniard's fascination

with death. Andalusia was, said Sheedy, at times a stoic place, yet it also staged events of great public emotion and excitability. It was a private, proud, secretive place, yet – still the contradictions – the families of small communities could by sheer physical circumstances have no secrets from one another, only from the outside world. It was a land of family, where women ruled in the home but men remained unchallenged on the streets.

She quickly developed a passion for the food – the cooking in garlic and olive oil, the big, firm tomatoes and crisp white onions, the fresh grilled fish, the roast meat, especially the chicken and the lamb and rabbit.

And she would always remember Sheedy, sitting on top of a hill, glass of wine in one hand, bread and *serrano* ham in the other, pointing out the tiny white towns sprinkled across the mountains like sparkling jewels in the sun, and reciting to her the words of his poet-hero:

> *Dry land,*
> *still land,*
> *of immense nights.*
>
> *(Wind in the olive grove.*
> *Wind in the sierra.)*
>
> *Ancient*
> *land*
> *of oil lamp*
> *and grief.*
> *(Wind on the roads.*
> *Breeze in the poplar groves.)*

No wonder that by the time they arrived in Ronda Kate felt sated with spectacle. There had been the view of the Costa del Sol and the Mediterranean from Sheedy's villa, the view of the Alhambra across the valley from the Albaicin, Granada's old Moorish quarter, the view over the roofs of Cordoba from the Bell Tower by the cathedral, the panoramic views of sunlit mountains and deep, shaded valleys on the San Pedro–Ronda road, the view from the bridge over El Tajo, the dramatic gorge that divides the old and new quarters of Ronda.

And now, in the late afternoon, she was looking at a magnificent view of the farms and the mountains to the south of Ronda from the balcony of their hotel, the Reina Victoria.

The hotel, built on the edge of a precipice, was plain but clean, the bed was soft, the water in the shower was hot, the view was intoxicating and, after she had flung herself into its swimming pool to cool down, she had, with some difficulty, persuaded a waiter to deliver to her room a jug of ice-cold sangria.

She could not imagine anywhere in the world she would rather be or anyone she would rather be with.

As she stood on the balcony she cast her mind back over her first few days in Spain. She had woken late that first morning and found him standing beside her with a tray of fresh orange juice, coffee and croissants. He had spent most of the day in Marbella, leaving her to swim and read and doze beside the pool. That evening, as promised, they had driven to Benahavis for a feast of *gambas pil pil, pollo ajillo*, and a huge salad at Los Faroles with Sheedy's colleague, Manuel, and his wife, Juanita, who lived in a *pueblo*-style building above the village. She had contentedly listened as over several bottles of red Rioja they had reminisced about their exposure of and encounters with some of the costa's less savoury operators.

For the first time she had come to realise that Sheedy was not universally popular. 'This is a dangerous man you're staying with, Señorita,' Manuel had told her. 'Did you know they tried to blow him up in his car once?'

Sheedy laughed. 'That lot are in prison now,' he said. 'Anyway, Manuel, from now on I'm going to assign all the dangerous stories to you. You speak the language better. You're more likely to talk your way out of trouble.' Juanita looked so apprehensive that Sheedy had to spend minutes convincing her that he was joking.

Kate had liked the Spanish couple. At first she felt envious of the shared experiences between Sheedy and his reporter, probably because it reminded her of their own friendship on the paper in New York, but she was more than consoled by the way both Manuel and Juanita treated her as if she was Sheedy's girl, as if they were lovers. Kate didn't know whether Sheedy was aware of their assumption but she was surprised how good it made her feel.

Slim, dark-haired, and good-looking, Manuel told her how Sheedy had enticed him from a Malaga newspaper to work on the programme, how the older man had shared with him his experience and techniques, how they had become a team talked about far beyond the English expatriate community Sheedy claimed was his only audience. 'I don't think he realises how famous he is becoming on the costa, Señorita, nor does he seem to care, one way or the other.' She told him Sheedy had always been like that.

It was a good evening, so good that it was nearly noon by the time they woke the following day. So the trip to the *sierras* was postponed. Sheedy decided instead to go up the costa to Fuengirola to set up a story for three weeks hence. He suggested Kate accompanied him.

'Fuengirola is the best place south of Nerja for *tapas* bars.'

Kate looked at him, uncomprehending.

'You don't know what *tapas* are?' asked Sheedy. 'Ah ha, you're in for a treat, Callaghan. Just because the Spanish don't have lunch till nearly two o'clock and dinner until nine in the evening, doesn't mean they don't get hungry. Especially if they're drinking. So they invented the *tapas* bar. *Tapas* are snacks. You can have a good meal just by strolling from bar to bar.'

And so they went on a '*tapas* crawl' of Fuengirola. By the time they called at the ninth bar they had drunk enough red wine and eaten enough *calamares, gambas, boquerones, pulpo, busanos, coquinas, navajas, habas con jamón, albóndigas,* and *patatas ali oli* to make lunch and dinner superfluous.

On Wednesday they had driven east to Malaga and turned inland for the climb to Granada where they went without their siesta and spent the afternoon in the splendour of the Alhambra and the evening climbing up the steps and wandering the tiny back streets of the Albaicin, the old quarter on the facing hill.

As they looked back across to the Moorish citadel, Sheedy told her how the last Sultan, departing the Alhambra for exile, had wept and said 'here are the keys to paradise'. His mother had been unsympathetic. 'Do not weep like a woman,' she snapped, 'for what you could not defend as a man.'

It was in Granada that Sheedy had his brainwave. He proposed that he and Kate collaborate on a coffee table book called *Lorca's Andalusia.* Sheedy would select the poems and Kate would take the photographs. So enthusiastic did they become that they sat up half the night re-reading the poems and planning the journeys they would make. Kate had begun taking photographs the following day, in Cordoba.

Finally, this day, there had been the journey across to Ronda. All the way she had found herself falling back in love with the calm, easy-going, kind man who was her friend and guide. And sharing his enthusiasm for Andalusia, especially for Ronda. The town was all he had described and more, a dramatic fortress on a hill, welcoming yet secretive behind its walls, full of life and colour.

She had been stunned by the gorge, El Tajo, and had stood for nearly an hour on the Puento Nuevo (the new bridge, albeit 200 years old), looking down into the chasm with its waterfalls and ruins.

Sheedy told her of its extraordinary history, of how many of those who built the bridge or cut the steps in the wall of the gorge had fallen to their deaths, including the bridge's architect; of how until about fifty years ago the horses killed in the bullring had been tossed from the bridge onto the rocks below, later to be followed by men who had angered one side or another at the time of the Spanish civil war.

After lunch on the edge of the ravine he took her to the place he loved best, the oldest and most beautiful *plaza de toros* in Spain, built in the mid-eighteenth century, the Plaza de la Real Maestrania de Caballeria. They sat in the shade while he shared with her what Miguel and the Rabbit Man had told him.

It was in this bullring that men had first abandoned their horses and fought bulls on foot, armed only with a sword and cape. The pioneer had been Francisco Romero, whose exploits were commemorated in a bullfighting museum under the circular stands, together with those of his grandson Pedro, a legendry artist of the *corrida*.

'It was Pedro who established the rules of the Ronda school of bullfighting.

'*The* matador's *honour lies in his never fleeing nor running before the bulls, provided he has sword and muleta in his hands.*

'*The* matador *must never jump over the fence after the bull has entered the ring.*

'*The* matador *must rely on his hands, not his feet, and faced with the bull should kill or die rather than save face or humble himself.*'

Kate was unimpressed. 'Sounds like macho bullshit to me.'

Sheedy laughed. 'The English writer Kenneth Tynan said there was no point in preaching the virtues of bull-fighting, that the aficionado should never apologise, never explain. I don't intend to. You will just have to come and judge for yourself. If you don't like it, leave.'

Kate looked at him, surprised. It had happened before: just when she was convincing herself Sheedy was a soft-hearted romantic, he would suddenly show his uncompromising side. Somehow it was reassuring.

Still she pressed him. 'OK, but even if you accept it for what it is, it's still cruel. Isn't it?'

He sighed, but good-humouredly. 'I knew we were going to have to have this argument,' he said. 'That's a hard question to answer. Especially as the bulls can't answer it for themselves. If they could, it's possible they would say they prefer dying with honour in the bullring to being butchered in their adolescence in order to become the steaks people eat while decrying bullfighting over the dinner table. But I don't expect anyone to take my word for that.

'I acknowledge there could be a case for stopping the *novilladas* that sometimes take place on the costa, if only to protect the reputation of bullfighting. They often involve poor or inexperienced matadors and even poorer bulls. But I can only say that when I sit in this bullring as the sun sets over the mountains in the background and watch the drama that takes place in the ring, the struggle between man and bull, then all of it, even the killing of the bull, becomes – at least to me – acceptable as part of the culture of this country in a way that I concede it probably wouldn't be in, say, Madison Square Garden. It *is* Spain, part of its character, its history, even its language.'

'But they say it's unfair,' said Kate, 'that the bull

'doesn't stand a chance.'

'He doesn't. At least he doesn't stand a chance of living. Even if he wins, even if he injurs or kills the matador, he dies, just as every animal bred to be butchered for the dinner table will die. What people forget is that the matador can die too. Or be badly injured. I saw some statistics recently. In 1987 there were 814 bullfights and forty-nine matadors gored. That works out at roughly one goring for every sixteen bullfights. A good matador will fight between thirty and thirty-five times a season and stands to get a horn at least twice. Obviously a bad matador is more likely to get gored than a skilful one, but some of the greatest were killed in the ring. Manolete for instance. It's partly a matter of luck; Pedro Romero fought 5,500 bulls and was never hurt, whereas another star of the last century, El Espartero, was gored eighty-two times.'

Sitting in the sun he recited Lorca on the fatal goring of a matador:

At five in the afternoon.
It was five sharp in the afternoon.
A young boy brought the white sheet,
at five in the afternoon.
A basket of already waiting lime,
at five in the afternoon.
The rest was death and only death,
at five in the afternoon . . .
. . . on the corners, groups of silence,
at five in the afternoon.
And the bull alone with a high heart!
at five in the afternoon . . .

. . . The wounds were burning him like suns,
at five in the afternoon.
and the throng was breaking the windows,

at five in the afternoon.
At five in the afternoon.
Oh, what a terrible five in the afternoon!
It was five on every one of the clocks!
It was five in the shade of the afternoon!

Soon after they had returned to the car and driven to the hotel.

Now she dragged herself away from the view from her balcony and banged on the door of the adjoining room. 'Hey, Sheedy, come and have some sangria.'

Like Kate, he was wearing a dressing gown. She poured him a glass of sangria and, taking his arm, led him into the balcony. 'Just look at that.'

He laughed. 'I know. I have the same view, idiot.' He pointed to the balcony just beside her own.

'Oh, of course.' She laughed too. 'But isn't it marvellous? I love the little white farmhouses, what do they call them in Spain . . .? *Cortijo?*'

'Well, your Spanish is coming on. Not bad. Not bad at all.'

He sank into one of the bamboo chairs on the balcony and put his feet up on the balcony rail. He looked across the plain at the foot of the cliff, a plateau within a circle of hills, and imagined the Rabbit Man slowly making his way across the fields of corn and between the olive trees, past the *cortijos*, over the Rio Guadalevin, and then up to the ridge and beyond it into the mountains, observed on his lonely journey only by the occasional eagle or hawk. He wondered how long it took the Rabbit Man to make the part of the journey that was within sight of the hotel. He could imagine himself sitting there having breakfast, lunch and dinner, and still man and mule would be in sight.

'Yes, it's one fantastic view.'

'I'll say,' she said, grinning as his dressing gown

slipped away revealing sun-tanned legs almost up to his private parts. He hastily pulled it around him and blushed, causing her to chuckle mischievously. 'I've seen legs before, Sheedy.'

'Well, that's all you're going to see,' he said. Normally his sense of humour would have more than met the challenge but the attention she was paying to his legs was causing a physical reaction the dressing gown was not designed to disguise. Holding his glass in both hands, he rested it on his lap, hoping it would cover the evidence.

She had moved to the railing, and was leaning over to look down to the foot of the precipice, pulling her dressing gown tight around her so that he could see she was naked under it, could clearly see the contours of her body. While her back was turned he quickly stood up and walked into the room and towards the door, his own dressing gown now even more revealing. 'I'm just going to finish unpacking,' he called to her as he went.

'Bill . . .'

There was an appeal in her voice that stopped him in his tracks, his heart beating fast. He paused with his hand on the door knob, his back still to her.

Then he heard her come towards him, and turning, found her walking into his arms.

'Bill, I think we should have a siesta. Together.'

He searched her eyes, not daring to believe what he thought she was saying. Then he was swept by a tide of emotion, of relief that the tension that had been building up within him was about to end, of gratitude that she had spared him the responsibility, the risk, as he had perceived it, of taking the initiative.

He wrapped her in his arms, buried his face in her hair, and for a moment rocked her back and forth. Then she pulled away, just a few inches, and smiling into his face, slowly opened his dressing gown and, as it dropped to the floor, ran her fingers over his bare shoulders and then down his chest until they reached and rested on his erect cock. He gasped at the touch and then, as she fondled it, still looking into his eyes with a teasing smile, he put his hands inside the top of her gown and caressed her breasts. They were as firm as he expected, having been painfully aware of them bouncing unsupported under the tee shirt she had been wearing all day, and the feel of them unleashed in him all the pent-up passion of their time together.

Moving swiftly now he pushed the dressing gown back over her shoulders so that it, too, slipped to the floor and, picking her up, naked but relaxed in his arms, he took her to the bed, swept off the cover and laid her down. She reached for him and rolled him onto his back and her head disappeared between his legs, her red hair lightly touching his balls as she kissed and gently sucked his cock. He closed his eyes and began to touch and tease her nipples. Then she was above him, her green eyes flashing, still smiling happily, but now rocking back and forward with him inside her. He ran his fingers over her bottom, feeling its rise and fall in his hands.

'Oh God,' he thought. 'Oh God, don't let this stop.' But it did, too soon, his balls tightening and then almost exploding with pleasure. He let his head fall back deep into the pillow and pulled her down on top of him, stretched out now, so that he could run his hands down her back and over and into the crevasse between her buttocks.

After a while she lifted her head from his shoulder and looked down at him. 'Not bad for an old man, Sheedy,' she said.

'You've no idea how much I wanted you, Kate,' he said.

'I think I have, Bill,' she said, 'because I wanted you too. Bill, I love you. I've always loved you.'

'And I love you too.'

'That's good then, isn't it?'

He rolled her off him, onto her back, and leaned over her, cupping her breasts in his hands and kissing them one by one, several times, then he said, so solemnly that she nearly laughed, 'Kate, I'm only going to say this once. I'm a fair bit older than you and it really doesn't make a lot of sense for you to love me in any longterm way. If you want to just take what I have to offer while you're in Spain and then move on, I'll understand and I won't make it hard for you.'

She gently pushed him away and onto his own back. Putting a finger to her lips, she said 'Sssh, Sheedy, stop being the good guy for once and get on with living. I'll decide whether you're too old without your help, and, judging by the way this is rising already, it doesn't look to be a problem to me.'

With that her head disappeared once more between his legs and he felt her tongue licking his balls under cover of her red hair. This time he rolled her over so that her head was on the pillow. Moving quickly between her thighs, and taking her into his arms, he entered her, still soft from before, and began to make love to her with an urgency and power that caused her to cry out. She wrapped her legs round his back and arched up, taking his bottom in her hands and pulling him deeper into her. This time it was she who came first, biting and crying into his shoulder. He quickly followed, the accumulated love juices of too many lonely, unfulfilled years pouring from him until, spent, he slid off her and lay beside her, her head on his chest, until they were discovered that way, half asleep, by an embarrassed and blushing maid some time later.

As the door closed they giggled at her hasty apologies, and he kissed her softly and asked: 'You OK?'

'Of course, I'm OK ... idiot.'

'Stop calling me an idiot.'

'Stop behaving like one. Anyway you called me an idiot earlier.'

'Do you think all first-time lovers end up talking nonsense like this?' he asked.

Then he suggested they shower and change and get ready to meet Miguel and the Rabbit Man and, after another hug, rose from the bed and, naked with the dressing gown flung casually over his shoulder, walked out of the room.

Kate lay still for a moment, her heart feeling as warm as the space between her legs, and then, putting on her dressing gown, she poured a glass of sangria, and went once more to the balcony.

It was dark now and lights twinkled in the windows of the farmhouses. She felt a great sense of peace and space, and also of pleasure that things had worked out, that she and Sheedy were now really together.

She thought of the men she had experienced in New York, younger, yes, maybe sexier-looking, but she thought too of her insecurities with them, of the demanding egos, of the competitive tensions, of the letdowns.

Sheedy she trusted. Sheedy would never knowingly hurt her. Sheedy had self-confidence, didn't need his ego boosting all the time.

And Sheedy was an attractive man in the fullest sense of the word.

'Hey, Sheedy,' she called.

He appeared on the neighbouring balcony.

'I've been thinking about what you said ... about just being together for a short while.'

'And ...?'

'Bullshit,' she said.

And went to have her shower.

Back in the main square, the Plaza de España, the last

of the tourist buses rolled away, back over the bridge, back to the costa. The ornate wooden doors to the bull-ring were slammed shut, leaving the golden sands of the arena to the ghosts of matadors past. The shutters came down over the souvenir shop windows in the Carrera de Vicente Espinel. And, with dusk, the church bells began to summon people to mass.

Ronda, the sunny mecca of tourists from the costa during the day, drew, as it became dark and the night got cooler, into itself, secure on its hill and behind its walls.

Cruickshank had done his best to surprise and disconcert the American.

Recognising the advantage of staging the confrontation on his home ground, he had arranged to meet Jordan in the bar of his Pall Mall club, and asked two of the members to join them for pre-dinner drinks, a member of the House of Lords and a senior civil servant. Jordan needed to be reminded who he was dealing with, and so far it was going according to plan. The American had clearly been impressed by the other guests and by Cruickshank himself, for, determined to give the impression he was unperturbed by the turn of events, that he was still in control, and looking particularly distinguished in formal dress, the Englishman had appeared relaxed and at home in these exclusive surroundings.

Not that Jordan appeared out of place himself. About sixty, he was tall and walked with a limp, had a parchment-white but intelligent face, and was completely bald. Yet, in a dinner jacket, he too looked a man of substance, and, after his initial surprise at finding himself in such company, more than held his own in conversation, deploying all the charm and courtesy that had so beguiled Cruickshank in their previous dealings. And Cruickshank, vastly experienced

65

in diplomacy, was not a man to be easily beguiled. As he watched the American he conceded that whoever the forces were behind Jordan, they had picked their front man well.

The Englishman, having agonised over the matter for twenty-four hours, had decided to negotiate a deal that would keep the project in being while strengthening his own hand and disciplining the Americans, especially Canning. He had planned the evening carefully. He was thankful that he had kept his cool during both his brief telephone conversations with Jordan. Canning may have seen him flustered, but Jordan had not, and, for all Canning's influence on site in Spain, Cruickshank guessed he was of no account at Jordan's level. With this man he could make a fresh start with the benefit of a weekend to recover from the shock and to prepare his ground.

He had decided, too, not to make an issue of the morality of the situation. Clearly, and he shuddered at the implications, this was not an argument likely to impress the American.

So, once in the dining room with its dark oak panels and oil paintings shining in the light from the chandeliers, the dinner and wine ordered, he built on the advantage he felt he had already established.

'Mr Jordan, let me come, if I may, to the matter at hand. I am not happy, to put it mildly, with the way your man Canning has dealt with our problem, but deal with it he has. I will say only this about it: we are all fortunate that his ... his behaviour ... is likely to go undetected. Whatever may be acceptable to you and your associates, and I dread to think, this is not, I repeat not, the way to do business in Spain, let alone anywhere else. If there is even a tiny hint of impropriety in connection with the project, all the necessary approvals will be withdrawn and we'll be out. I remind you that the socialists are in power in Spain now and while they are far too realistic to cut back on foreign investors on the Costa del Sol they would not want, nor could they afford to turn a blind eye to any criminal behaviour.'

Convinced by the other's silence that he was re-establishing his authority, Cruickshank continued. He and the company may have lost the majority share-holding but they were no less essential to the project than before. 'I would go so far as to say that my involve-ment is vital if its full potential is to be achieved, if only because of the standing I have with the Spanish author-ities. If you are in any doubt, ask yourself what the effect would be if I were to withdraw, especially if I was to explain exactly why.'

Jordan looked at him expressionlessly. 'And?'

'I'm prepared to stay involved on four conditions: I want to know exactly who you and your associates are. I want a legally-binding contract between the other share-holders and myself that establishes my chairmanship of the company, my ownership of villa no. 1 and my presidency of the community for a term of no less than ten years. I want your assurance that from now on the project will be developed in a legal and straight-forward manner ... that what has happened will prove to be a once-only aberration. And I want Canning removed, not just from the project but from Spain.'

The American looked at him thoughtfully. 'Sir Brian, I'll give you English credit. You have style.'

'It's not a question of style, Mr Jordan. I am, with many qualms, adopting a pragmatic approach to the position we find ourselves in. You should understand, however, that I have weighed carefully in the balance my duty as a citizen to have criminal behaviour dealt with by the law and, on the other hand, my duty to everybody who can benefit from the project, not just investors but the local workers. I have narrowly decided in favour of the second, but, of course, any further criminality would tip the scales overwhelmingly in favour of the first.'

Jordan smiled. 'You not only have the British civil servant's style, Sir Brian, but also his penchant for hypocrisy. However, I see no profit in discussing your motives. Suffice to say we respect your achievements and your remarkable abilities, and we value what you bring to the project ...'

'*Bring*, Mr Jordan?' Cruickshank was provoked into indignation. 'May I remind you who devised the project. It is you who *bring*, Mr Jordan, and you bring little that I am grateful for ... just additional finance I could have obtained elsewhere and with it, unfortunately, the morality of the Mafia.'

Now it was Jordan's turn to look pained. 'Not the Mafia, Sir Brian.'

'Well, who then?'

They were interrupted by the waiter. Once he had served their appetisers, Jordan leaned forward, his voice low but, to his listener, chilling: 'We have a lot to discuss and I don't wish to waste time on character analysis, but as you have been frank, let me be equally so. You have decided to stay involved despite what has happened. You may, if you feel the need, pretend to yourself that you're in some way a superior being to me and my associates, but do not pretend to me that it is so. In New York we have a saying that whores may be $500-a-night whores operating from luxury East Side apartments or $10-dollar back-alley whores soliciting on 42nd street, but they are both whores. At this moment we are both planning to take advantage of Canning's impetuosity in equal measure and that, Sir Brian, puts us on the same level, whatever that level may be.'

As the Englishman half rose in protest, Jordan, now in charge, waved him back to his chair.

'Let me reply to your four points.

'Yes to the conditions for your own involvement. We are, of course, content for you to remain the top man and be seen to be so. I will not insult your intelligence by denying the strength of the case you make. We would be at a disadvantage if you were to withdraw.

'Yes, of course, to your desire that the project is proceeded with on a legal basis. I should say, by the way, that for the sound reasons you have yourself spelt out, we do not entirely approve of Mr Canning's ... shall we say ... hasty action.

'That brings me to your other points. Despite the reservations I've mentioned, we would not be happy to withdraw Jason Canning. I think you will accept that until last week you found him suitable in every way. He can be given firm instructions about the standards of behaviour we both require. May I commend to you the old saying "better the devil you know"?'

'Are you suggesting that his replacement could be worse, Mr Jordan?'

'I am suggesting that if you're able to reconcile yourself to the act, you should also reconcile yourself to the actor. Jason will be pleased to work with you on the old basis, with you clearly in charge. We would request that at least you try to make that arrangement work.'

'Who is "*we*"? Who are you? What exactly is it you want?'

'We are the same organisation you checked out from the beginning, Sir Brian. We invest on behalf of a portfolio of clients who wish their funds placed in a number of countries, including Spain. Our interest in the project is, in fact, a tribute to you. We believe it to be a brilliantly-conceived and potentially immensely profitable one. Our increased shareholding simply reflects the increased demand from our clients for opportunities to invest in it.'

'You're not exactly the organisation I checked out, Mr Jordan. That organisation, as represented to me, did not engage in murder.'

Jordan looked at him coldly. 'I hoped we had moved on from expressions of moral indignation. I don't deny that some of our investors have accumulated considerable funds in ways that may not generally be thought to be socially acceptable. But that need not concern you ...'

Before he could continue, the waiter once more intervened.

Cruickshank thought rapidly.

They were willing to confirm his position and he would make damn sure the deal was water-tight.

They were giving him assurances about future conduct and, while these counted for little in themselves, Jordan did appear to understand that there was no need for criminal behaviour, that it could be counterproductive. Also, now he, Cruickshank, knew the kind of people he was dealing with, he was forewarned and could probably prevent other excesses.

As for Canning, well on that point Jordan was right. Given that he was dealing with criminals, albeit at a distance, better the devil he knew. And at least he had something to hold over Canning, even if he were not now equipped with the evidence.

As to who they were, Jordan had told him what he guessed. They were laundering money through the project. Money undoubtedly earned by crime.

But, then, who ever did know exactly where invested funds came from? Probably half the world's most respected businesses were partly financed by the profits of crime invested at one stage removed. Undoubtedly there was already a lot of illicitly-earned money being invested on the Costa del Sol.

The whole business was, of course, deeply disappointing. Despite his continued involvement in the project, and his desire to live in Spain during the winter months, it would have to be downgraded on his list of priorities. Instead of shedding many of his other business interests so that he could semi-retire into the presidency of the community, he would need to maintain them so that, should any serious problems arise in Spain, he could brush them off as of little consequence compared with his wider concerns.

For a moment he felt despondent. Then, reminding himself that he still had the upper hand in this conversation, he began to deliberately fuss over his selection of vegetables and the tasting of the wine, showing no inclination to renew the conversation until he had tucked into his roast lamb. Jordan, shrewdly realising that his host was considering all that had been said, also made no attempt to force the issue.

Finally the Englishman spoke. 'Mr Jordan, I will say two things to you. First, you have satisfied me as to who you are and I do not like it, even less do I like Canning's continued involvement. But, on the basis of your assurance that there will be no more criminality and provided the contract I will give you at the end of this evening is signed, I will proceed.

'Second, I am placing a sealed envelope with my bank so that should I find it necessary, or should I suffer a so-called "accident" myself, the full facts will be provided to the appropriate authorities in the United States, Britain and Spain. It may not represent evidence that would hold up in a criminal trial but it would be adequate to persuade the authorities to stop the project and cause investigations into you and your organisation that you would find more than embarrassing.

'If you are prepared to proceed on that basis, I suggest we cease discussion of the past and look at steps we need now to be taking to facilitate the enterprise.'

It was Jordan's turn to take his time. 'May I?' he asked, reaching for the wine.

'Of course.'

'It's a splendid wine. A splendid dinner, Sir Brian. A splendid club. Perhaps if I spend more time in Britain you would consider nominating me for membership.'

Cruickshank almost choked on his food. The audacity of the man. A criminal in his club. It was an unspeakable idea.

Jordan, who had been joking, but showed no sign of it, suppressed a laugh at the horror on the other's face and continued: 'I think we understand each other. May we proceed to other matters?'

'Very well. Our first step must be to see how we can make the best of the fact that the old man . . .' Cruick-shank faltered for a moment.

'Is no longer alive?'

'Quite.' He stared at the American accusingly, affronted by Jordan's indifference to his own sense of moral outrage. 'I'm afraid Canning's solution is not even as clear-cut as you seem to think. As the man is not yet officially dead, and hopefully will never be discovered, we need to persuade the authorities to presume him dead. Or, if we can't do that, we may have to facilitate the finding of the body; that means testing Canning's claim that there is no evidence of foul play and that's a risk I, for one, would prefer to avoid.'

Jordan concurred. 'You're right, it would be better if he is not found. Personally I hope we can find a relative or heir of some sort, because a straight-forward deal is the easiest course and it's unlikely anyone else would be as difficult as the old man. However, if no-one is forth-coming I have no doubt you can manage the authorities with the same skill you have shown in managing all the other arrangements.'

Cruickshank meditated for a moment, then

concluded the discussion. 'I will be spending three or four weeks in Spain to handle this matter myself. I think we can proceed with reasonable confidence that the remaining problems can be overcome.'

The two men moved to the library for coffee, and it was there that Cruickshank raised the outstanding question in his mind. 'I take it, Mr Jordan, that despite not having the majority shareholding I still have full power of decision as in the past? Otherwise, of course, it would be impossible for me to continue.'

'We have no problem with that. Our increased stake is a show of confidence in your management, not a criticism.'

'Very well. I will await your signature on this.' He handed the other a contract he had had drawn up earlier.

Jordan carefully read it. Then, without a word, he signed it.

Cruickshank was spared having to shake his hand by the intervention of a friend. Accepting an invitation to join him and others in the bar when their business was concluded, he coolly, almost abruptly, dismissed the American.

Jordan showed no sign of being offended, just as he had shown little sign of emotion throughout the evening. A dignified figure, he limped slowly to the stairs and disappeared into the night.

Cruickshank, trying hard to appear affable and at ease with his old colleagues, watched the American go. He had achieved his objective, yet he felt only a sense of loss.

As he looked at the other members, peers, MPs, civil servants, businessmen, all in dinner jackets, united in their bonhomie, a reassuring show of Establishment strength, he thought once more of Jordan's hint that he should be nominated for the club and of his, Cruickshank's, horrified reaction.

But what now made him any more worthy of membership than the American?

He looked up to a bronze plaque above the bar containing the club motto:

'*Better to die 10,000 deaths than wound my honour.*'

And he wondered whether he would die those deaths, one by one, day by day for the rest of his life, for in one respect Jordan had surely been wrong.

Not all whores were the same.

Some, like Jordan, would come to terms with being a whore and some, like Cruickshank, never could.

SATURDAY, MARCH 24

It was a warm evening for March and the streets of Ronda were packed and humming with anticipation of the following day's corrida. In the bars and *bodegas* the men were talking loudly, talking, it appeared to Kate, at each other rather than with the give and take of conversation. Each appeared totally confident of his own judgement about the attributes of the matadors they would soon see.

They strolled down into El Mercadillo, the relatively modern part of town, up the popular trafficless shopping street Carrera de Vicente Espinel and then left into the Piazza del Socorro. There the teenage señoritas were out in force, eyes flashing, dresses swirling as they walked in threes and fours round the colourful old square under the watchful gaze of some of the younger *hombres*, leaning on their motorbikes and trying to look macho with their Coca Colas, and before the more world-weary eyes of the old men and women gossiping in its inner courtyard.

Sheedy led Kate through the crowds to a big three-storey building at the top of the piazza. 'This is the casino. Despite its name it's not a gambling place. Casinos in Spain are gentlemen's clubs. Most *pueblos* have one, but this is bigger than most. It's where they held the court martials during the civil war. If you were found guilty you were taken straight to El Tajo and thrown into the depths below. It was an inexpensive form of execution. As you can see its a bit down at heel now. They've changed the name to the Circulo de Artistas and opened a bar that allows women, but to locals I guess it will always be known as the casino.'

Ignoring the sign *Privado* and nodding at the doorman who appeared to know him, Sheedy led her into a big covered courtyard, its roof made of glass, its fringes lined with old leather armchairs. From the centre of the glass ceiling hung an impressive chandelier and on the wall was a giant clock.

He showed her the series of rooms adjoining, one with an immaculately-preserved snooker table, one for chess, the boards all set up and waiting for players, one for playing cards, its small square tables covered in green baize cloth, one a tiny library with newspapers and books and a notice saying *Silencio*.

Then he led her into a bar also full of men talking about bullfighting and wagering with each other on the coming *corrida*, on which matador would win an ear, or two ears, or even the coveted honour of two ears and a tail.

In the far corner of the bar, smoking the biggest cigar Kate had ever seen, sat an enormous elderly man in the green uniform of the Guardia Civil. He was not just rotund but tall, so that he towered over the low table and made the leather chair seem ridiculously small.

'Hey, Señor Bill,' he cried, waving the cigar and pointing to two men sitting with him. 'These two desperados will make space for you. I warned them they must.' The two rose, nodded politely to Sheedy and

Kate, and went to the bar.

'Miguel, this is Señorita Callaghan. Kate.'

The giant Spaniard raised himself with some difficulty from the chair and bowed extravagantly, kissing her hand, and then calling for more wine.

Kate liked him immediately. His big round face was full of humour and mischief. There was about him an aura of good living and laughter. If the *Guardia Civil* had a tough, even sinister image, it had not been created by men like this one.

'And where is El Conejero?' Sheedy asked.

The old policeman spread his hands in puzzlement.

'Who knows? I have not seen him. He has not come to town. It is strange. I have never known him miss a *corrida* before.'

'Maybe he mistook the day.'

'Impossible. He has no timepiece and no calendar but he can tell you the exact hour of any day. Don't ask me how, but he can. No, it is truly strange. But ...' (and his face lit up at the thought) 'he may yet come. Let's hope so. He doesn't say much but I miss him. A good audience for my stories is hard to find.' He roared with laughter. 'And I miss my *conejo*, fresh from the valleys.'

'And so,' said Sheedy, settling himself into a chair and lifting his glass to the other, 'do we have a good corrida ahead?'

'I think so, Bill, I think so.' He puffed on the cigar and almost disappeared in a cloud of smoke. 'We have our own Ronda *novillero* Pepe Luis Martin. I think he is improving. Good enough to be a fully-fledged matador. He will want to be a success in front of his home crowd. I think it will be good. Pepe tells me he will be in his bar later. We will call in to toast his success.'

The noise in the bar grew, and the smoke thickened, and eventually Sheedy persuaded Miguel to go with them to the Restaurante Pedro Romero opposite the bullring where he had booked a table. 'For three, not four,' he told the waiter. The manager came running over. 'Señor Miguel, where is El Conejero? We have no *conejo* left.'

Miguel explained that he didn't know and, cheated of their rabbit, the three settled for a feast of *rabo de toro* preceded by *jamón serrano*, and accompanied by bottles of red Marques de Riscal.

'This ham is good,' Kate said, chewing with relish.

'I'm told there is none better anywhere in the world,' Miguel replied forking another slice for himself. 'It comes from Huelva province to the south-west. You can tell by the black hoof and dark pink meat that it is probably an Iberian pig, not a factory pig but one that is allowed to run wild for a year or two and is fed on acorns.' He explained how the pigs were killed in winter and the hams were then packed in sea salt for at least two weeks to dry out the moisture. They were then cured for eighteen months to two years. The cold winter caused the fat to break down and the meat to become firm. Then the hot summer played its part, causing the fat to melt into the meat so that the whole ham got its special taste. The curing process ended in a dry cellar or cave where the hams developed the mouldy coat they have when you see them hanging in the charcuterie.

'Well, I love it,' said Kate.'

'*Si*, Señorita. It is good. But when you order ham ask if it is *pata negra* and if in doubt look for the black hoof.'

Kate was enthralled by the conversation of the policeman who waved his hand at scores of bullfighting posters and pictures on the walls, for the restaurant was itself a virtual museum, and told stories of matadors and picadors and corridas and great Ronda occasions, until, full of food and wine, they stumbled into the street at nearly midnight.

'Now we must go see Pepe Luis Martin,' said Miguel,

leading them out of the square and up a side-street to the Club Taurino, the bar owned by the matador. As they entered Kate noted the bulls' heads on the wall, posters advertising Martin's 1988 appearances in Spain's great bullrings: Madrid in March, Cordoba in April, Seville in May, and Malaga in August. A noticeboard provided details of his recent results and on another piece of paper there were the signatures of aficionados who wanted to go in the club bus to see his fights.

Near the door was a big life-size colour picture of a good-looking, dark-haired young matador dressed in red and gold.

The bar was crowded but Miguel drove a path for them through the crowd towards a densely-packed corner. 'Pepe?' he called loudly as he reached it.

'Hey, Miguel,' Kate heard a voice call. 'Make way, *caballeros*, for my friend Miguel.'

The crowd parted and she saw a slim young man in red shirt and white jeans sitting in the corner surrounded by admirers. It was the matador in the picture.

'Pepe, this is my friend Bill Sheedy of whom I have talked. And this is Señorita Kate, his friend.'

The young matador rose courteously and shook hands.

'We wish you well for tomorrow, Señor Martin,' Sheedy said.

'*Gracias*, Señor.'

Kate looked keenly at the matador. What was it about his eyes that she found so disconcerting? Was it the lack of bravado? She had expected them to be bold, maybe even arrogant, but it was not so. Of all the men in the bar, Martin was the one entitled to an aura of machismo; yet of them all, he was the one who seemed to eschew it. Was it vulnerability she read there? She couldn't believe it was fear. No it wasn't exactly fear ... more like caution. And loneliness. That was it.

Surrounded as he was by fans, this man was lonely. Kate could guess why. Alone of the men in this crowded, noisy bar he would be in the arena tomorrow; alone he knew what it was like to face the bull. Not for him the unending debate about whether bullfighting was right or wrong, cruel or fair. Only the knowledge that no matter how the dice were stacked in his favour, one mistake, one lapse of concentration, and he could be impaled on a horn propelled at him at speed by half a ton of fierce animal. She remembered the words Sheedy had recited in the bullring earlier:

Bones and flutes sound in his ears,
at five in the afternoon.
The bull now bellows near his brow,
at five in the afternoon.

How much exhilaration did the matador feel? How much apprehension?

The matador called for a bottle of wine for his guests, chatting for only a few minutes before excusing himself, saying he must get some sleep before the next day's fight. Miguel, Sheedy and Kate stayed on to finish the bottle and listen to the arguments all around them. When they left the streets were still full and Kate saw the two men were nowhere near to calling it a night. For her the journey, the love-making, the food and wine had, however, had its effect and she told the men to continue with their reveries while she returned to the hotel to sleep.

They walked round the backstreets to a smaller piazza dominated by an old church, Miguel stopping every few yards to speak to someone he knew, until they found the bar Los Zanos where they had made it their habit to end their evenings with the Rabbit Man before corridas. But he was not there. Over their fifth bottle of the night, they talked on, joined frequently by other friends of Miguel's, until in the early hours Sheedy finalised arrangements for meeting the following day, said *buenos noches* and strolled a little unsteadily back to the hotel where he found the door between his room and Kate's left ajar.

She was asleep, her face picked out by the moonlight through the half-open window.

He quietly undressed in his own room and then, moving next door, slipped into bed beside her.

She half woke, turned and slipped into his arms. Her still unfamiliar touch was enough to cause him to harden. As she felt it she murmured something that sounded like 'you're a bull yourself Sheedy' and went back to sleep.

His heart full he, too, gratefully fell asleep beside her.

Chapter Four

Canning sounded the same as usual when Cruickshank telephoned – cool, efficient, but slightly mocking.

Cruickshank was determined to demonstrate he was back in control, albeit a little discomforted by not knowing what Jordan had reported to the younger American after the previous night's meeting.

'Jason, I have no doubt Jordan has told you that he shares, or at least understands, my concern about the way matters have been handled recently, and that we have reached an accommodation that enables me to continue my involvement with the project.'

'I'm pleased, Sir Brian.'

There was no sarcasm in the voice but Cruickshank flushed with sudden fury at the other man's nerve.

Struggling to keep the anger from his voice, he said 'I have a matter I wish you to deal with. The old man ... I wish you to find him and if there is any difficulty recruit the assistance of the authorities. Do you understand what I am saying?'

There was a pause as Canning, appreciating Cruickshank's care over the telephone, read between the lines.

'Yes, Sir Brian. I will *let it be known* I am seeking him.'

'I need hardly say that this matter must be handled with discretion.'

'I understand. I share your concern.'

I bet you do, Cruickshank thought to himself as he hung up without saying goodbye.

He summoned his secretary, one of a number of staff members called in to work this Saturday morning, and told her he intended to spend the weekend reviewing his full file of activities and delegating as much as possible. He then planned to spend three or four weeks in Spain in order to get the project moving. He asked her to arrange for him to have all the current files, fix a meeting for twelve noon with those departmental heads and project heads who were in the office, and call a board meeting for 9 a.m. on Monday. Also to arrange a flight to Gibraltar and contact Hobbs and arrange for the villa to be ready for his occupation. All communications equipment, fax, computers, telephones etc would need to be in good working order at both the yacht and the villa.

He watched her elegant figure leave the room and for a fleeting second felt an unfamiliar flicker of desire at the sight of long legs accentuated by a short, tight skirt. Then the phone rang and he became submerged in the business of the day.

SUNDAY, MARCH 25

They woke together and lay close for nearly an hour, hardly exchanging a word, each silently, happily adjusting to the fact that they were now lovers. And to confirm it they made love, this time slowly, warmly, almost lazily. Over coffee and rolls afterwards Sheedy outlined his plan for the day. In the morning they would wander down to the foot of El Tajo and look up at the bridge and the gorge from below. Then they would stroll up to La Ciudad, the old town. Then, he suggested, they would have a relatively early lunch, rest ('likely story, Sheedy,' she giggled) in the hotel for an hour or so, before meeting Miguel and hopefully the Rabbit Man for the corrida.

They spent the morning as planned in an increasingly crowded and excited Ronda, adding to their itinerary a market at the foot of the hill near the stone gates to the old town. There they strolled between baskets of tiny squeaking chickens, displays of colourful ceramics, piles of clothing, stalls of fruit and vegetables, racks of cheap electrical equipment, all part of a travelling 'high street' – Ronda today, some other town tomorrow.

They climbed back up the hill and stopped at a *tapas* bar for lunch. They were just tucking into some rabbit stew when an elderly man burst into the bar and cried '*Ha tocado! Ha tocado!*'

Immediately there was uproar. Others crowded round him, slapping his back. Drinks were ordered for everyone.

Kate was amazed. 'What the hell is happening? What does *Ha tocado* mean?'

'I have touched it,' Sheedy replied. 'It's their way of saying they've won some money on the lottery.'

Frantically shouting to be heard over the noise, he told her about the Spanish love of lotteries. The big one was the Christmas lottery. It was called El Gordo, the fat one. The tickets cost 25,000 pesetas each, so most people purchased a share in one, usually a tenth, a *decimo*. But many people divided that into lots of smaller *particiones* and sold them to friends. There were 50,000 million pesetas in prize money with a huge top prize of 250 million pesetas. The draw took place on TV over five hours and the whole of Spain tuned in. There had been some extraordinary wins. The last such story Sheedy had heard was in 1986 when the village of Herrera el Duque in poverty-stricken Estremadura won nearly 3,000 million pesetas. Nearly everyone in the village became a peseta millionaire. But there had been other remarkable wins. For instance, in 1977 the poor mountain hamlet of Criales hit the jackpot. Its ticket, purchased by a grocer and sold in shares, netted more than 450 million pesetas; that was four and a half million pesetas for every man, woman and child in the village.

Escaping with some difficulty the celebrations for what appeared to be just a small win, they made their way back to the hotel for their siesta before, at a quarter to five in the afternoon, they went down into the town and found Miguel surrounded by shouting aficionados outside the *plaza de toros*.

'Any sign of the Rabbit Man,' called out Sheedy above the uproar.

'No, Señor Bill. He has not come. But you come, come now, we go inside. Ah, Señorita, you have picked a good day for your first corrida.'

The crowded old *plaza de toros* made a magnificent spectacle. Its carefully-swept sand was near-golden, the *barrera*, the fence round the arena, a newly-painted red and yellow. The colourful crowd were in tiers from ring level all the way up to the topmost cheaper seats. Over the top of the brown tiled roof of the circular stand they could see the mountains to the east.

Into this arena to a fanfare from a small band came two gaily-dressed marshals on horseback to receive the nod from the president to allow the drama to begin. To a roar of applause the three *novilleros*, young matadors, entered the ring side by side. Kate, finding the scene a photographer's dream, recognised Pepe Luis Martin as the one in the middle. Behind them in a line came their aides. Miguel leaned over to explain. 'Each matador has his *cuadrilla* of five. Those three walking behind Pepe are his *banderilleros*. You'll see them helping him in the ring, drawing the bull away if there's a problem, and eventually placing the *banderillas*. The two on horseback are the picadors. If the matador is the star and the *banderilleros* popular supporting actors, then the picadors are the villains of the piece. But you will see.'

After doffing their hats to the president, the matadors retired to the narrow passageway behind the *barrera*. Then the first, Pepe Luis Martin, stepped into the ring, each of his three *banderilleros* positioned to help. The president waved his white handkerchief to an old man who then leaned over from the front row and opened a heavy gate and waved his hat to attract the attention of the animal behind it.

For several seconds there was silence and then a gasp from the crowd as half a ton of bull came racing out at speed, its head down and its horns aimed straight at the slim figure of Martin, standing alone in the centre of the ring. Kate felt her throat go dry. But as the bull was almost upon the matador he made a pass with his cape, drawing the bull away from his body as if it were hypnotised, so that it ran harmlessly by.

The bull turned and charged, a huge, black, snorting tank of an animal hurling itself at the slim figure in front of him, but for a second time it was diverted by the leisurely swing of the cape.

Five times this was repeated and then Martin dramatically turned his back, leaving the bull seemingly rooted to the spot. The crowd roared appreciatively.

'Those passes are called *verónicas*,' Miguel whispered. 'That last pass was a *media-verónica*. It's intended to force the bull to turn so suddenly that it stops it dead. Pepe has established his control of the bull.'

Then after the sound of the bugles the gates opened

and into the ring, to hisses and boos, came the picadors, big men (Kate thought ugly, but Miguel told her that all picadors looked ugly) on horseback carrying lances. 'This is the *sureta de varas*,' explained Miguel. 'You may not like this.' And Kate didn't. And neither did the crowd. Twice each picador jabbed the bull with his lance, drawing blood and weakening the animal. 'It's a test of the bull's courage,' said Miguel. 'If it continues to attack it is a brave bull.'

'It's cruel,' said Kate. 'Look how the crowd are booing. They think so too.'

'Actually that's not so,' said Sheedy. 'They're booing because they think the picador is over-doing it and making it too easy for the matador.'

The bugle sounded a second time and the picadors withdrew to a storm of hissing.

Then came the placing of the *banderillas*, with each of the matador's aides in turn standing on tip-toe and then running diagonally across the face of the bull to place the sticks with their sharp steel points in the muscle of the bull's neck. Each succeeded brilliantly and retired to cheers.

Finally, Martin faced the bull alone. Now he changed his colourful red and gold cape for a simple red one, the *muleta*, and, draping it across a sword, began a series of thrilling passes. One drew the crowd to its feet, as the matador, the *muleta* in his left hand, appeared to walk almost into the horns and then leaned away, confident he had so dominated the bull that it would follow the cape. 'A *natural*,' cried Miguel to Kate. 'The classic pass.'

Eventually it came time to kill and Martin, having won the approval of the president, and subdued the bull by what appeared to Kate to be a series of highly dangerous passes (in fact, Sheedy told her later, the bull was weary now and confused; the matador had him beaten), now stood directly in front of it and raising the sword to eye-level ran forward, leaned directly over the horns and plunged the sword in. For a moment the bull stood defiant. Then it toppled to the ground.

The crowd rose, cheering and waving white handkerchiefs, demanding the award of an ear, two ears, even a tail to the local hero. As the bull was dragged from the ring the president seemed unmoved but eventually he indicated the award of an ear. Now the matador with his *cuadrilla* walked slowly round the ring as people tossed in flowers, hats and cheered their local matador to the echo.

Kate sat back, exhausted by the experience. She had not liked the picadors, not liked the blood, not liked the killing. But it had been a magnificent, emotive spectacle and as the men around her removed their evil-smelling cheap cigars from their mouths and waved their cardboard sun-visors, their handkerchiefs, their arms at the president, and cheered the matador on his circuit of honour, she found herself abandoning her camera and standing and applauding him too.

The second and third fights were a bit of an anticlimax by comparison and when Martin came back to another roar, Kate felt sorry for the visiting matadors. They were clearly a supporting cast today. It was the local man the crowd was willing on. This time he confronted a big grey animal, more aggressive than the earlier ones and, thought Kate, Martin handled it with some care even after the picadors and *banderilleros* had done their work. The kill, too, was not as clean as the first and, despite the demands of the crowd, the president declined another ear. But it had been a good day for the local hero, two performances clearly to the liking of the crowd, the award of an ear, and he was alive and uninjured.

The day ended well, thanks to one of the visiting

matadors who turned on a brilliant series of passes with the *muleta* and then killed cleanly.

The crowd poured from the arena, excited, talkative, satisfied, Kate amid them, emotionally drained by all she had seen.

'Well?' asked Sheedy.

'I don't know what I think. Except that I'm glad I saw it,' she replied.

'And,' she added, 'I got some terrific pictures for the book.'

It was about 8.30 and they went straight to a restaurant in the alley-way opposite the *plaza de toros* until Kate once more left Sheedy and Miguel sitting in the bar, not saying much now, exhausted, slightly drunk, but happy men. Miguel called for two glasses of *Magno*, the Spanish brandy. 'Ah, Bill, our old friend missed a good one. But I tell you, I am worried. I have been a policeman many years, too long . . . I have, what do you call it, a . . . a . . .'

'Sixth sense?'

'*Si*. A sixth sense. I think something is wrong.'

'Well, maybe we can go and find out. I know roughly the part of the *serranía* he comes from, because he once told us, but do you know exactly where his *cortijo* is, and how to get there?'

'I think so. I think we can get within two, maybe three hours walk of it by taking a car to Atajate, but it's a hard walk. Can you ride?'

'Yes.'

'Good. I have a friend who has a *finca* near Atajate. He could lend us horses. I tell you what, we will go the day after tomorrow. I will come to your hotel at, say, eleven o'clock.'

'You're on. Well, I'll be getting to bed.'

Miguel's eyes lit up. 'Ah, Señor Bill, if I had been you I would never have left it. The Señorita. She is beautiful.'

88

'Yes, Miguel, she's beautiful. And too young.'

'No, Señor. It is good for a man to have a young woman. Keeps him alive, keeps him full of ... what do you call it? ... Vitality.'

'But is it good for her, Miguel?'

'She may be young, but she is not a child, Señor Bill. Leave that for her to decide.'

'Maybe you're right. See you in the morning.' He gave the man a slap on the shoulder and left him calling for yet another *Magno*.

Cruickshank closed the door and, it now being late in the evening, went to his drinks cabinet. 'A drink?'

'Thanks. Gin with ice.'

'No tonic?'

'No thanks.'

Cruickshank poured himself a whisky and walked across to the window. 'It's been a long day. I've been clearing the decks for a month or so in Spain.' He looked at the surrounding buildings, dimly lit on a Sunday night. 'Have you seen my view?'

'Yes, once before. It's magnificent.'

'Oh, yes, of course, I remember, at the time of the Middle East business.'

Cruickshank had been involved in the financing of a complicated construction deal in the Middle East and, at a time when he was frequently travelling there, had been warned by the Foreign Office that he was said to be on the kidnap list of an Arab terrorist group. He had turned to Jim Miller to protect him.

'I gather from our brief telephone conversation that you're free.'

'Yes ... or can be.'

'I need someone. Loyal, discreet. You'll be with me or representing me down in Spain. It will pay well and you'll have no complaint about the other conditions.'

89

'Sounds good. What do you need?'

'A combination of fixer, bodyguard, and investigator.'

'Bodyguard. In Spain?'

'I have a problem.' He paused. 'I need hardly say that this could not be more confidential.'

'You know you can trust me.'

Cruickshank hesitated, then deciding that he had little choice, plunged on. 'I've discovered that our biggest shareholder has been using the project to launder the profits of American crime. I don't know exactly who's involved but I suspect the worst. That need not in itself be a problem except that they seem particularly anxious to protect their money or get an early return on it. They've put a man in to watch their interests, ostensibly as an executive aide to me, but really he's their man. He's dangerous. In fact . . .'

Once more he hesitated. He had not wanted to share this secret with anyone.

'. . . in fact, he has already killed a man who got in the way.'

Miller raised his eyebrows. 'Not like you to get involved with people like that,' he commented.

'Naturally it was my instinct to get out but it's become too complicated and there's too much at stake for too many innocent people. I must try to save it if I can. But I need someone to watch my back, to watch this man Canning and to act as an early warning system for any further trouble.'

His listener sat watching Cruickshank thoughtfully, turning his glass in his hands.

'How long would this be for?'

'At least a year – maybe longer.'

'The money?'

'£50,000. Plus keep.'

Miller put down his glass. 'You're on.'

'Good.' Cruickshank handed him an envelope.

90

'Here's some cash to help sort yourself out fast. Meet me at Gatwick tomorrow morning; Miss Chambers can tell you the check-in time. In the meantime I want you to guard this envelope and on your way to the airport take it to my bank and hand it personally to the manager.' He gave him another envelope containing the contract Jordan had signed.

Pleased and relieved the deal had been made, and noting the other man's glass was empty, Cruickshank suggested he help himself to another drink before he left.

Miller poured himself a second gin.

An enormous one.

Once more he drank it without tonic.

Cruickshank frowned. He hoped his newly-appointed 'minder' hadn't taken to drink since they were last together. He looked at him more closely. He did look thinner, pale, even a bit seedy. Should he have Miller himself checked out?

But as quickly as the idea came to him he dismissed it. It was late on a Sunday night and he was tired and in no mood to begin setting a watchdog on his own watchdog.

Anyway, the man was a professional ... had always been reliable.

No, he had no cause to worry. He was in safe hands with Jim Miller.

MONDAY, MARCH 26

Miguel had telephoned the Reina Victoria at about eleven in the morning and suggested lunch in Setenil, a town some twenty kilometres from Ronda. It proved a revelation. Unlike most *pueblos*, it was not built on the top of a hill or on a convenient mountain ledge, but in a ravine-like valley. Many of the homes were, in effect, caves, built into the sides of the valley so that only the white-washed facade and the door were visible.

They meandered down narrow streets sometimes completely over-shadowed by rock, Kate unable to resist peeping into the doorways and the darkness inside. She could see how cool these homes must be in mid-summer because already, in March, it was hot in the open but cool, even chilly, in the shaded alleys and under the rock verandahs.

Over lunch she asked Miguel about the *Guardia Civil.* There were, he said, four kinds of policeman in Spain. Generally speaking, all towns of more than 5,000 people, and some busy towns of less, employed their own *Policía Municipal* to enforce local laws. They were responsible for parking and traffic control and neighbourhood policing.

Larger towns, especially those of 20,000 or more, were also policed by representatives of two national forces, the uniformed *Policía Nacional* and the plain-clothes *Cuerpo Superior.* These were to be combined into one. But for the majority of Spaniards, and undoubtedly in Andalusia, the *Guardia Civil* was the law. Recognisable by their green uniforms and, to foreigners anyway, rather ridiculous-looking black patent leather tricorns, the *Guardia Civil* had been established in the 1840s to control banditry. They were usually the only enforcers of the law in rural areas and had special responsibility for guarding roads and frontiers.

In peacetime in the last century and the earlier part of this they had devoted much of their energy to trying to control smuggling and to catch those who transported by mule and even by dog the contraband whisky, cigarettes, coffee and even contraceptives from the costa up into the sierras.

Because they traditionally sided with authority and were para-military in nature, being subject to military discipline, having military-type titles, and being entitled to military decorations, they came to be seen by many as more than just enforcers of the law, more a political force. Even in the late nineteenth century they were used to repress anarchist uprisings and in the twentieth, at least in Andalusia, tended to support the nationalist rebels in the civil war whereas their own colleagues in the cities were more inclined to support the republic.

Their past unpopularity had led to a tradition that they always travelled in pairs, were armed, and were never stationed in *pueblos* or towns where they were born or where their families lived.

These days, as memories of the past were dimmed and the *Guardia Civil* modified their behaviour, they had become more accepted. Some, like Miguel, no longer lived apart from communities, and even, like Miguel, became popular members of them ... as Sheedy and Kate discovered that evening in Ronda as, in the company of the giant policeman, they meandered from bar to bar and drink to drink until they staggered to bed after midnight.

'I like him ... I really like him,' Kate said as they lay together in bed.

'Yes,' said Sheedy. 'One day I hope to get him to tell me more about his past. I have a feeling there's a terrific story there.'

He chuckled to himself.

'What are you laughing about?' she asked.

'Well,' he said, 'I've not been able to draw him out after five bottles of wine. And that's my limit. My fear is that after about six bottles I'll finally get at the truth, but I'll be so drunk that the following morning I won't remember a word of it.'

Jim Miller felt as if his head had become a cement mixer. When he put his shaking hands to it, the surface was still, but the inside was revolving round and round.

With each turn of the inner cylinder there was an

awful thump, the noise rebounding off the inside of his skull, as if an oozing mixture of sand, gravel, water and other muck that was once his brain was being thrown from side to side before sliding in a molten lump from the top of his head towards his mouth and throat. There it had dried and hardened, turning his mouth into a dry, rough concrete cavity. His tongue had disappeared, presumably cemented into the roof.

He rolled off the bed, falling painfully to his knees, and began to crawl, crab-like, towards the bathroom door. But it had gone. He turned round, still crawling, and began to move slowly in the opposite direction. There, to his relief, he saw the door. He must have previously been crawling towards the bare wall. Reaching his destination, still on hands and knees, he inched his way to the bath, turned on the cold tap, and put his head under it, turning it occasionally to pour cold water down his throat, hoping to be able to breath without the awful rasping pain.

After several minutes he progressed from firmly believing he was dying and headed for some kind of cement mixer's hell into feeling just plain bloody awful.

This he could handle.

This for Jim Miller had become the norm.

It hadn't, of course, always been so. A brilliant Special Branch officer who had moved into the more secret of the security services, he had met Cruickshank when he had been No. 2 at the Northern Ireland office and Miller had been assigned to protect him.

The word in the 'business' was that Miller was destined for the top. In his mid-thirties at that time, Miller had a suitably unmemorable appearance for his self-effacing work – he was medium height, medium build, had medium-fair hair, and in even a small group of people he could, when he wished, go completely unnoticed. The wags in MI5 used to say that his only party piece was an imitation of a piece of wallpaper. Within that medium-sized head there was, however, a considerable mind, a computer-like memory for detail, and remarkable powers of observation. Miller never forgot a fact or a face.

Few people knew what happened to Miller, why he had become this shadow of his former self. Even those who were better informed only knew the little he would reveal. Or that his conscious mind would allow him to recall. Those details were that he had been sussed out and captured by the IRA while on an undercover assignment in Belfast. Only he, or his sub-conscious, knew what they did to him while they had him, but by the time he miraculously escaped his nerve was shot forever. Such courage and peace as he now found, he found in drink.

He was quickly and quietly pensioned out of the service and set himself up as a private security advisor, most of his clients also abandoning him because he had too much to drink at the crucial time. He had taken to writing to those retired civil servants who had gone into industry. His letter had arrived on Cruickshank's desk just at the time of the Middle East affair. Cruickshank, who had felt safe with Miller in Belfast, had no reason to think the man had changed, nor did the Middle East experience give him any clue. In fact it proved one of Miller's few private enterprise successes, partly because no-one actually made an attempt to kidnap or kill his employer, and partly because he couldn't get his hands on much drink in the Middle East and remained relatively sober.

Now, as he sat, his throbbing head in his hands, his elbows resting on the kitchen table, breathing in the steaming black coffee, he told himself he had to make a supreme attempt to conquer the problem. He reckoned he had hit the jackpot this time. The pay was at least

£20,000 a year more than he would have asked for and, on this rainy March day in London, a year in Spain sounded like the answer to a prayer. He also doubted whether the work would be that exacting. He couldn't see why the Americans would want to make Cruickshank's life any more difficult. There was no profit in it. He could live well in the sun without facing any danger whatsoever. And without the danger, he believed, there would be no need for the drink.

Just the same, he made a detour on his way to Gatwick to a small, basement shop in the backstreets of Camden Town. Its owner, who had taken what seemed an age to shuffle to the door, locked it behind them. Tiny, rotund and round-faced with big spectacles, and at least seventy years old, he peered badtemperedly at his visitor. 'Mr Miller, you know that I don't like to be disturbed so early in the day.'

'I'm sorry, old friend. But I have a plane to catch.'

The old man sniffed with irritation. 'What is it you want?'

'A gun. But I want to pick it up in Spain. Do you have a contact there? Can you arrange it?'

'Spain ... Spain ...' The old man scratched his head. 'What kind of gun?'

'Small. A small pistol. I want to be able to carry it in the inside pocket of a lightweight jacket.'

'Wait a minute.' The old man disappeared into a backroom. Miller looked anxiously at his watch. He was cutting it fine. The old man shuffled back. 'Where can you be found in Spain?'

Miller handed him a card with the phone number of the villa on it.

'I believe I can help. You will have to pay the supplier direct. I shall, of course, require a facility fee.'

'I understand. I think you will find this adequate.' He handed the man an envelope. 'When can I expect a call?'

'It will take two or three days.'

'Fair enough.' And he was on his way.

In the City, Cruickshank had been chairing an edgy board meeting. The news that Anglo-Spanish Investors Ltd no longer owned the major shareholding in the Costa del Sol project had not been well-received by his fellow directors. They had, in any case, never shared Cruickshank's unqualified enthusiasm for the scheme, probably because it was he, not them, who stood to gain most personally. There could only be one Villa No. 1 and one Presidency of the Community and they weren't candidates for either.

They wanted to know how, after investing so much of the company's own money in the scheme, and persuading it to borrow more, Cruickshank could allow it to lose control. Cruickshank responded as positively as possible. The company had never had a majority shareholding, he reminded them – only the most shares. They had always known the opportunity was there for the Americans to seize control if they wanted to.

The way he put it, it was almost as if he had planned the American buyout of the small shareholders.

He stressed that he was still in charge in Spain and argued that if it were a success the board's profits would be unaffected.

'This is a vote of confidence in our idea. And if more money has to be invested it will fall to them to give a lead. What have we lost?'

Only one crusty, rather elderly non-executive director gave him real trouble. If Cruickshank didn't care, why had he gone to so much trouble to spread the ownership around?

'I didn't say this is ideal,' Cruickshank replied curtly. 'I said it has its bright side and, as we have no option, it is on the bright side we should look.'

He was tempted to add, look, if you think the share-holding's a problem, how do you feel about a landowner murdered in the company's name and a syndicate hitman on its staff? Restraining himself, he instead introduced a promising market survey about the project.

Drawing on a reservoir of respect from the rest of the board, he soon calmed the atmosphere. He had taken the precaution of putting the item on top of the agenda and adding several other unrelated matters for decision, all of them to do with company ventures that were highly profitable. This had the effect of restricting the time available for discussion of the Spanish project and ensuring that the meeting ended on a positive note.

From it he travelled by chauffeur-driven car to Victoria to catch a train to Gatwick where he met Miller as planned. The two flew to Gibraltar where they were picked up by Green to whom Cruickshank barely nodded. Once at the yacht he told the chauffeur to take his bags on to the villa and went directly to the study, calling for coffee and Canning.

The brief meeting was for Cruickshank a vital one. He was determined to show that the events of the past few days and in particular his unfortunate confrontation with Canning had not affected his confidence or his power. If Canning expected a cowed figure, he was in for a surprise.

He began by telling the American he wanted Green replaced and that he would himself do the choosing. 'I appreciate that the crew and probably half our other employees are your handpicked men, Jason, but I can't be bothered to remove them unless their specific behaviour warrants it. However, I will not be driven around by a man whose loyalty I cannot trust.'

Canning nodded unenthusiastically.

Cruickshank then gestured towards Miller. 'This is Mr Miller. He will be working directly for me as an aide and it should be understood by all the crew and the company staff that when he speaks he speaks for me.'

Canning looked at the Englishman closely, his eyes narrowing. 'Perhaps you could define more clearly Mr Miller's duties, Sir Brian.'

Cruickshank had already decided to be open about Miller's role. Why pretend? And it would signal to both Jordan and Canning that he meant to call the shots from now on. 'To counterbalance you, Jason. I make no pretence of any other role. I have no doubt you are efficient but you are no friend of mine and you can hardly expect me to operate in an atmosphere of distrust.'

'But I understood my role ...'

'Your role will remain the same. I don't deny your competence. You will continue to handle business affairs and to report direct to me. But yours will be a company role. You will be my executive aide; Mr Miller's support will be personal.'

Canning, unhappy, looked as if he were about to protest, but, noting the determination on Cruickshank's face, stopped himself and merely nodded compliance as the Englishman continued. 'One final point, Jason, before we proceed to business. I don't know how Mr Jordan explained matters to you or what your instructions are but I have been direct with him and I intend to be direct with you. It's as well you know where we stand. And it may mean that we can get on without further reference to the past. I want you to understand that I am running this project and will brook no insubordination or countermanding of instructions. In particular I will tolerate no act of criminality of any sort ... not even a parking ticket ... From now on this project will be developed impeccably.'

Canning, inwardly furious at being lectured in front of the new man Miller, had nevertheless now got his feelings well under control. Cruickshank's reference to his instructions from Jordan was a reminder of what he had been told from New York; that the project needed Cruickshank and Canning was expected to keep him happy. So he lamely replied 'Of course, Sir Brian. Mr Jordan has explained the arrangement and it is one that I am happy to be part of.'

Cruickshank bit his lip, equally angered by what he interpreted as the other's damnable cool, and then said 'Very well, let's get to business. What has happened over the past two days?'

'Not a lot. It's been a bullfight week in Ronda and I felt it was best to get that over before I went up there. In the meantime I've had to get our lawyers looking into the procedure if the old man can't be found. I hope there will be a report on your desk in the morning. We can then decide exactly and at what pace to proceed.'

Cruickshank, refusing to use the chauffeur even once more, asked Miller to drive him to the villa.

The two Englishmen climbed into the Rolls and on reaching the main road turned west. Instead of turning off to the villa, however, Cruickshank asked Miller to continue. 'I want to have a look at the site.'

They drove past the turn-off to Benahavis and a few kilometres further, then, turning north, made their way up into the foothills on an increasingly rough road until Cruickshank indicated a dusty track between some olive trees. After 150 yards it came to an end and they parked the car and climbed between the trees until suddenly they were out in the open on the brow of a hill.

For a moment they stood in silence. Miller had turned down all offers of drink on the plane and damn-near drowned himself in black coffee. He was now desperately wishing he had sun glasses to counter the glare and to deaden the pounding in his ill-treated head, but he could still marvel at the view of the surrounding hills and valleys and of the coast.

Cruickshank was also feeling once more the thrill of pride he always got when he came to this place. 'We own almost all that you see, Jim. There will be a series of small *pueblo* villages on the side of each of those three hills, a five star, membership-only hotel over there, a golf course in that valley to the east, and over there to the right, on the valley floor, the costa's only race-course.'

'A racecourse?'

Cruickshank explained. All the horses would come in from England, Ireland and France especially for the meetings. There would be three meetings a year, timed to help trainers to tune up their horses at appropriate times of the season. And the prize money would be such that it should attract the best. There would be special regulations to allow gambling and the company would split the take with the state, 50–50. The income would alone repay in only five years much of the money invested.

Sprinkled throughout the valleys there would be swimming pools built like small lakes, each with its own bars and restaurants, tennis courts, and a variety of other facilities.

It would be highly exclusive, literally out of bounds to anyone who needed to even look at the prices. But there would be special guests of the company, leading politicians and other influential people, so that it would not only be a place the rich and famous would want to come to for a holiday but also to meet the powerful.

Miller was stunned. 'How have you managed to pull all this off?'

'It's taken some time, because we did much of the buying up of the land in small parcels before we even began to talk about our plans.

'As for the authorities, we've been more than generous in the arrangements we have made, both in terms of the public purse and guarantees of special memberships etc for those who matter.'

'Incredible.'

'Yes, I'm rather proud of it ... Jim, would you mind waiting at the car for a few minutes.'

Cruickshank watched the other descend and then made his way down a winding dirt path and up to the brow of another small hill nearby.

This was to be the site of Villa No. 1, his villa, the home of the President of the Community.

For a short time he stood where it would be and as he did so, as he took in once more the beauty of the area, the views of the mountains and the sea, even of the Rock of Gibraltar in the distance, and as he was reminded of the size of the project, he felt the problems of the past few days begin to dwindle in proportion to the prize within his grasp.

This was too grand a project to be destroyed by the behaviour of Canning.

If there had been a way to rescue the old man he would, of course, have done so. But he couldn't. He couldn't save him and he couldn't bring him back.

What he could do was guarantee there was no repeat of his criminality.

He had been right to continue.

As had always been the case when he came to this place, he returned to his car in buoyant mood.

If he had been forced to tell the truth, he would have had to admit that his buoyancy, at least at this moment, was tinged with relief ... relief that the problem of the old man had been solved.

Fortunately he was not forced to tell the truth, least of all to himself.

Sheedy had left Kate asleep in bed that morning, laying

on her side in the position she had been in earlier when, having woken already excited by the warmth of her soft round bottom pressed into him, he had gently aroused her and entered her from behind, loving her rhythmically, slowly, until they climaxed satisfyingly together.

He went to his own room, showered, and after a cup of coffee walked to meet Miguel who had commandeered a small green *Guardia Civil* car for the day. Sheedy hid a smile as the big man squeezed himself into the driver's seat, his gigantic thighs getting in the way of the gear lever. They drove over El Tajo and down into the old town and at the gate to Ronda turned onto the Gaucin Road, the C341, heading west but mainly south until they reached the town of Atajate, a small white *pueblo* dominated by a big whitewashed church built on a hill above the main thoroughfare.

Miguel continued to the far end of the town and parked outside a bar-restaurant, roomy, modern, clean with a polished wooden bar. They ordered coffees and afterwards Sheedy wandered up the main street and climbed the steps to the big wooden door of the church, but it was closed. He was watched with ill-disguised curiosity by three old men, one with a shepherd's crook, sitting in the shade on the street corner opposite.

He returned to the car and they drove half a kilometre beyond Atajate before turning down a dirt track to an old, flower-covered *cortijo* surrounded by a field containing a number of grazing horses. There, after the usual Miguel performance of hugs and slaps on the back and shouted greetings, they picked up two horses and a string of directions from the owner who, Miguel explained, knew the Rabbit Man and had been to his *cortijo*.

'He says that he last saw El Conejero seven or eight days back, on his way into the hills. He has been expecting him these last two days. He usually comes at least this far once a week to sell some rabbits and pick up some supplies, and he always comes past on his way to the corrida.'

They left the town and the road behind and rode east, initially shaded by trees until they climbed beyond them, negotiating barely discernible paths over the hills and down into small valleys, sometimes riding across hard rock, sometimes through shrubland. Sheedy, unaccustomed to the exercise, felt the sweat pouring in rivers down his neck and back, turning his shirt into a wet rag clinging to skin already irritated by insect bites. His jeans were sticking to him uncomfortably and his backside, not accustomed to the exercise, was beginning to feel raw. His throat was dry and his eyes were aching from the glare. Just when he was about to suggest a rest to the well-padded Miguel, who despite his age and weight seemed unaffected by what was to Sheedy an ordeal, they came to the brow of the hill and he found himself looking down into a beautiful, wild valley, one that he would never have guessed was there. Running across its centre there was a ravine, a crude gash in the valley floor, as if a giant had taken a jagged knife and cut a slice out of the ground. On the other side was a white stone building, surrounded by what appeared to be orange and lemon trees.

'*Bueno,*' cried Miguel. 'That's it, I'm sure that's it.'

They encouraged their horses down the hill, round the end of the ravine, and across the grass and small flowers of the valley until they reached the *cortijo*. Dismounting, Miguel called out '*Hola* . . . are you there? Señor Conejo?'

There was no answer.

The policeman walked over and pulled aside the piece of heavy cloth across the door and he and Sheedy went inside. Miguel looked around with expert eyes. '*Si.* It's his place, Bill. That's one of his guns. And look at the

104

rabbit skins. But he's not been here for a few days, maybe for a couple of weeks. Look at the dust, and this bread ...' He picked up a half-eaten loaf – 'it's hard as a rock.' He shook his head. 'It doesn't make sense. He left Ronda for this place nearly a week back.'

'Could he have had an accident on the way?'

'Maybe, but I doubt it. I think we would have seen him or the mule. We came the way my friend described, the way the old man always came.'

Sheedy looked at a pile of papers on the table. 'I wonder why he gathered all these together ... what he was looking for.'

'What are they?'

'Receipts. One or two brief notes. A couple of old newspaper pictures of bullfights. And some photographs. That's all.'

The two went out into the fresh air and sat down under a lemon tree to drink from a leather *bota* of wine that Miguel had slung across his back before leaving the village.

'What do you really know about him, Miguel?'

The policeman sat silent, looking into the distance. Eventually he said 'Not much. You know how little he said, Bill.'

'But you must have picked up a few things.'

'He was a simple man. He killed rabbits and he cooked some for himself and he sold the rest, he drank vino until he fell asleep, and he loved the corrida, the *toros*.'

'Did you never learn his real name?'

'*Si*. It was Pepe ... Pepe Rodriguis. That was it, Pepe Rodriguis.'

'Who were his other friends?'

'He was a loner. He knew many people, sold them his rabbits, bartered goods with them, slept on their floors, but who really knew him? I think, no-one.'

'Did people talk about him, wonder who he really was?'

'There was talk, but I took no notice. I think he was a peasant of this hard land. He trusted his valleys and mountains and his mule more than he trusted people. People gave him nothing. The valley and mountains gave him his living, the mule was his faithful servant.'

Sheedy sat quietly for a minute. The perceptive American sensed that the Spaniard had chosen his words with unusual care. There was a story in this that Miguel was not telling. But he had no wish to press it. He had no doubt the policeman had his reasons for being discreet.

'You told me earlier he had a brother. Do you think he could have gone to see him – in Casares?'

'At the time of the spring corrida? Miss the corrida? If there was a passion in the man, Señor, it was a passion for this. He loved that *plaza de toros* and he loved the corrida. Loved it, he told me, from childhood. Go away at such a time? Impossible!'

'Unless he got a message that his brother was sick, or in some trouble.'

Miguel touched his chin thoughtfully. '*Si*, Bill, that could be the answer.'

For a while they sat quietly in the sun, Sheedy not in any hurry to climb back on the horse and begin the painful journey back. He looked across the valley and revelled in the peace of the place.

But the more he looked across it the more he felt that something was wrong, something was not as it should be. He looked slowly from left to right, the whole length of the valley, but he couldn't see anything to justify the feeling.

And yet it persisted.

'Miguel, this is probably crazy, but the more I look out from here, the more I feel I'm seeing something that

106

doesn't make sense, that's out of place. And yet I don't know what it is.'

The policeman stood up and for a long time looked, as Sheedy had done, from left to right. 'I can see nothing, Bill.'

'Maybe not.'

Eventually they climbed on the horses and began their journey back. At the top of the hill they stopped and looked down on the lonely *cortijo* and across the peaceful valley. Then they turned west and headed slowly back to the village, the car, and eventually, driving north and slightly east, to Ronda.

Cruickshank's villa was built a few feet above and beyond the narrow, stony beach. Surrounded by a security fence and guarded day and night, it enabled him and his guests to swim either in the sea at its front or in a swimming pool at the rear, the latter set in semi-tropical gardens.

The villa itself was built on two levels. The interior rooms were all large – Cruickshank liked space – and furnished in Spanish style and in the best of taste. His master bedroom suite was on the top, with its own balcony, and it was to this he went on arrival, to shower and change into a navy-blue silk dressing gown. Having done so he settled into a soft chair on the balcony with the usual cigar and Scotch. Even in Spain he engaged in the ritual of his 'special hour'.

He was more relaxed than he had been at any time since Canning's call about the murder. That had been unfortunate, distressing, but he was convinced there wouldn't be a repeat.

The board meeting had gone well, and so had his meeting with Jordan.

And he had enjoyed humiliating Canning that after-noon. If the young American had expected to be calling the shots he could forget it. Cruickshank was back in command and going to keep it that way.

Somewhere nearby someone was grilling sardines on the beach. It smelled delicious. Cruickshank began to look forward to dinner. He had just picked up a pair of powerful binoculars to watch a yacht pass by on its way to take shelter in Puerto Banus for the night when his attention was caught by a sound from the beach. He swivelled round, catching his breath as the binoculars focused on a horse and rider picking their way along the narrow path between the villa and the beach.

She was sensationally beautiful, with the long, black hair of a classic Spanish señorita, and under her pink blouse firm-looking breasts bounced without the aid of a bra, breasts slightly larger than were appropriate to her otherwise slim body. Using his binoculars, Cruickshank, unusually but unashamedly a voyeur of the girl's solitary ride, could actually see her dark nipples protruding under the thin blouse. Silhouetted against the silver sea and still-blue sky on a black horse, she looked like an oil painting.

His binoculars gripped so tightly that his knuckles turned white, he watched her until she was out of sight and then slumped back in his chair, Scotch in hand, stunned by the effect she had had on him.

Women had never played a big part in his life. His first experiences of sex had, in fact, been at boarding school, not with a girl but with a member of the school cricket eleven. Cruickshank had idolised him. Being allowed into his bed at night had been, as he saw it at the time, an honour. Unfortunately, they were discovered one night, Cruickshank a small naked bundle at the foot of the bed with his head between the other's legs. The older boy was expelled, the school losing a useful number four batsman, and Cruickshank was so savagely beaten that he had been sexually repressed ever since.

He had married a colleague in the civil service as much for the comfort and convenience as for love. He had been working closely with her for a couple of years and, while she was not a beautiful woman, he found her both attractive and companionable. And marriage made sense. Their wedding took place at Caxton Hall one lunch-hour. As he rose in the civil service she got left behind and, instead of rejoicing in his success, became sour about it. When he was working late or out of the country she drank heavily. He was welcomed home with bitter remarks and was denied both affection and support. All this was reflected in a decline in her looks. He began to be embarrassed by her, then ashamed of her. To be fair, he tried to talk it out, to persuade her to ride his success with him, not to resent it. But she wouldn't listen. He was not proud of it but told himself that in ending their marriage he was freeing her, too, from an intolerable prison for both of them.

Since then he had from time to time called on a woman in Maida Vale who discreetly and with considerable dexterity met his physical needs.

He was, however, a fit fifty-three-year-old, and, liberated from his London persona and enlivened by the free and easy atmosphere on the costa, had more than once been attracted by a young woman, without having the time or the nerve to act upon it. He had hoped, however, that he would one day meet a suitable companion, someone to share his villa in the sun. Without consciously thinking about it, Cruickshank, the repressed romantic, was ready, for the first time since school, to fall in love.

Of course he had not actually fallen in love with the girl on the horse.

He didn't know her.

But he had been mightily attracted by her.

Attracted enough to slip on a pair of white trousers

and a tee shirt and, taking the binoculars, half run downstairs and out into the front garden to the beach. He was just in time to see her turning off the sand and up a track, between the last of the villas and the open stretch of sand and stones that became, a hundred yards further on, San Pedro beach. He realised she was going to the stables nearby, from where you could rent a pony, but he suspected her horse was too good for that, was probably looked after by the stable especially for her.

He began to make a mental note to make enquiries and then, thinking that he was acting like a teenager, chuckled to himself and, feeling suddenly light-headed, went back into the village to dress for dinner.

Sheedy woke from his siesta and sat up so abruptly that he accidentally struck Kate with his arm.

'What's the matter, Bill?' she asked sleepily, rubbing her head.

'I've got it. How extraordinary – it came to me in my sleep. It was the track.'

'Track? What track?'

'At the old man's *cortijo*. I knew there was something out of place and I couldn't figure what it was. It was the track ... There was a track, probably made by the mule, running from the *cortijo* to the ravine.'

'So?'

'So there wasn't a bridge. Why would a track lead straight to a ravine and stop?'

'I don't know. Why would it?'

'I don't know either. Unless there was a bridge there. But there wasn't one when we were there.'

'How old was the track?'

'I don't know that either, but it didn't look that old. Look, maybe the old man had made some kind of bridge and it collapsed under the weight of him and the mule.'

110

He sat for a moment, thinking. Then ... 'I'm going to go back.'

Kate grinned. 'Holy shit, Bill, aren't you making a bit much of this. The old man could be anywhere. He's probably killed all the rabbits where he lives and moved on.'

He leaned over her, drawing back the sheet to uncover her breasts and gently running his fingers over them. 'I know. I'm sorry. But it won't take much time. You come too. We'll borrow the horses and you can have a ride. The scenery's terrific. Worth the trip for that alone.'

She groaned. 'Oh God, it's the old obsessive Sheedy. Why did I ever get involved?'

'Because you like this,' he said, running his fingers slowly down her front and between her legs and planting little kisses on her neck.

'Well ... seeing as you're here,' she giggled, drawing him down.

It was some time before they surfaced, their intimacy shining from their faces, but when they met Miguel at the Casino Club for what was intended to be their last night together, Sheedy was once more the hunter. 'I just can't go back to the costa without looking down that ravine, Miguel.'

The big policeman was for once silent, looking down into his glass. 'It was careless of me not to look today, Señor Bill. I will come with you.' Then he added, 'But if he is not there, and I waste a day, you will pay for all the vino tomorrow night.'

'It's a deal.'

Cruickshank had arranged a small dinner party, just a local banker, a legal advisor, and the architect who would design the project's *pueblo* villages. They were to be accompanied by their wives and, in the case of the

111

architect, also by a friend from Seville who was staying for the summer.

Rejoicing in the warmth of the evening, he told Hobbs he wished to dine al fresco, and awaited his guests in the garden.

The banker and lawyer and their wives came together and were drinking a vintage Jerez sherry when Cruickshank's other guests arrived. Julio, the architect, flamboyant as ever, greeted the Englishman with an extravagant embrace but Cruickshank, who would usually have reacted with distaste to the lack of reserve, hardy acknowledged either Julio or his wife Isabella, so astonished was he by their companion.

It was the girl on the horse, now wearing a short white dress, still – he could hardly take his eyes off her full, upright breasts – without bra.

The architect introduced her as their family friend, Maria Garcia from Seville.

Cruickshank bowed with all the old-world courtesy he could muster considering that, uncharacteristically, he felt like abandoning all restraint, ordering the others to leave, and keeping only the girl for himself.

'Señorita, it is an honour,' he said, looking deep into her dark-brown eyes.

'And for me, Señor,' she replied, her voice as soft as the breeze in the palm trees swaying above their heads.

For what seemed an age he stood, captive to her eyes, while his other guests looked on. Had the butler Hobbs not come forward with a tray of drinks the evening could have stopped there, as if in a time warp. After the drinks were served, Cruickshank drew Hobbs aside. 'The young lady – see she is sitting on my left. Change the table plan accordingly.'

The girl had settled herself in a deck chair, her long legs crossed, her brief white dress halfway up her bronze thighs. If she was aware of Cruickshank's fascination with her, she gave no sign. With a huge effort, he pulled himself together and concentrated on his older guests, turning on the Cruickshank charm, deploying his gift for giving each in turn just enough of his full attention to make them feel they were particularly special to him that evening. But dinner could not come too soon, for then he had her beside him, and could for the first time talk to her directly.

'What do you do with yourself in Seville, Señorita?'

She answered him shyly. 'I manage a boutique, Señor. It is owned by my guardian.'

'Guardian?'

Julio, the architect, sitting on Cruickshank's right, joined in. 'Not just an ordinary shop. Maria has had the good fortune to become a member of one of Seville's best-known families. For three generations they have been famous for raising fighting bulls and horses, and, contrastingly, for their trade in antiques, but the present head of the family has expanded into fashion, top quality clothes and jewellery. He was a close friend of mine at university. We have kept in touch.'

'For how long are you visiting the Costa del Sol?' Cruickshank asked her.

'For some weeks, Señor.'

'That is our good fortune.' He smiled into her eyes and was rewarded by a shy lowering of the eyelids that made him want to laugh out loud with delight.

'Julio,' he said. 'You must bring Maria out on the yacht. I was planning to spend the weekend at sea. Will you come?'

The architect could not have been more pleased. For him the project was an unprecedented opportunity and Cruickshank was a client to be treasured. 'We would be delighted, Sir Brian, delighted.' He beamed up the table at his wife, while Cruickshank smiled, idiotically he felt, at Maria. Then, afraid he was in danger of disconcerting

113

the girl with excessive attention, he dragged his eyes from her and encouraged the conversation to become more general.

Later as he saw his guests to the gate he walked at her side once more. 'Thank you for coming, Maria,' he said. 'You have made the evening a specially enchanting one. I look forward to seeing you at the weekend.'

'It has been an honour, Señor,' she said.

'An honour? he replied, speaking quietly so that only she could hear. 'I hope not. I hope you will come to feel that time spent in my company can be fun.'

Suddenly she lifted her head, tossed back her hair, and looked straight into his eyes. He lost a breath and almost choked at her beauty in the moonlight. 'I like men of honour, Señor,' she said. And was gone.

That night he lay in his bed, the words *I like men of honour* going round in his head.

He fell into an uneasy sleep and in it saw an old peasant on a donkey falling ... falling down an endless pit.

Then the girl was there on her horse, falling too. They were both falling silently until she looked up and called to him ... to him, standing at the top ... '*but I like men of honour*'.

Then she was naked and Canning was there and he was naked too and they were coupling even as they fell. Canning was laughing ... laughing at him. They were both laughing at him. Then there was Jordan, limping towards him, Jordan standing looking down into the pit, Jordan telling him not to worry, that a whore, too, could have honour.

Then once more they were there, falling still, naked still, Canning with a huge erection, Canning whispering in her ear and looking at Cruickshank, and then she, her brown eyes, reproachful, looking at him too, and shaking her head and saying '*but I like men of honour*' ...

That night and with that nightmare he suffered the first of the many deaths he would suffer alone in his bed at night.

The first of the 10,000 deaths.

TUESDAY, MARCH 27

They looked down at him, all three of them, Sheedy, Kate and Miguel, standing in silence, side by side on the rim of the ravine.

Only his head was visible, his body covered partly by the dead mule and partly by the wooden slabs that were once a bridge.

Kate moved away first, distressed, but also sensitive to the deeper feelings of the two who had been his friends.

'Poor bastard,' Sheedy said, more to himself than to the others. 'Poor old Rabbit Man.'

'Should we leave him, Señor Bill?' asked Miguel after a while. 'Should we leave him in peace in his valley?'

'I don't know.' Sheedy turned away and, with the policeman following, walked slowly back to their horses to collect the leather *bota* of wine. Calling to Kate, they sat together on the grass, each thinking their own thoughts.

Sheedy looked sympathetically at the Spaniard, suddenly older and greyer, all the humour gone from his face. 'I'm sorry, Miguel, I know you had a special friendship.'

'*Si*, Bill. He didn't say much but I was used to his company. We drank a lot of vino together, saw a lot of corridas together ... even argued over your hero Lorca together.'

'I guess his bridge just fell apart.'

'*Si* ... his bridge and his world.'

115

'I don't think we can leave him down there, Miguel. We'll have to get help and some ropes. If we go back to the village now we could arrange to collect him tomorrow.'

Miguel nodded forlornly. '*Si.*'

They stood up and Sheedy walked up to the big man. 'Miguel, you and I will stay friends. We'll keep his memory alive. We'll remember him as we eat our *conejo* and when we meet for the corridas.'

'*Si*, señor.'

Sheedy opened his arms and they hugged each other.

Kate, watching, marvelled at the friendships Sheedy struck up with the most unlikely people, and loved him for his compassion.

Urging their horses over the rough ground, they rode as fast as was possible back to the village and Miguel arranged for a local policeman and two or three farm workers to accompany them the following day. Then they drove back to Ronda from where, Miguel said, he would also find a doctor to go with them to the ravine.

Tired from the journey and aware they had to repeat it the following day, Sheedy and Kate went early to bed, lying awake in each other's arms for an hour or two, saying little, growing closer in their shared experience.

Miguel spent the evening in his customary corner of the Casino Club, drinking brandy and becoming increasingly morose.

The last to leave, courteously removed by the manager, he could be seen in the early hours, his uniform awry, standing in front of the plaza de toros, a half-drunk bottle in his hand, tears rolling down his face.

Turning away he crossed the road to the pavement outside the Restaurante Pedro Romero.

On the window there was a small notice: *No conejo today.*

He stood looking at it for several minutes, then said softly, 'It will do for your gravestone, old friend ... it will say "Pepe is dead – no conejo today".'

Chapter Five

WEDNESDAY, MARCH 28

It was a classic Costa del Sol day, albeit more like July than March. The sun was blazing from a cloudless sky and all the way down the costa, from Torremolinos to Benalmadena to Fuengirola to Marbella to San Pedro to Estapona, the invading army descended upon undefended beaches. They came slowly, plodding in ill-fitting flip-flops or hopping insanely in bare feet on hot sand ... ungainly Englanders, olive-skinned French, fair-haired Germans, loners and lovers and families with squealing children, sun-bathers and swimmers, water-skiers and wind-surfers. They came with beach bags, beach balls, beach mats and beach umbrellas, with sun lotion and sun glasses, with paperbacks and Walkmans.

And on the beach near Puerto Banus they looked out to sea, envying Sir Brian Cruickshank's magnificent yacht, the sun causing its blue, green and white waves to sparkle as it sailed south from the port towards the African coast.

Reclining in a deckchair by the pool on the top deck,

a glass of chilled champagne in his hand, Cruickshank had at last been able to forget the trials and tribulations of the past week and concentrate on the beauty of the young woman from Seville.

She was wearing a pink bikini. He remembered the pink blouse she wore when he first saw her. It was obviously her favourite colour. He asked Hobbs to collect any pink flowers he could find in the vases scattered about the lounges and bedrooms and make up a bouquet to put beside her bed.

He was surprised that, while shy in conversation, she was physically uninhibited. The bikini was revealing and she had joined in the pool games enthusiastically.

When sitting reading, her hair was pushed back and this, together with her dark sun glasses, made her look both sophisticated and older than what he had guessed were her twenty-eight-or-nine years.

Cruickshank himself was wearing white trousers and a blue sleeveless shirt, too sensitive about his pale skin and thin legs to sunbathe in her presence. This was in contrast to Julio, whose small red bathing costume enabled him to show off what Cruickshank disapprovingly, if irrationally, thought was an unnaturally muscular body for a middle-aged architect. Once he imagined he caught Maria secretly smiling at his own comparatively conservative appearance and he decided to engage in some private sunbathing at the villa at the earliest opportunity.

On the whole, though, it was going well. She was the only unaccompanied woman on the trip so it had been natural for Cruickshank to place her near him at lunch, and his attention to her needs and sensitive drawing out of her opinions had won, he dared to believe, at least one warm, grateful smile before they retired to their cabins for a siesta and shade from the full heat of the sun.

Now it was late afternoon but still hot, and he had

come up on deck to find her alone in the pool. He sat watching until she swam to the edge, right by his chair, and looked up. 'You are a fortunate man, Senōr, to have such a beautiful yacht, to live such a good life.'

'Yes,' he said, feelingly unusually tongue-tied as he looked down into her face and struggled to keep his eyes from straying to the barely-covered bosom just below the surface.

'But you have no-one to share it with? No wife?'

'No.'

'You have never been married?'

'I was once.'

She rested her forehead on the side of the pool, her eyes closed, as if considering what he had said, so he took the chance to switch the focus to her.

'And, you, Maria, do you have plans to marry?'

'Of course.'

'Oh.' He must have sounded disappointed because she looked up and smiled at him, and then said, shyly, 'but I have not yet found the man.'

'Oh.' He sounded happier this time. Then, aware of being alone with her for the first time, warmed by the sun, the champagne and her smiling face looking up from the pool, he went a little further than he had intended. 'Maria, may I tell you that ... that your company on the yacht makes me feel immensely happy.'

Once more she dropped her forehead to the pool's edge, then she looked up, her brown eyes serious. 'I am pleased that you are happy, Señor.' With that she pushed herself backwards and, as she drifted away, called out 'It is good to be happy.'

The moment of intimacy was broken by the arrival of Julio, fresh from his siesta, full of energy for the pool, his pleasure at being a guest on the yacht making him even more flamboyant than usual. He took two or three steps and leapt in, landing beside Maria with a huge splash. She laughed with child-like abandon and, as he surfaced, put her hands on his head and pushed him back under until he came up spluttering and gasping for breath.

Cruickshank joined in their laughter, grateful for the diversion.

He needed time to think, to regroup after his untypical loss of restraint.

Was there hope in her reaction? Had she appreciated the passion, the yearning that lay behind his words? Or had she put it down to gentlemanly courtesy?

He didn't know, but he was not discontented with the encounter. No harm had been done, and just possibly a first careful step had been taken.

But just by him? Or had her questions, her share of the conversation been a small sign of her interest too?

Apart from the crew, there were nine people on the yacht, Cruickshank, Miller, Maria, Julio and his wife, and two English directors of the Anglo-Spanish Investors who were on a few days' holiday with their wives. That evening they all had dinner in the superb oak-panelled dining room, the movable wall panels taken away so that they could look out to the sea and stars. Cruickshank was at his best, hospitable, witty, almost light-headed in his relief at recapturing his confidence after the near-disaster of the past week and in his delight at the presence of Maria, who looked dazzling in a long white dress with a dark brown pendant highlighting the colour of her eyes.

The Englishman had made a calculated decision to put Maria at the far end of the table from where he was seated. If he had too recklessly exposed his feelings that afternoon, this would help her relax, allay her fears that he was coming on too strong too soon. If, on the other hand, she had welcomed his words, then it would do no harm to show he was a man in control of himself, to

121

demonstrate his strength of character by his ability to relax with his other guests even while in her dazzling presence.

Also he was in no doubt that Julio and his wife had observed his inability to take his eyes of the girl; this would, at least for a few hours, reduce any concern they felt. Not that he was too worried about Julio's reactions. The architect was ambitious. If he thought that by introducing Cruickshank to Maria he would be held in higher esteem he would not get in the way of any friendship that developed. Isabella could, however, be a different matter. While the architect would not give their comparative ages a thought, his wife probably would. She clearly felt responsibility to their friends in Seville to watch over the girl and had, thought Cruickshank, been quick to join them when he and Maria had found themselves alone or at a small distance from the others. He went out of his way to be particularly charming to her over dinner and hoped that this, together with Julio's influence, would at least neutralise her.

After dinner the party adjourned to the yacht's small cinema to watch a new Michael Caine film specially flown in from America. Cruickshank waited until it had begun and slipped out, preferring to take a quiet walk on the deck and smoke a cigar.

The yacht, he thought, must be almost halfway between Morocco and the Costa del Sol, a few knots from Gibraltar, for he could clearly see the lights of both the African and Spanish coasts and, ahead, the concentration of light at the foot of the giant shadow that was the Rock.

He hoped that at night he would be able to see the lights of Africa from his villa overlooking the project.

The project?

Why did they keep calling it that?

It was time to give it a name.

122

He was disturbed by a sound behind him. He turned to see Maria, stunningly beautiful in her white dress in the semi-darkness. She came over and they stood beside each other, looking out at the lights in the distance. Neither spoke, and the longer their silence, the more meaningful Cruickshank felt it becoming. And the harder to break.

In the end, with superhuman control, he chose to perpetuate the slight distance he had created over dinner and, resisting a nearly overwhelming desire to turn and try to take her into his arms, he said in a detached, conversational way 'That must be Sotogrande over there. Have you been there?'

'No, but I have heard it is a big resort.'

'Maria,' he said, 'it will not compare with the project we are building. Not be in the same class.'

'What will your project be called, Señor?'

'Brian.'

'You will call it Brian?'

He laughed. 'No. No, that is my name. I was asking you to call me Brian.'

'But is it not Sir Brian?'

He turned and looked at her and then, drawn in by her eyes, her watchful, cautious, beautiful brown eyes, he dropped his calculated manner and said softly. 'I would be deeply hurt if you ever called me Sir, Maria. Please, just Brian.'

Disconcerted by his change of mood, she turned away, looking back out to sea. 'And your project, Señor Brian, what will it be called?'

He was about to reply that it had no name when he had an idea. He knew now what he would call it. But, before he could tell her, they were interrupted. The film was over and the others were coming out on deck, glasses in hand.

Cruickshank called for Hobbs to bring another bottle

of champagne and two glasses for Maria and himself and
the group settled down in chairs and chatted until one by
one the couples slipped away. As Julio and his wife rose,
so did Maria. Cruickshank was disappointed but not too
much so; age brought with it the benefit of patience and
he knew there was no more he could have said or done
that night without pressing her too far. But left on the
deck alone, he poured himself one last glass of champagne and found himself analysing the position in his
usual way, point by point.

He wanted her. He had never known such desire,
such need. He wanted her urgently. But also forever.
Just for himself.

Yes, just for himself. The very thought of anyone else
having her, holding her, making love to her, sent a
shockwave through his entire system.

They *must* marry.

They *would* marry.

He was surprisingly confident about that.

But, then, why shouldn't he be? He had made clear
his feelings and she had not avoided him or backed
away; on the contrary she had left the others and come
looking for him. That did not necessarily mean she felt
drawn to him but it probably did; perhaps his remote-
ness from her at dinner had worked and she felt a need
to re-establish contact, be reassured about his interest.

Despite the age difference, he saw no reason why she
shouldn't be physically attracted to him. Cruickshank
possessed his share of vanity but this had its advantages;
it ensured he kept in shape and cultivated his distinguished appearance, and it gave him the assurance now
in coping with a much younger and beautiful woman.

She was, he knew, no ordinary woman. He suspected
that she was more cautious than shy; he sensed intelligence and a powerful will behind the big brown eyes
that, when turned towards him like searchlights, had the

effect of paralysing his own brain so that he had to deliberately talk more slowly to avoid incoherence. No, this was no ordinary woman. He would be proud of her and devoted to her if she became his.

He went down to the library and turned the light on over the model.

It had been more than ten days since Canning had killed the old man and there was no sign that anyone had missed him or cared.

He had cross-examined the American further and was satisfied that, if and when the body was found, it would be taken for granted that the old man was the victim of an accident.

He was confident the project was back on course and every day, helped by his developing obsession with Maria, he was finding it easier to forget the shadow that hung over it.

For some time he stood looking at the model, then removing the card beside it, the one saying '*the project*', he replaced it with a new one, with, in his handwriting, the name he had decided upon.

It would be called the Valle de Maria.

It had been a long day. Sheedy and Miguel had left Kate photographing Ronda and made their third journey in three days to the hills and valleys of the *serrania* this time accompanied by a doctor and two men from the village.

Sheedy, stiff, sore, and sunburned from the earlier journeys, found it even tougher going and marvelled at the way Miguel, who must have been at least twenty years older and God knows how many stones heavier, appeared untroubled by the ride. Once at the ravine, Miguel, calling upon the combined strength of all of them, had been the first to be lowered to the body, followed by the doctor, then Sheedy. The journalist found Miguel keeping the doctor at bay, standing over the body, looking puzzled.

'It's not right, Bill ... somehow it's not right. Look how the wood is piled on top of him. The bridge must have fallen first. Would it not be spread about, some of it under him?'

Sheedy's eyes narrowed. He carefully moved some of the planks and beckoned the doctor to examine the body. Several minutes passed before they received his opinion. 'Fortunately the body has been sheltered from the sun by the walls of the ravine and by the wood from the bridge ... I would guess he's been dead about twelve to fourteen days. He's been killed by the fall. It appears he landed on his front as you find him now. The impact crushed the front of his head and I would expect a post-mortem to reveal serious internal injuries.' Then, asking them to come closer, he said 'There is one inconsistency. This cut and the bruise on the back of his head. I don't believe it could have come from the fall.'

'Could he have landed on his back and bounced onto his front?' asked Sheedy.

'Not possible, Señor. The back of his head would have been far more damaged.'

Sheedy knelt down and looked at the cut. 'Of course, it could have been caused by one of the falling planks. I guess his greater weight would have caused him to fall faster than the bridge, so that one or two bits of wood could have landed on him.'

The doctor looked unconvinced. 'It is a sharp cut, Señor. More likely to have been caused by a falling rock, perhaps dislodged when he fell.'

Miguel began a careful search. 'There is no log with blood on it. But there is this.' He took off a bandana from around his neck and picked up a sharp-looking stone, big enough to fill his giant palm. Part of it was discoloured with what appeared to be dried blood. He looked at it suspiciously, then wrapped it up and began a careful search of the ground and, with the aid of binoculars, the walls of the ravine.

Then beckoning to Sheedy to help, he wrapped the body in the threadbare blanket from the dead mule's back, tied it up in the rope, and waved to the men above to pull it up.

The doctor went next. While they waited Miguel looked at the mule. 'Leave it to nature. We will uncover it so that the birds of prey can see it. They will dispose of it.'

He suggested to Sheedy that he go up to the surface next. 'It will need your combined strength to pull me up.'

Left alone he looked around once more, and then piled up the planks to one side of the dead animal. Just before he grabbed the rope to leave he noticed an object spotlighted by a small circle of sunlight that had penetrated the depths and the gloom of the ravine. He walked over and picked it up. It was a match-book, empty, but on the front the name of a club – Alexander's.

While the doctor and the other two took the body back to the village, Sheedy and the policeman walked back to the *cortijo*.

The doctor had said he would do the necessary paper work and arrange with the priest that there be a funeral.

'Let him be cremated,' Miguel said, 'so that his ashes can be spread in the valley.'

He also told the doctor, 'Describe him as dying from wounds caused by the fall, Señor, but do not use the words accident or accidental death.'

At the *cortijo* the two men made a careful search of the old man's belongings. Before they left Miguel picked up all the papers and photographs from the table and put them in his saddle bag.

127

Then for what Sheedy devoutly hoped was the last time they made the tortuous journey back to Ronda. A long hot bath later, in the case of Sheedy, and three or four brandies, in the case of Miguel, and they were dining with Kate at a restaurant in the Piazza del Socorro, the two men tired and sombre.

No-one mentioned the old man until they had finished their main course, then Sheedy said, 'So, what do you think Miguel?'

'Most probably it was an accident, Bill. That is the most likely explanation. After all, who could have a motive for killing him. He had no enemies, harmed no-one ...'

He paused, hesitated, then added, 'at least not these forty years.'

Sheedy could see Kate picking up on the hesitation. He gave her a warning glance and said 'So you will leave it at that?'

Miguel went silent. 'I have a ...'

'Sixth sense again?'

'*Si*, Bill. It is the sixth sense. It tells me that something is not right. He was a careful man, a survivor. He would not let his bridge deteriorate until it fell apart like that.

'And I did not like the way the bits of wood lay on top of him, as if they were thrown one by one.

'Then there was the stone with blood on it, the one that probably caused the gash in his head. It did not look the same colour as the stones in the walls of the ravine, but I did find stones like it on the surface nearby.

'Then there was this.' He took from his pocket the match-book and gave it to Sheedy. 'The old man didn't frequent the bars on the Costa del Sol. Where would he get this?'

'Where did you find it?'

'Near the body. And it could not have been in the ravine for many days, Bill. It is still crisp, nearly new.'

Sheedy looked thoughtful. 'You said it was probably an accident, Miguel, yet you speak as if it were not.'

'Let me put it like this. If I had not known this man, if I had just been called to the scene, I would have written it off as an accident without a second thought. And, of course, that is still what it could have been. But because I knew him, because I could not visualise this happening to the man I knew, and because I cared enough to look more closely, I have seen other things. Maybe I am not objective and am seeing things that are not there. And yet . . .'

Sheedy responded decisively. 'No, Miguel, you're not imagining things. The position of the logs, the stone with blood on it, the match-book that shouldn't have been there, each on its own means little. But taken together they add up to grounds for suspicion.' He put down his knife and fork. 'On the other hand, as you say, it seems so motiveless.'

Kate listened intently. 'What will you do, Miguel?'

'I will make some enquiries. See if someone knows anything that happened to him recently . . . if someone knows anyone who would have cause to want him dead.'

Sheedy said 'Maybe I can help. Why don't I do a brief report on the next show, ask anyone who knows anything to come forward? The company won't mind; they'll think it's a good human interest story – the death of the Rabbit Man of Ronda.'

'Not many people in Ronda will see it, Bill.'

'I know. But it's worth a try.' Sheedy stood up and hugged the big Spaniard. Kate, too, hugged him and kissed him on the cheek. He smiled expansively, the first real Miguel smile of the night. 'Ah, Señorita Kate, if I were a younger man, if I were not so full of vino and mutton stew' – he patted his stomach – 'I would have to fight this man for your hand.'

'Gracias, kind Señor,' she said. 'But that is not neces-

129

sary. Say the word and I will leave him for you immediately.'

'Holy shit,' said Sheedy, 'and I was worried about those skinny young things down on the costa. Come on, let's go.' And pursued by a gale of laughter from Miguel they headed back to the hotel and bed where, if Sheedy had harboured any doubts, Kate dispelled them with a combination of affection and uninhibited agility that was to remain one of his heartwarming memories of Ronda forever more.

THURSDAY, MARCH 29

Cruickshank waited until Maria was below decks and then slipped into the pool. While he was there she came back and soon he found her splashing beside him, the proximity of her semi-naked body causing him to thank God he was wearing a loose-fitting swim suit. He moved a fraction closer. 'Maria, would you have dinner with me during the week? Alone. It would give me great pleasure.'

She looked away, then back at him. 'Gracias, Señor. I would be honoured.'

'Maria,' he said firmly, 'I beg you, do not be honoured. Just come.'

'Then I will be happy to come.'

'That's better. Friday?'

She looked surprised. 'But that is tomorrow night.'

'I assure you the time will drag.'

Cruickshank, embarrassed by the contrast between her magnificent brown body and his paleness, did not want her to see him get out of the pool. He was, therefore, relieved to see her climbing the steps to the deck. 'Maria,' he called out, 'would you be good enough to go to the top of the gangway and call Hobbs?'

130

She walked round the corner and he quickly climbed out and wrapped himself in a towel dressing gown.

Julio, glass in hand, strolled over and the two stood leaning back on the railings, while Cruickshank lit a cigar. 'Maria is a beautiful girl, Sir Brian.'

'Yes, beautiful.'

'It was kind of you to ask her.'

Suspecting the hint of a question in the other's voice, Cruickshank turned and looked at him coldly, but, remembering his need of Julio, forced a smile and said 'She referred to a guardian the other evening?'

'Yes. I believe she is an orphan, or at least has no known family. The Garcias of Seville – as I told you, an old and respected family – unfortunately could not have children and they adopted Maria from an orphanage. My friend Juan Garcia told me that she had originally been found on the steps of the orphanage after an Easter fiesta. That suggests she was left by a gypsy family. She has been fortunate, Sir Brian, she has had the best education and been raised in a fine home by a family who love her as one of their own.'

'What would normally happen to such a young woman?'

'How do you mean, Sir Brian?'

'What is the custom in Spain. Would a marriage be arranged?'

'No, not arranged. But her parents, or adoptive parents, will take care that she meets young men from the right kind of family. We are honoured that they trust her to us.'

'But she must be at least twenty-eight. Surely she can take care of herself.'

'Thirty, Sir Brian. But of course. She is not under lock and key. She is in charge of her own destiny. It is her upbringing that is the guarantee of a good marriage. And her loyalty to and her respect for her guardians. But who is to blame loving parents for wanting their daughter to be in the care of trustworthy friends?'

'Quite.' Cruickshank thought for a moment, then suggested they stroll to the other end of the yacht from where, he said, they could now see the hills where the project would be. Once there, he turned to face the architect and said 'Julio, I would appreciate a word in confidence.'

The architect was flattered. 'Of course, Sir Brian.'

'Maria. I am attracted to her. Not,' he added hastily as he saw the architect's face fall, 'in a frivolous way. I would like her to be the woman I marry.'

Julio looked stunned. 'Marry, Sir Brian. But that ... why that would be a splendid thing.'

'Julio, I don't yet know and may not for some time whether Maria could feel the same, whether she would be content with an older man. But in the meantime I would welcome your advice on how I should establish myself with her adoptive parents.'

'They are coming to Marbella for a weekend at the time Maria is due to return, Sir Brian. Why not have them as your guests on the yacht for a day. They will be left in no doubt about your suitability socially and materially, and I have no doubt that, when they come to know you, they will come to respect your other great qualities as I have.'

Cruickshank, embarrassed now and wishing he had never begun the conversation, nevertheless plunged on. 'I don't know whether I will be in a position to say anything then, whether Maria will have responded favourably to my ... my ... advances.'

'It would be a mistake to raise the matter then, anyway, Sir Brian. It would be better to go to Seville later and if all is well to raise the matter with my friend Juan then.'

'Julio, I am grateful to you. I can trust your discretion?'

132

'Of course, Sir Brian.'

'Good.' He looked at the Spaniard's eager face and added 'I'm pleased that you'll be working with me on the project and ... who knows? ... other things.'

The Spaniard flushed with pleasure. 'You are too kind, Sir Brian.'

He made a note to do all in his power to encourage Maria to respond to the Englishman's advances.

It would be as close as he could get to having his distinguished and powerful companion marry into the family.

Not that he was thinking in purely mercenary terms. Julio genuinely thought Cruickshank a great man. His friends the Garcias should be proud to have their daughter marry him.

FRIDAY, MARCH 30

'Holy shit, Sheedy, look at those boats.'

'*Yachts*, for Christ's sake! Ships! But not *boats*. Their owners would spit if they heard you call them boats.'

'Well, who cares?'

Sheedy had taken Kate to Puerto Banus. Settling her in a wicker chair underneath a palm tree at the Salduba Bar opposite the biggest of all the yachts he told her, 'This is really pseuds' corner, but it's fun to sit and watch the world go by. Hang on while I go and book a table.' He left her and walked down to Los Bandidos restaurant.

On his way back a red and black illuminated sign caught his eye. It was advertising Alexander's. He climbed the flight of stairs but the door was closed. He guessed it was too early.

He returned to the bar where Kate was being chatted up by a young Spaniard in sailing gear. She winked at him and he deliberately dawdled at the bar so as not to spoil the fun. But then, noting the young man's slim physique and good looks, he had second thoughts. Seeing the two of them together reminded him that he was significantly older than Kate. He settled in the chair beside her and the Spaniard, looking disappointed, moved on – to another girl about two tables away. Sheedy chuckled. 'Sorry, Callaghan, but my arrival doesn't seem to have broken his heart.'

'That's OK,' Kate said. 'I told him my father was returning.'

'Bitch.'

She giggled. 'Whose is that yacht, there? The dark blue one?' She pointed to a yacht towering over the others, *La Gaviota.*

'The Seagull? I don't know. Not bad, is it?'

They wandered down the rows of yachts and then into one or two of the boutiques, where Kate ignored Sheedy's warnings about the rip-off prices and bought a tee shirt.

Over dinner she asked him what was next on the programme.

'Well for me it's just that – the programme. I have to start work tomorrow. Manuel has been researching a couple of stories for the first show and I have to put them together.'

'Are you going to do an item on the old man?'

'Yes. But low key. After all, it could've been an accident. And I'm going to hold back the only clue we've got. The match-book. By the way, I thought we would have a drink in Alexander's after dinner. Get the feel of it.'

'I see. And I thought you brought me down here for a romantic evening. I should have known better.'

'It *is* a romantic evening.' He looked at her lightly-freckled, sun-tanned face and his eyes softened. 'That reminds me, you do know that I'm crazy about you.'

'I know you're crazy.'

'Don't be flippant.'

'Don't be pompous.'

'Oh shit.'

'Shit to you too.'

'Did anyone ever tell you that your language ill befits a lady.'

'Did anyone ever tell you I'm not a lady.'

'I noticed that last night. No lady . . .'

'Don't you dare say it, Sheedy, or I won't do it again.'

'You win,' he said so hastily that she giggled again. 'Let's get out of here before I get into more trouble.'

As they walked to Alexander's he asked her what she would do while he was working. 'Listen, since I arrived you've been rushing me all over Andalusia. This was supposed to be a holiday. I've had only one swim. I want at least a week reading and swimming and I can cope happily on my own, thank you.'

'OK, but if you're sunbathing at my pool wear a bikini top. The gardener has never been the same since the first day you were there.'

'He's not the only one.'

The door was closed but it opened at a push. The club consisted of one space, with a semi-circular bar extending the length of two walls. There were plenty of bar stools and comfortable armchairs around a semi-circular disco floor. The lighting was so designed that those sitting on bar stools or standing at the bar would be in half-light, those sitting round the edges of the dance floor would be in quarter light, and the dance floor itself was fully lit. The music was loud but not too loud to drown conversation. It was fairly empty, but then it was still early in the evening for Spanish discos. There were, however, two women sitting together, dressed in a way that was both old-fashioned and provocative at the same time. One was in her early twenties, and wore a white outfit, revealing an expanse of contrasting black skin between a top barely able to contain an enormous bust and a mini-skirt so short that, when she was perched on a barstool, it all but disappeared. The other, white-skinned with dark hair, had been poured into a shiny, green dress, revealing little bust but legs that appeared to Sheedy to go on forever. They looked curiously at Sheedy and Kate who chose to sit on barstools too, he ordering a Bells whisky with ice, she a chilled vodka and tonic.

'I've got a feeling that you're not as welcome as I am in this place,' he whispered to her.

'What do you mean?'

'Those girls. I don't think they like amateurs getting in the way of their business.'

'You mean . . .?'

Sheedy grinned. Skilled at making friendly contact with barmen, he was soon in conversation with the one man behind the counter, a Spaniard whose English was impeccable.

'I guess most of the people who come to this place only come once or twice,' Sheedy speculated. 'Holiday-makers.'

'Actually, no, Señor. For about half of our customers that is so. But we have a regular clientele, from the yachts and from the costa.'

Sheedy, skilful at not appearing too inquisitive, nodded and made a pretence of losing interest. As he anticipated, the barman, now committed to the conversation, was the one not happy for it to stop. Not while the club was so quiet. 'Do you come from round here, Señor?'

'From near San Pedro. But I spend a lot of time near Ronda.' The opportunity had been created. 'I guess you don't get many people from Ronda in here?'

'Not really, Señor. I can't think of anyone I know.'

The barman was joined by a second. For a moment he looked at Sheedy curiously, then suddenly his face brightened. 'I know your face. You're Bill Sheedy. I watch your programme.'

The first barman became even more friendly. 'Of course. I have seen you too. You're welcome Señor Sheedy.'

'Well, thanks. But don't spread it around. Not everyone likes me.'

Others began to drift in, two or three women in what Kate described as 'varying states of undress' and several men, some alone and some in groups, one clearly well launched into a night's drinking. Sheedy, not wishing to push his interest too far, threw several 500 peseta coins on the bar and, telling the barman they would be back some evening soon, steered Kate to the door.

As they were leaving they bumped into a tall young man, immaculately dressed, conspicuous for his blond hair, bleached almost white.

'Sorry,' he said as he stepped aside.

Sheedy noticed that he had an American accent.

Cruickshank had booked a table in the courtyard of Pantiles, the old farmhouse restaurant, and Maria was enchanted by its pink walls and the flowers and trees growing around the candle-lit tables. Dressed in a light-blue casual suit with even lighter blue shirt and a dark blue tie, with colour in his face from an afternoon working on his papers in the sun, the Englishman looked fit and handsome and more than appropriate company for the young woman, who had combed her hair back and chosen a sharply-tailored black dress with high collar that made her look older than her age.

Cruickshank was still trying hard to appear cool, to put her at her ease, although he himself was far from

137

relaxed. His diplomatic and business career had taught him how to control feelings, to determine the pace of relationships, but the analytic mind, and the nerves of steel that had served him well for more years than he liked to remember had, in the young woman's company, all but proved inadequate. He had to struggle to control a child-like eagerness to please and impress, so afraid was he of making a mistake and alienating the object of his desire.

Trusting that Julio had not mentioned their conversation, he feigned ignorance of her background, wanting to hear it from her. 'Tell me about yourself, Maria. You mentioned a guardian. Are your parents not alive?'

'No, Señor. My mother died giving birth and my father died when I was three.'

'I'm sorry. It must have been a terrible start to your life.'

'I was too young to really understand what was happening, Señor.'

'Brian.'

'*Sí*. Señor Brian.' There was the darting glance from the corner of her eye, the shy smile again. He laughed resignedly.

'Anyway, where did you live then?'

She looked vague. 'In the mountains.'

'Did you not have other family?'

'*Sí*. My father had two uncles. But they did not feel able to bring me up so I was placed with another family, a gypsy family. They were good to me but they had many children and they were poor. I think it became too much. When I was twelve they took me to Seville and I was put in an orphanage. Then Señor Garcia and his wife came to adopt me and I have been living with them since.'

'And you have been happy with them?'

'Very happy. They have been like a real father and mother to me.'

'That's good. And you work in the family business?'

'*Si*. I manage one of the boutiques.'

'What do you do the rest of the time?'

'We have a busy social life. I ride. We have a small horse ranch, and also an interest in a cattle ranch. And I swim; we have a beautiful pool. I read and listen to music.'

'What kind of music?'

'The Garcias love opera and have helped me to learn to love it too.'

'That is a pleasure we share, Maria. In London my company has a box at the Royal Opera House. I have not missed an opera for some years. Where do you go to opera – not, I think, in Seville?'

'No, alas there is no opera house in Seville. Senõr Garcia has many recordings and also we go for a few days to the seasons in Madrid and Barcelona.'

'Is your home in the centre of Seville?'

'No, it is a small *hacienda* on the outskirts.'

'Sounds to me as if you have been very fortunate. But ...' he could no longer resist the question ... 'why is it that the young men of Seville have not been fighting for your hand in marriage ... such a remarkable young woman?'

She blushed at the compliment. 'Some have, but I have been happy at home and felt no pressure to marry. I have not met a man I would wish to live with, a man who shares my pleasures and who is grown ... not old ... but ...'

'Mature?'

'*Si*, Senõr. I do not respond well to the machismo of many young Spanish men.'

Cruickshank felt his hopes rising. He struggled to refrain from pressing the advantage but, deliberately or otherwise, Maria herself enabled him to keep their conversation where he wanted it to be: 'And you, Brian? Why are you not married?'

'As I told you, I was once, Maria. Not happily. My wife and I decided we were making each other unhappy and parted.'

Noticing a little frown, one that quickly came and went, he suddenly saw a problem. Was she a Catholic? Almost certainly. Would his divorce block the way? Panic. His self-discipline broke. He pressed. 'It is a tragedy I deeply regret, Maria, for if I were to wish to marry a Catholic it could cause a real problem.'

'I expect not if the woman wanted you enough, Señor Brian. It would be difficult, yes, but not insuperable.'

He relaxed. Reclining back in his seat he looked straight at her. For a moment her eyes dropped, then she looked up and straight at him.

For a moment neither spoke.

Then he knew, as he had always known in negotiations over the years, that accord had been reached. Somehow, without a word being exchanged, they were both silently acknowledging that there was more to this dinner than the food, than gentlemanly hospitality.

He felt a great soaring of his spirits. Leaning forward, holding her eyes with the full force of his personality, he now spoke quietly, sincerely.

'Maria, I wish to say something to you. From the moment we met the other evening I have been captivated by you. I am not a teenager. I do not fall rashly in love with every woman I meet. Nor am I a philanderer. In fact women have not played a big part in my life. But I know now that whether I waited to say it for a week, a month, a year or ten years, I would feel the same as I do now. I am deeply attracted to you. I want to share all that I have with you, have you in my life, have you as my wife. Is it possible ... is there even the smallest chance ... you could overlook the difference in our ages, that you could feel at least a little as I do, that it might be possible ...?'

140

The girl looked down at the table, and then back up, straight into his eyes. 'I have been aware of your interest, Brian. And I am honoured ...' she waved her hand to stop him protesting. 'Yes, Brian, *honoured* by your interest. And I find you a kind and attractive man. But I cannot say to you now what I may come to feel. It is too soon for me. I would like to be your friend and I would like to spend time with you. Is it so urgent that I should respond?'

'Of course not,' he lied.

Cruickshank was fighting panic.

Had he pushed it too quickly?

'Of course I understand. And *I* am honoured ...' he returned her smile 'yes, I am honoured too – that you would even consider me. How long are you here for ...?'

'Three weeks yet.'

'Then can we see a lot of each other?'

'I would like that.'

'Good.'

He reached out and took her hand. 'Perhaps tomorrow you will allow me to show you the place where our project will be built. We could ride up into the hills.'

She looked surprised. 'You ride, Brian?'

'Of course.' He was doubly pleased. That time the Brian had come naturally. And the riding lessons he had taken some time back, and that had since appeared to have been a waste of time, had paid off at last.

He signed their bill and they walked out into the warm night, strolling along to where the Rolls was waiting. 'If you don't mind, my chauffeur will drop me off at the yacht on its way to taking you home, Maria. I have to take a call from the United States.'

They sat silently in the back of the car, holding hands like teenagers. As they arrived at the port he said: 'Tomorrow? Will it be convenient if my car picks you up at about 11 o'clock?'

'*Gracias*. I will look forward to it.'

He reached out and gently drawing her to him kissed her on the cheek. 'Until then.'

He stood and watched the Rolls until it disappeared from sight and then walked back to the yacht to await its return to take him to the villa.

As he climbed up the gang plank he passed Canning leaving.

'Damn you, Canning,' he thought. 'If it weren't for you life would be as good as it could be.'

Chapter Six

SATURDAY, MARCH 31

Sheedy's office in Marbella consisted of one big room occupying the whole of the floor above a bar. From there Manuel and he did their research, wrote their scripts and organised the programme. The film crews would come up from Gibraltar when required.

In one corner Sheedy sat in an old leather chair behind a desk stacked high with newspapers, letters, files, photographs, old scripts, an over-flowing ashtray and half-drunk coffee cups. Half buried in the chaos was a battered old typewriter. Manuel's desk could not have looked more different; it was neat, the few files carefully piled on top of each, and in the centre, his pride and joy, a brand-new Apple 11GS word processor.

Between them sat their part-time secretary, Rosa, struggling to get their calls via an unreliable phone system. Altogether, there was an atmosphere of cheerful mayhem.

It was a programme day. Sheedy was just preparing to leave for Gibraltar when Miguel called from Ronda.

Sheedy asked what was new.

'Not a lot. As we knew, El Conejero had no enemies in these parts. But there is one thing. I put the word about that I wanted to hear any out-of-the-ordinary gossip about him. Yesterday a man who owns a bar just outside the town called me. He said that El Conejero had looked in to leave some of his catch and to have some wine and that he had been in conversation with a foreigner. He said it was either "an *ingles* or an *americano.*" He said it was so unusual for El Conejero to talk to anyone, let alone a foreigner, that he remarked upon it to his wife that evening.'

'Did he hear what they said?'

'Only one thing. This is what is peculiar. He heard the stranger say "*you'll be hearing from me*".'

'Were they arguing?'

'The barman says not. But who could argue with Señor Conejo? It takes two to argue and he was always so non-commital. The only thing he argued about was bullfighting.'

'What else did the barman hear?'

'Nothing else. That was it. Apparently they spoke for about ten minutes then the foreigner and El Conejero left at the same time.'

'What did he say the foreigner looked like?'

'Maybe thirty, maybe a bit more, expensively dressed and fair-haired.'

'H'mm. Any chance it was just a casual conversation, tourist wanting to chat to local character, that kind of thing?'

'*Si.* At first the barman thought that, especially as the young man did most of the talking. But what about the remark at the end?'

'Maybe he was arranging to get some rabbits, maybe he was a buyer for a restaurant, from the coast or some-where?'

'That's possible, Bill . . . unusual, but possible.'

'OK. Well, let me know anything else you pick up. By the way, we're putting out a piece on the programme tonight. I guess you won't see it in Ronda. I'll keep a video for you to see when you're next down here.'

'*Gracias.* Take care.'

'You too.'

Sheedy sat thinking. He knew that the first step to solving any mystery was to look for things people did that were uncharacteristic, for things that didn't fit the pattern.

The Rabbit Man just didn't get into conversations with strangers in bars. No way. It didn't fit.

If they were talking it was because they had business together.

But what kind of business?

Sheedy believed the answer to that question would produce the missing motive . . . the reason why an apparently harmless old peasant had been singled out for murder.

The horse Maria had been riding when Cruickshank first saw her was owned by Julio and kept at a stable near the beach. From it he now hired a horse for himself and the two rode down the beach until they reached an under-pass that took them beneath the main highway and into the fields beyond. Soon they were climbing into the hills.

Cruickshank had risen early to pick up some suitable riding gear from a shop in Marbella and, with his sun tan coming on nicely, looked like a prosperous rancher. Maria was wearing a white tee shirt and jeans tucked into leather boots and appeared so desirable that just looking at her made Cruickshank ache.

When they reached the brow of the hill overlooking the valley at the heart of the project, they dismounted.

Cruickshank opened a small saddlebag and took out a corked jug of *sangria*. Handing her a glass, he said 'Well, there it is ... the Valle de Maria.'

She looked puzzled.

'That is what I have decided to call it.'

For a moment she looked disconcerted, and, quickly realising what she must be thinking, he said 'Don't worry, my dear. If ... and I hope it will not be so ... but if you decide not to accept my proposal, I would still wish it to be so named. It will be a beautiful place and it should be named after a beautiful woman.'

She blushed and looked down at her glass. 'I am ...'

'I know ...' he interrupted, laughing, 'You're honoured. You can't keep on being honoured, Maria. I just want you to be happy.'

'But it *is* an honour, Brian.'

He began pointing out the sites for the mini-villages and the other features of the project and finally, drawing her to her feet and leading her by the hand, he took her up the winding path until they reached the place where his villa would be.

'This is where my home will be, on this hill. It will be a beautiful home, and should you feel one day able to share my life with me, it would be your home too.'

She turned and walked right up to him, took both his hands and looked into his eyes. 'You are a kind, a generous man, Brian. I can understand why in your country they call you a Knight. You would have made a great Spanish nobleman.'

She leaned forward and kissed him gently on the lips. He felt a great longing building up in him and was just going to reach out and pull her to him when she drew back and taking just one of his hands began to lead him back to the horses.

'But it is becoming hot,' she said. 'It's time to return.'

He rode behind her, watching her shapely bottom

bouncing up and down on the horse in front of him, wishing for the chance to do things that he good-humouredly admitted to himself were anything but noble.

He wondered what his fellow directors in London would think if they could see him now, riding full of desire behind this beautiful *señorita*, his interest in balance sheets and board meetings waning by the minute.

They would think you had gone mad, Cruickshank, he thought good-humouredly, and maybe they would be right.

He laughed out loud.

At the sound, she turned in her saddle, and smiled at him.

And he knew then he didn't care. Didn't care what they would think.

If this was madness, he wished for no other state.

The programme always began with Sheedy talking to camera. Then the credits. Then would come the one or more items of the week, film reports, or studio interviews, or a combination of both.

Kate had travelled to Gibraltar with Sheedy to see it being made and sat now in the director's box as the show went on the air.

'Hi there, this is Bill Sheedy, tonight we look at how developers are trying to get round the new laws prohibiting building too close to the beaches of the Costa del Sol. We update you on plans for more flights into Gibraltar's airport. How will that affect the surrounding area? And we say farewell to the Rabbit Man of Ronda . . . and ask how did he die? Did he fall . . . or was he pushed?'

Up came the title: *Sheedy on the Costa del Sol.* And the programme was under way.

With three minutes left, the second film report now

ended, Sheedy appeared live on the screen.

'Now, a mystery.

'If you've been up to Ronda and perhaps had rabbit for lunch or dinner, *conejo* as it's called in Spanish, the chances are it was hunted and killed by this man (an old picture of the peasant, taken by Sheedy at a bullfight, appeared on the screen) ... Pepe Rodriguis ... known as El Conejero, the Rabbit Man, or Señor Conejo, Mr Rabbit.

'For years he has come to that town from the mountains and valleys of the Serriano do Ronda, his mule laden with rabbits, all ready for the roasting pot.

'Pepe – the Rabbit Man – lived alone in a farmhouse in a mountain valley about three hours from the village of Atajate. (Picture of the valley and *El Cortijo* taken by Sheedy appeared on the screen.)

'He had no family we know of and few close friends, although he was a popular character in the area.

'Last week he was found dead. At the bottom of a ravine near his farmhouse. The bridge had apparently collapsed.

'Poor old Pepe. He died alone.

'Just one question: how did he fall?

'He was a careful man. Would he have let his bridge fall into such disrepair that it would crumble under him? It seems unlikely?

'But if he was pushed, who by and why? Who would want to kill this harmless old man?

'Probably no-one. Probably it was an accident.

'But if you know anything ... anything at all ... about the Rabbit Man that may clear up the mystery, and especially if you know anyone who could have wished him harm, why not give me a ring?

'In the meantime, farewell Pepe, *adiós* Rabbit Man. You'll be missed.'

★

Cruickshank stood in front of the television set, his face white with shock. Miller had disturbed his 'special hour', running upstairs to alert him after he heard the opening headlines on the set in the downstairs bar. They had watched the final segment together.

Miller had never seen the normally imperturbable financier look so angry.

'Christ, Jim, that ... that bastard Canning told me that everyone would assume it was an accident. Why is this man Sheedy suggesting otherwise? What has Canning overlooked?'

Agitatedly, he paced around the room. 'Damn, damn, damn. I should never have let them convince me to let it pass. I should have known better.'

He poured himself another Scotch and gestured to Miller to help himself. Miller, who had been making a superhuman effort to reduce his intake by pouring himself tiny gins and drowning them in huge glasses of ice and mineral water, called instead for a black coffee.

Cruickshank asked him. 'What do you think, Jim?'

'Well, the presenter was pretty laid back. I didn't get the impression he had any evidence to suggest it was other than an accident. Remember, it was hardly a major item on the programme, more like what we in the trade call a fishing expedition. My advice would be not to over-react.'

The financier walked onto the balcony and looked out to sea. 'You know, Jim, when I was a kid I was told by my father that one lie always led to another. I have a terrible feeling this one act, of which I'm innocent but which I've elected to ignore, is going to come back and hit me again and again.'

'I still think this man Sheedy had nothing to go on,' said Miller. 'If anyone had seen it happen or they had any real reason to know it wasn't an accident, he wouldn't have been so tentative. Don't forget the only point he made was that it was unlike the old man to let the bridge fall into disrepair. Well, that's a bit weak.'

Cruickshank cheered up. 'And he did say it was probably an accident.' He stood thinking for a moment, then, decisive once more, said 'Jim, I want you to do two things. Get together with Canning and go over the whole thing again. Test his story. See if you can satisfy yourself that his account stands up. And find out a bit more about this man Sheedy, and why he's interested in this ... this Rabbit Man.'

SUNDAY, APRIL 1

The two men eyed each other without warmth. Canning, already resentful that the unhealthy-looking Englishman had taken his place as Cruickshank's confidant, was even more annoyed to find that Miller and not Cruickshank was questioning him now. Recalling Cruickshank's attempt to record their earlier conversation he insisted they discuss the matter while walking on the beach and only then after he had carefully checked Miller was not wired.

Canning was impressed, though, with the Englishman's professionalism. As Miller took him through his story, he kept tossing in little trip wires, checking detail after detail, so that Canning was amazed at what he was helped to remember.

Miller took him back to the moment of the murder. 'OK, three things I want to check. First, what was the condition of the ground. Was it soft, muddy ...?'

'Hell, no, it was hard as rock.'

'Was it dusty?'

'No, more stony. I guess you're concerned about footprints. There won't be any.'

'Second point. Why for Christ's sake did you dismantle the bridge?'

'To make it look like it fell under him?'

'Why not make it look like he fell off it?'

'I didn't really have time to think. But, anyway, people would be more likely to wonder why he should fall than they would be surprised that a rickety bridge gave way.'

'How did the logs and the planks fall? All over the place or in one pile?'

'I guess they fell in a pile around him and on top of him.'

'On top? Doesn't that strike you as odd-looking? If the bridge fell first, he would be lying on top of the wood, not the other way round.'

'Not necessarily. He was heavy and the mule was heavy but the wood was light. It would make just as much sense for him to fall through the bridge and then for the wood to fall with him and after him.'

'OK, now what did you do afterwards?'

'I went to the farmhouse ...'

'No, before then. Did you stand there looking down?'

'I guess so. I just wanted to check he was lying still ... that he was dead.'

'Did you do anything else but look?'

'How do you mean?'

'Well, light a cigarette, or do anything at all.'

'Yes, I guess so. Yes, I lit a cigarette.'

'So there could be ash around the place where the bridge was?'

'No, because I only took one or two puffs and then walked off. There would be no ash there.'

'And the match?'

Canning marvelled at the man's thoroughness. 'Well, I ... I ... don't know ... I ... I guess I threw it down into the ravine.'

Miller looked at him coldly. 'Great. Bloody terrific. So there could be a dead match in the ravine?'

'For Christ's sake, that could have been dropped any time. By anyone. Even if it's found it proves nothing.'

Miller looked at him even more coldly.

'Now let's go to the farmhouse. You say you collected every bit of paper?' Canning described what he found, the receipts, cuttings, photographs.'

'Why did you leave them there?'

'There was no reason to take them. Anyway, it would have looked strange if there was no paper in there at all.'

'But you left it all on the table?'

'Yeah, I guess that was a bit careless, but it could simply mean the old man had been looking for something himself. I tell you, Miller, there's no problem. We just have to keep our heads.'

Miller considered what Canning had said. His head was beginning to ache as it did whenever he went out into the sun, and his whole being was yearning for a gin, an ice-cold gin, a big gin.

He took his frustration and pain out on the American. 'Look, Canning, you have fucked up on this ... fucked up properly. I tell you now that if a real professional was investigating the man's death, if I was, I would have rated it more than highly suspicious by now, especially as I would soon establish a motive, that the old man was blocking action on the project. I would be calling on Sir Brian within about three days and on you not long after. Fortunately all we're dealing with here are the Spanish police who, I suspect, won't be taking it too seriously, and a TV reporter who has probably forgotten the story already. But don't come on all fucking cocksure with me. Because from me you get no points at all. Is that clear?'

The American flushed with anger. 'Screw you, too, Miller.' He stalked off, back to the villa and his car, and, roaring the engine in his rage, drove out onto the main road.

He arrived back at the port just as Cruickshank and his lunch guests were climbing into the Rolls. Canning noticed that the architect Julio and his wife were accompanied by a young woman. He was struck by her beauty. Obviously Spanish, she was younger than the others, yet the way Cruickshank was helping her into the car he clearly fancied her and Canning couldn't blame him. He decided that if Cruickshank was getting involved, this was a good thing. A romance with a lovely Spanish girl would further tie him into the area, commit him to the project.

As the car went past, the girl looked out of the window and just for a moment her eyes and Canning's were locked together.

The American was left with a feeling that he knew her, that he had seen her somewhere before.

He stood thinking for a moment, then shrugged. Maybe she had been into Alexander's or Capone's sometime. No, she didn't look the Alexander's type. Maybe Capone's? Or maybe he had seen her at some other club on the costa? After all, the costa was really just a big village.

Anyway, he was bound to meet her with Cruickshank. He could ask her then.

Sheedy was woken by the phone ringing. As always after a programme, he and the others who had worked on it had wined and dined well and 11 o'clock the following morning was too early, far too early to be taking calls. He groaned, clutched his head, crawled out of bed and reached the phone just in time. '*Hola.*'

'Señor Sheedy . . .Bill Sheedy?'

'Yes.'

'I am a regular viewer of your programme, Señor. I

saw it last night. I have some information I believe you would find helpful. I wonder whether we could meet soon ... maybe lunchtime today?'

This was the kind of call Sheedy had no choice but to take seriously. This was how half of his stories began. Of course it meant that occasionally he was exposed to a real nutter, but it was a risk he had to take. The worst that could happen was that he would spend lunch indulging someone's paranoia and that Rosa would then spend the next week keeping the caller off the phone.

Still this was a Sunday – couldn't it wait? The caller apologetically explained that it was difficult on week-days. Sheedy reluctantly arranged a drink at one o'clock in San Pedro. The man suggested a *tapas* bar behind the town hall.

'How will I recognise you?'

'It's no matter, Señor. I will know you from the tele-vision.'

'Then may I know your name?'

'Could it wait till we meet, Señor?'

'Of course. One o'clock then.'

Sheedy looked at his watch. He had just over an hour and a half. He telephoned Miguel's office in Ronda and left a message for him to ring. Ten minutes later he did.

'Miguel, I think we need to review the matter of the Rabbit Man, whether I should do another item or let it drop. Why not come down to the costa tonight? We'll have dinner together at my villa and you can stay the night. Plenty of good food and wine and a council of war.'

Miguel having enthusiastically accepted, Sheedy rang Manuel and asked him to come too, and then drove to San Pedro.

Pepe Almejero's was a fairly new bar-restaurant off the piazza at the top of the main street of San Pedro. Sheedy had hardly settled at a table, glass of wine in

154

hand, when a short, dark-haired man in a navy-blue suit but open neck shirt came bustling in, looked around and then came over.

'Señor Sheedy, I am Ramon Aparitico.'

Sheedy shook hands and ordered a bottle of white Don Faustino and some *calamares*, while Aparitico, looking around to assure himself there was no-one in the bar he knew, unfolded a map. Sheedy saw that it covered the costa from Marbella to Estapona and about ten kilometres inland.

'Señor, I work for the authority that considers all applications by developers and others who wish to build in this area.'

Sheedy groaned inwardly. He needed another planning story like a hole in the head. Still he feigned interest.

'See this area here, Señor?' The man pointed to a section of the map bounded by a blue ink line. 'It covers about ten square kilometres and at its heart is a beautiful undeveloped valley.

'Over the past eighteen months all of the plots of land, the *fincas* and the few villas nearby, have been bought, bit by bit, by one company, Anglo Spanish Investors Ltd. In every case they have paid premium prices without complaint.

'And every contract has specified confidentiality for twelve months, a most unusual requirement in my experience.

'Señor, they plan a project that is more ambitious than any of its kind on the costa. Billions and billions of pesetas are involved. It is going to make Sotogrande look small by comparison. It will be like a . . . a mini-state . . . and it will have every facility the rich could want. They even plan to build an English-style horseracing track there.'

He now had Sheedy's full attention. 'Holy shit. You

are right, Ramon, this could make a good story for the programme. How has it all been kept secret?'

'They have powerful friends, Señor. And they have been generous to the right people. But, I stress, apart from that ... that generosity ... and that's part and parcel of the way things work here ... they have done nothing wrong. Just bought the land without fuss.'

'They now own it all?'

'Ah, that's the point, Señor. All but this small plot here.' He pointed to a small oddly-shaped area within the blue lines. 'The owner would not sell.'

'That must be extremely irritating for them.'

'More than irritating, Señor. It's the ideal place for the main entrance to the whole area. While they can get round it, it won't be easy and it spoils their master plan. They want it ... desperately. It's already costing them money, because, until they know whether they can get it, they can't go ahead with much else.'

'Presumably,' said Sheedy, 'the owner is just holding back for a huge sum of money. This could make him a millionaire.'

'No, Señor. It's more complicated than that. The owner wouldn't sell at any price. They tried to persuade us to compulsorily purchase the land and sell it to the project but that is not our way. So they have been greatly frustrated.'

Sheedy's interest grew, 'Bloody hell. Well, who is the owner?'

'That's the point, Señor.

'That's why I came to see you.

'The owner was the man about whom you spoke on television last night ...

'... the owner was Pepe Rodriguis.'

Canning drove down the highway to the turn-off to La Siesta beach club. Near to the club, on the edge of the

156

beach, there is a *conferencias internationales,* a small international telephone bureau from where holiday-makers can call their home countries. Canning called New York. For nearly thirty minutes he talked to Jordan. When they had finished he placed a call to Malaga. A Spanish voice answered the phone. '*Hola.*'

'*Hola.* Señor Castillo?'

'*Si.*'

'I am a friend of Mr Jordan's.'

There was no reply.

'We need to talk.'

Still there was no reply.

'There is a bar in Istan. On the street whereby you enter the town, at the front. Please meet me there at one o'clock tomorrow.'

Only then did the other speak. '*Si,* Señor. I will be there.'

Sheedy was pleased by the stunned silence around the table. A storyteller by profession but also for pleasure, he had enjoyed building up to the climax and got his reward from the surprise on the faces of those around him.

Miguel was first to speak. 'A motive, Bill. We have a motive.'

'You're telling me,' Sheedy replied. 'Billions of pesetas worth of motive.'

'But why wouldn't he sell?' asked Kate.

'Aparitico said that the old man talked about keeping it in trust. "I'm holding it in trust, Señor," was all he said when he was asked.'

'In trust for who?' Kate asked.

'Who knows? But presumably if he was keeping it in trust there must be a will. Miguel, you're positive there was no will in the papers?'

'No. But I think we must go back to the *cortijo* and

157

look. We weren't that thorough because we didn't know we were looking for papers.'

Sheedy, groaning at the idea of another painful journey to the *cortijo*, looked round the table. 'So let's sum up what could have happened. And,' he said warningly, 'I stress *could* have happened.

'Now, the old man was in the way of these people, Anglo-Spanish Investors.

'A man goes to meet him in a bar in Ronda. He is made what was probably a last offer and says no.

'The man follows him out to the valley and kills him with a rock, throws him and the bridge to the bottom of the ravine, but also throws the empty matchbook down there.

'So we have two real mistakes: he was seen talking to the Rabbit Man, and he left the matchbook. I have a feeling if we investigate who's involved in the company we'll find a man who fits the Ronda barman's description and also goes to Alexander's.'

He looked at his audience for questions but there were none.

'Right, there's work to do.

'Miguel, would you be prepared to get a detailed statement from the barman? And could you go back to the *cortijo* and search again? The old man would not have gone to all this trouble to protect the land for somebody without leaving a record or telling someone for whom it was intended.

'Manuel, I want you to find out all about Anglo Spanish Investors. Who and what are they?

'I'll follow up the matchbook. If he was killed, that matchbook was probably dropped by the killer.'

'What about me?' said Kate. 'I want in on this too.'

'I reckon we're going to need you. For a start I'd like to get the TV company to hire you to work on one or two other stories while Manuel and I concentrate on this. Would you mind?'

'So much for my holiday ... but, sure. I'm surprised you're not afraid of the competition?'

He grinned. 'Cheeky cow.'

Miguel interrupted. 'We're still short of evidence, Bill. Even if we show motive and connect someone in the company to the old man, it's too circumstantial.'

'Maybe, but there's more than one reason to investigate it. If the land has been left to someone else, that person has to be found. For one thing he could be in danger. For another, if we can't prove the murder, we can at least avenge Pepe by stopping his killers getting the land or by making them pay a fortune for it. Also, it's just possible that if we build up enough pressure we could cause them to attempt some other reckless act that would give the game away on the Rabbit Man's murder.'

Some time later, after Manuel had gone back to Benahavis and Miguel had emptied the last bottle of Rioja and retired to bed in the spare room, Kate cleared away the remains of the langoustines, salad, and a glass of sangria Miguel had missed and went out onto the balcony to find Sheedy standing, tense, looking out at the lights of the costa.

'I remember you were always like this when you were onto something big in the old days, Bill. You change. You get all tense and single-minded. You're as much a hunter as the Rabbit Man was.'

'Maybe we're imagining it all, Kate, but if that poor old bugger was killed so that some shit of a developer could make a few more bucks, then I'm going to get him.'

'OK, but in the meantime, remember me?' She put her arms round his waist and kissed his nose.

He smiled back. 'Yes ... yes ... I think I do ... just remind me where it was ...'

' Swine!'

She suggested a swim and within a few minutes they were both in the unlit pool, moving quietly in the water so as not to disturb anyone in the surrounding villas.

For a moment they were separated. As the moon appeared from behind a cloud Sheedy looked round him.

Kate had disappeared.

He was just about to call her name when he felt a hand tugging at his shorts. He grabbed at them but it was too late. She already had them over his ankles and was coming up for air, gasping and laughing and tossing them onto the grass out of reach.

'What the hell . . .?' he began but she had disappeared a second time and now he felt her hands between his legs. Abandoning all resistance, he put his own hands under the water and drew her up, kissing her as her face emerged in front of him. Then he quickly slipped her costume off so that she was naked too, glistening in the moonlight.

Throwing her arms round his neck, she athletically encircled his waist with her legs, and then lowered herself in the water, drawing him into her. He leaned back on the side of the pool and allowed her to ride up and down on his cock below the surface until with a gasp she buried her head in his shoulder and bit his neck as she carried them both to a stunning climax.

For two or three minutes they clung to each other in the water than he whispered in her ear 'I've always wanted to do that.'

'What?' she said. 'Fuck me? Or fuck someone in a pool?'

'Fuck you,' he said.

'In a pool.'

Cruickshank sat, glass in hand, in the garden of the villa and looked at the two men facing him. 'What's your evaluation, Jim?' he asked.

'If someone really wants to dig, really wants to prove the old man was deliberately killed, he could find one or two bits of possible evidence ... the position of the wood from the bridge, possibly a match book thrown into the ravine by Canning, maybe a footprint or two. But none of it would be conclusive. Even if some fanatical policeman or the reporter Sheedy convinced himself it was a killing, none of it would be sufficient to incriminate us. I think you're OK.'

'What about the barman?'

Miller looked puzzled. 'What barman?'

'The one who saw Canning and the old man talking.'

Miller looked at Canning with anger. 'You never told me about that.'

'You never asked me.'

'Tell me now.'

'I had a conversation with the peasant for a few minutes about a week before. How else do you think I established he wouldn't sell? It was in a bar outside Ronda. My guess is the barman won't remember.'

'Well, my guess is that he will,' said Miller, 'especially if someone bothers to ask him when he last saw the Rabbit Man. Christ, Canning, it's one thing to be a bloody criminal, but do you have to be a bloody incompetent one as well?'

Canning flushed with anger and began to respond but Cruickshank, who had been listening to this without expression, now surprised both men by interrupting calmly.

'Jim, I've given this some thought. There is no way we can avoid the link between the peasant and the project because we ourselves need to draw it to the attention of the authorities. Otherwise we can't move things forward. I propose, therefore, that Canning goes to the planning office today and tells them that he spoke to this man recently and was at last promised the right to

161

purchase the land. Unfortunately, he can say, we discovered from the television programme that the man died before his promise could be confirmed.'

'Will they believe that?'

'Maybe, maybe not. But Canning should make it clear that we're not expecting our word to be taken on this and we're happy to await the necessary enquires into a possible will, or other family ownership. The more open and forthcoming and innocent we appear, the less it will look as if we have anything to hide. Only if we hold back or deny any interest in the man will it look suspicious.'

Canning, pleased to be extracted from the cross examination by Miller, was eager to agree, but pointed out the peasant had already been contacted by the authorities and had told them he wouldn't sell.

'No problem,' replied Cruickshank. 'We'll just say we upped the offer to a point where he couldn't refuse. That would explain your contact with him in the bar. And it's entirely credible. No-one is likely to believe that he didn't have a price. Everyone has a price – isn't that what you people say, Canning?'

Miller stayed after Canning had left, sitting still and thoughtful in his chair.

Cruickshank asked him, 'What is it, Jim, you don't look happy?'

'Well, for a start, Sir Brian, I think you probably just saved that barman's life.'

'What?' Cruickshank was shocked.

'You gave Canning an out. My guess is that without it the barman, too, would have suffered a nasty accident.'

'Christ,' the financier moaned. 'I thought all this was over. I was assured they had learned their lesson.' Then, looking sceptical, he asked, 'But what makes you say it?'

'I've met his type before. They're completely without

162

scruples. And they don't take prisoners. They don't take them because they don't trust anybody. They don't trust anybody because they can't be trusted themselves. Once in a moment of anger you called him a psychopath. My guess is that's exactly what he is. I have a feeling I'll have to spend most of my time watching him from now on.'

Cruickshank began to walk around the room, agitated. 'God, I hope you're going over the top on this. But please do, Jim. Don't let him out of your sight.'

'There's one other thing that worries me.'

'What's that?'

'Sir Brian, what else do you know about the people behind Canning?'

Cruickshank frowned. 'Not much more than I knew before all this happened. To be honest, Jim, I had assumed that this business with Canning would probably have a restraining effect on them. That from now on they would settle for the long-term financial benefits of the project and behave themselves. It never crossed my mind to have them investigated further.' He paused and then apologetically added 'I'm not even sure I want to know.'

Miller shook his head. 'I don't like it. I have a funny feeling about these people. I can't understand why they wanted to go for all-out ownership. They're supposed to be clever and discreet investors seeking a safe place for their money. They don't need the power as well. In the circumstances I would have expected them to keep in the background. Why have they taken control?'

'My guess is that it's plain greed, Jim. They like the project and its potential and just want more of it.'

'But if they think like that they could have done the same with a lot of the American businesses they've taken shares in, and my impression is that they haven't, preferring a safe, respectable front and a safe return on their funds. Are you sure they don't want to use the land for any other purpose?'

Cruickshank laughed. 'What? Do you think they've struck oil? No, Jim, they've supported all the plans for the project so far, and it's this project and only this project that we've got planning permission for. Honestly, apart from acts of utter stupidity such as Canning's, I don't see what harm they can do. Obviously I dislike being involved with them but I'm satisfied that once it's rolling they'll see it's best to leave well alone.'

For a moment they sat in thoughtful silence then Miller said 'Let's say the authorities find a will, or another member of the family. What happens if they won't cooperate?'

'I think they will. He was keeping it in trust for them to sell. Surely. What other value could it have? Anyway, I'm having the planning team work on a different way of establishing access. If there are any more problems we'll just go ahead without it. That's what we should have done anyway. It's a bloody nuisance, it will cost a lot of money, but it's not the end of the world. Another murder would be.' He considered his own words for a moment. Then added: 'And there won't be another murder. Canning may be mad but Jordan knows any further violence simply wouldn't make sense. He'll see it doesn't happen.'

MONDAY, APRIL 2

Manuel had spent the day on the phone, often a frustrating business in Spain. More than once Rosa had blanched at his language when he had been cut off. When Sheedy arrived back from Gibraltar where he had been recording part of the following week's programme the younger man's usually tidy desk was covered in bits of paper and scrawlings.

'What have you got?'

'Anglo-Spanish Investors Ltd is a British company. Its chairman is a Sir Brian Cruickshank. He owns a villa down the costa and the company also has a yacht in the port. It looks highly respectable, Bill. Apparently Cruickshank was a British civil servant, very high up. He has a lot of his own money in this and I gather there's also American money but I haven't been able to get to the bottom of that yet.

'Apart from keeping the project under wraps in a way I would have believed impossible in Malaga province, they seem to have acted properly in every way.'

'Is Cruickshank based in London?'

'Usually yes, but he's down here at the moment.'

'Is he just? Maybe worth a visit. But first, Manuel, try to find out a bit more about the other investors. Whether there's any Spanish money involved. And who the Americans are. And we need to know who's working for them ... and whether there's anyone who fits the description of the man in the bar.'

Manuel nodded. 'I thought I would wander down to the port and take a look at the yacht, see if any of the crew turn up in a bar.'

'OK, but take it easy. I don't want them to know we're digging – not yet.'

Sheedy picked up the phone and made a number of calls to journalist friends in London. From each the story was the same. Cruickshank was highly respected, well connected, and, in the words of one city reporter on *The Guardian*, 'about as straight as these people can be'.

'Just one thing,' the *Guardian* man added. 'The word in the City is that Cruickshank has climbed into bed with an American outfit, the International Investors' Trust, headed by a man called Theodore Jordan.'

'Yes?'

'Well, I was over in New York last year and there was a kind of rumour ... not much of one and probably unfounded ... that as well as a lot of respectable money the Trust was accepting a lot of cash from some rather shady sources.'

'How shady?'

'Well, like I say, it was not a terribly reliable rumour, but the way I heard it, about as shady as you can get.'

'Christ!'

'Don't act on it, Bill. You would need to know a helluva lot more than I've got. And even if there's truth in it, it's possible that Cruickshank doesn't know.'

'OK. Listen, thanks. I owe you one.'

'Yeah, well, take care.'

Sheedy put down the phone and sat thinking. Then he asked Rosa to get him Teddy Gray on *The New York Times.*

Istan is a *pueblo* village so far largely untouched by the foreign invaders on the Costa del Sol. Perched on the top of a hill, it is approached by sixteen kilometres of winding road between La Concha, the bare, grey mountain that dominates the view inland from the beach between Marbella and San Pedro, and the Rio Verde valley with its dam and reservoir.

Jason Canning had to abandon his car on entering the village because the streets were so narrow. He walked along the street at the front, oblivious of the magnificent view, until he came to a relatively modern bar. Outside it sat a man, alone. Canning settled himself at the same table and called for a San Miguel beer. Only after he had it in front of him and had lazily lit a cigarette, did he speak. 'Señor Castillo?

'*Si.*'

166

'The time is approaching when we will need to activate our plans.'

'I am ready, Señor.'

'You have people in place?'

'In Morocco. And on the costa. Good people.'

'OK. Jordan will be over in a few days. He'll want you to meet him in Tangier.'

'No problem.'

'Two other things. I need some phones tapped. And I need two or three good men available to me at any time.'

'When?'

'The phones? Like yesterday. The men – from tomorrow. You have a place within, say, thirty minutes of the port where they can stay?'

'*Sí*, in Fuengirola. We have a safe place there. Here's the telephone number.' He left a piece of paper lying on the table for Canning to casually pick up. 'Good. I'll be in touch with you in two to three days. In the meantime, I want these two lines tapped pronto.'

Castillo rose, his drink only half-finished, picked up a piece of paper Canning had also dropped on the table, and wandered down the road to a telephone box.

Canning leaned back, comfortable in the sun, and lit a cigarette.

It was his last match.

Carelessly, he tossed the match-book into the ashtray ... a match-book from Alexander's.

Soon the man from Malaga returned and the two strolled back up the street, climbed into their respective cars and left.

As they did so a man emerged from a doorway nearby. He walked slowly to the table where the two men had been and, picking up the match-book, looked at it thoughtfully.

Then Jim Miller, too, went to his car and drove back to the Costa del Sol.

*

Kate was dozing in front of the pool when the man from the phone company came. 'Do not disturb yourself, Señorita,' he said. 'There is a fault on the line. I know where to fix it.'

It took him less than five minutes to place the bug.

When he came out of the villa she was asleep, the phone engineer already forgotten. Ignoring Sheedy's strictures she had slipped off her bikini top.

For a moment the man paused and looked at her half-naked form. 'Holy mother of Christ,' he muttered, 'I would rather tap into you, Señorita, than your telephone.'

And he was gone.

Miller had only been back an hour when the phone rang.

'Señor Miller?'

'*Si*,' he said. It was one of his only Spanish words. He hoped it would not lead, as it sometimes did, to a torrent of Spanish from the other end.

'I am a friend of a friend of yours in England. I have the gift you ordered.'

'Good. Can you meet me tonight – at Puerto Banus?'

'*Si*, Señor. I will be in Duques at 10 o'clock … at the bar in the back.'

'How will I recognise you?'

'You have been described to me, Señor. I will find you. But just to be on the safe side you can buy a copy of today's London *Times* from the bookshop at the port and put it on the bar in front of you. And order a bottle of champagne.'

'Champagne! Are you mad? Do you know what it costs there. And I don't even like the stuff.'

'But I do, Señor.' The other man laughed and hung up.

Miller cursed. 'He'll be bloody lucky if he gets an *agua mineral*,' he said to himself. Going to the kitchen he picked out the biggest glass he could find, poured himself a tiny gin ... then added a tiny bit more ... then filled it with ice and topped it up with mineral water, then went to his room and lay down, balancing the glass on his chest and promising himself that when this business was over he would, for old times' sake, have just one bender down at the port.

He could cope with that.

It had been hell but he was getting the drink problem under control.

And over the past few days he had, for the first time in years, begun to feel near to his old form, to feel once more the thrill of the chase.

At six in the evening the yacht slipped out of the port. Cruickshank had decided to take Maria for dinner at sea. They relaxed side by side in comfortable armchairs near the edge of the deck, Cruickshank with his feet up on the railing. Both seemed content to sit without conversation in the late afternoon sun, drink champagne, and look back at the coastline and the hills beyond.

Finally she asked 'Have you been busy today, Brian?'

For a moment, as the memory of his meetings with Miller and Canning returned, he frowned. Then, recovering himself, he smiled at her, pleased at her new-found ease with his Christian name. 'A busy day, Maria. But now a beautiful one, made beautiful by you.'

'Julio says you have some problems with a plot of land.'

He frowned again. Julio talked too much. 'Yes. We had difficulty finding the owner and now, sadly, we find he has suffered an accident and is dead. It may take time to sort it all out. But it is he we should feel sorry for, not

169

ourselves. Our problems can be solved.'

'I'm glad. I would not like any problem to get in the way of your villa on the hill.'

His heart leapt. Was this a hint that she was warming to the idea of the villa as her home too?

'My parents are coming for a brief visit soon, Brian. I hope you will meet them.'

'I insist, Maria. Perhaps they could be persuaded to have lunch on the yacht.'

She looked pleased. She stood and leaned over the side, her bottom almost within reach of her companion's fingers. She was wearing a pink blouse again, this time with black trousers matching the black hair cascading over her shoulders and down her back. Cruickshank felt a great desire building up within him.

As he looked at her he thought bitterly of the nights of arid hostility he had experienced in his marital bed. He remembered, too, the woman in Maida Vale. She had seemed to know by instinct, more even than he knew, what was necessary to relieve him of the tensions that had driven him there. Sometimes it had been a gentle massage and then equally gentle lovemaking, as if to meet a need for affection. Sometimes he had taken her, urgently, roughly, selfishly, as if his need was purely physical. Sometimes she would take charge, encourage him to do things beyond his own imagination or nerve. There was no act they had not at some time performed together. Cruickshank admitted to himself it was only possible because for some reason he trusted her. Yet every time he had left her flat he had felt degraded and swore to himself that it would be the last time. And then a week, maybe a fortnight later, late at night or after a heavy day in the office, the need would return and back he would go.

He now knew, as he looked at this woman with her back to him, that while he had had physical experiences, he had never had physical love, never had the chance to pour his love into the depths of a woman who opened herself up to him because she wanted him, just him, and because she wanted to make him happy.

And only now, in his wanting, did he know what he had missed.

He wanted this young woman as he had never wanted before in his life.

He wanted her tenderly. He wanted to hold her and protect her and warm her.

But he also wanted her carnally, wanted to do things to that beautiful bottom leaning over the rails. He wanted to see it naked, hold it, enter it; he wanted her to draw him into her arms, to bury his face in her breasts, he wanted to sleep with her and wake with her and lie with her and love her.

He *wanted,* deeply and desperately.

'If I can have this,' he thought, 'just this, I will never use the word *want* again.'

Suddenly, as if feeling his intensity, she turned and looked at him. He went red, knowing his face revealed his feelings. Yet she pursued them. 'What were you thinking, Brian?'

It was no good lying. 'I was thinking that you look magnificent, that I want you.'

She stepped over and sat beside him, so close that he could hear her breathing, smell her scent. 'Brian, what do you want of a woman, of a wife?'

'A companion. A lover. Someone to experience all the things of life with me. Someone to sit with in the evenings, to start the day with and end the day with. Someone who will end the loneliness I now realise I have been living with for too many years. Someone to give purpose to all that I am building and creating.'

'Was none of this possible with your first wife?'

'No. We were companions for a while. We were poor

lovers. And we ended up avoiding each other most of the day and all of the night. I felt sorry for her and she hated me, and I don't blame her. I didn't love her and I didn't know how to pretend that I did. It was my fault ... by my ignorance I spoilt both our lives. It's only now I realise what I have missed. And what I caused her to miss.'

'But why is it that you want me?'

'Because I believe if I spend every hour of every day with you for the rest of my life I will still be discovering new things, still be excited by you, still be proud of you. That you will enhance every moment of my life, whether I am with you at every moment or not.'

She looked thoughtful. And serious. Then she said: 'Yes, Brian, *enhance* ... that is the word. Enhance. I believe you would enhance my life too. I never felt that about the young men I have met; I always felt that I would be their possession, that I would exist to enhance their lives. You are the first man I have met who I believe would enhance mine.'

For one weak moment Cruickshank found himself fighting back tears. 'Maria, does that mean you think it is possible ...'

'Yes, Brian, it is possible. I have thought of little else for the past two days. And this morning ... up in the hills ... I knew I would be proud to have you as my husband, not because of what you showed me, your project, but because riding on horseback in the open air I saw your ... your nobility. That and your kindness, they are rare qualities in a man.'

In the distance, in the depths of the yacht, a phone rang.

Barely aware of it he took her gently in his arms, kissed her, and began to talk of all his hopes, his plans for them both.

'At this moment there is no man in the world I would

172

rather be,' he said. 'And there is no woman in the world I would rather be with. At this moment I know what it is to be totally happy.'

He was about to kiss her once more when, from the stairway, he heard the butler's voice.

'Sir Brian.'

'Yes, Hobbs.'

'There's a Mr Sheedy on the phone.'

Cruickshank felt as if a small dagger had been plunged into his heart, a heart that a few seconds before had been so full.

'Take a message,' he said dully. 'I'll call him back.'

Chapter
Seven

TUESDAY, APRIL 3

Felipe Blanco stood naked in front of the mirror drying his black hair and narcissisticly admiring his own physique. Barely eighteen, he was only five and a half feet tall, slim and with the kind of Latin good looks that make the hearts of teenage girls throb ... alas for him in vain, because since coming to the Costa del Sol from the *sierra pueblo* where he was born Felipe had found sexual, if not yet emotional fulfilment elsewhere.

He had been eagerly awaiting this evening off work ever since he spent nearly half his first month's pay on the pair of skin-tight white cotton pants he now pulled up over his otherwise bare backside. They were so close-fitting that he could only just fasten them. At the back they tucked revealingly into the crevasse between his buttocks; at the front they produced a bulge he now surveyed with pride before slipping on a navy-blue tee-shirt. After one last self-admiring glance, he left his tiny cabin and climbed the ladder-like stairs to the deck of the yacht.

Canning was sitting in a leather armchair in the open lounge area near the gangplank, a Martini in one hand, cigarette in the other, his feet carelessly resting on a drinks table. He leered at Felipe as he went by, his contempt only too clear. The young crew member felt himself blushing. '*Bastardo*,' he muttered under his breath.

He hated Canning, all the more so because when he had first come to work on the yacht he had fallen hopelessly in love with the tall, blond American. Spotting this, Canning had missed no opportunity to humiliate him.

But, Felipe decided as he proudly paraded down the jetty, not even Canning was going to spoil this night. Arrogantly dismissing admiring looks from young women and the occasional meaningful glance from a lone man, he walked silkily towards the lights of the bars and restaurants on the front.

In his self-absorption he didn't notice another dark-haired young Spaniard who had been sitting at an open-air bar just opposite the yacht, and who now quickly dropped some pesetas beside an untouched drink before following him, unobtrusive amid the growing crowd of after-dinner strollers.

Felipe slipped down an alley-way between restaurants into the back street, Calle Ribera. From there he climbed a dimly-lit stairway and walked along a first floor landing until he came to one of the few doors without a neon sign, just a small brass plaque at its side. He pressed a buzzer. The door was opened a fraction, he was inspected, and then allowed to enter.

A moment later the other Spaniard arrived at the door, pressed the buzzer, and was also admitted.

The Pink Coconut club had just one bar running the full length of a narrow, dimly-lit room, with a row of stools and just enough space to walk between them and the wall. At the end of the bar there was a small, round dance floor, raised a few centimetres from the ground, and to its left a doorway into a pitch-dark back room. Every stool was occupied, and other customers leaned by the wall, their drinks resting on a high shelf, so that Felipe had to squeeze his way to the end of the bar. As he did so he felt exploratory fingers touch his backside. He pretended he didn't notice but his heart thumped with anticipation. In this bar Felipe was much-desired and he knew it and loved it.

At the end of the bar, from where they had been looking back up its full length, and from where they could see everyone else in the club, two men were abandoning their stools and heading for the back room. Felipe slipped onto one of the stools and ordered a cold San Miguel. The other was also quickly taken, this time by a man Felipe guessed was six or seven years older than him, also dark-haired and slim, with a warm, friendly smile that had the effect of engulfing Felipe as he turned and looked at him.

'*Hola*,' the stranger said.

Felipe, who was determined not to succumb to the first approach of the evening, at least not too quickly, for he hadn't got himself looking so desirable to immediately disappear out of sight into the gloom of the back room, did not return the greeting but curtly nodded.

If the man was disconcerted, he didn't show it. Instead he casually ordered a San Miguel too and busied himself lighting a cigarette. Then he offered one to Felipe who, satisfied he had made his point, accepted, albeit with a rather ungracious shrug.

'I haven't seen you in this place before,' Felipe eventually said, speaking Spanish.

The other repeated the warm smile that the boy found so extraordinarily difficult to resist. 'No. First time.'

'You're on holiday?'

'No. I live down the costa.'

'Ah.'

'And you?'

'I'm with a yacht in the port.'

'Really? Which one?'

'*La Gaviota.*'

The other looked surprised. 'Really? You must be incredibly rich.'

Felipe laughed. 'No, I don't own it. I . . .' and he exaggerated, 'I'm an officer on it.'

His companion suppressed a sceptical grin. 'Really? I bet that's a good life. I wish I was you.'

Felipe was gratified. He looked around the bar. There were three or four men sitting nearby who he would usually have been happy to attract, men with more obvious machismo than his neighbour, and Felipe liked his men big and tough, but he felt an unusual affinity with this easy-going stranger.

The Pink Coconut meant a lot to Felipe. Because of the importance of machismo to the younger men in his *sierra* village and their contempt for *marica* (their word, full of distaste, for effeminate homosexuals), Felipe had been forced to suppress both his personality and his needs. Despite a rather pathetic attempt to appear even more macho than his peers, he had inevitably become a lonely and isolated boy. When he came to the port and another crew member on *La Gaviota* introduced him to the Pink Coconut Felipe found himself for the first time able to relax in friendly, uncritical surroundings. He thrived on the sense of belonging, even more on the discovery that he was not only accepted but desired. Yet for all the easy companionship of the evenings he spent in this place, the boost to his ego from the men he picked up, the physical release, Felipe was still unsatisfied. He had never really met anyone with whom he could build a friendship, with whom he could sit drinking in the bars at the water's-edge, gossiping and making catty remarks about the passers-by, with whom he could go to parties or even for a day out in the country or swimming at the beach. Often on his way from the yacht to the club he would see two men dining together in one of the expensive restaurants, absorbed with their own company, and he would wish that he had a friend who could afford to take him there. So far it hadn't happened. The men who picked Felipe up in the Pink Coconut wanted him just as long as it took to satisfy their needs in the darkened back room, or at their hotel, or even on a remote patch of beach. And that was it. Just '*gracias y adiós*'.

So when the young man offered to refill his glass and began to chat without any of the usual sexual come-on, treating Felipe as a friend, Felipe began to feel immensely happy. Sitting cross-legged on the stool, waving his cigarette in the air, and drinking too quickly, he laughed loudly at the other's jokes, and looked at the poker-faced men down the length of the bar as if to say, Look at me; I've got a friend: I'm having a good time; not for me a night of solitary drinking and eye-contact assignations in the back room. Felipe was showing off.

'I think I met someone else from your yacht the other evening,' said his new friend. 'I was having a drink in Alexander's. A tall, blond guy. Hair almost white. I don't think he was gay, though.'

'Oh that would be Canning, he's in Alexander's a lot,' Felipe said with distaste. 'He's an *americano*. He's not with the yacht. Not one of the crew. He's with the business that owns it.' He looked at the other, surprised. 'But what were you doing in Alexander's? It's not a gay bar.'

The other took a leisurely sip of his drink and then, grinning, said 'A friend of mine was playing a joke at my expense. Told me it was a gay bar. It's about as non-gay as you can get.' He lit yet another cigarette and then picked up the earlier conversation. 'Anyway I think that was the man, I think he said that was his name. Tony Canning.'

'No, not Tony. Jason. Jason Canning.'

'Right. *Si*. Of course. It was Jason. And he's not gay?'

'No. If you ask me he's not even human.'

'Oh, why do you say that?'

Felipe happily launched himself into an attack on the character of his enemy. 'Cold as ice. Thinks he's God. Doesn't like anyone and no-one likes him. The others on the yacht say he spends hours in Alexander's drinking alone and watching people. He's always watching people.'

'Is he the top man?'

'No. The Englishman is the top man. Cruickshank. Canning just works for him. There's been a lot of talk on the yacht that the Englishman hates him too, but he can't get rid of him.'

'Why's that?'

'I don't know. And I don't care.'

The other, not wishing to push the matter too fast, took his time lighting a cigarette, and then deliberately moved his stool closer until his arm and that of Felipe were touching. The young Spaniard felt a hardening in his crotch and began to wish the new white pants were not quite so tight. He moved his hand to adjust himself and the other let his eyes slip down to the bulge then back up to Felipe's face. He smiled again, an intimate smile, a smile full of warmth and understanding. Felipe's heart lurched.

The stranger now re-opened the conversation, this time approaching similar territory but from a different direction.

'You must have a good life. How much time do you spend at sea?'

'Oh, we get out most weekends, especially when the Englishman is here. And sometimes for an evening. Occasionally we have a longer trip, across to Tangier or even as far as the Italian Riviera or the Greek islands.'

'Do you have your own cabin?'

Felipe's smile faded. This was a familiar question, usually the opening gambit in the game of sexual proposition and counter-proposition that comprised the twilight life he led in this and the other gay bars. Maybe he was being illogical, but he was disappointed. 'Yes, but we're not allowed to take friends on board,' he replied coldly.

'Ah.'

There was a moment's silence, then the other asked 'So how big is the yacht? How many on board?'

'About seven crew members, some cooks and stewards, and then in the offices there are the Englishman, Canning, and some administrative people. The planners and architects operate from their own offices.'

'What planners and architects?'

Felipe looked vague. 'Oh, they're involved in some project the company is building in the hills. They say it will be *super grande*. Hotels and golf courses . . .'

He was getting bored with the subject and the other saw it. He put his hand on Felipe's thigh. The crew member's hand shook as he reached for his cigarette. The pressure within his now too-tight pants was becoming unbearable. He couldn't resist a glance towards the back room, yet it was not an eager glance. Felipe felt an ambivalence towards the back room; it was, of course, exciting, ideal for uncomplicated, raw sexual relief, but usually it meant that his search for love had once more ended in a soulless physical encounter with a man whose face he couldn't even see. And he hated returning to the bar to the knowing look in the ever-watchful eyes of the others sitting in the gloom, and then to the yacht feeling abused and soiled and desperately alone.

But this was different. Felipe wanted this man, wanted to do things in the back room that even in there would not be anonymous, then wanted to come out proudly, hand in hand, and leave with him, perhaps to go back to his place, more likely to make a date for another evening and the friendship and affection he craved.

So when the other turned and began to talk more quietly he was ready to acquiesce to anything. What he heard was the last thing he expected.

'Look, I have to go now.'

Felipe's face must have revealed shock and indignation at the crushing of his hopes, for the other continued quickly. 'But I really would like to meet you again when we can spend more time together.'

Once more he rested a gentle, suggestive hand on Felipe's thigh and the younger man melted at the touch.

'When is your next night off?'

'Tomorrow. I have tomorrow off also.'

'Tomorrow then? About nine?'

'*Si.*'

With that Manuel slipped off the stool and quickly left the bar.

Near the exit to the port he slipped into a telephone booth and rang Sheedy, catching him just after he had arrived at the villa.

'Bill, the man we're looking for: his name is Jason Canning. He works with Anglo-Spanish Investors, fits the description of the man who spoke to the Rabbit Man in the bar at Ronda, and he drinks most nights at Alexander's.'

'Well done, Manuel.' Sheedy chuckled. 'I trust this information hasn't cost you too much, that we don't have to tell Juanito that you've been seduced by a sailor.'

Manuel bridled. 'Listen, I hate this whole thing enough already without your jokes.'

'OK, OK. You did well. For when did you fix the next meeting?'

'Tomorrow night.'

'Right. I'll talk to you in the morning about how we handle it.'

Back in the bar Felipe was wrestling with conflicting emotions. He was elated that he had made a friend. Someone who had been happy to spend time with him despite knowing a sexual encounter wasn't possible that night. Someone who was anxious to see him as soon as possible. Tomorrow. Perhaps tomorrow after having a drink they could go out and have dinner.

Felipe wondered if the other had money. He tried to guess what work he did. Then it struck him: they hadn't even exchanged names. As usual, he had been too happy being the centre of attention to ask about his companion ... even to ask his name.

Yet he trusted the other.

He would come tomorrow.

Felipe remembered the warm smile and knew he would.

In the meantime he was frustrated, and discomforted by the other's sudden departure. He felt he had lost face, especially after his exhibitionist behaviour at the bar. And he felt physically let down. He had waited a week for this night off the yacht and the encounter with the other man had excited him further.

Endeavouring to maintain as much dignity as he could, he rose from the stool and wandered to the edge of the dance floor, aware that his provocatively-exposed figure was under lascivious surveillance from the men lounging against the wall.

He paused at the door to the back room and leaned against the wall, cigarette dying in his hand.

A big, fair-haired man clad in blue jeans, denim shirt and black leather jacket came over to the doorway, turned and looked hard at Felipe and then disappeared into the gloom. Felipe, his heart thumping under his tee shirt, followed. As he too was enveloped in darkness he felt a hand guide him further into the room. As he obediently responded he bumped more than once into other men, and his protective hand felt naked arms and backs. He was now totally under the control of the other's guiding arm, his own will dissipated by the combination of physical need and the pull of a stronger personality. He felt himself being turned round to face the shadowy figure of the larger man. As rough, demanding hands reached down and began to fumble with his top button he closed his eyes and gave in to the forces of desire, egoism, loneliness that had brought him here to this uncaring darkness.

Later as, eyes downcast, he climbed the gangplank of the yacht he heard a sardonic chuckle. He looked up and saw Canning still sitting, smoking, in the leather chair, his face a picture of malevolent innuendo. Felipe flushed and half-tripped in his haste to escape the other's gaze.

Canning laughed.

The young Spaniard fled to his cabin, his heart full of hate. '*Bastardo*,' he muttered. 'I'll get you one day ... one day I'll make you pay.'

Only later, much later, after he had showered and climbed into his bunk, did he open himself to happier thoughts ... about the nameless man with the warm smile who he would meet tomorrow.

Cruickshank could not have been happier. Maria's guardians Juan and Cristina Garcia had come unexpectedly to the *Costa* del Sol and were now welcome last-minute guests of honour at a garden party and barbecue he had organised for influential local people.

It was all set up at the front of the villa, over-looking the beach. The chef from the yacht and two others were cooking over charcoal fires, filling the night air with an enticing aroma as giant Mediterranean prawns, lobsters and other fish sizzled at one end, whole chickens on skewers at the other, and steaks, chops and sausages between them. A trio of guitarists were playing on the balcony overlooking the garden. At the candle-lit tables, decorated with displays of red roses and bowls over-flowing with fresh fruit, guests were choosing from quality wines and the best Spanish champagne.

At one table in the centre of the lawn sat Cruick-shank, the Garcias and Maria, Julio the architect and his wife, and the mayors of Estapona and Benahavis and their wives. Maria, as she often did in the evening, had dressed in white and looked sensational.

The Garcias were impressed by the enchanting scene and flattered by the special attention of their host. Cruickshank had positioned Juan Garcia on his right and after dinner he took the Spaniard by the arm and under the watchful gaze of Cristina and the apprehensive one of Maria strolled down to the end of the garden. There he talked of the pleasure Maria's company had given everybody and how much inspiration she obviously drew from the Garcias.

As intended, Juan Garcia was charmed. Cruickshank, he insisted, must come as their guest to Seville. It was an invitation accepted with alacrity.

Later Maria said to Cruickshank 'My adoptive mother has been watching us. I think she may guess. She asked me what I thought of you.'

'What did you say?'

'That you are generous, that you have been kind to me, and that you are a man of honour.'

'Oh God,' he groaned. 'Honour again.'

Maria laughed, a gentle laugh that warmed his heart.

'Well, it pleased her, even if it doesn't please you. Anyway, I changed the subject and she has not pressed further.'

Cruickshank took her arm and drew her closer. 'You look magnificent this evening, Maria. I wish I could order all these people away and have you alone to myself.'

'I wouldn't do that, Brian. I do not think my guardians would be at all impressed.'

Now it was his turn to laugh. 'Very well. For that reason alone I will allow them to stay.'

With that he began to expertly circulate, 'working the room' as his political masters used to say, ensuring as always that every guest left feeling they had been special to their host that night.

When at last they had all departed he strolled alone down onto the beach and looked out at the sea, black satin under moonlight diluted by light clouds. It was a warm night and the only sound was that of the small waves breaking on the stony shore. I could be happy in this country, he thought. Happy with Maria.

He thought of London, the struggle to meetings through increasingly heavy traffic, the cold, damp winters, the hundred and one irritating problems that arose in his office every day, the same faces in the City and at the club, the boredom of the 'games' that had once excited and enthralled him.

How could that compare with the colour, the warmth, the gentle pace of this place? Or with the life he could lead in his villa above the valley, the life he could lead there with Maria?

He resolved to progress the project with renewed vigour in the morning.

It was time he got things really moving.

Nothing, but nothing, must upset his plans.

★

After he had spoken to Manuel, Sheedy checked his answer-phone. There were two messages.

The first said 'Señor Bill. This is Miguel. I have found hidden in *El Conejero's cortijo* what I believe to be the answer to the mystery. Can you come to Ronda tomorrow? If you can, leave a message at *Guardia Civil* headquarters.'

The other was from a secretary telephoning on behalf of Sir Brian Cruickshank. Sheedy was invited to conduct his interview over lunch on *La Gaviota,* the company's yacht, also the following day.

'Well, I can't be in both places,' Sheedy said to Kate. 'Miguel will have to wait.'

'No need for that, Bill. Why can't I go and see him? I want to build up my portfolio on Ronda. And I want to photograph Gaucin. I can find out what he's turned up and you'll save a day.'

Sheedy liked the idea. After leaving a message for Miguel he left Kate reading and drove down the hill.

The busy restaurant Dos Pinos is on the main coastal road a few kilometres east of Malaga. Over a dinner of prawn cocktails and suckling pig Sheedy asked Ramon Aparitico to tell him what was happening on the costa. 'I'm seeing Cruickshank tomorrow and I'm a bit out of touch. Who's developing what? Is the pace slowing down?'

'Don't you believe it, Señor,' said the Spaniard. 'There's no stopping it. People from the north of Europe seem to have decided this is their equivalent of your California and the developers are queueing up to build for them.'

Some land prices had doubled in just two years, he said, and that was an increase on what were already astronomic levels. The number of Costa del Sol golf courses alone was likely to increase from fifteen to over thirty before the mid-1990s.

'Señor ... er ... Sir Brian Cruickshank is not even alone with his idea for horse racing. A Spanish company is investing at least 35,000 million pesetas on a huge project in Mijas-Costa and has been seeking a licence from the authorities for a track.'

Sheedy whistled. 'I wonder whether Cruickshank knows about that. That lends some urgency to his activities. No wonder they're worried about the delay in getting the remaining piece of land.'

The Spaniard nodded. 'You know, of course, about the huge Disneyland-like park planned for between Benahavis and Estapona, not far from the land Cruickshank has purchased?'

Sheedy nodded. 'I did an item on the programme about it. But what's the latest word?'

'It's going to be called Magic Mountain and will be run by your American Six Flags company. It's going to be financed and built by a French company. But the man behind it is a Lebanese. I believe they expect to spend about 100,000 million pesetas on it. They're aiming for one and a half million visitors a year.'

'It's even bigger than I realised. Well, what do you think Anglo-Spanish Investors are spending on their project?'

'I don't know exactly, Señor, but I believe it could be as much as 120,000 million pesetas, including the land. I'm told they are sparing no expense'.

Sheedy whistled. 'Christ, that's over 1,000 million dollars. That's a lot of money.'

He sat quietly for a moment.

'Yes, that's a lot of money. I guess a man would do a lot to protect that sort of money.'

It was a cold night and Miguel shivered and pulled his big leather jacket around him as he left the bar and began to climb the hill to the bridge over El Tajo, stumbling once or twice because, truth to tell, he had drunk a brandy too many.

The bars had been quiet and Miguel had lacked his usual company. Drinking alone had made him morose, and spotting two lovers whispering to each other on one of the stone steps by the bridge made him feel even more empty and sad. The civil war and then his duties with the *Guardia Civil* had cut him off from community life when he was younger. He had missed out on the chance to court a señorita, to marry and have children. In this respect he knew life had passed him by. He would have liked, by now, to be a jolly grandfather, sitting in front of the fire on cold winter nights surrounded by grandchildren spellbound by his stories of the war. Now it could never be.

The Plaza de España was quiet and dark, the bars now closed and he meandered up the main thoroughfare, the Calle Virgin de la Paz, past the *plaza de toros* and the Restaurante Pedro Romero. As he did so, as he did every night now, he thought of his oldest friend, El Conejero, and he felt sadder still. Often they had talked about Miguel retiring, about sharing their last years hunting together, drinking wine and dozing under the lemon trees at *el cortijo* during the hot summer evenings, and coming to town only for the *corridas*. Now that, too, could never be.

Now he was past the Alameda park, and walking up into the back streets until he came to a small alley between two rows of white-washed houses. At the end of the alley he paused. He wasn't ready to go home. He suddenly felt terribly alone. And tired. And old. He yearned for the noise and smoke and argument and laughter of the bar. But even if he had the energy to walk back into town those bars that were not closed were all but empty.

At that moment, standing at the entrance to the alley,

Miguel took a decision. He would not go on like this. It was time to retire. He should have done so years back. He would tell them tomorrow that he would not wait for the fixed date. They wouldn't mind; they had already been indulging him, letting him stay on years after he should have gone.

The decision made him feel better. Now he was no longer reluctant to go to his bed.

His home was at the end of the alley. As he fumbled for the key he half-leaned on the door and to his surprise it gave way.

Miguel paused.

This was not right.

He had locked the door. He remembered doing it.

Struggling to sober up, he reached down, unbuttoned the leather holster, and slipped the old wood-handled revolver into his hand. He stepped into the dark and listened. There was no sound.

He took another step and the door slammed behind him. He swung round only to feel the sharp end of a knife at the back of his neck. A rough hand pushed him forward so that his face was pressed against the door.

'Drop the gun or you're dead,' hissed a man's voice. Miguel let it drop with a clatter on the stone floor.

He was aware now of a man on each side, the one to his left holding the knife that was sticking uncomfortably into his neck.

He heard a third man moving on the other side of the room, heard him lighting the lamp on the table. 'Turn him round.'

As the lamp flickered into life Miguel saw that the men on either side of him were Spaniards, not, he thought, from Ronda. The man lounging back in Miguel's old armchair was tall, slim, blond, almost white-haired. His accent was American. Miguel guessed this must be the man who had spoken to his old friend El

Conejero in the bar . . . the man who had probably killed him. He looked at him in silent anger.

One of the Spaniards had picked up the gun and tossed it to the American who now sardonically waved it at Miguel almost as if it were a toy.

'Do these still work, Señor Policeman?' he asked. 'Well, you believed it would save you so presumably it also has the capacity to kill you. Let's hope we don't have to find out.'

Miguel found his voice. 'What do you want? Why are you in my house?'

'Papers, my friend. Papers and photographs. You took them from the old man's farmhouse.'

'You mean El Conejero? His *cortijo*? I did not. They are still there. They were his. Why do you want them? What are they to you?'

The smile left the American's face.

'Don't lie, Policeman. You took the papers and photographs. You have them. We know that. I want them. And I want them now. We've searched this place and they're not here. Where are they?'

Miguel shook his head defiantly. 'I think you killed him. Why? Because he wouldn't sell his land? Is that why? Do you need money so much that you must kill an old man for a bit more?'

The American's smile faded. Miguel felt a chill radiating from his grey eyes.

'Hold his arms.'

He walked over and transferring the gun to his left hand, prodded it in Miguel's considerable stomach while reaching with his other for the knife. Once he had it in his hand he poked it between Miguel's legs.

'Now, Señor Policeman, I don't think you understand. I am a busy man and I want the papers now. I am going to count to ten and if you don't tell me where they are I am going to cut off your *cojones*. One . . . two . . . three . . .'

Miguel's stomach turned to water. There was a lack of humanity in this man's eyes, a madness. He didn't doubt the American would do exactly what he threatened. He tried desperately to think, wishing he had not drunk so much brandy. 'Wait,' he said. 'I don't have them but I can tell you where they are.'

The other smiled slowly. 'That's better. Talk.'

'I posted them.'

'Posted them? To whom?'

'To the reporter. To Bill Sheedy.'

Miguel had decided there was no point in lying. The American undoubtedly knew of Sheedy's interest. If he also knew that Sheedy had the papers he would be discouraged from killing Miguel; there would be no point.

And if he, Miguel, could get out of this, there was plenty of time to warn Sheedy.

'When did you post them?'

'Today.'

The American looked at Miguel suspiciously, but finally, to the Spaniard's relief, said 'I think you're telling the truth, Policeman.'

'Then give me back my gun and go.'

The American laughed humourlessly. 'I'm afraid I can't do that, Policeman. You know that. You know too much. But what I can do is give you one of the bullets. Would that help?'

Miguel knew the time for talk was past. With a tremendous effort, and drawing on all of his weight, he threw the two men off him and lunged towards the American.

He nearly made it but one of the Spaniards grabbed his arm, pulling him off balance. This enabled the American to bring the gun barrel down onto the back of Miguel's head with great force. As he hit the ground he was struck a second time. And a third.

Telling the Spaniards to eliminate any signs of a struggle while they waited with the unconscious policeman, the American slipped out into the darkened street and round a corner to where his car was parked. He quietly drove it to the entrance of the alley and signalled to the two men to bring Miguel out. This proved easier said than done. Sweating and cursing they slowly dragged the enormous inert form of Miguel to the car and with enormous difficulty bundled him onto the back seat. The Spaniards then climbed uncomfortably into the single passenger front seat and the car slipped quietly away.

When it reached the Plaza de Espana it was driven under the archway with the big clock and into the empty car park alongside El Tajo, a place where there is only a low stone wall between the Ronda plateau and the ravine.

There Miguel was taken out. The American poured brandy into the unconscious man's mouth and a little on his clothes. Then the three dragged him to the edge and threw him over the wall.

Silently they watched him disappear into the black hole that was El Tajo.

Watched him begin his lonely, unwitnessed last journey ... the fall onto the rocks 900 feet below.

And there, where many of his fellow countrymen had died before him, priests and revolutionaries and soldiers ...

... there Miguel, who had himself survived the civil war and fifty years as an officer in the *Guardia Civil* ...

... there Miguel, smiling, food-loving, fun-loving, wine-loving Miguel ...

... there Miguel died too.

WEDNESDAY, APRIL 4

Sheedy had as a news editor always urged his reporters not to prejudge anyone. 'Approach every story as open-mindedly as possible. The facts should dictate the story, not your prejudices.' Despite these views he had formulated in his mind a picture of Cruickshank and he didn't expect to like him, not at all. As a result, he was taken by surprise.

For a start, he recognised Cruickshank. He was the man who had been on the plane with him and Kate the other day. But the tall, thin, rather severe-looking man Sheedy had only half-noticed then greeted him now with a warm smile. The eyes looking at him over the half-moon glasses were intelligent but also full of good humour. This was a man, the reporter concluded, who it would not be difficult to like.

Cruickshank ushered him into the library, poured two glasses of champagne, and let Sheedy set the pace.

'I've heard rumours about your real estate purchases and how you plan to develop the land, Sir Brian. If they're correct it's an unusual and impressive project. I would like to film a report on it for my programme.'

Cruickshank looked – and was – surprised. He had assumed Sheedy had come to talk about the Rabbit Man. Could it be that the reporter had no idea of the connection? That this was a relatively innocent visit, just about the project itself?

Or was the reporter leading up to the real story slowly? If so, this approach could work to Cruickshank's advantage.

'You're well informed, Mr Sheedy. Yes, we do plan a major project. To be frank with you, we've not publicised it till now because the land values would have been raised even higher than they already were. I don't blame the landowners for that. That's their right. But we

193

equally have the right to protect ourselves from an excess of greed. However, we have the land we want now and we've been planning to announce our plans soon. When did you wish to do your programme?

All journalists liked to be ahead of their rivals, Sheedy replied. He would like the story to be screened before the project was officially announced.

Cruickshank nodded. 'I understand that, but you won't be surprised that the company would like to announce the details itself in its own way.' He refilled Sheedy's glass. 'I wonder whether there is a compromise. If we can reach accord on the timing I could announce the project late in the afternoon of the day of your programme. Thus while it won't be a scoop – I think that's what you journalists call it – most people will hear it first from you. And, of course, we could assist you by recording an interview in advance.'

Sheedy rose and held out his hand. 'It's a deal.' He walked over to the model. 'Is this it?'

Cruickshank joined him. 'It is ... this is the Valle de Maria.' He began to describe it in detail and, Sheedy noted, with infectious enthusiasm. This, the American decided, was no ordinary developer. This man was a dreamer.

Over lunch of fresh fish and salad Sheedy asked question after question and Cruickshank, open and friendly, answered them in a direct way that impressed the reporter. He commented upon it: 'You're surprisingly helpful, Sir Brian. I'm accustomed to greater reticence from developers.'

'I come from a career in public life, Mr Sheedy, I understand your profession. I'm also, you may have observed, proud of this project. And, to be frank, we will need a friendly response from people on the costa; fair and accurate publicity can only be helpful. So I have every reason to cooperate.'

Sheedy laughed. 'You make me feel I'm involved, Sir Brian. That's a rare talent. But I don't know that I want to be *that* involved. I don't know whether I approve. Tell me, what benefit is there to Spain in projects like this? I can't imagine many Spaniards can afford to be members. And won't the profits go into the pockets of foreign investors?'

'There'll be work,' Cruickshank replied, 'both in building the project and in staffing it.'

'You mean servants to the foreign rich? Is that such a good thing?'

'Look, Mr Sheedy, there are many aspects of the holiday and tourist explosion on the Costa del Sol that I don't like. I think the lack of planning control, the allowing of monstrosities to be built near the beach, the creation, at least for a time, of a safe haven for British criminals, the exploitation of many local workers in the catering and hotel industries, all this has been bad. But that's as much the fault of the Spanish authorities as it is of foreigners.

'For my part, I'm building a project of unprecedented quality.

'I'm building it on a piece of land that has not been good for agriculture. And I'm creating work. You may sneer about the Spanish being servants but Andalusia still has high unemployment and this will be reasonably well-paid and secure work. I suspect the Spanish won't be sneering.'

Sheedy threw up his hands. 'OK, Sir Brian ... let's not argue about it, at least not now. We can always do so on camera. Incidentally I wasn't sneering ... just asking.'

Cruickshank was not, however, easily appeased. 'Tell me, Mr Sheedy, where do you live? I expect in a villa that has been built by Spanish labourers on Spanish land. And I suspect your cleaning is done by a Spanish maid. And do you not eat in Spanish restaurants and drink in the Spanish bars manned by the same allegedly underpaid workforce? Don't you think your questions would be more valid if you were not taking advantage as much as anyone else?'

Sheedy laughed but didn't attempt to answer, preferring to ask where the money was coming from.

'Anglo-Spanish Investors is not at present a public company, Mr Sheedy, it is a limited company. It is, in effect, a consortium of private investors, some in Spain, some in the UK, and some in the United States.'

'Who in particular in the United States?'

Cruickshank hesitated. 'I think it only fair that before I name them, I advise them I'll be doing so. I'll have to come back to you on that.'

Sheedy pressed. 'Fair enough. But I imagine you have to be careful. I imagine this is just the kind of overseas project that would be attractive to people who have questionable funds to invest.'

Cruickshank was more than up to the challenge. Smiling, he replied, 'Good heavens, Mr Sheedy, next you'll be suggesting our money comes from the Mafia.'

Then to change the subject, he rose and suggested they return to the library for coffee and a brandy. There the American asked Cruickshank for details about himself. The Englishman briefly described his career, missing, Sheedy observed, none of his achievements, yet covering them in a deprecating way that made the point without pressing it immodestly. It was impressive and, Sheedy thought, unless the man was a consummate actor, it was more than just a performance. The man's ego was well under control.

Cruickshank, too, had been sizing up Sheedy. He, too, had taken a liking to the man from the start. The reporter had an open face. Cruickshank felt there was a good chance the American was clever but not devious,

196

sceptical but not prejudiced. He was the kind of man he liked to deal with.

On the other hand, he thought, if Sheedy did stumble onto evidence of the murder, there could be no question of his being persuaded to stay silent.

Offering the reporter a cigar, he asked Sheedy about his own career. The American briefly described it.

When he had done so Cruickshank, fascinated, said, 'The Costa del Sol seems a long way from Vietnam, or for that matter the streets of New York. Don't you find it comparatively unexciting?'

'We all get older, Sir Brian. I've had more than enough gunfire for one life.'

The Englishman laughed. 'I know what you mean. I must admit I look forward to living in Spain myself. Are you married, Mr Sheedy?'

'My wife died.'

Cruickshank looked genuinely compassionate. 'I'm sorry.'

'Thanks. Time heals. I have a friend.'

'Then the two of you must spend a weekend at sea with me soon.'

'That's kind. We'd love to.'

Sheedy rose and walked across to the model.

Steeling himself to ask the key question, he turned towards the developer.

But to his surprise Cruickshank beat him to it. The Englishman had known it had to come and perceptively guessed when Sheedy rose that this was the moment. A master at getting an opponent off-balance, he spoke quickly, before the reporter could.

'By the way your programme the other night was of some relevance to my project.'

Sheedy was taken aback. 'Oh, why?'

'The man you spoke of. Señor Rodriguis. We had just negotiated with him to buy the last parcel of land we

197

need. His unfortunate death makes things a bit more difficult, I'm afraid. We may have some delay and no doubt his beneficiaries will ask for even more, so it will also cost us money. By the way, do you really think he was deliberately killed?'

Sheedy thought quickly. Either Cruickshank was incredibly clever or the Rabbit Man's death was a coincidence. To his surprise the American found himself hoping it was the second. And he had to admit the story sounded entirely plausible. If the Rabbit Man had reached a deal with Cruickshank's man, there was no incentive for Cruickshank to want him killed.

On the other hand there was the evidence – the stone that probably killed him, the position of the bridge planks, the match-book. All explicable, of course, but not to be lightly discounted.

'It probably was an accident, Sir Brian. After all who would want to kill him? Obviously not you.' He laughed to take the edge off the remark.

Cruickshank was equally light-hearted. 'Obviously not. Apart from my sympathy for the man, it's a damn nuisance.'

'Still,' Sheedy said, 'it's a coincidence. I take it you know nothing about the man that could explain it?'

'No.'

'How on earth did he come to own the land?'

'I can't help you, I'm afraid. We discovered the name of the owner of the land and it took my staff months to find him. At first he didn't want to sell but eventually we made him an increased offer, far more than we should have paid, and he simply couldn't refuse.'

Cruickshank looked at his watch and, explaining he was flying to London later that afternoon, guided the reporter to the gangplank.

Sheedy walked thoughtfully back to the car and drove to see Manuel at the office.

198

'Well?' the young Spaniard asked impatiently as he entered.

'Well, I don't know. He could not have been more open. He even raised the death of the Rabbit Man before I did. He said the old man's death is an inconvenience to them, will cause delays and cost them more money.'

'Did you believe him?'

'Either that or he's a brilliant actor.'

'So what are you going to do?'

'Wait until we hear what Kate brings back from Miguel and until we've had our little encounter with your boyfriend tonight.'

'He's not my boyfriend.' Manuel looked furious and Sheedy laughed.

'OK, OK, no more jokes. Now let's see if we can get Teddy Gray on the phone and find out what we can about this man Canning.'

While Sheedy had been with Cruickshank, Kate had driven up into the *sierras* en route for Ronda, calling first at Gaucin, a key stop-over point on the old smuggling trails. As her tiny hire car chugged up the hill and into the village, she could imagine the scene in the earlier days of the century – the shadowy figures of mule and man making their laborious way up during the night to disappear into the narrow streets and to shelter behind the big wooden doors, there to be fed, rested, and warmed in exchange for a carton of cigarettes or a bag of coffee.

She parked the car and walked up the narrow streets wondering what family dramas were being played out behind the silent, unrevealing white walls, the beaded curtains, the thick wooden doors.

In which of them was the peace being broken right now, at this moment, by the cries of babies, the laughter of children, the moans of lovers, the snores of slumbering old men, the prayers of black-clad widows?

In which of these houses had smugglers been made welcome, fed and rested?

Which of these old men chatting in the square or sitting on their steps had robbed, killed or even tortured in the civil war days ... who were the heroes and who were the cowards?

Kate marvelled that this noisy people who lived so much of their lives in the bars and on the streets were yet also so enigmatic, sceptical, watchful, their secrets hidden behind layer after layer of caution and privacy.

She felt Gaucin was an ideal place to illustrate Lorca's poem 'The Village':

Upon a barren mount,
a calvary.
Clear water
and century-old olive trees.
In the narrow streets,
men hidden under cloaks;
and on the towers,
weather vanes spinning.
Eternally
spinning.
Oh, lost village,
in the Andalusia of tears!

After taking many photographs she drove on to Ronda, parking on the edge of El Tajo, in too much of a hurry to notice the two *Guardia Civil* officers who were, unusually, guarding part of the car park and keeping it free of vehicles. She soon located the headquarters of the *Guardia Civil*. The Spanish flag was draped over its doorway. On the tiles above it, on a yellow strip between two strips of red, were printed the words '*Guardia Civil ... Todo por la Patria*', All for the Fatherland.

She guessed that there was some kind of flap on; there were three cars outside the station, one bigger than the usual *Guardia Civil* vehicle, and several officers were standing in a group talking quietly, some obviously distressed.

She pushed past the group and, entering the office building, asked a sergeant at the desk for Señor Miguel. He looked at her questioningly for a moment, then asked her to wait.

Soon she heard a door open and turned with a smile to greet Miguel only to find herself facing another policeman, immaculately dressed in what she assumed to be the uniform of a senior officer.

Having established her identity he led her into a smaller room. Bare-looking and uncarpeted, it contained two tables, each with just a canvas chair behind it. In front of one was an old leather armchair in bad need of upholstering. The officer indicated she should take it. She looked around. On a shelf beside her was a row of files that appeared to contain updates on *Guardia Civil* regulations. Hanging on a nail was a bunch of keys, beside it a black and white picture of King Juan Carlos. On the other desk was an old typewriter. Sitting behind it, oblivious to Kate and the other officer, an aged policeman was typing out a report, painfully slowly, and with occasional muttered curses as with a machine-gun-like ratatattat he put a series of crosses through a mistake.

For a moment the officer sat silently looking at her, then he asked 'Why do you want to see Officer Ayala?'

'Who?'

'Officer Ayala ... Miguel Ayala.'

Kate realised she had never heard Miguel's last name before.

'I had arranged to call on him today. Just a social call. Is there a problem?'

201

'When did you arrange this, Señorita?'

'Yesterday afternoon.' Kate began to be alarmed. 'What's the matter? Has something happened to Miguel? Why are you asking me these questions?'

'In a moment, Señorita. But first I must ask you some more. How long have you known Officer Ayala?'

'Only two or three weeks. But my friend Bill Sheedy has known him for much longer.'

'When did you last see him?'

'Oh, about a week ago, when he came to our home near San Pedro.'

'Where were you last night, Señorita? In Ronda?'

'No. At the villa in San Pedro. Señor Sheedy's villa. He was there too.'

'I see.' Again he looked at her silently, then, his voice softening, he told her Miguel was dead.

Kate felt tears spring to her eyes. 'But where? How?'

'I'm afraid he was found at the foot of El Tajo, Señorita. This morning. It could have been an accident ... but ...'

'My God.' Kate struggled to grasp what she was being told.

'He had been drinking, Señorita, so he could have accidentally fallen, but we can't think why he would have gone to that place. Unless it was suicide and no-one who knew him could believe that. So we are for the moment treating it as a suspicious death. Do you know of any reason why this should have happened?'

Kate tried to think. What would Bill want her to do? Then, unable to see any point in not telling the truth, she said 'I only know that he was investigating the death of the man they called El Conejero, the Rabbit Man. Oh God ...' She was struck by the coincidence. 'He also died by falling into a ravine. That, too, was made to look like an accident. It's all repeating itself.' She wiped her eyes, then added 'Miguel had been collaborating with

Bill Sheedy over that investigation ... He is a television reporter.'

The officer looked thoughtful. 'I see. Had you come to talk to Officer Ayala about this matter?'

Kate was having difficulty associating the formal name with the friendly Miguel. 'Not really. Except that he had some information for Mr Sheedy that I was to take back.'

'What kind of information?'

Kate decided a small lie wouldn't matter. 'I don't know. You will have to ask Mr Sheedy.'

Satisfied, the officer made a note of her and Sheedy's address and telephone number and led her to the door. 'Will you be all right, Señorita Callaghan, or should I have one of my men drive you back?'

She thanked him but declined the offer, and walked back into the piazza and into the Restaurante Meson del Puente on the cliff edge where she asked to use the telephone. From there she broke the news to Sheedy and arranged to meet him at the villa in the hour it would take her to drive back.

She found him sitting on the balcony looking out at the sea with unseeing eyes, whisky glass in hand. 'I'm sorry, Bill,' she said, and sat at his feet, putting her head in his lap. For a while they sat like that, wordlessly, he gently stroking her hair. When he spoke he sounded grim.

'Bloody hell, Kate, a couple of hours back I was ready to accept that it was all a coincidence, that Cruickshank and his bloody project had nothing to do with the Rabbit Man's death. But they've got to be, Kate. The two so-called accidents have got to be connected and they've got to be connected to Anglo-Spanish Investors and their bloody project. And they're going to pay for it. We're going to get these buggers. Don't doubt it.'

'You think Cruickshank is personally involved?'

'I don't know. If what Teddy Gray in New York tells me is correct, one of the big investors in this project is about as bad news as you can get. He could be looking after his interests independently of Cruickshank. On the other hand the project is Cruickshank's baby and he doesn't strike me as the kind of man to relinquish control to anyone. Anyway, whatever the level of Cruickshank's involvement, this man Canning is the executioner.'

He stood up and restlessly paced about, going into the villa and then coming back out onto the balcony. 'Listen, Manuel and I have some work to do tonight. We'll be through by about 10 o'clock. We'll come back for a planning session.'

'Be careful.'

'I will.' Sheedy grabbed a jacket and the car keys and walked out of the room.

Kate looked after him, thinking it was strange how Sheedy the hunter took on a harder, younger physical look than when relaxed around the house or pool. She liked these two shades of the man, the 'softie' as she called him when he was relaxing with her, and the restless tough guy when it came to work, yet as she heard the door slam and the car roar as his foot hit the accelerator, she thought she liked the relaxed Sheedy best. This one she felt she didn't really know.

Sheedy drove quickly down the hill, through San Pedro then left onto the main road to Marbella. Pulling up at his office, he carelessly left the car on a no-parking line and climbed the stairs two at a time. He found Rosa looking puzzled at a big pile of papers and photographs lying on his desk.

'What's this?'

'It came in the post, Señor.'

Sheedy picked up a few of the papers and recognised

them immediately. They were the ones from the *cortejo*. With them was a brief note scrawled by Miguel on *Guardia Civil* letterhead: 'Bill, I tried to reach you or Señorita Kate at the villa to say that I was posting these after all. There is a chance I may be sent out into the country in the morning. I know that Kate will not have a wasted journey because she has her photographs to take. I went back to the *cortijo* and found a letter together with about 20,000 pesetas in notes in an old leather pouch stuffed up the *chimenea*. I'm sending it with the other stuff. Will ring you. Miguel.'

Sheedy momentarily rested his head in his hands, the memory of the big policeman holding court in the corner of the Casino Club almost more than he could bear. Then he asked Rosa 'What is a *chimenea* – is it the chimney?'

'*Si*, Señor.'

Turning to the papers, he moved the pile to one side of the desk and began to transfer them, one at a time, to the centre, so that he could study them with care.

There were several notes clearly given to the Rabbit Man on his trips to Ronda on the lines of 'Restaurante Pedro Romero orders fifty *conejo* soon as possible.'

There were some old bullfight cuttings.

There were photographs, some old and faded, some more recent, some of the bullfighters, some of the Ronda fair, including one of Miguel and the Rabbit Man taken by Sheedy himself, some of people Sheedy couldn't identify, and the one he remembered of the girl, the dark-haired child dressed in traditional Andalusian costume.

After careful inspection Sheedy set aside two items.

One was a photograph of the Rabbit Man with another man, taken on a bank overlooking a hill capped with a white town. Sheedy recognised it as Casares, a *pueblo* thirteen kilometres in from the costa between

205

Estapona and Gibraltar. The other man looked sufficiently like El Conejero for Sheedy to guess it could be his brother.

The second was an old yellow press clipping showing a group of young men on horseback, each holding a rifle. Sheedy guessed it probably dated back to the civil war. He couldn't, however, identify which of the men was the Rabbit Man.

He put the photographs on top of the pile of papers and put them all in a brief-case, then asked Rosa if she would give top priority to translating and typing out the letter Miguel had found – the handwriting looked very difficult to decipher. Then, looking at his watch, he bounded back down the stairs to the car and roared off in a cloud of dust towards Puerto Banus.

Felipe was just about to turn into the alley to the backstreet of Puerto Banus when he heard someone calling and, turning round, saw his new-found friend from the Pink Coconut walking towards him.

'*Buenos noches*, my friend. Do you know, I did not ask your name?'

'Nor I yours,' replied Felipe.

'Then I am Manuel.'

'And I am Felipe.'

'*Hola*, Felipe. I was thinking, let's not go to the Pink Coconut . . . Let's go to a happier place. What about one of the beach clubs?'

Felipe was pleased. This was how he had hoped it would be. Manuel's proposal that they should not go to the gay bar was reassurance that the other liked him for his company and conversation, was proud to be seen with him anywhere. That he didn't just want Felipe for sex. '*Si*, Manuel,' he said. 'Let's do that.'

'I have a car. We will drive there.'

Felipe brightened up even more. So this man had a

car, and that meant money, maybe enough for them to be able to go out for dinner and to the better clubs.

'*Bien*,' he said. 'Let's go.'

Manuel led him to a blue Seat, just a couple of years old. Winding down the windows and turning on the radio, he steered it out of Puerto Banus and onto the main road south. Soon they turned left and drove down towards the beach until they stopped by a wooden building on the edge of the sand. It was brightly lit and from it came the sound of loud music.

They walked into the bar.

'Manuel ... Manuel ... come, have a drink. Bring your friend.'

Felipe looked to the bar and saw a big, friendly-looking man waving to his companion. He frowned. Who was this? A rival? Perhaps an older lover?

Manuel introduced him as Bill. He was American but spoke Spanish. Felipe found him vaguely familiar. Perhaps he had seen him in the Pink Coconut. The big man insisted on buying a bottle of wine for the three of them and ushered them to an empty table. Despite his irritation that his intimacy with Manuel had been disturbed, and his fear of rivalry, Felipe soon relaxed. After all, had he not always pictured himself sitting in places like this with his own special friend, but also surrounded by others? And the big man was popular, judging by the number of people who waved to him or stopped briefly at their table. Anyway, he was difficult to dislike. He had gentle eyes and did not appear to be competing with Felipe for Manuel's affections. In fact he seemed pleased for Manuel that he had a new friend.

They had been chatting and drinking for nearly half an hour before the big man said 'Hey, boys, I know you two would prefer to be on your own, but why not let me buy you dinner first. We could go to Toni Dalli's.'

Felipe was thrilled.

Toni Dalli's!

He, Felipe, was being asked to go to *Toni Dalli's*.

Manuel looked doubtful. 'I don't know ...' he began, 'maybe Felipe would prefer ...'

Felipe, not to be denied, interrupted. '*Si*, Manuel, *si*, we can go. Let's go.'

Manuel shrugged. 'OK. If it makes you happy, Felipe.'

They decided they would all go in the car belonging to Bill, the big man having promised to drop them back afterwards.

Felipe was too excited to notice as they entered the elegant restaurant that their host seemed expected, and that a table for three had been reserved in the centre section.

It was not until they were on the main course that Manuel said 'By the way, Bill, I think Felipe knows the man you have been enquiring about, what's his name ... Canning ... Tony Canning?'

'Jason,' Felipe said without thinking. 'It's Jason.'

Sheedy looked amazed. 'Is that right? But how do you know him Felipe?'

'Felipe is an officer on *La Gaviota*,' Manuel said, as if proud of his friend.

Felipe blushed with embarrassment; the lie that he was an officer may have had some plausibility in the unreal atmosphere of the Pink Coconut but it seemed only too transparent when repeated in this place. Fortunately the big man didn't appear to think so.

'*An officer*? Is that right? You have done well.' The American looked at him admiringly. 'But I'm sorry to hear Jason Canning is a friend of yours.'

Felipe couldn't wait to reassure him. Over-excited by his new experiences, and already having had more wine than he was accustomed to, he unleashed his anger at the humiliations he had suffered at Canning's hands,

208

pouring out his grievances. 'He is a bully, Señor. He is always sneering at me, making life difficult. If I could fight back I would. But I have always dreamed to work on a yacht. I daren't risk losing my job.'

Bill looked at him sympathetically. 'Well, this is an extraordinary bit of luck for both of us, Felipe. Because I don't like your Mr Canning either. I think we can help each other.'

Just at that moment there was a stir in the restaurant. Felipe looked round. The owner, Toni Dalli, an Italian singer, once an international star, had come near to their table and, accompanied by a guitarist, was breaking into song. When he finished there was loud applause and then, to Felipe's amazement, Dalli came over to their table and greeted Manuel's friend Bill warmly. The big man then introduced Manuel and Felipe.

Well after the entertainer-restaurateur had moved on, Felipe was still speechless. This was unbelievable. What would the others on the yacht, and the men he met in the Pink Coconut think of this?

'You know Toni Dalli well, Señor?'

'For years,' Sheedy replied casually.

'But you know him *well*?'

Sheedy, struggling to suppress a grin, shrugged and said 'Well, what's well? I guess as well as anyone.'

Manuel glanced at Sheedy who gave him a barely discernible nod. He turned to Felipe. 'Bill is a celebrity himself. He has a television programme. You may have seen it. *Bill Sheedy on the Costa del Sol.*'

Felipe, almost too excited to sit still, looked hard at the American. 'Yes, yes, I knew I had seen you.'

Sheedy leaned over the table. 'Well, it's my programme that I think you can help.'

Felipe was overwhelmed. This evening was exceeding his wildest dreams. 'But, of course, Señor, but how . . .?'

Sheedy began to talk about Canning, building on the

209

young man's hatred of his American tormentor while flattering him by drawing him into the plot. 'He's a bad man, Felipe. And we can deal with him. You could be rid of him forever. All you have to do is pick up what information you can. We need to know how many times he has been to Ronda and when. We particularly need to know where he was last night. We need to know who he talks to. And what he and Sir Brian Cruickshank say to one another. Whatever you hear will help. You can be our man on the yacht.'

For a moment Felipe hesitated. Manuel leaned over and touched his arm gently, looking into his eyes. 'Don't do it if you don't want to, Felipe. Bill will understand. Won't you, Bill?'

The big American nodded. 'Of course. But I think it will help Felipe too if we can get Canning off the yacht.'

Manuel leaned even closer to the crew member. '*Sí*, I guess it will. Why not have a go at it Felipe?'

Felipe was impressed by their consideration. 'Have a go. *Sí*, I will have a go.'

'Great.' Bill rose. 'Let me give you a lift back.' On the way he told Felipe where to telephone if he had any information. 'Just leave a message that you rang and I or Manuel will meet you at Joe's Bar in the port at nine o'clock the same night.'

Felipe could hardly credit all that had happened.

The beach club. Toni Dalli's. Meeting the singer himself. His involvement with the friendly TV reporter. And Manuel ... his new friend Manuel.

Such was his excitement that he was in his bunk before he realised that the two had dropped him off and gone away together, that he had not ended the night with Manuel as he had expected.

Still, so heady had the evening been that he didn't care too much. He was exhausted and anyway he knew his new friends were here to stay ... as long as he had something to tell them about Canning.

He thought of the cruel, sarcastic American.

Canning would pay for the way he had treated Felipe.

He resolved to start his enquiries first thing in the morning.

Chapter Eight

Cruickshank was tired. He had taken the four o'clock plane from Malaga to Gatwick, travelled to Victoria by train, and been working in his office for over two hours. Now he pushed away the last of the stack of letters, memos and messages that had awaited him and, placing on top of them the dictaphone cassettes containing his comments and replies, he summoned his secretary. 'I would like these typed by the overnight secretary and ready for me to check and sign at 7.30 in the morning. I shall be returning to Spain on the late morning flight.'

She nodded. 'Mr Jordan is downstairs.'

Cruickshank looked at his watch. It was 9.30 p.m. 'Show him up.'

While he waited he looked out at the City lights and reviewed, not for the first time, his meeting with Sheedy on the yacht. It had gone well. He could not have handled it better. Provided they survived the next couple of weeks without further setbacks all would be well.

He had liked Sheedy and believed the feeling was mutual. The reporter could be useful. He would cultivate his friendship.

His thoughts turned to the other American, Jordan, now on his way up to the office. He remembered how impressed he had been with the authority and elegance of the man when they had first met in New York. How was he to treat him now – as ally or adversary?

Deciding it was vital to keep control of the moral high ground, he shook the American's hand unsmilingly and coolly bid him to sit down, abandoning his severity only to offer him a drink.

The two sat in the window. Cruickshank liked to entertain foreign visitors in this way. The spectacle of the new tower blocks, competing with St Paul's cathedral to dominate the skyline, was impressive in itself, and his position overlooking it conveyed a sense of power and influence.

Jordan wanted to talk about the race track proposal. Was it really practical?

'Of course. In fact, I hear that planning permission has been requested for another one, further east, near Mijas.'

'Is that good news for us?'

'I think so. We only planned three or four meetings a year; the other will help to develop the appetite for horse-racing. Provided we make a deal with them on the timing of meetings, and that makes sense for them too, each company will benefit from the existence of the other.'

'But is the appetite there? For gambling?'

'Of that there's no doubt. Apart from your fellow countrymen and, I believe, the Filipinos, the Spanish spend more money on gambling than anyone else in the world.'

'But on what do they gamble now?'

'Nearly half of it's spent on slot machines ... one-arm bandits. And bingo is tremendously popular. I believe that in Andalusia alone nearly 10,000 million pesetas are

213

spent every year on bingo. Then, of course, there are the lotteries. The Spanish are lottery-mad.'

'If that's so,' said Jordan, 'why not add a casino to our plans?'

Cruickshank looked askance. 'Apart from the fact that there's one at Nueva Andalucia, much more accessible than one on our land, I personally think it would lower the tone. The point about the race track is that we would be promoting the sport of kings in a setting and atmosphere appropriate to the project as a whole.'

'A casino need not be a sordid place,' Jordan replied. 'It could be small, intimate, comfortable and very, very profitable.'

Cruickshank's eyes narrowed further. Resort casinos conjured up unattractive images of Las Vegas and Atlantic City and the accompanying 'industries' of prostitution and drugs, and this in turn resurrected memories of Canning's criminal behaviour and the way the Americans had taken financial control of the operation. He didn't like the sound of it.

He rose and went to the drinks cabinet to refill Jordan's glass, but really in order to buy time to think. He was in no doubt that a casino had to be resisted. But it would be better not to have an argument with Jordan now, not until he had re-established his full authority over the project. There was a further point: if he handled the Spanish authorities well, it was possible he could get them to forbid a casino without it being necessary for him to make a personal stand at all.

As he handed the American his drink, he managed a relaxed smile. 'I will explore the idea, Mr Jordan, but I would be surprised if you convinced me.'

Jordan smiled in response, leaving Cruickshank unclear whether or not he had already succeeded in discouraging the American. His visitor now asked about the Rabbit Man's land. Cruickshank revived his severe look. 'As I warned you, Canning's so-called solution has not been that helpful,' he said. 'For a start, questions have been raised about the old man's death. Canning was not as careful as he claimed. While there was, of course, no evidence to link the death with us, there apparently was evidence of foul play. And already the connection between the peasant and our project has been exposed. I am, of course, taking the line that the ... accident ... was a considerable setback to us and that we have more cause than anyone to regret his passing. But it is vital we give no other grounds for suspicion. That is why I must ask you to keep Canning well under control.'

Jordan moved to reply but Cruickshank was enjoying the opportunity to rub home the down-side of Canning's homicidal behaviour. 'All this means we can't press quite as hard as we would like,' he continued. 'If we're too anxious to get the problem solved it will look uncaring and that is contrary to the image I have been creating. At present it is the intention of the authorities to adver-tise for relatives of the peasant to come forward, informing them that there may be a small legacy. Once they do – if they do – we shall immediately make them an offer they can't refuse ... to use your jargon.'

Cruickshank enjoyed that bit of sarcasm. If Jordan hadn't taken on board the unacceptability of Canning's actions by now, Cruickshank would make damn certain he had before he left the room.

'If no-one comes forward,' he said, 'the land will be taken over by the authorities and sold to us. I have taken care of that. My plan therefore is to proceed at full pace on the assumption the land will become ours in six to nine months.'

Jordan nodded appreciatively and, to Cruickshank's irritation, without any sign of anger at the Englishman's pointed remarks.

They turned to other matters, notably the availability

of funds at appropriate times, and then the American rose to leave. For a moment they paused in front of the model. Cruickshank looked at it with his usual sense of pride. Jordan looked at it without expression, then shook the Englishman's hand. 'It has, as always, been a pleasure, Sir Brian.'

Cruickshank, feeling increasingly confident that all was back on course, did his best to maintain his severity and did not reply.

As he picked up his briefcase Jordan added 'We'll look forward to hearing from you about the casino.'

Then he was gone and Cruickshank was left alone feeling disconcerted.

Damn them. Why was it that just when he felt he had the upper hand these people always succeeded in leaving him with uncertainty?

That last remark had not been a casual one.

Jordan had been telling him that the matter was not resolved. The question was still open.

Jordan wanted that casino.

And that 'we' to Cruickshank spelt trouble. Who in God's name was 'we'?

He looked again at the model. The casino would be out of place. He would be damned if he would let Jordan and company distort the project, cheapen it with their damn casino. What would they be suggesting next. A high class bordello?

He sat down in the window with another Scotch. That last thought had led to another ... the woman in Maida Vale. Suddenly, for the first time for weeks, he felt an urge.

There was, he knew, no question of making love to Maria until they were married. He was sure she was a virgin and would want to be until after their wedding. And that's the way he wanted it too. His marriage to her must be perfect.

Just the same, proximity to her, the powerful desire she aroused, was frustrating. And now he had the woman in Maida Vale on his mind he couldn't forget her.

For nearly thirty minutes he wrestled with his conscience before making a call on his private line.

As always he left the taxi at the corner of the street and walked slowly up to the block of flats. He rang the bell and waited self-consciously while he was inspected via the small security camera above the door. Then, in response to the buzzer, he pushed the door open and, moving quickly now, climbed the two flights of stairs to her flat.

She was in her late thirties, shorter than Cruickshank, dark-haired and curvy, friendly and sexy. The flat looked just like he imagined the home of a single woman to be, and that he valued, because Cruickshank had come to terms with his visits by imagining her as a mistress rather than a whore, by thinking of the envelope he left on her dresser as a gift rather than a payment for services rendered, by closing his mind to the possibility, indeed the probability, in fact the reality of other men and other envelopes.

'It's been a long time,' she said. She never used his name. He liked to think she didn't know who he was, shutting his mind to the probability that as she sat alone waiting for her clients she watched television and was only too aware of his identity and importance.

'Yes,' he said, 'it's been a long time.'

'A drink?'

'Scotch.'

She poured him one and, while he sat sipping it, she said 'I'll be back in a moment. Why don't you undress?'

Usually this is what he would have done, but tonight he couldn't bring himself to move, just stayed in the chair, drinking the Scotch, looking round the room, until she returned, dressed now only in the black transparent nightdress he had always liked.

If she was surprised to find him sitting there, fully clothed, she didn't show it. Instead she sat on the arm of the chair and looked at him. He was acutely aware of her scent, her eyes smiling at his, her white breasts stretching the negligée. He reached out a hand and cradled one, succumbing to her proximity and to the scent as if injected with a drug.

Yet still all he could think of was Maria, her big brown eyes searching deep into his soul, her soft voice talking of honour and trust.

Suddenly he knew he shouldn't have come. He stood up abruptly and began to reach for his coat, apologising clumsily. But she rose, too, slipping the negligée over her shoulders so that it fell to the floor. Naked, she walked up to him so that her dark, firm nipples were touching his chest. 'You're troubled,' she said. 'Can't I help you relax?' She put her arm round his neck and gently kissed him on the lips.

But all he felt now was foolish. He picked up his coat and, reaching into the pocket, took out an envelope. 'This was going to be my last visit. I won't be returning. I would like you to accept this gift. I have been grateful for your kindness and your discretion.'

She rose and taking the envelope, slid her finger under the top and opened it, gasping at the wad of banknotes inside. 'But there must be . . .'

'Yes, but I owe you much. Ours may have been a business arrangement but I've not felt uncomfortable with it. You have been a friend. And I have trusted you. Please accept it.'

Still naked she came back up to him and gave him a hug. Then she kissed him on the cheek. 'Thank you.'

As he began to walk to the door she said: 'You are

218

going to marry, aren't you?'

'What makes you say that?'

'I don't believe that you're changing to another business girl. And an unmarried man of your kind doesn't just have an affair. You're going to marry.'

He smiled, said goodbye, and left, pausing in the darkened doorway for a moment before walking quickly down the street and round the corner into St John's Wood Road where he called a taxi to travel the short distance to his town house near Regents Park.

She had been a good friend. He would miss her. And he was pleased it had ended this way ... that he had not succumbed to the desire that took him there. He would always know that from the moment he met Maria there had been no-one else.

Still, he was grateful to the woman. He didn't begrudge the £1,000 he had given her. With it he had, he felt, paid a debt and at the same time earned her further discretion.

After he had gone the woman tossed the negligée onto the bed and pulled on a dressing gown. She put the money in her handbag. Behind her a door opened and a man's voice said 'Well done.'

She looked at him and shrugged. 'I'm sorry. You didn't get much. But what could I do? The man's fallen in love.'

The man grinned. 'Don't worry. The scene was explicit enough. I'm just glad I got here before him. He must have left his office directly after his telephone call.'

He handed her an envelope, her second of the night. 'My clients will be pleased.' Then, slipping a small cannister of film into his overcoat, he walked to the door. There he paused and looked back.

'They never learn, do they?' he said. 'That there is no such thing as a whore with a heart of gold.'

'Just for that,' she replied, 'next time you'll pay double.'

'Just for that,' he said, 'there won't be a next time.'

She went to the window and watched him walk down the street.

Actually, he was wrong, she thought.

Well . . . a bit wrong.

She felt sorry for Cruickshank.

Well . . . a bit sorry.

Once home, Cruickshank telephoned Julio in Marbella and asked to speak to Maria. He lounged back in an armchair, Scotch in hand, delighted as she told him with enthusiasm what she had been doing during the day.

As he listened it struck him that this was the first such telephone conversation he had shared with her. He sensed that she had been looking forward to him ringing, storing up the things she wanted to say. He rejoiced in the sound of her voice. How marvellous it would be to be able to ring her every time he was away, from wherever he was on business, and talk in this way.

After he put the phone down it struck him that she, too, was lonely.

He felt his heart fill with love for her, with joy at what lay ahead, of what they would share together.

Thank God it was all coming right once more.

The woman in Maida Vale was in the past.

The project was back on course.

The reporter was no threat. It was obvious from their meeting that Sheedy had no evidence to link him or the project with the murder. Nor would there be any.

He had Jordan's word there would be no more 'indiscretions' and, while he now knew that Jordan's word wouldn't ordinarily count for much, he believed the American had the sense to accept that strongarm tactics just couldn't work in Spain.

So all he had left to do was squash this casino idea, fast and firm. That would be no problem.

There was now nothing on the horizon likely to spoil his happiness with Maria.

And nothing was going to be allowed to.

Nothing.

Full of new confidence he went to bed and for the first time in over a week he slept well.

It was a relatively chilly night and Kate had built a fire. She and the two men, home from their dinner with Felipe, settled in front of it with a bottle of Rioja.

Kate reminded Sheedy that he should expect a visit from the police. 'What will you tell them?'

Sheedy thought for a moment. 'Well, obviously that Miguel believed the Rabbit Man had been murdered and was making enquiries and that there is a possibility, in fact a probability, that whoever committed the first murder also committed the second because Miguel knew too much.'

'And the link with Anglo-Spanish Investors?'

'I don't know about that. At the moment they don't necessarily think they're in the frame. If the police descend on the company they'll be on the defensive. I reckon I can get more out of them at this point than the police can.'

Manuel looked concerned. 'Wouldn't that be with-holding evidence?'

'Maybe for a few days.'

'Bill, what did Miguel find in the papers?' Kate asked.

'I don't know yet. I left the new letter with Rosa. I hope to get the translation tomorrow.'

Manuel picked up the two photographs Sheedy had set aside and looked at them. 'And these?'

'I think one is the Rabbit Man's brother. It was taken at Casares. We'll have to go up there and talk to him.

And this other picture, the old one of the group of men, I don't know ... probably means nothing. But I just wondered whether Miguel had seen anything in it that could have been a motive from the past, nothing to do with the Cruickshank project at all. Miguel was holding something back the other day, something I suspect from the deep past, perhaps involving them both.'

Kate said: 'So how close are we to proving that Anglo-Spanish Investors were involved, that this man Canning killed them both?'

'It's all so bloody circumstantial. If, as we believe, the Rabbit Man was murdered, it's too much of a coincidence to suggest that Miguel's death is unconnected. We know Cruickshank's outfit had a motive – a fortune's worth of motive. We know Canning goes to Alexander's and that a match-book from Alexander's was found near the Rabbit Man's body. Yet we still have the problem that no-one seems to have seen either killing. My guess is that the police will find it all a bit weak.'

Kate asked, 'Don't you think that to help the police will mean that more people will be looking into it properly, there'll be more publicity, and a much better chance of getting at the truth?'

'It's possible. But we have to consider Felipe. He's one of our best prospects of getting more information and once the police get involved he'll be frightened off. We need to give him some time.'

Manuel had been listening carefully. 'Look, Bill, I don't like it. I don't like holding back from the police, and I don't like what we're doing to the kid on the yacht. He's harmless and we've been conning him. Doesn't it strike you that his life's at risk? And maybe yours and mine too?'

Sheedy poured another glass of wine. 'Manuel, these bastards have killed two harmless old men to save themselves a bit of inconvenience or a bit of money. They're getting away with it. And if they do, why shouldn't they just keep doing it? I know we can get them. I know it. Let's at least give it a few more days.'

Kate was troubled. 'I feel the same as Manuel. It's one thing for you not to go to the police voluntarily and another to hold back when they come to you. After all, you're only responsible for a television programme. Their job is enforcing the law.'

Sheedy looked at her sharply. 'It's not just the bloody programme. If it hadn't been for me the Rabbit Man's body probably wouldn't have been found and Miguel would still be alive. I have a responsibility too.'

'And what will you say if the boy on the yacht is killed? That you're even more responsible? That you have even more reason to go it alone? For Christ's sake, Bill, stop acting like the Lone Avenger.'

Sheedy rose to his feet, flushed with anger. 'I don't need this shit, Kate. These men were my friends and I believe I can prove who killed them. Doesn't that matter?'

Kate stood too, her temper flaring. 'And Felipe? You don't give a damn about him. You're just using him. Why? Because he's gay. Do you think because he's gay he doesn't matter so much, that he's expendable. You're just exploiting his vulnerability. What happened to Sheedy, crusader for the little man?'

Sheedy put his glass down and, ignoring her, turned to Manuel. 'Let's call it a day. I'll talk to you tomorrow.' And he walked out of the room onto the balcony.

Kate and Manuel looked at each other. The Spaniard shrugged. 'Forget it for tonight, Kate. He's upset about Miguel. Maybe he'll see it differently tomorrow.'

When Manuel was gone Kate threw another log on the fire and calling Sheedy in, pulled him down to where she was sitting on the carpet with her back resting on the sofa. Gently she massaged the back of his neck as he sat leaning back on her. 'Sorry, Bill, I didn't want to argue with you. It's just that I think you're in danger of losing your perspective on this. You're too involved. And I'm frightened ... for you ... and for us.'

When he didn't reply she added 'I know you. You're capable of making a deal with the police and working with them. You always did in New York. Why can't you do it now?'

Still he was silent. Kate moved her hands over his back, then put her arms round him, pulling him back to her, hugging him. 'You're getting too tense, Bill,' she whispered. 'Time to relax ...'

At last he turned and looked at her, then said 'I'm sorry I shouted at you. I guess it's because you suddenly reminded me of ... of Jan ... telling me what to do. For a moment I resented someone else doing that. But I don't really.' He kissed her warmly. 'I'd forgotten what it was like to have someone who cared enough about me to argue. I'm grateful.' And they rolled over on the carpet and in the warmth of the fire they made love, first gently, then with mounting passion, until as the blaze gathered force in the grate they reached a climax together and lay in each other's arms becoming increasingly drowsy until he rose and picked her up and carried her off to bed.

Julio and Isabella had a long-standing engagement and the Garcias and Maria had chosen to spend a quiet evening together at the architect's home, one interrupted only by the call from London.

Now, as the time neared for them to retire to bed, Cristina looked at Maria, resting back in her chair by the log fire, lost in thought, her beautiful face illuminated by the flames. She had never seen the young woman look happier.

'Doesn't our child look beautiful, Juan?' she said.

224

Maria sat forward and blushed.

'And happy,' said Juan. 'You've had a good time on the costa. You should come more often.'

Cristina looked at her husband and then at Maria. 'I don't think the costa is the reason, Juan,' she said. 'I think our child is in love.'

Juan Garcia looked up sharply. 'In love. In love with whom?'

Maria looked at Cristina, half annoyed, half embarrassed, and then at her impatient-looking guardian.

'I did not say I was in love. Mama did.'

'But are you?'

She sighed. Then, standing, she poured a coffee and walked to the fire, her back to them. 'Sir Brian has honoured me with a proposal of marriage.'

Both man and woman gasped. It was Juan who responded first. Rising and walking over, he turned her to look at him. 'And you?'

'I want to accept, Papa. He is the kindest, most intelligent man I have ever met ... except for you. And a man I could trust.'

'But he's so much older than you?'

'That is no matter. I don't want to marry a man of my own age. They don't please me.'

'Juan,' it was Cristina, 'Sir Brian is a distinguished man and would give our Maria a good life. And he seemed a kind and considerate man. If Maria loves him ...'

'But she hardly knows him ... I am not opposing this, but I would wish Maria to know him better, and I would like to know him better.'

Maria stepped between her guardians. 'Please don't worry. Sir Brian will not wish me to hurry and is anxious to get to know you as well. But, Mama and Papa, I do care about this man.'

Cristina gave her a hug. 'Don't you worry, our dear

225

Maria. We will rejoice if he is the man who can make you happy.'

Juan sat down, looking thoughtful. 'I'm surprised Sir Brian did not say a word to me about it when we talked at his villa.'

'Sir Brian is not Spanish,' Maria gently reminded him. 'I think in England men assume that women can speak for themselves. He is too much of a gentleman to raise it with you until I have spoken to you.'

'And when were you going to do that?' Juan asked.

'When I was brave enough,' she replied.

'Do you need courage to speak to me,' Juan said, looking hurt.

'No, Papa,' she replied. 'Just to overcome my shyness.'

He looked at her and smiled. 'And yet you are not shy with this important Englishman?'

'No,' she said. 'No. Does that not say a lot about him?'

THURSDAY, APRIL 5

The sociologists would have had real difficulty with Jason Canning. He didn't fit the usual pattern. There was no chapter in their textbook that applied to him.

He didn't take drugs, so didn't need extra money to satisfy a dependency.

He didn't come from a criminal background, so wasn't born into law-breaking like many of those who operate in the middle-management of organised crime.

He hadn't been raised in poverty or in slums, hadn't had to fight his way out of them, so wasn't rebelling against an unjust society.

On the contrary, he was the only son of an affluent businessman, had apparently been content at home, had emerged from college with academic honours, and was just beginning to make a career for himself on Wall Street when he took a conscious decision to make a career in crime. That's what the sociologists would not have been able to fathom. Most people drift into crime, or are bullied or dared or talked into it, or are driven into it by desperation, by need of money, or to protect themselves from some threat. But Canning's was an intellectual decision. He simply decided he wanted to work in crime ... just as his peers decided they wanted to go in for commodity-broking or some other form of money-making.

No doubt if they could dissect his brain, the scientists could one day come up with an answer to the conundrum but, until it was found, there was only one word to describe Jason Canning.

Amoral.

He believed rules were there to keep others in check, to create an ordered society in which a rule-breaker could thrive. In a society in which everyone patiently queued, he reasoned to himself, a skilful queue-jumper couldn't fail, provided he didn't mind being disliked. And Canning didn't.

He kept his distance from other people, shared his thoughts with no-one, lived alone. Not without physical needs, he satisfied them with whores. He figured you made your deal with them, you took what you wanted, you paid them and they were gone. There was not a whore in Puerto Banus he hadn't had once; there was no-one he had slept with twice. He wouldn't give even them the chance to get too close. Not that they wanted to; the same compulsion to concede nothing meant he was in his sexual encounters with them cold, hard, even brutal.

People only had meaning for Canning if they could help him, in which case they were used for that purpose and then dropped; or if they were in his way, in which case they were removed.

Or they were there to be toyed with. Canning liked to play with people as you would play with poker chips, pick them up, turn them over, juggle them, drop them, gamble with them, and then cash them in – you win some, you lose some.

He had first been attracted to Capone's Bar because of the name. It appealed to his perverse sense of humour. It also suited him because, rather like the Pink Coconut, it consisted of a long bar with stools at the end, round the corner from all the others, and from this dark corner he could watch people at the bar or on the little dance floor.

He had then moved on to using Alexander's more. Men tended to make fools of themselves at Alexander's and Canning liked to watch them do it and record it in his memory in case he could make use of it at a later date.

Canning liked to watch. For all his indifference to them, he understood what made most people tick. He liked to think he could work out what everyone in the bar at a particular time wanted ... what they wanted that night, what they wanted from life. Canning reckoned if you knew what people wanted you had them.

This night, however, things were quiet. Alexander's was not yet open and he had been drinking in Capone's. He tossed a handful of 100 peseta coins on the counter and left, wandering up Calle de las Alegrias, the small alley that led from Capone's into Calle Ribera. From there he planned to make his way to the car park. Canning didn't live on the yacht, preferring as always to keep his distance; he lived in an apartment on the Nuevo Andalucia complex nearby.

Now, as he neared the end of the Calle Ribera he saw

a familiar figure, the little fag from the yacht, the one he liked to toy with and to bully. Felipe. He was climbing some stairs to the first floor of the second row of buildings in the port. On an impulse he followed, reaching the top just in time to see Felipe pushing open the door of Joe's Bar.

Not his usual territory, thought Canning.

He paused for a moment, then with a few quick steps was himself in the bar. At first he couldn't see the slight Spaniard but then spotted him with his back to the bar, sitting on a small round stool talking to two men who were listening intently. Canning recognised Sheedy immediately.

He ducked onto a low stool at the far end of the room where he could just see the three but was side-on to them and out of their line of vision. From there he settled down to his favourite game – watching.

Felipe was doing most of the talking. Every now and then Sheedy would speak, apparently asking questions.

After a few minutes Canning slipped back out. He quickly climbed the steps of the block of the flats above and, lighting a cigarette, stood in the dark, waiting.

It was some thirty minutes before the big man left. Felipe was still inside with the other. Canning continued to wait.

Another fifteen minutes passed and the two younger men came out. They stood close, talking quietly. Canning could see Felipe was upset, clearly trying to encourage the other to go somewhere with him. The other was seeking to reassure him. He heard the other say 'Next time ... we will ... I promise ...'

Then he watched Felipe begin to walk disconsolately down the backstreet, then up the alley in the direction of the yacht.

Canning stayed for a few more minutes finishing his cigarette. Then thoughtfully he strolled back to his car and drove home. Once there he put in a call to the Spaniards in Fuengirola.

Maria was out, dining with Cruickshank, and Juan took the opportunity to tell Julio and Isabella of Cruickshank's proposal to his ward.

The architect responded enthusiastically. Cruickshank was a man of distinction and integrity, rich and generous. Yes, he was older than Maria, but by no means an old man. If the young woman loved him it would be, said Julio, a good marriage.

Juan said he wished it could have been a younger man. But Cristina gently suggested that the choice of an older man could be partly Juan's fault. 'You have been such a kind and sensitive guardian to her, Juan, that she has looked for a similar man. She is proud of your integrity, your sense of honour, and that is why she sets such store by it in Cruickshank.'

'You mean she wants a father figure?' he asked.

'No, I don't mean that. Maria has great inner strength. She doesn't need someone to look up to, but she does need someone she respects as she respects herself. You have set a standard and the young men who she's met have not been able to match it. Sir Brian has.'

'One good thing about that, Juan,' said Julio, 'if Maria marries Sir Brian you will have no worries about her future. He is a man of great integrity.'

Juan looked reassured. '*Si*, that is so. That is one thing we don't have to fear.'

Pleased with that thought he suggested they opened a bottle of champagne to toast the absent couple – his dear ward Maria and her Knight.

Jim Miller was not happy. Things had been slipping out of his control and it was partly his own fault.

When he had gone to pick up the gun on Tuesday

night he had lost Canning. He had checked at the yacht, looked into Capone's and then Alexander's, and eventually parked his car in the dark near Canning's apartment and waited for him to return. It had been nearly 3 a.m. when Canning got back. Miller had a feeling he had been in the wrong place at the wrong time.

Then there had been tonight. He had nearly missed Canning leaving Capone's from his own vantage point in the window of the bar on the corner of the alley. Then he had only just avoided being seen by Canning when the American had slipped up some stairs to stand in the dark watching Joe's Bar.

Miller had not felt any happier to see Sheedy come out of the bar. Was it the reporter who Canning was watching? If so it could be for no good reason.

He had followed Canning home and only when he was sure that the American was settled in his apartment did he return to the villa, picking up a copy of *El Pais* on his way. Miller made a practice of struggling through the Spanish newspaper each day to improve his Spanish.

Once home, he bathed and, climbing into bed, switched on the bedside light, flicked through its pages and began to slowly read the stories that captured his interest. It was on page six that he saw it. Just three paragraphs.

'An officer in the *Guardia Civil*, a civil war veteran, Miguel Ayala, was found dead last night at the foot of El Taja, the ravine dividing the town of Ronda.

'Police say they have no reason to believe it is a case of suicide. Ayala had been drinking and an accident was not ruled out. But for the moment it is being treated as a suspicious death.

'Ayala, believed to be in his early seventies, had been given special dispensation to continue his career in the *Guardia Civil* but was due to retire in a few weeks time.

He had become a popular local character. His most recent investigation had been into the death, believed to be by accident, of his close friend of many years, Pepe Rodriguis, known as the Rabbit Man of Ronda.'

Miller sat up in shock. This was too much of a coincidence. '*Last night*' ... that was the night before last, Tuesday night, the night he had lost Canning's trail, the night the American had not got back till 3 a.m.

Miller threw the newspaper to the ground. 'Shit!' he said. Then repeated it. 'Shit.'

He got out of bed, put on a dressing gown and lit a cigarette, looking out of the window across the garden to the sea shining in the distance. 'Shit,' he said for a third time. 'The man's mad.'

He looked at the clock. It was 1.30 a.m. Cruickshank would be back in the morning. What would he tell him?

It was bad enough that he had let Canning loose for a night, but another murder?

Of course there was a chance it was a coincidence but Miller didn't believe in coincidences.

Why had Canning done it?

Had the policeman been onto him?

Surely the American wasn't just mopping up ... eliminating anyone with an interest in the affair.

If so, who was safe? The Ronda barman? The TV reporter, Sheedy?

Miller suddenly recalled that Canning had that night been watching Sheedy.

'Christ,' he thought. 'I'm right. He's mopping up. He's starting to eliminate them one by one. This is crazy. It's got to be stopped.'

He lay back on the bed but the headache had returned, worse than ever. He felt on the edge of panic. Somewhere in the deepest recesses of his brain he felt a stirring of memories, things he didn't want to remember

... Belfast ... fear and pain.

He got out of bed and paced up and down. Then, deciding that keeping his nerve was paramount, he went downstairs to where the drinks were kept. There, gleaming seductively amid the other bottles, was an unopened quart of Beefeater's.

He picked up a glass, half-filled it, and drank it.

Without ice.

Without tonic.

Neat.

Neat gin.

He felt it work its way into his blood stream, into his brain.

Slowly the memories faded and feelings of panic were stilled.

He felt better.

It had been the right thing to do.

He had just one more ...

Sheedy slipped quietly into the villa so as not to wake Kate, poured himself a Bells, and sat down to think.

Felipe had come up trumps.

Canning had visited Ronda at least twice. Felipe hadn't been able to get an exact date but at least one of the trips was after he had been seen with the Ronda barman. So there was a real possibility of a second meeting with the Rabbit Man ... at the *cortijo*.

But there was more. Felipe said the talk was that Canning had been involved in a row, some kind of show-down with Cruickshank, and that since then Cruick-shank and Canning had hardly been talking. The Englishman had a new aide, a man called Miller.

Sheedy reckoned there was a real chance that the row had been over the murder of the Rabbit Man. There was no way Cruickshank would have authorised that. On the other hand, if that was the cause of the row, it meant

Cruickshank had been lying when he met Sheedy. He may not have been part of the murder but he was most definitely part of the cover-up.

Felipe's most interesting revelation was that of the seven crew on the boat, only he, Felipe, and one other, a relatively new sailor, had not been employed by Canning; the rest were, according to Felipe, involved in some kind of secret bonus scheme he had been unable to get to the bottom of.

Anglo-Spanish Investors Ltd., Sheedy concluded, was up to its eyes in something nasty.

Only two problems remained: how to get proof that Canning was the killer? And how to discover whether Cruickshank approved the murder or was just covering it up?

He decided the time had come to lean on them. He would please Kate by mobilising the Ronda police and the *Guardia Civil.* And in the day or so that it took the police to get their act together to approach Cruickshank he would put together a programme linking the project with the killings and raising questions that would force it all into the open.

FRIDAY, APRIL 6

Cruickshank had organised a party on the yacht as part of the buildup to the official public relations launch of the project, an event that Sheedy's inquiries had now made inevitable. He had invited the editors of local Spanish newspapers and also the editorial staff of English magazines based on the costa, hoping to soften them up for the launch by establishing friendly relations.

The decks of the yacht were brightly lit and a small string quartet was playing on the upper deck. On the jetty a small crowd of evening promenaders gathered to gaze at the scene and to speculate about the guests as they arrived.

Cruickshank's executive team and others in the know, including the architect Julio, and Maria, were briefed to be discreet about the project itself. They could hint there was a big story coming up, but that was all.

Cruickshank himself was delayed at a finance meeting in Malaga and only just beat his guests to the yacht, hurrying to his cabin to change. Hobbs told him that Miller wanted to see him urgently but Cruickshank said it would have to wait. 'Tell him I'll have a word later, after the party and after Señorita Garcia has gone home.'

The party was in full swing when Sheedy and Kate came up the gangway. Cruickshank, who had been standing by the railing on the top deck chatting with the *Lookout* journalist, David Baird, excused himself and quickly descended the steps to welcome the American couple. After a few smiling words to Kate, he took Sheedy's arm and drew him aside. 'Just one word, Mr Sheedy. If I'm to help you achieve your exclusive I take it you will assist me by not sharing the news of the project with your colleagues tonight. I would appreciate your discretion.'

Sheedy looked at him grimly. 'I'm afraid things have changed since we met, Sir Brian. In view of the second death I have no choice but to bring my story forward. I intend to cover it in tomorrow's programme.'

Cruickshank stared at him, uncomprehending, and then with growing alarm.

'Death ... *second* death?'

Sheedy observed him closely. Either the man was an unbelievably good actor or he didn't know what Sheedy was talking about. The American believed it was the latter and was surprised at the strength of his sense of relief.

Before Cruickshank, clearly stunned, could press him further, some new guests arrived, effusive in their greetings. Their host did his best to make them welcome, his eyes apprehensively following Sheedy, as the American, aware of an advantage, deliberately climbed to the upper deck and with Kate joined a group of other journalists who were sitting in a circle of deck chairs gossiping and laughing at the stories of one of their number, Perrott Phillips, a travel journalist and contributor to *Lookout* who was on a research trip from London.

Phillips was celebrating being allowed to donate a bottle of wine to Madrid's famous Bottle Museum. This, he explained, was a less generous act than it appeared. Of the 22,000 bottles in the museum his bottle of Konyagi from Tanzania was probably the most undrinkable. It was, he said, almost as bad as Mick's Red Rotten, an outrageous brew sold from grim, flagon-size bottles at a journalists' pub in London. The label said it all: 'An unusual rough-guts red wine that has the distinctive bouquet of old and ill-cured animals. It is best drunk with the teeth clenched to prevent the ingestion of seeds and skins. Avoid contact with the eyes and open cuts. Keep away from naked flames.'

As the group broke into gales of laughter, Sheedy noticed out of the corner of his eye Cruickshank looking desperately at him while half-heartedly conversing with other guests. For a while he avoided the Englishman's eye but eventually he took pity on him and chose a moment when Cruickshank was hovering nearby to stroll over to a waiter to collect another drink. The Englishman moved quickly to his side.

'Mr Sheedy, you referred to another murder. What did you mean?'

'Did I say murder?'

'Sorry.' Cruickshank bit his lip. It had been a careless

remark. 'I meant death.' He groaned inwardly; the correction sounded even worse.

Sheedy told him 'The Rabbit Man had a close friend, an officer with the *Guardia Civil* called Miguel. On Wednesday morning he was found dead in Ronda. Also at the foot of a ravine, this time El Tajo. Too much of a coincidence, don't you think?'

Cruickshank was shocked, but responded decisively.

'Mr Sheedy, I don't see why your programme on the project should be related to your concern about these accidents. I hope you're not suggesting that I have any connection with either death. That would be outrageous. As I've told you, the death of the man you called the Rabbit Man and his connection with my project are purely coincidence. And as I also explained to you, it causes us considerable inconvenience. As for this other man, the policeman, if there is a link between the two deaths and they weren't accidents, this would suggest some other affair entirely, as we had no interest in him or dealings with him at all.'

'Except that he was investigating the old man's death,' said Sheedy.

'Well, I for one did not know that. Come, Mr Sheedy, be reasonable. Do you really believe I'm the kind of man to have people assassinated all over Andalusia?'

'Frankly, Sir Brian, no. But there is a link, albeit coincidental, between your project and at least one of the deaths and that is a story and I'm afraid I have no choice but to tell it. I'm a journalist and that's my job.'

'And will you make it clear that I am not the kind of man to be associated with violence of any kind?'

'Sir Brian, I will, if you like, quote you as saying that. But it is not for me to make the judgement. "Associated with" is a vague phrase. My experience is that the best people sometimes find themselves "associated with" the worst kind of behaviour, not by design but because a

237

drift starts and at the key moment, when it can be checked, they hesitate and end up betraying their own standards.'

'I'm beginning to wonder whether you're a journalist or a novelist,' Cruickshank snapped. 'Assuming the former, I must at least assume you're educated in the laws of libel and slander.'

'Indeed.'

'When does your programme appear next? Tomorrow you say?'

'Tomorrow night.'

'Then you must not be surprised if I also do what I feel I must, Mr Sheedy. You say our arrangement is outdated by events. I will, therefore, announce the project in my own time, probably tomorrow morning.'

'That is your right, Sir Brian, but you may wish to consider one thing. If I am reporting on both the project *and* the coincidence of the two deaths, there will be a better balance on the programme than if the project is already old news and the only new story I have is the coincidence of the deaths.'

Cruickshank struggled to keep his temper. 'I hope you're not blackmailing me, Mr Sheedy.'

'Not at all. I'm telling you what any journalist would have to do in the circumstances you describe.'

The Englishman sighed. 'Whoever is responsible for these deaths, presuming they're not an accident, has a lot to answer for, Mr Sheedy.'

'Yes, Sir Brian, but not just inconvenience to you. Also two lost lives.'

Cruickshank looked chastened. 'That is a fair point, but you must appreciate I didn't know these men, whereas the project has dominated my life for over eighteen months. And I'm not accustomed to being accused of complicity in murder.'

Before Sheedy could reply Kate was at his elbow,

238

anxious to introduce him to Cruickshank's fiancée.

Sheedy turned to find himself facing a young woman of exceptional beauty: dark, wearing a simple white dress and smiling warmly at his host.

Cruickshank, looking pale and annoyed, smiled half-heartedly as the introductions took place. Then almost immediately he excused himself. For a fleeting moment Sheedy saw the young woman's smile fade. She was clearly not accustomed to Cruickshank being preoccupied in her company. Sheedy guessed she was taking his abrupt departure personally, that she was unaware of the pressures he was under.

Cruickshank had gone looking for Hobbs. 'Where's Canning?'

'He said he had to make some calls to the United States, Sir Brian.'

'Get hold of him and tell him and Miller to go to the library at the end of the evening and wait for me.'

Then with a superhuman effort he concentrated on his guests for the remaining hour or so until the majority, including Sheedy and Kate, had drifted away. Urging the rest to stay as long as they wished, he bid them goodnight. Taking Maria's arm, he told her he had some urgent business that would preoccupy him for some time. 'I think it best if the chauffeur takes you home, my dear. I *am* sorry. I had so much looked forward to chatting with you. Let's have a long lunch together tomorrow.'

Taking her in his arms, he warmly embraced her, begging a last smile before she left. Then he watched her disappear into the night before going quickly to where Miller and Canning were waiting, drinks in hand, eyeing each other with hostility.

'All right,' Cruickshank said without ceremony, 'Sheedy tells me there's been another murder. This time a policeman. What do you have to say about it?'

Canning spoke first. 'I can tell you nothing, Sir Brian, except that from what Miller tells me it was probably either an accident or suicide.'

'Accident?' Cruickshank looked at him with fury. 'That's what you said about the old man.'

'No, with respect Sir Brian, I told you exactly what happened to the old man. I said his death would *look* like an accident, not that it was one. Now I am telling you that I have no knowledge of this policeman or what happened to him.'

'Jim?' Cruickshank looked at his minder who, he noted with irritation, was pouring himself another drink, a substantial gin.

Miller sounded sober enough however. 'Here's the newspaper story, Sir Brian. As far as I can see there's no *evidence* of murder. Sheedy was wrong to use the word. On the other hand he probably thinks it's too much of a coincidence and I don't blame him. May I question Canning?'

'Please.'

'Canning, where were you the night before last – until you returned home at about 3 a.m.?'

The American turned white with anger. 'Have you been following me Miller? How dare . . .?'

Cruickshank interrupted. 'Answer the question.'

'Well, if you insist, Sir Brian. I was with a companion. A young woman.'

'Where?'

'For a while at Alexander's Club and then at her flat.'

'Will she confirm this story?'

'Of course. But it shouldn't be necessary.'

'Who was the man I saw you meeting the other day at Istan?' Miller asked.

Canning looked at him with hatred. 'So you have been following me. This is the personal service you perform for Sir Brian.'

Cruickshank interrupted again. 'Canning, you're trying my patience. Answer the question.'

'I don't know. I went up there for a drive and he just happened to be at the table where I was having a drink. I've no idea who he was.'

Miller scoffed. 'You never go anywhere just for a drive Canning. You went there to meet him.'

'Prove it.'

It was Cruickshank who replied. 'Miller doesn't have to prove it. This is not a court of law. I'm happy to accept the balance of probability and that is that you went to meet this man. Did you instruct him to kill the policeman?'

Canning rose. 'For Christ's sake, I've had enough of this. If you wish to discuss this matter properly, I will. But I'm not going to be cross-examined by you two. The police report says the man had been drinking. He probably just fell over the edge. It happens.'

'Unfortunately it usually happens when you're around, Jason.'

Before the American could reply, Cruickshank turned to Miller. 'The reporter Sheedy is going to do an item on this. What is the most he can say?'

'He can only point to the coincidence. He's got no evidence to link the deaths and even less evidence to link us to them. The worst he can produce is innuendo.'

Cruickshank nodded. 'At least we're forewarned. We must have a statement ready to release after the programme. It can frankly acknowledge the coincidence but point out that we're the big losers by the old man's death. We can offer a reward for anyone who can produce information. That way, we go on the offensive.'

Miller warned Cruickshank that the police were bound to call. 'If you're going on the offensive, you may wish to do so with them too. You could call them before they call you. Then you can state publicly that you've

241

been in touch with the police and are doing all you can to help. The offer of a reward is a good idea. And you could say that you're hoping to identify relatives of the old man in order to buy the land; this would show that you're ready to pay its market value and that there was no profit for you in his death.'

Cruickshank looked at Miller appreciatively. 'That's helpful Jim.' Miller, pleased, struggled to resist the temptation to celebrate his employer's goodwill with another gin.

Both men now looked at Canning. Cruickshank was the first to speak. 'Jason, I have no reason to believe you. You killed the old man. Now the policeman who was investigating the murder is dead. I don't know how to get through to you but you've got to understand that if the project has to be abandoned that will have to be the price we pay to stop this.'

'I didn't do it.'

'I wish I could believe you.' He stood and walked to add ice to his drink while thinking furiously. How could he get to this man, make him understand the insanity of his behaviour? With a change of tone, authoritative, but friendlier, he made an attempt to appeal to the intelligence he knew was there: 'Look, Jason. Can you not see that we're on course? The project *will* happen. There will be no problems. Unless we make them for ourselves. I've compromised far more than I would wish by not uncovering what happened to the old man, because whatever I did would not bring him back, and because I believed I could do more for the people of the area, perhaps make amends, by continuing. But it was clearly understood that there would be no repeat of this behaviour – that it would put me in an impossible position and jeopardise the project. Now, I know you say you were not involved in the death of the policeman, and maybe . . . maybe . . . you're telling the truth, but it is indicative of the position we're in that you can hardly blame us for our scepticism. Now this is the last time ... *the very last time* ... I'm going to say this: one more step out of line, one more act outside the strict letter of the law, one that we even suspect, let alone can prove, and I am going to cut my losses and get out. And, believe me, I'll take everybody else with me. Will you ... can you ... understand that – and cooperate?'

The American looked at him coolly. 'I understood your position when you spoke to me after the death of the Rabbit Man. You have no reason to believe that I have done other than respect it since.'

Cruickshank sighed. He was tired and he felt weighed down by it all, by his feeling of impotence in the face of Canning's obstinacy. Eventually he told the American to go but keep the yacht informed of his movements. He asked Miller to stay.

'Look, Jim, did he do it? Is he out of control?'

'I'm sorry, Sir Brian, that I lost him the other night. But I have to say that I have no doubt.'

'Jim, don't leave his side. Even if you have to sleep with him. I'll speak to Jordan and I'll see the police when they come and then we'll have to think hard about what we do.' He began to pace around the library.

Miller felt sorry for, even affectionate towards, the financier. 'Sir Brian, assuming Canning killed them both, there's one thing that has to be said for him, not that it's a lot of consolation to you. He's not given a lot away. The police can't even prove the deaths were deliberately caused, or that they were connected, let alone identify a possible killer. All they have are two unrelated deaths, possibly accidents, possibly suicides, possibly but unprovably murders by a person or persons unknown. You can afford to act as if that is the case.'

As he left, Cruickshank smiled at him weakly, not apparently willing to be uplifted by such a pragmatic message. He walked slowly out onto the deck, lighting a cigar. It was a clear night and the stars twinkled brightly from the sky.

He felt deeply despondent. No matter what he did, this psychopath got in the way.

He remembered his hopes as he had stood on the balcony of the villa only a few days back, and his optimism in London.

He had, he thought, been extraordinarily naive.

He was being dragged down into a mire of amorality.

Even half of his conversations tonight had been concerned with coverup rather than helping justice take its course.

His failure to act after the first murder made it more difficult to act after the second.

But if he didn't speak out now, what would his position be when a third occurred?

And Maria? He had so looked forward to being with her tonight and now she was gone. He had had hardly a minute alone with her. He had not even had a chance to ask about her parents' reaction to the news of their engagement. No wonder she had looked sad when she left.

His hands gripped the ship's railings till they were white.

Damn, damn, damn.

Felipe lay on his bunk in the cabin covered only by a towel. He felt like crying. He couldn't understand his new friend, Manuel. Why did he appear so affectionate yet keep Felipe at arm's length?

He leapt up, dropped the towel, and inspected himself in the mirror. Manuel would not find a more beautiful boy on the costa. What was the matter with him? Was there someone else? Was it his other friend Bill? Were they lovers after all?

He picked up a magazine and flicked over a few pages before throwing it petulantly into a corner of the cabin. He turned his small bedside radio on and off. He lit a cigarette and, pulling the curtain aside, looked out of the cabin at the bright lights of Puerto Banus.

To hell with it. If Manuel didn't want him, there were plenty of others who would.

He tossed the towel onto the bunk and wriggled into his tight white pants. Stuffing a 1000 pesetas note in his top pocket he switched off the light, climbed the ladder to the deck and, pleased not to have to endure Canning jeering at him, left the yacht and began to walk round to the Pink Coconut.

As he did so he became aware of another man walking alongside him. He turned and found himself staring into the face of a dark-haired Spaniard of just above medium height, but powerfully built, muscles rippling under a sleeveless tee shirt. The stranger smiled at him. Felipe looked sharply away but, a few yards on, couldn't resist another darting glance. The man was still there. Another smile, and this time he spoke.

'*Buenos noches*, pretty child,' he said.

'I'm not a child,' Felipe said indignantly. 'And I would be happy to prove it.'

'Want to come for a drive then?'

'Sure.'

He followed the other round to the car park and was impressed to find himself being helped into the passenger seat of a powerful-looking low-slung sports car.

This, he thought, would teach Manuel to treat him with indifference. Why, he, Felipe, could get anyone he wanted. And he was going to.

Defiant at life in general and Manuel in particular, he wound down the window, switched on the radio and lit a cigarette as the driver guided the car out of Puerto

Banus and east towards Estapona.

After a few kilometres they turned right and headed towards the hills.

'Where are we going?'

'Just a place where we can be on our own,' said the other, reaching out a hand to touch the young man's thigh.

The road wound up a hill and down into a valley out of sight of the costa and got rougher and then all but disappeared. Felipe realised they were driving across open ground to the ruins of an old *cortijo*. For the first time he felt slightly apprehensive. 'Where is this?'

'Just a place where we won't be disturbed ... where you can show me you're not a child,' smiled the other.

He pulled the car to a halt and they both climbed out and entered the open door of the deserted farmhouse.

It was dark inside except where the moonlight, coming through the windows, created spotlights on the dirt floor. The man gently steered Felipe, now trembling with anticipation, into an unlit corner and stood him facing the wall, his hands moving round to touch the front of the white pants.

Felipe felt himself hardening. The hands came from behind, moving slowly up to his chest. One of them appeared to be clutching a hard object ... like the handle of a ...

Felipe tried to cry out but it was too late. With one sharp movement the knife was pulled across his throat. For a moment he was held as life faded from his body, then he was allowed to slip to the ground.

Moving quickly now the other went outside and began to gather wood. This he took into the *cortijo*, building a bonfire around the body.

Then he went to the car and took out two drums of gasoline. One was tipped over the body and the bonfire, the other over all the wooden parts of the building ...

Standing well back, he set fire to a bit of brush and tossed it through the window. Within seconds the *cortijo* was an inferno.

He quickly climbed into his car and drove back to the rough road and down towards the costa.

A kilometre away a woman looked out the window of her bedroom and called to her husband. 'There's a fire. The old *cortijo* is on fire.'

Grumbling, he climbed out of bed and walked to the window to look at the blaze. 'It was no use to anyone,' he said. 'Forget it.'

He got back into bed. 'It will be just ashes in the morning,' he said. 'You won't be able to tell what was there.'

Then I realised I had been murdered
They looked for me in cafes, cemeteries and churches . . .
but they did not find me.
They never found me?
No. They never found me.

247

Chapter
Nine

SATURDAY, APRIL 7

At the heart of old Marbella is the sixteenth-century Plaza de los Naranjos, the square of the oranges, named for the small orchard in its courtyard, a square within a square. The orange trees shade nearly half a million people a year who come for coffee or wine and *tapas* served by waiters from the bars and restaurants that surround them.

Kate had spent a pleasant hour there, drinking coffee and writing letters, and now began to meander into a maze of Moorish alleys, past more bars and restaurants and bazaar-like shops, until she came to the main Marbella produce market.

Once inside the two-tier building she wandered past the imaginatively-displayed, cleaned and polished fruit and vegetables and headed for the *pescadería y mariscos*, the fish market, passing by a row of lottery sellers and fishermen selling from wooden boxes their overnight catch of tiny anchovies, silvery-blue sardines and small rosy-red mullet. Turning hurriedly away from the stare of an evil-looking, one-eyed octopus, she went inside to photograph the proprietors of the twenty or more stalls as they gutted, scaled and sliced or filleted the disconsolate-looking fish on marble counters, using big sharp knives with wooden handles. She found the shiny displays of fish mesmerising. There were big swordfish and tuna, their wide tails creating the appearance of grounded aeroplanes. There were wide, flat sole, huge lobsters with their claws still wriggling frantically in complaint at their fate, red and orange jumbo prawns and grey and brown langoustines, whole bags of live, moving tiny crabs, blue and yellow amberjacks, pink-gold dorada, olive-grey flounders, good-looking silver sea bass and hake, ugly bright-red furnard, black, sinister-looking mussels with seaweed still clinging to their shells, squid and octopus, menacing with their bulbous heads and tentacles.

After the fish market she paused at stalls devoted to herbs and spices, saffron, rosemary, sage, basil, estragon, oregano, thyme, coriander, pure bee honey, burghol, tahine, aniseed, basmati rice, nuts and raisins of every kind. So absorbed was she by the aromas and atmosphere that she almost didn't respond when another young woman greeted her. Then she recognised Maria, Cruickshank's fiancée.

The young Spanish woman seemed pleased to see her and Kate suggested they walk back to the Plaza de los Naranjos for a drink. They were soon chatting happily in the sun, Kate talking about photography, about working with Sheedy in the States, and about her first few days in Spain, Maria content to encourage the talkative American, fascinated by stories of New York, full of questions.

'You should go there, Maria. In the spring, that's the best time.'

'But it's also the best time in Seville.'

'Then go in the Fall, when the trees in Central Park are all gold and red and brown and the squirrels are out collecting nuts, when everybody is just back from summer vacation and in good spirits.'

'I would like to ... maybe I should go to New York in autumn and you should repay the visit by coming to Seville in spring, for *la Semana Santa*, Holy Week, and for the fair that follows.'

'It's a deal,' Kate promised.

She suggested lunch. Maria hesitated, and then, deciding, smiled and nodded.

They wandered back into the old shopping area and up the Calle Virgen de los Dolores to El Cortijo, a restaurant with decor like that of a Spanish kitchen. Once they had ordered, Kate a plate of grilled fresh fish, Maria a simple lettuce and tomato salad, the food to be accompanied by a bottle of rosé, Kate said, 'Now, Maria, tell me about this fiancée of yours. When are you going to marry?'

Maria looked shyly down at her lap for a moment, then answered. 'I don't know exactly. It's all happened rather suddenly. There are details ...'

Kate interrupted to encourage her. 'You know, we're in the same boat ...'

'The same boat ... what boat ...?'

'Sorry, just an expression. I meant that you and I are in a similar position. Bill is also older than me, twenty years older. We've only really come together recently. So you can see that you and I are probably both experiencing many of the same feelings.'

'Feelings?' enquired Maria cautiously.

'Happy, and content, apart from just a little regret it didn't happen earlier. Isn't that how you feel?'

Maria answered her question with another. 'Do you plan to marry, Kate?'

Kate laughed. 'Sheedy? I doubt whether the idea has

entered his head. I think he's just getting used to the idea that he can be happy with someone other than his wife. She died some years back. But I guess we'll make it. It's just that he's one of those people who's too busy living each day to actually stop and think where he's going and what he should do about it. Maybe one day I'll suggest it to him.'

Maria was amazed. '*You* would suggest it to *him*?'

Kate laughed. 'I guess that's not on in Spain. But surely men don't still rule in this country in the way they once did?'

'Kate, it's no coincidence that machismo is a Spanish word. While the status of women has dramatically improved over the past twenty years or so, it's still largely a man's country, especially away from the cities or tourist areas. The woman is only really equal in the role of home-maker and mother. But with that privilege goes all of the work. And there's a lot of hypocrisy. For instance, while a man who sleeps with a single woman or even another man's wife is often respected for it by other men, the woman is just as likely to be written off as a whore.'

'No wonder you prefer an Englishman,' Kate said dryly.

'Oh, the Spanish are not that bad. And things are much better than they were.' She changed the subject. 'Anyway, your Bill seems a friendly man.'

'But I liked your man too, a real gentleman,' Kate replied.

'He is.' Once more she looked shy.

Kate smiled at her. 'Maria, I hope we can become friends.'

Maria looked pleased. 'I would like that. I would like that very much. Let's hope your Bill and my Brian become friends too.'

For a moment a shadow passed over Kate's face. 'Yes,' she said thoughtfully. 'Yes, I hope so too.'

251

The red light came on and Sheedy began talking.

'Hi, this is Bill Sheedy.

'Tonight two stories that may be connected.

'First, I have news of a remarkable project being planned for the Estapona–San Pedro area and when I tell you that it will even put Sotogrande into the shade you'll have some idea just how ambitious it is.

'And then more news of El Conejero, the Rabbit Man, whose death I reported a couple of weeks ago.'

Sheedy then described the proposed Cruickshank project, showed a map of the area, and, using still pictures of Cruickshank because an interview had in the circumstances been frostily refused, spoke of the personalities behind it.

This segment was followed by interviews with the mayors of Estapona and Benahavis, both municipalities affected by the project, and also with a local resident who objected to the plan and argued there should be controls on further construction on the Costa del Sol.

Then there was a filmed discussion between Sheedy and two local personalities about whether it was right that gambling on horseracing should be encouraged in the area.

The report concluded:

'Undoubtedly this project will go ahead ... but it has been made easier by what its sympathisers hope is just a bizarre coincidence, or series of coincidences.

'Remember my item about the Rabbit Man of Ronda, El Conejero? I asked whether his death in a ravine near his lonely *cortijo* was an accident, or whether there could be some other explanation.

'It now emerges that El Conejero, Pepe Rodriguis, was the owner of a piece of land that was crucial to the new project. And he was refusing to sell. You can imagine how frustrating that was for Sir Brian Cruick-shank and Anglo Investors Ltd.

'Now his untimely death has opened up the way for the project to proceed – provided, that is, that El Conejero's heirs will sell it.

'There will be those who say this is a particularly convenient coincidence, but – and I stress this – there is no evidence to suggest a connection.

'However the possibility that Pepe's death was an accident has been lessened in the eyes of some by the death of his closest friend Ronda policeman Miguel Ayala just a few days later – a death that also appears, on the surface, to be the result of an accident.

'Were they the victims of coincidental accidents? It's possible of course. But likely?

'Did Miguel commit suicide as a result of distress at the death of his friend? That's possible too, although, knowing him, I have to say it's extremely unlikely.

'The police have much to think about, and this reporter will be turning his files on the case over to them immediately after this programme.

'If you can help, contact me, or the Ronda police.

'That's all for now. This is Bill Sheedy. Good night.'

Cruickshank, Canning and Miller had watched the programme together and, as he switched the television set off, Cruickshank turned to the American and, his voice heavy with sarcasm, said 'Whatever the truth about the policeman, Jason, I hope you're proud of your handiwork. What should have been a big moment, the launch of the project, is totally ruined. Instead of positive publicity about what we're planning to do, we begin on the defensive, not merely answering the usual critical questions about developers but also having to deny we killed a harmless old peasant. Congratulations.'

Canning looked uncomfortable. 'I understood we

were not going to continue with these recriminations,' he snapped back. 'It's clear no-one can prove we were involved in the man's death and if you act decisively we should kill the story stone dead. For a start you could informally warn the rest of the media that you're considering legal action should anyone suggest a connection between the deaths and the project.' He produced a sheet of paper. 'I've prepared our comment as you requested.'

'Let's hear it.'

Cruickshank had to concede that it was cleverly worded:

'Anglo-Spanish Investors confirms the report on a Gibraltar television programme that it is about to announce plans for a major project in the municipalities of Benahavis and Estapona that will create employment and in other ways benefit the economy of the area and of Spain generally.

'However, with respect to the tragic death of one of the land-owners with whom it has been negotiating, Anglo-Spanish resents the programme's suggestion that it has been a beneficiary of this accident.

'While naturally deeply regretting his fate, and offering his relatives sympathy, we are forced by comments made on the programme to point out that, rather than benefitting from his accidental death, the company is greatly inconvenienced by it. Not only will it cause expensive delays but it is likely to lead to an increased price for the parcel of land involved.'

Miller wondered whether it was an over-reaction but Cruickshank argued that the programme couldn't be ignored. 'If we couple its release with a private warning to the media that we'll take legal action if there is any further innuendo we should be all right.' He turned to Canning: 'Fax it now to the daily papers, local radio and television. That should stop the story being repeated tomorrow morning.'

'I notice the release doesn't refer to the policeman,' Miller said to him after Canning had left.

'No. Canning's right there. We shouldn't risk acknowledging by denials that there are grounds for even considering a possible connection between the two deaths, let alone any possibility of our involvement. Our position is that the policeman was unknown to us, as in fact he was – except, perhaps, for Canning, and we'll come to that in a minute. As far as we're concerned he's a stranger who was involved in an accident far away from where we're operating.'

'But you surely don't believe Canning?'

'I don't know what to believe. I know what I want to believe . . . I want to believe that it's just a coincidence. That the old policeman just drank too much and wandered over the edge. I gather from the newspaper reports that this is possible.' He looked at Miller hopefully but the latter looked sceptical.

'Look, I'm sorry, Sir Brian, I know that's what you want to believe but you're overlooking the other coincidence – that Canning came back at three o'clock in the morning and his only alibi is a whore he claims to have picked up in Alexander's and has no doubt paid to back up his story. And Canning's meeting with the Spaniard in Istan . . . what was that about if it was not to set up the killing of the policeman?'

Cruickshank paced around the room. 'Christ, Jim, I don't know. I don't know what's going on. And, frankly, you haven't been a lot of help.'

Miller looked embarrassed. His head was beginning to ache and he was in desperate need of a drink. 'I'm sorry, Sir Brian. It was incredibly bad luck. But from now on he won't change his underwear without me knowing about it, that I guarantee.'

Left alone, the Englishman called to Hobbs for a whisky with ice and sat out on the balcony. It was a warm night, the sea was still and in the distance he could see fishing boats, their lights bobbing up and down.

He began his methodical review of the position. Two men dead now. Probably both killed by Canning or someone sent by Canning. By not going to the police after the first one he had made it extremely difficult to go to them now, especially as he had no evidence whatsoever concerning the second one. He imagined the scene:

'What evidence do you have that Canning killed the policeman, Sir Brian?'

'None.'

'Do you know whether he was in Ronda that night? Can you disprove his alibi? Do you know whether Canning had even heard of the policeman?'

'No.'

'Then why are you making this charge?'

'Because he did admit killing the first man.'

'But that was weeks ago. Why did you not report it then?'

'I . . . I . . . decided not to.'

Great. That would sound just great. He remembered what he had told Miller, that one small lie always led to another. He had allowed himself to be trapped in a web of deceit, one murder had led to another, and he no longer knew how to extricate himself. It was even possible – he felt a deep sense of shock at the idea – that he too, could be charged, if not with murder, at least with conspiracy to murder, or obstructing the course of justice. That would be the end – not just of the project but his whole career.

He thought about Jordan. Jordan was the only hope. The man wasn't a fool. Surely he could see this had to stop. Surely he would recall Canning now.

He called to Hobbs to telephone the American at his home number in New York State. Convinced now that

Jordan held the answer, he paced up and down waiting to speak to him. Eventually Hobbs returned. 'They say he's not there, sir. That he's out of the country. That he's in Europe.'

Cruickshank looked at him sharply. 'Where in Europe?'

'They said they didn't know, sir. Just that he didn't return from your meeting in London but was intending to go on from there to somewhere in Europe.'

Cruickshank felt alarm bells ringing. Europe? Where in Europe except Spain did Jordan have an interest? Was he on his way? Was he already on the Costa del Sol somewhere? If so, why? And why hadn't he told Cruickshank he was coming?

His eye caught the picture of Maria he had placed beside his bed. Oh God, he thought, Maria. Would she have seen the programme? Then he remembered the reason they were not together that evening was that she was attending a dinner party in Malaga with Julio and Isabella. She wouldn't have seen any television. Thank God for that.

Thinking of her made him want her, want the feeling of renewed confidence he felt when in her company, want the way she reminded him of who and what he was.

Maria was on a different plane from these other people, Jordan, Canning, even Miller, all people Cruickshank should never have to deal with.

Maria. He compared the sordid nature of the problems that engulfed him with the purity his love and imagination had invested in her. It seemed to him that, whereas before the murder of the peasant all had seemed possible, now a chasm was building up between the hideous reality of his position and the dream he had nurtured – a chasm that was widening every hour.

★

After the programme Kate and Sheedy drove back into Spain with Brian Hunter, the company's director of news and documentaries, for dinner at Meson Arni's, a small, back-street restaurant Sheedy had discovered in Estapona. After feasting themselves on spare ribs and fresh vegetables, and homemade apple crumble, all cooked in a cave-like baker's oven, they were having coffee with the American-born proprietor, Arnie, when a telephone call came from the television station for Hunter. After jotting down a lengthy message he handed it to Sheedy. 'They didn't waste any time.'

'Hell no,' said Sheedy after reading it. 'Look at this, Kate.' It was Cruickshank's press release.

Hunter lit a Don Julian cigar and, leaning back in his chair, looked at Sheedy thoughtfully. 'You know we don't have a lot to go on Bill. We'd better be careful with this one.'

'You don't have to tell me,' the American replied. 'I know the evidence is circumstantial. But I'm convinced that Miguel and the Rabbit Man died because of Cruickshank's project. The problem is to prove it.' His listeners looked at each other, both amused at the way his eyes lit up at the challenge. Sheedy continued, 'I'm hoping tonight's programme may lead to someone coming forward with fresh information, as Ramon Aparitico did.'

'OK,' said Hunter, 'but just the same they're threatening legal action if there's even the slightest suggestion they've been guilty of murder and I don't blame them. If they're innocent they've every reason to be furious. You've ruined the publicity launch of their project for no reason. And if they're guilty they've every reason to be furious too. Bill, you know we'll back you up as far as we can, but one libel action could close the station and we're a Gibraltar station, not Spanish, so a libel action would be easy to bring.'

Kate asked, 'Apart from that, you don't think Bill is in danger too, do you Brian?'

Hunter looked taken aback. 'Christ, I hope not. I hadn't even thought of that.' He pondered for a minute. 'I guess if they've killed two people they wouldn't stop at more. But it would be so obvious. Everyone would know who was behind it.'

'Actually that's what puzzles me about the whole business,' Sheedy said. 'It *is* obvious. And it's hard to believe they gain that much by it all. Which is why I can't believe that Cruickshank is so stupid as to allow it.'

'And I don't think he's so immoral, Bill,' Kate added. 'He strikes me as being someone of real stature. I just don't think he's that kind of man to let all this happen.'

'Well that only leaves two possibilities,' said Hunter. 'Either the deaths of the two men have nothing to do with Anglo-Spanish Investors, or Cruickshank is not in control of what's happening. And if he isn't, who is?'

'Ah ha,' said Sheedy, 'that was going to be my next story. Brian, do you think we could invest some additional money in research for a few weeks? I want to pay someone in the States to look into the American investors. It's possible there's money going into this project from organised crime, maybe even Mafia money.'

'Christ, Bill,' said Hunter, 'don't even think of broadcasting that till all the angles are covered and that includes protecting the station. In every way. Listen,' he added, half laughing, 'I tell you, I'm trying to run a quiet profitable little TV station, I don't want the place blown up, let alone bankrupted by a huge libel suit.'

'Don't worry,' said Sheedy, 'I take your point. Anyway, there's a long way to go yet. We may get some inside information from the yacht' – he waved a dismissive hand to the curious Hunter to indicate there was no point in questioning him about the source – 'and

Kate has become friendly with Cruickshank's fiancée. She may pick up a few facts too.'

'Look Bill,' said Kate, 'forget it. I'll be damned if I'm going to involve Maria. Jesus,' she looked at him, exasperated, 'there's no stopping you.'

'OK, OK,' he said placatingly, in too good a humour, as he always was after the programme, to take offence, 'but maybe a question or two. She may even be able to help clear Cruickshank if he's not involved himself.'

'Listen, Bill,' said Hunter, 'have you thought what Cruickshank must be feeling and thinking. Let's imagine he was not involved ... that this man Canning killed both men without authority from Cruickshank. The Englishman is, as you say, no fool. He knows of the deaths, he knows you're linking them with the project. Surely he would be furious and would be investigating Canning's behaviour and pressing for information too.'

'That's what I'm hoping – that there'll be a row between Cruickshank and Canning, or whoever Canning works for, maybe on the yacht. And that we'll get to hear of it.'

'But wouldn't Cruickshank go to the police if he got any evidence?'

Sheedy sat silent. 'Well now, that's the question, isn't it? That's when we find out just how much a man of honour Cruickshank actually is.'

SUNDAY, APRIL 8

The two officers from the *Guardia Civil* came to the villa at about ten o'clock. The senior, the one who had spoken to Kate in Ronda, introduced himself as Colonel Rivas. Kate, who had arranged to go swimming with Maria, made some coffee and orange juice and left the three men to talk.

Sheedy told Rivas of his friendship with the two old men of the *sierras*, of the Rabbit Man's death, of his and Miguel's suspicions, of the project and the possible motive for the Rabbit Man's murder, about Cruickshank and what little he knew about Canning and the man in New York, Jordan.

'It's a pity you did not come to share this with us before, Señor Sheedy.'

'It wasn't for me to do so,' Sheedy replied. 'After all, Miguel was one of your officers. Naturally I assumed that if there was sufficient evidence to justify official action he would have told you. In any case, had you begun investigating the project, the company would have shut up like a clam, whereas there was a chance my unofficial investigations would provoke them to make a mistake.' Observing the policeman frown, he hastily added, 'Of course, once Miguel was killed I realised that you had to be fully involved. I intended to make contact ... today. In fact I said as much on my programme last night.'

Rivas was unimpressed. 'Unfortunately we do not see your programme in Ronda, Señor Sheedy. In any case coming to the police after you have taken your television audience into your confidence hardly suggests you're taking us seriously. What evidence have you discovered that the two men were murdered because of the project you describe?'

'That's the point. None that you can act on. There was the evidence around the body of the Rabbit Man suggesting that it may not have been an accident and there was the observed meeting between this man Canning and the Rabbit Man. But, to be fair, Anglo-Spanish Investors admit that link.'

Rivas rose, saying that it was his intention to see Cruickshank and Canning later in the day. 'Can we hope Señor Sheedy you will cease your freelance policing of the area and leave it to us?'

'I'm afraid I can't promise that, Inspector. I'm a reporter. I have a duty to follow this story now I've started. And I'm also under a personal obligation to two friends.'

'We have a greater *public* duty, Señor Sheedy. It would be unfortunate if you were to get in the way.'

'With respect, not only have I not done so but what little you know is entirely due to my work.'

'Had we been acting as a police force, Señor Sheedy, it is possible that Miguel Ayala would still be alive.'

'That was his decision.'

The inspector looked at him coldly. 'May I ask what you plan to do next?'

'We have a connection within the company. I can go no further, because he must be protected. I hope he may come up with some new evidence. But I give you my word I will share it with you. My only wish is to see that whoever killed my friends comes to justice.'

Sheedy watched the police car go down the hill and then rang Manuel in Benahavis. 'Any news from Felipe?'

'Not a word. I've looked out for him for two nights now and there's been no sign of him, either on the yacht or on land.'

Sheedy felt apprehensive. 'Look, they don't know you. Why not go to the yacht and say you're a friend and ask to see him?'

'Bill, I can't do that. Felipe would panic. It would be betraying him. We don't have the right.'

'I know there's a risk but I don't like the sound of this. We had him excited. Why should he have cooled off? I think enquiring after him is the best of two unpalatable options.'

Manuel reluctantly said he would have another look for Felipe that evening and, if he didn't show up, he would go to the yacht.

★

West of Marbella there are a string of beach bars and clubs of varying degrees of luxury. Some are built round swimming pools and have their own entrance to the beach so that customers can either swim in the pool or in the sea. Others, usually built with wood, are on the beach itself, and sell cold drinks and a lunch of grilled fish or paella.

Kate and Maria chose the beach just west of Puerto Banus, in front of the extraordinary Arabian Palace-like giny d'Albion complex. Maria had suggested one or two more exclusive clubs but Kate said she wanted to be around people who were not sweating money out of every pore and by noon the two of them were propping up the wooden counter of one of the noisier bars drinking ice-cold San Miguels.

Kate felt a bit guilty about questioning Maria but the memory of Miguel's round, smiling face stiffened her backbone, so she began to probe gently.

'Tell me, Maria, why is Sir Brian down on the costa so much? I would have expected him to leave the details to others while he's wheeler-dealing in London.'

'I don't know,' Maria said, puzzling, 'except that this project means a lot to him. It's not like the other business deals he's involved in. It's a kind of dream. He plans to live in the valley some of the time, and retire there eventually. That's probably why he has to be close to it now.'

'Maybe it's you he wants to be close to, Maria.'

The Spanish girl blushed. 'I would like to think so. But I think he is too practical a man for that to be the only reason. Anyway, I think he's had one or two problems with it, so that's probably another reason why he's been on the costa so much.'

Kate sipped her drink for a moment, not wishing to

appear too interested, then, as if remembering, said 'Oh, yes, Bill said that one of the landowners was killed.'

'Yes, an accident in the mountains. It has caused a delay I think.'

'Sir Brian must be upset.'

'Upset? I don't think so. He didn't know the man. I think just, how do you say ... irritated? Yes, irritated.'

Kate decided to press one more time.

'Bill met someone else from the company. Canning? Would it be a Mr Canning?'

'Maybe. I haven't met him. Why?' Maria looked at Kate questioningly, and the latter decided it was time to drop it.

'No reason. Bill just mentioned it.' She felt sorry for the Spanish girl, in love and blissfully unaware of the dark clouds assembling around her fiancée's head.

The two young women walked back down to the water's edge, dropping their shoulder bags on the beach and hopping about as they abandoned their sandals and felt the heat of the sand. Maria asked a young Spanish woman lying nearby to guard their belongings and, clad only in the briefest of bikini bottoms, their breasts proudly displayed, they both waded into the water.

All over the beach men sat up, pretending to stretch, look out to sea, put on sun lotion ... all actions to explain to their wives and girlfriends why suddenly their paperbacks had lost their appeal.

'You know what this reminds me of, Jim,' Cruickshank said as the two of them and Canning gathered in the library of the yacht before lunch. 'It reminds me of Watergate, of how Nixon got involved in the cover-up of a relatively petty and totally unnecessary break-in and the whole business grew and grew as a result of journalistic investigation until he spent most of his time in pathetic plotting meetings with Haldemann and Erlichman. Remember the Watergate tapes and the level it all sunk to?' With mounting anger he said, 'I let myself cover-up for you, Jason, for your totally unnecessary violence, and now I'm spending all my time in these bloody meetings. I feel as if a net is closing in and I'm powerless to act. Damn it, will your criminal inter-ference with what should be a relatively straight-forward business operation never end?'

Taken aback by the anger on his face, the others didn't speak immediately. Miller looked contemptuously at Canning and the American looked equally contemptu-ously at Cruickshank. It was Canning who eventually replied: 'Perhaps if you stopped panicking we could all get on with other things. There wasn't a word in the papers this morning about the deaths, only details about the project. It was all presented positively. Our strategy is working. They'll never prove our connection with the old man's death. And we have no connection with the policeman, so why don't we just get on with our work?'

Cruickshank snapped back. 'Because the police are on their way here now, Jason, that's why. I am about to be reduced to answering questions from some half-illiterate Ronda policeman because you've been running round the countryside like a Spanish version of Baby Face Nelson.' Then, remembering, he said, 'By the way, where is Jordan?'

Canning looked shifty. 'What do you mean where's Jordan? In New York, I presume.'

'No, Jason, he's not in New York. He's in Europe, probably on his way to Spain or in Spain. I want to talk to him and I want to do it now. So where is he?'

Canning stood up and walked to the port-hole, looked out for a moment, and then turned to the Englishman. 'I'm sorry, Sir Brian, I'm not authorised to say.'

'*Not authorised*!' Cruickshank was on his feet, furious, almost out of control. 'What the hell do you

265

mean, *not authorised*? This is a business we're running. Jordan is part of it. I want to speak to him. You find him and get him on the phone or I will turn you over to the police before the day is out. Now get out.'

Canning rose and abruptly walked to the door. Turning, he looked coolly at Cruickshank.

'Bullshit,' he said.

Then he left.

Cruickshank sank into his chair, too angry and unhappy to speak.

That last word had been a blow. He had convinced himself he was back in charge. But he wasn't; that was made only too clear by his impotence when confronted by the arrogant young American.

It was Miller who broke the silence. 'I'm sorry, Sir Brian, I can't help you on this. I tapped his phone but he's been making his calls from bars and call boxes. He's clever.'

Cruickshank looked amazed. '*Tapped his phone.* You *tapped his phone*? My God, it gets worse and worse.'

Miller, startled at his employer's discomposure, gently drew his attention back to the forthcoming meeting. 'Sir Brian, if I may suggest from my experience as a former policeman, you should not be too charming in dealing with the police. Your position is that you have been slandered by the very suggestion of a connection with these deaths. As an innocent man, you are an aggrieved party and have a big interest in the matter being cleared up. You must demand that they establish whether the deaths were accidents or not, and if they were not, they must arrest the killers. Your whole approach must be one of a senior, respected businessman who is both angered at the inconvenience caused by all this and by the challenge to your integrity. And you should hold the police responsible for not moving faster. Don't be insulting – remember the strong Spanish pride – but do

266

be impatient and demanding. That way they'll be on the defensive rather than you.'

Cruickshank reached for the coffee on the sideboard and poured himself a cup. He looked at Miller gratefully. Perhaps he had misjudged him. Maybe his minder drank too much these days but he was still thinking more clearly than Cruickshank. 'That's good advice, Jim.'

As Miller was leaving the villa a few minutes later, fortified from a bottle of Beefeater gin now kept in his room, he heard Cruickshank's voice from the library. He was evidently talking to Colonel Rivas of the *Guardia Civil* in Ronda. 'Now I hope you're going to get this business cleared up, Colonel. Frankly, I'm shocked that these irresponsible journalists could link my good name and that of my company with these tragic accidents and I'm counting on you . . .'

Miller was pleased. Cruickshank was acting on his advice. He still had his employer's confidence.

As he went in pursuit of Canning he resolved to do all in his power to get Cruickshank out of the mess he was in.

He liked the man.

And for himself he saw the possibility of a bright future.

The project would need a security service, and the security service would need a chief . . .

Sheedy had a leisurely swim and then, alone in the garden, settled into a deckchair in front of the pool, and began to review recent events. He recognised the distinctive sound of Manuel's motorbike as it came up the hill. It was deafening.

'For Christ's sake, Manuel,' he greeted his colleague, 'can't you get a silencer on that thing? It's a public menace. Or abandon it and use your car. How can I run a campaign about the noise caused by motorbikes when you're running around on that?'

For once the young Spaniard did not respond to the badinage. 'Bill, Felipe's gone.'

'Gone?' Sheedy sat up.

'When I asked at the yacht they said he had left. Gone home.'

'When?'

'They said a couple of days back. They said he just left a note that he was homesick and left without even picking up his back pay. But took all his belongings.'

'Did anyone see him go?'

'Well, I couldn't question them too closely ... but no-one mentioned seeing him.'

'Who did you talk to?'

'A couple of guys guarding the gang plank.'

'Did they ask who you were?'

'I just said I was a friend from the Pink Coconut and that we had arranged to meet. They seemed to accept it. There was no big deal about it.'

Sheedy was worried. He asked where Felipe came from.

'North, somewhere near Cordoba.'

'OK, I think the best thing is to get the *Guardia Civil* to check out whether he got home. I'll talk to Colonel Rivas later. I want an excuse to ring him anyway, to ask how he got on with Cruickshank.'

He walked in and got a couple of bottles of San Miguel beer from the fridge. He opened the bottles and carried them without glasses back to the pool. The two sat drinking silently for a few moments. Then Sheedy looked at the young man. 'I'm sorry, Manuel. I don't think I've handled this well. It's becoming a terrible mess. It's just that nothing adds up. I never thought Miguel was in danger and I thought we could keep Felipe safe and I was wrong on both counts. And I still don't know what to make of Cruickshank, I find it hard to believe he's involved. Yet it's equally hard, logically, to believe he's not. I accept we've got to work with the police now but my fear is that the police stumbling around will cause the killers to tighten up their operation and it'll be even more difficult to get at the truth.'

'Well, maybe this will help.' Manuel handed him an envelope. 'It's from Rosa. It's the letter. She had a helluva job translating it.'

With that the Spaniard left with another deafening roar that caused Sheedy to wince and look apologetically at the windows of the surrounding villas. Then, putting his feet up on the other chair, he opened the envelope.

On top of the typescript there was a note:

TO: SEÑOR SHEEDY

I have done my best to translate this letter. It was not easy. Some of it is indecipherable. For some reason the hand-writing of the opening and closing is particularly bad, probably because the old man wrote these few words himself, so I cannot make out who the letter is addressed to or the signature at the end.

ROSA

Sheedy put the note aside and began to read the letter ...

Chapter Ten

'My . . . (indecipherable) . . .

Your great grandmother showed me how to write a few words but at writing I am not good. To help me tell my story an old friend will write for me. I hope one day soon to discover where you are and to send this letter by messenger.

My dear niece, I am your father's brother. We had another brother, Diego; I have not seen him for many years but I think he has a cortijo *near Casares where like me he hunts the rabbit. He and I were left to care for you when your dear parents died when you were small.*

It was not because we didn't love you that we asked old friends, a good gypsy family, to look after you as one of their own. It was simply that our lives were hard and we wanted more for you than we could offer. It was not right for you, a little girl, to share the lonely life of a hunter in the mountains without other children to play with, with no woman to understand your needs, with no chance to go to school.

I was at first deeply upset and angry to hear that our friends had experienced bad times and abandoned you, but, just as I was setting out to find you, I learned that you had been adopted by a good man and woman who had many pesetas. Do not fear, my niece, I will not embarrass you by coming to see you. This letter will tell you all you need to know ... about the life of your family and about me, your uncle.

Did you know that the Rodriguis family has lived for over 200 years in the sierras west of Ronda, for nearly a century in the pueblo of Grazalema where your father and I were born? You may even have been there. If so, you will know that it is said to be the wettest place in Spain. This is because it is nearly 3,000 feet above sea-level and is built under a mountain that stops the clouds swept by the winds from the oceans. As they cannot pass, they fall as rain.

Your great grandfather, Pepe, and his son, my father Antonio, worked at the beginning of the century in a wool mill making blankets and ponchos. Many in the village did this. The ponchos were sold to shepherds and also to other men, middle men, who sold them in faraway countries, even one called Argentina in South America. As a boy I would help my father take stacks of ponchos by mule all the way to the port in Cadiz, over 110 kilometres on rough tracks, sometimes no tracks at all, over high hills and across hostile country. We did this no matter what the heat of the summer day or the cold of the winter night.

Sometimes my father would return with his mule loaded with contraband smuggled in from Africa via Gibraltar or unloaded late at night on the beaches of the costa, usually coffee or tobacco. This he would buy from the contrabandistas or carry for them. Everyone who helped us on the journey, with water for the mule or food or shelter, would be paid with a carton of cigarettes or some coffee. Near the village the goods would be transferred to other men with a truck and we too would be paid. Please do not judge harshly, dear niece, for in those days smugglers were not seen as bad or dishonest but as heroes, people who outwitted the wealthy merchants on the coast and the Guardia Civil and gave to the people not just goods they would never otherwise have had but also their dignity in the face of these scoundrels and oppressors.

Then in the 1920s, when I was still a small boy, people began to buy fewer woollen ponchos. They could more easily buy clothing made of cotton. The mills in the village began to close. The family was forced to do other work. Some became shepherds, protected from the cold in the hills by the same ponchos they used to make. The sheep they guarded provided the wool for the few who still tried to survive by blanket or poncho-making and the sheep's milk was used for cheese.

But these were hard years, especially in the winter when it was cold and wet in our pueblo, and especially for the older members of the family.

Of course it was not so hard for me. I was a child. I think maybe all childhoods in Spain are happy, for children have no reason to know life can be better, nor that their loving mother and father are going hungry so they can eat, or lying cold at night so they can be warm. I played bandito games in the hills around the pueblo with other children. We played late into the evening, oblivious at the time to the activities of the adults around us, the mothers and grandmothers sitting in the doorways, the courting couples talking to each other through the grills over the windows, the men arguing and philosophising loudly inside and outside the bars.

Once when I was nine I was taken with the men of the family all the way to Ronda to sell ponchos, go to the fair, and then see a corrida. I will never forget how excited I was. The journey by mule took three days but I was so proud to be with the men that I hardly noticed. We slept in the gardens near the plaza de toros and while the men drank in the bars I walked the streets, looking into the windows of shops and staring in wonder at beautiful señoritas promenading in the evening air. We sat in the cheapest rows at the top of the plaza de toros. It was hotter than I had ever experienced for we could not afford seats in the shade. But I will always remember that first corrida and how we shouted for the bravest of the matadors to be awarded two ears and a tail that day, my cries louder than anyone's. And he was. On the way back I was too tired to hurt from the riding. My father said I slept for three days on the mule's back.

The best day of the year in our pueblo was at the time of the Fiesta del Carmen in July. At about seven o'clock in the morning we would line up to run from the bull that would be let loose at the top of the hill and allowed to charge down the narrow, winding lanes of the pueblo. All the previous night the young men would drink to build up their courage. All day the village was full of people, many of the men fairly drunk, and there was much noise and excitement. I am told the bull is still let loose at the fiesta to this day.

Alas, my dear niece, such happy times were few. When the cold damp winter in Grazalema killed your grandmother, we decided to move east away from the rain. Your father, my brother Mario, was to learn to be a charcoal-burner. It was decided I should learn to make cal – whitewash. I was put into the charge of the man we knew as old Fernando, the elder brother of your mother, who took me with him high into the hills to collect bits of wood from olive or pine trees to bring down by mule. He lived in a lonely cortijo on the side of a bare hill and into the side of that hill we built a calera, a furnace, taking two weeks to do it. It was a small cave with a hole only big enough to enable us to throw in wood to maintain the heat. Inside we stacked the cal stones we had collected. For three days we would stay there, building and rebuilding the fire until it was white-hot, then we would take turns to guard it for another few days until it cooled so that we could extract the cal stones and break them down into white, crumbly stones or powder, ready to be sold for the making of whitewash. It *was hard back-breaking work.*

Then, my dear niece, came the civil war. How can I explain to you why we fought, Spaniard killing Spaniard, Andaluz killing Andaluz, why such horrors were committed, except to tell you what life was like before. Hundreds of thousands of peasants in Andalusia were living at the mercy of the caciques, the autocratic landowners who took advantage of the poverty to hire labourers a day at a time for little money. Somehow my family became in debt to them so that all we earned from them with our labour had to be used to pay the interest on their loans. Your father Mario, when only ten years old, was working twenty-four hours a day as a shepherd, sleeping with the sheep, having to eat only bread, maybe a little soup, and stewed chickpeas. When the politicians in Madrid decided we could share ownership of the land and we tried to possess it we were badly beaten and denied further work. I knew little about politics except that the Republican politicians in Madrid had at least tried to help, to give us some land, and that the nationalists were the supporters of the landowners who refused to implement the policy and who instead met our legitimate demands with violence.

One day the pueblo near where I was struggling to survive with my parents was taken over by an extreme group of Republican guerrilleros and they killed those Nationalists they could find. A day later the Nationalist forces arrived and exacted their revenge, killing nearly sixty of the villagers. I fled to the hills and joined a band of guerrilleros fighting for the Republican cause. I will not attempt to tell you of what I saw in those years, of the cruelty and the horror of the civil war, or of my confusion at the wars within wars, for even those who professed to be Republicans were divided. I only know that there seemed no choice but to be what I was and that not a night went by without my praying that I and my parents and my brothers, Mario and Diego, would survive. For three years I never

274

slept easily at night; always we were in danger of being captured or killed. That we were not killed was a miracle, for it is said that more than half a million people died in the three years of the war.

One day a group of us were ambushed in a small valley from where there was no retreat. Soldiers blocked off the entrance and came riding in and shot and killed everyone but me. I had slipped into some bushes only a moment earlier to relieve myself. I lay there, under a thick bush, shocked and terrified and, thank God, they missed me. Our numbers in that part of the sierras had been getting fewer and I now spent many weeks alone, hiding in a tiny cave in the hills, living on a few berries and on my skill in trapping rabbits or the occasional goat that had wandered from a herd. Even then I had to cook the meat quickly, away from my cave, so that the smoke would not give me away. I would then scurry back like a wild animal with its captured prey.

In the winter it became unbearably cold. Twice at night I woke just in time to avoid being attacked by hungry wolves. I finally decided to try to creep into Ronda and find some food and perhaps somewhere I could stay. I knew the chance of capture was high but I believed I would die if I stayed out any longer. I had walked for three days across the hills, twice narrowly evading soldiers on horseback, when I found a small clutch of trees in a valley and tearing off some branches made a kind of tent to sleep in overnight. I woke to find a light in my face. Standing over me were two Nationalist soldiers . . . My blood froze. One was thin, with a sharp nose and hard eyes. He pushed me down and held me there with his boot at my throat. The other was different. A big man, fat, he had a kinder face, one that gave me hope. He was, I suspected, no older than I.

I was so weak by now and so shocked when the older man, the thin one, said, 'What are you doing in this place, you bandido, are you a Republican?' that I blurted out 'Si.'

'Let's not waste our time dragging him back to be tried and executed,' said the thin man. 'Let's shoot him on the spot.'

I was terrified. I thought I was about to die. I began to pray for my mother and for my family. But, thank God, the big man would have none of it. The two argued and then reluctantly the thin man roughly tied my hands behind me and tied a rope around my neck. They climbed on their horses and the thin man made me walk in front. For hours I stumbled across rocks and shrubs with him jerking the rope.

Eventually he pulled me to the ground and told me to lie there. They got off their horses and sat under a tree, unwrapping some food and drinking from a bota of wine. The thin man ignored me but the fat man walked over and gave me a piece of bread and a swig from the bota. I looked at him gratefully but the older man just laughed and called him a weak young fool.

Then they tied the rope to a tree and lay down to rest. I must have fallen asleep because next I knew the thin man was leaning over me cutting the rope and telling me to run. 'Run, bandolero, run,' he kept saying. I could not understand why he had changed towards me but I began to run. I had got only about ten metres when I heard the click of a trigger and realised I had been tricked. He had helped me to escape in order to have an excuse to shoot me. There was a bang and I felt a terrible pain in my side. I fell, twisting round as I did so. He was raising his gun and aiming it at my head. There was another bang and then to my amazement the gun toppled from his hand. A terrible look of pain mixed with surprise came onto his face, and then he fell forward on the ground. The younger soldier had shot him.

I do not remember much about the next few days except that we were in a cave and the soldier who should have been my enemy helped me to recover, bathing what was apparently not a serious wound, and feeding me with meat obtained by shooting wild goats and rabbit. Then he told me that I was to go, taking both horses. He would walk back and tell his superiors that they had been attacked by Republican guerrillas, that his colleague had been killed and that he had escaped and been forced to return on foot. He even gave me his gun.

I asked him why he did this. He simply smiled and said, 'We are all Spaniards. The difference is that you and I are not of the past. We still have our lives to live. We can still do good, and he was a man who never would. The war is nearly over. You and your friends have lost. I see no reason why you should die now. So go and be safe.' With that he was gone.

Three weeks later I met some other Republicans in the hills. The war was over. Some were going home. A few were planning to keep fighting, to become guerrilleros, living in the mountains. They said there would be no pardon. That we would all be punished, maybe killed. I did not know what to do so I chose the guerrilleros. And I did hear of many killings of those who went home, of much retribution. For many more years I lived in the mountains armed with a shotgun, but never a full member of one of the Communist guerilla bands.

Our enemy now was the Guardia Civil. There were attacks on Guardia Civil headquarters and kidnappings by guerillas and, I know, some killings, but I saw little of this. Then one day I was riding with a comrade in the hills when we saw some Guardia Civil officers coming down the valley. We hid above the pass and watched them go by. One of them was told to remain and guard the entrance to the valley. My comrade drew a knife and signalled to me that he was going to jump down upon him from a rock above his head; he made a gesture with the knife across his throat to indicate what he had in mind. Then the policeman turned his head and I saw his face; it was the man who in the civil war had saved my life. In the split second that it took my comrade to jump I called out a warning. The big *policeman turned, pulling his horse away, so that my comrade hit the ground. As he did so the policeman hit the back of his head with the butt of his revolver. He then looked up and our eyes met. For a moment he said not a word then he slowly smiled. 'I knew that one day you would do good, my friend,' he said. I dragged my comrade to our horses while the policeman rode on as if it had never happened.*

I'm told more than 2,000 guerrilleros were killed and 25,000 guerrilleros or so-called accomplices were arrested in those years. But once more I survived. Years went by and I became part of the land itself. By the time a full amnesty was announced in 1959, about the time you were born, I had been living, half-human, half-animal in the sierras for more than twenty-five years, most of it an outlaw, yet not known to the Guardia Civil for I had always evaded capture and not been with any one band enough to become well-known or be betrayed.

Yes, I had survived, but my younger years had gone.

In the years after the war, while I was still an outlaw, things had been no better for our family. Andalusia was desperately poor. Whole families left for the big cities to live in poverty in shacks on the outskirts. Many smallholders abandoned their cortijos and left them to decay. Your father Mario, who had returned to charcoal-burning and cal-making after the civil war, suffered much illness probably caused by getting the dust and smoke in lungs already damaged by the cold and damp of his childhood. Mario, who was born in the 1920s, six or seven years after me, was nearly thirty-five when he married your mother and you were born two years later, about 1960. Tragically your mother died giving birth to you.

My dear niece, your father was a good man, a good brother, and though he was poor in those years he always gave generously to me when, putting him at risk in my desperation, I crept late at night from the hills looking for food or warmth. He never recovered from the loss of your mother and I believe died as much from a broken heart as from the effects of years of struggle.

My dear niece, you must forgive these ramblings of an old man, but I have never before had cause or desire to remember or recount all these things. It is right you should know what has gone before in your family. And also you need to know some things that I pray will make your life an even better one.

Your mother's uncle who lived in Malaga came to Mario's funeral and talked to me. He said that he owned some land near the costa. It was not worth much because it was unfit for growing things. But he wanted it kept for you, his only niece. As he was old and ill it was decided it should be registered in my name and that it would one day be given to you. Now things have changed; there is much building of grand houses on the costa. I'm told it's possible that the land is now worth many pesetas. If you go to your other uncle, Diego, near Casares you will find he has the details and the written authorities transferring its ownership to you.

My dear niece, you come from a family that was always loyal to each other, that lived in hard times but was as honest as it was possible to be and survive. For my part, I know only one life now, the life of the sierras. I can read or write only a few words, I have never known the warmth of a woman in my bed, and for me the inventions of my life-time, radios and television, even electricity itself, are things I see when I pass other people's houses or when I am invited in for food. But I do not want you to think I write in complaint for I love this magnificent country, these hills and mountains, the flowers in the valleys, the peace I share with the eagles and the conejo and my faithful old mule. I am, too, at peace with myself. I have only one duty and that is to fulfil my obligation to your father and to you, so that you will live a better life, for in your good fortune lies the hope

279

that our family will never know hardship again.

So, my dear niece, take care and live a good life. Think kind thoughts of your old uncle. I write with love on behalf of your mother and father,
your loving uncle,
(name indecipherable).
P.S.

If you ever need help from the police see my good friend Miguel. He is a captain in the Guardia Civil in Ronda. You may guess from the above story that we share many memories.

Chapter Eleven

Sheedy let the letter drop from his fingers to the ground beside the deckchair and, closing his eyes, pictured the two old men, Miguel and the Rabbit Man, sitting in their customary corner of the Casino bar in Ronda, Miguel full of energy, expansive, talkative, the other sitting completely still, listening, watching. He remembered them differently in the *plaza de toros*, Miguel leaning back, relaxed, beer in hand, the Rabbit Man tensed forward, his face alert, his eyes on fire.

What lives the two men had shared. What loyalties. What secrets. Now he knew why Miguel had been so reticent about the Rabbit Man's past. Each had betrayed his allegiance by saving the life of the other; as a result each must have been at risk of being executed by his own comrades. To the end the Rabbit Man, his suspicion entrenched by years of living outside the law, had felt it necessary to keep his past from the *Guardia Civil*; to the end Miguel must have feared he would face a court martial if ever his killing of a fellow officer became known.

How sad that having survived the civil war and the

severity of life in the *sierras*, having survived into their seventies, that they should now be killed by a casual foreigner for so trivial a reason.

With a sigh, the American picked up his drink and the pages at his feet and walked back into the villa. He showered and changed and made himself a coffee, then sat at a table on the balcony and, picking up a ruler, placed it vertically on the last page of the old man's letter.

Using a formula that had served him well in the past, he began to slowly move the ruler across the signature, trying to isolate each letter of each word. He quickly identified two words, one with four letters and one more difficult to work out, but probably nine or ten.

Now he moved the ruler slowly from letter to letter, endeavouring to work out what each one was. He was, of course, helped by knowing what the signature *should* be; that the two words should be Pepe Rodriguis. So he looked first for the letter *P* then the letter *E* and so on. It wasn't difficult. If you knew the letter was *probably* a *P* it was easier to see that it *was* in fact a *P*. And there was no doubt about it; the signature was Pepe Rodriguis.

Now he turned his attention to the greeting at the top. This was more difficult because he didn't know what he was looking for. Once more by moving the ruler slowly along he was able to work out that there were three words, one with just two letters, one with six or seven, and the last and most difficult possibly four, five or six letters.

The first he distinguished as *Mi*, my, and the second as *quehido*. *Quehido?* He reached for his Spanish dictionary and it wasn't there. He checked other possible words. Then he saw it. *Querido* – dear, beloved. '*My dear...*'

But the most difficult word was the last. It was written in a scrawl as if his hand had lost energy at the end of the line. He knew the best he could do was guess. The first letter was completely indecipherable. The second was either an *a* or an *o*. The third was either an *r* or an *h*. The fourth was once more either an *e* or an *i*. The final one was either an *o* or an *a*. Five letters. *Ario?* No, it had to be *Aria* if it was addressed to a girl. Was the first letter an *M* – *M* for *Maria?* Yes, that must be it. Maria.

Deciding he had done as much as he could with the letter he returned to the other papers, this time concentrating on the photographs. Were these old faded ones of the Rabbit Man's family? Were the two men pictured with the Rabbit Man his brothers, one of them the girl's late father? And was this the Rabbit Man with his brother, Diego, the one who lived near Casares? Sheedy put it aside to take with him when he went to search.

Finally he moved to the top of the pile the colour picture of the smiling dark-haired girl in Andalusian costume, pictured with a fair in the background. The longer he examined the picture the more the background looked familiar. He realised that it was a corner of the huge fairground at Seville. Could this be the Maria to whom the letter was addressed?

Behind him he heard a car pull up in the drive. Leaving the papers he walked into the villa to give Kate a hug as she came in. 'Hi, lover,' she said, 'had a good day?'

'You sound like a New York telephone operator.'

'OK, did you have a lousy day?'

'So so.'

'I'm dying for a drink. Shall I open a bottle of wine?'

'Sure. I put some Faustino dry white in the chiller. Bring it out on the balcony.'

Sheedy returned to his chair and, picking up the picture of the girl, looked at it thoughtfully.

Kate came onto the balcony, put two glasses of wine

on the table, and standing behind him threw her arms round his neck and kissed the top of his head. 'What are you up to?'

She reached out and took the photograph from his hand. 'Hey, where did you get this picture of Maria?'

Sheedy looked at her in surprise. 'What did you say?'

'I said where did you get this picture of Maria?'

'How did you know her name was Maria?'

'Well for Christ's sake, Sheedy, it's obvious. It *is* Maria.'

'Maria who?'

'*Maria.* The Maria we've met. The Maria I've just spent the day with. Cruickshank's Maria.'

Sheedy slumped back in his chair. 'Well, for Christ's sake. How did I miss it? I know I only met her briefly but I should have remembered. You're right. It's her. And it ties in with the name on the letter.'

He stood up and paced up and down. 'I wonder if Cruickshank knows. Heavens, Kate, what's going on?'

Kate looked bewildered. 'Bill, what on earth are you talking about?'

'Sorry – read this.' He tossed the letter to her and went in. 'While you're reading it I'll get some food together. Fancy *gambas a la plancha* and salad?'

'Sure.' She sat and began to read. By the time he called her to eat she had been sitting quietly for some time, looking out at the lights of San Pedro, beginning to twinkle in the dusk.

'Bill, are you thinking what I'm thinking?'

'What's that?'

'That Cruickshank and company could have had the Rabbit Man killed so that Maria would inherit the land ... that Cruickshank has been cynically wooing her for the land.'

'I was trying not to think that.'

'But otherwise it's all a fantastic coincidence.'

'Coincidences do happen. I've been increasingly coming round to your point of view that Cruickshank just isn't the kind of man who would authorise murder. Or the kind to court Maria to get her land. It isn't consistent with his record or his personality.'

'Look, Kate,' he continued, 'I don't know what to think any more. But we're getting closer to the truth ... Let's consider the options.'

'If neither Cruickshank or Maria know the old man was her uncle, then when Maria does discover she owns the land she'll naturally be happy to let Cruickshank have it. Happy end to story.' He paused, then added, 'Apart from two dead.'

'Maybe three,' interrupted Kate, thinking of the missing Felipe.

'OK, maybe three,' Sheedy acknowledged reluctantly. 'Inspector Rivas tells me Felipe hasn't returned to his home village. He's just vanished. Not that that means a lot; boys like Felipe can spend years moving from place to place seeking ... well, only they know what they're seeking.'

He looked ill at ease for a moment, then pulled himself together and continued theorising. 'Option two: Cruickshank knows about the land and Maria doesn't. If Maria finds out Cruickshank has been keeping all this from her, that he stands to profit from their marriage, bang will go her belief in him as a man of honour. She'll break the engagement off. Then what? She won't sell them the land, so that leaves them with a choice ... they either get by without it or they eliminate her as well.'

Kate looked shocked. 'Surely not. They couldn't go on like that ... killing anyone who gets in their way.'

'One wouldn't think so. However, and this is option three, if Cruickshank doesn't know about the connection between Maria and the land, but Canning does, then we have real problems. Canning clearly has a ball game of his own going, and the stakes seem high enough for him to do whatever he thinks is necessary.'

But how, asked Kate, would Cruickshank or Canning have discovered that the Rabbit Man was keeping the land for Maria?

'I don't know. Except that Canning has seen this picture too. So he could have been cleverer than I, or seen a lot more of her than I, and recognised her and told Cruickshank.'

'Of course, that in itself wouldn't tell them about the land,' Kate said. 'Maybe they forced the details of the letter out of Miguel.' Then seeing Sheedy shake his head, she added 'Or maybe Canning made contact with the brother in Casares. Bill, we should have tried to find him before now.'

'Hell, I know. But first we have to get to Maria. If she's involved we'll soon know. If she isn't we can put her on her guard.'

'Bill,' Kate said decisively, remembering her conversation with Maria on the beach, and the idealism in the Spanish woman's eyes, 'it's inconceivable that she's involved. She's in love with Cruickshank; in fact I think she idolises him. She keeps talking about her man of honour.'

'In that case,' said Sheedy, 'we're back to square one: either Cruickshank meeting Maria is a coincidence or Cruickshank has deliberately set about wooing her to guarantee he gets the land. Either way, we've still got to talk to her,' He sprang to his feet. 'Maria is staying with the architect, Julio Aparitico, isn't she? Look, he lives in a villa between San Pedro and Estapona. Why don't you ring her and suggest she comes to Casares with us tomorrow. We could kill two birds with one stone. Talk to her over lunch and then see if we can find and talk to her uncle.'

Kate went to the phone book and found the architect's number. Maria was not yet back from dinner with Cruickshank. Julio was out but Isabella, his wife, said she thought Maria would love to go to Casares. If they didn't hear to the contrary, they should pick her up in the morning.

Tired, Kate went to the bedroom, slipped off her tee shirt, jeans, and knickers and, naked, walked back into the lounge and past him on her way to the bathroom. 'I'm going to take a shower.'

Sheedy watched her thoughtfully. He was still surprised at how quickly he could be aroused by seeing her undressed. He heard the water running in the shower. He couldn't rid himself of the image he had just fleetingly seen, the straight back and athletic legs, brown from the sun, the firm, round bottom, milky white. Getting up, he walked towards the bathroom, shedding clothes as he went, and pulling back the shower curtain, he stepped in, taking her in his arms.

'Sheedy . . . ' she laughed, giving him an unconvincing push. 'What are you doing here?'

'In Spain,' he said, taking the soap and beginning to lather her breasts, 'we save water where we can.'

'Save time more like it.' The chuckle came from deep in her throat. 'Hmmmm . . . '

Troubled as he had been all day by the death of the policeman and the possibility of Canning's involvement, Cruickshank had, as always in Maria's company, been able to relax and forget. Now, as he walked her to the car, the front gates to the villa opened and Canning's Porsche rolled in and up to the front steps. The American got out, looking, Cruickshank noted with irritation, as cool and immaculate as ever.

The Englishman did not introduce his young fiancée but observed, with even greater irritation, that Canning was inspecting her closely. 'Perhaps you would wait in the house, Jason,' he said coldly.

The American began to walk to the front door, then stopped and turned, and took another look at Maria. Cruickshank was just about to rebuke him when, with a final glance at both of them, he turned on his heel and entered the villa.

'I'm sorry about that, Maria,' he said. 'The man has no manners.' He leaned into the car and kissed her on the cheek. 'I look forward to seeing you tomorrow.'

Inside the house Canning was chatting with Julio and their newly-appointed site director. Cruickshank opened the meeting without ceremony. Ownership papers for ninety-five per cent of the land had now been signed. Work would begin. They must determine the priorities and finalise a timetable.

Not for the first time his anger at, and dislike of, Canning were matched by respect for the American's ability. The plans Canning now produced were well-conceived and, no matter what obstacles the architect or site director identified, Canning had an answer.

It was Julio who asked about the Rabbit Man's land. 'Do we act on the assumption we'll get it, or do we revert to Plan B and go ahead without it?'

Cruickshank hesitated. He knew the project would benefit considerably by acquisition of the land, that it was his responsibility to persevere. Yet he was so sickened by the whole affair that he was tempted to write it off and make the best of what they had. While he was thinking, Canning replied: 'We'll get the land. Act on that basis.'

Cruickshank looked at him, surprised at his assurance. But he let it go, uncharacteristically pleased that the question had been answered for him.

After the meeting Canning stayed behind. 'Sir Brian, I wonder whether we could have a private word.'

'If you insist.'

He took the American into a small sitting room off the main lounge where, his admiration for Canning's professionalism giving way to distaste as memories of their recent difficulties came flooding back, he snapped, 'Well, what is it?'

'Forgive me for asking, Sir Brian, but the young lady ...'

Cruickshank flushed, furious at this intolerable intrusion into his private affairs, and virtually shouted, 'What about the young lady. What business is it ...?'

Canning doggedly interrupted: 'Sir Brian, I believe I have seen her before. Or at least a picture of her.'

'So? That's not unlikely. She comes from a well-known family. Her picture appears often in magazines.'

Canning deliberately kept his voice low in contrast, trying to calm the Englishman down. 'I told you that when I was in the old man's hut, the man they called El Conejero, there were some old papers and some old photographs. One was of a young girl. Sir Brian, I would swear it was the same ... the same lady. Only much younger of course.'

Cruickshank looked at him uncomprehendingly. 'The same? Don't be ridiculous, man. How could it be?'

'Forgive me for asking Sir Brian, but what do you know of her background?'

Cruickshank rose. 'Damn you, Canning, this is too much. How dare you pry into my affairs in this way. Señorita Garcia comes from a respectable family in Seville. The suggestion of a connection with this ... this peasant ... is ludicrous.'

He stood over the younger man. 'Canning you despoil everything you get near. I tell you now that if you go anywhere near Miss Garcia or even mention her to me or anyone else, I will show you there are others who can act as violently as you. Now get out.'

Canning shrugged. 'Very well. But I have said

nothing to her discredit. I just wondered whether she could be related to the old man. And think about the possibilities if she was, Sir Brian. It would mean . . . '

'Get out, you idiot.' Cruickshank was almost incandescent with rage. It was bad enough that Canning was endangering his project but he was damned if he was going to allow him to intrude into the one untarnished part of his life – the part that he shared with Maria.

Canning looked as if he were about to argue further, then with a shrug, he rose, and walked from the house, climbed into his Porsche, and drove quickly to the nearest telephone booth. From there he rang a number in Tangier, and afterwards a number in Fuengirola.

Cruickshank went upstairs in a rage, stripped and showered, and then in a dressing gown lay on his bed listening to the sounds of the night. All the troubles of the day returned to plague his thoughts, but now compounded by what Canning had said. He tried to push the conversation out of his mind but he couldn't. On the contrary, the more he considered Canning's words the more he worried.

He struggled to recall what Maria had told him that night over dinner at Pantiles.

She had been raised by a gypsy family because her uncle or uncles hadn't been able to take care of her.

And she had been abandoned in Seville when she was twelve. The girl Canning claimed to have seen in a picture at the peasant's house had been, he said, eleven or twelve.

What if it were the same girl? Could it be possible? Was the old man her uncle?

It would be an incredible coincidence but then Cruickshank was beginning to wonder what in this whole business could surprise him any longer.

One thing he knew: Maria had no idea of the connection between her, the peasant, the land, and the project.

But she would soon. The way the reporter, Sheedy, was pursuing it, the questions would continue to be raised. Someone was bound to talk to her about it.

What would she think of him when it was suggested that *her uncle* had been deliberately killed . . . not by him, but *in his name*?

He sat up.

He must get to her first.

He must tell her the whole story.

Yes, that was it. He would tell her the truth, and even ask her opinion about what he should do. This was not just a business problem; it was also a personal one. He would share it with her. It was only right. This was how their life together must be, a partnership.

His mind began to work faster. Logic gave way to hope. Perhaps with her support he could still go to the police and reveal all. After all, with her by his side, what did it matter if he had to answer criticism for not revealing Canning's behaviour earlier? What would it matter if the project itself had to be abandoned? He could live without it. What he couldn't do was live without Maria.

He thought of going to her immediately.

But no, he had already arranged for them to have dinner the following evening.

Nothing would happen in the meantime.

He would tell her then.

Miller was taken unawares by Canning's abrupt departure. He had been relaxing in his room when the first group left, persuading himself that the tumbler of gin in his hand was definitely the last of the night. However, when it became clear that Canning was remaining, presumably engaging with Cruickshank in yet another of their interminable inquests into the so-called 'accidents', Miller decided to treat himself to another.

When he did leave, Canning moved at such a pace that Miller nearly missed him. Downing the gin on the run, spilling some of it onto his shirt, he stumbled to his car and had to make an almost suicidal entry into the stream of fast-moving vehicles in order to keep the Porsche in view.

He knew that following someone in a car and remaining unobserved looked easy in films but was usually damn-near impossible in practice, especially when the driver was someone as streetwise as Canning. Despite employing every bit of his experience and skill, he had an uncomfortable feeling that Canning usually knew he was there. Not that this appeared to worry Canning; either he didn't care or was confident that if he wanted to slip the net he could do so with ease. In a race the American's Porsche would leave Miller's modest Seat standing.

This time they didn't go far – just to the Andalusia Plaza hotel. Miller, following the other at a discreet distance, saw him disappear into the casino on the ground floor. He waited for five minutes to allow Canning to get to a roulette table and then attempted to enter himself, only to be stopped by a burly man in evening dress demanding to see either his membership card or his passport. Miller, who was not a member and didn't have his passport with him, was told in that case he couldn't enter. In a clumsy, half-hearted attempt to bribe the man he waved a 5,000–pesetas note at him but this elicited such a look of contempt that he hurriedly retreated, embarrassed and annoyed.

He now had a choice, either to hang around outside or to return to the villa for his passport. He gambled on the latter course and to his relief the American was still there on his return, playing at one of a number of roulette wheels in a huge cavernous room half-full of people, more of them spectators than players. Miller took an empty place at a blackjack table. It was ideal because, while he could see Canning, the American had his back to Miller.

Absent-mindedly he let the dealer change the whole pile of notes he had dropped on the table. There must have been 50,000 pesetas' worth. He was disconcerted by the stack of chips that appeared and looked at it with distaste. He didn't like gambling. Still, he figured, there was no problem. He would only bet the smaller ones and could change the others back.

There was one 20,000–peseta chip and he put that to one side of the stack of those worth 500 and 1,000 pesetas. His first bet was 500 pesetas. He found himself with a Jack and a four facing the dealer's Queen. Fourteen. He took another card. Another Jack. He was over twenty-one. The chip disappeared. He felt mildly irritated.

Hoping to break even on his opening two bets, he replaced it with a 1,000–peseta chip and drew a King and Queen – twenty. He rested, confident that the dealer with only a six would go over the top. In fact the dealer drew a seven and then an eight and finished with twenty-one. The chip disappeared.

And so it went on.

He abandoned any idea of doubling up, at least until he started winning, and he cut back his bets to 500 pesetas, but still he lost, his concentration not helped by the need to keep an eye on Canning.

After half an hour he totted up his chips; he had lost nearly 25,000 pesetas' worth. He was just considering taking up a less expensive vantage point (he had just observed a bar at the other end of the room) when he saw Canning move away from the roulette table and out of his line of sight. He cautiously turned to his left and saw the American heading for the door. He turned back to pick up his few remaining chips and to his horror saw that in his haste he had accidentally elbowed the 20,000 peseta chip onto the square. He did a quick calculation ... 20,000 pesetas, that was £100. The first card was already in front of him ... a six. Desperate to chase Canning but also concerned about his money, he groaned inwardly but tried to look calm as the dealer produced a seven for him, then an ace for himself. With only thirteen and the dealer with a good chance of getting a blackjack, Miller had no choice but to draw. It was ten. 'Over,' said the dealer and the chip disappeared.

Miller, humiliated by the amused gaze of the other players and in a hurry to find Canning, pocketed his remaining three 1,000–peseta chips and fled the table and the casino.

Canning was turning from the car park up the street that led to his apartment. Miller waited a moment and then drove up the same way. By the time he got there Canning's car was parked outside the building.

Miller waited a couple of hours, hungry now, thirsty, head aching, and cursing his misfortune at the blackjack table. Finally, half an hour after the lights went out in the American's window, he decided it was safe to call it a night.

As he drove back to the villa he reflected that the trip to the casino, the race back to get the passport, the loss of more than 45,000 pesetas, and the wait outside Canning's apartment had all proved unnecessary.

Worse, he had a feeling Canning had been performing for the last few hours for Miller's benefit. It was almost as if he *wanted* the Englishman to be with him. But why?

Miller's headache was now horrendous.

He was beginning to hate Canning.

After Kate had fallen asleep, Sheedy had driven down to

Puerto Banus to make a few of his own enquiries about Felipe. It was one in the morning by the time he drove the car up the San Pedro–Ronda road towards the villa. His upbeat mood after the discoveries of the day and his love-making with Kate had turned to unease. No matter how much he rationalised his behaviour, he knew the truth was that they had exploited the boy. Not only had they endangered him but they had done so without the boy fully realising it. They hadn't left him with a chance.

It was 3 a.m. when he turned up the approach road to the villa and swung the car into the small parking lot. As he walked past the swimming pool he began to sense that things were not as they should be. There were more lights on in the villa than usual and he could almost feel the tension in the air. He walked quickly but quietly up the steps and then, just as he was reaching the door, heard a woman's voice, Kate's voice, cry out 'No.'

He took the last two or three steps in one leap and flung the door open, taking in the scene at a glance. Kate was spreadeagled, naked, across the back of the sofa, face down. Around her, grinning with malicious pleasure, stood three men, one tall, an Arab, the other two shorter, Spanish. The Arab was standing behind her, his intentions only too clear. The usually even-tempered American became in an instant a man possessed. Not thinking or caring that he was out-numbered and roaring like a bull he leapt across the room, kicking the Arab in the backside so that he fell forward over Kate. Sheedy pulled him off, turned him round, and hit him so hard in the face that blood spurted onto the floor. The Arab reeled back, falling to the ground. One of the Spaniards moved threateningly towards him but Sheedy couldn't have been stopped by an army. He grabbed the man by both arms and hurled him against the wall. The third intruder took one look at Sheedy's face and raced out of the open door. By then

295

the Arab was staggering back to his feet. Sheedy picked up a chair and raised it to strike him. As he did so the remaining Spaniard, clambering back to his feet, hit him with an empty wine bottle from the table. He was swung off balance and fell dazed. By the time he was back up the other two were gone and Kate was kneeling over him, sobbing and laughing hysterically and thanking him all at the same time.

He pulled her up and held her tight, his face in her hair, his hands gently rubbing her back, his voice softly whispering in her ear until she quietened and then he picked her up and carried her to the shower, tearing off his own clothes, so they could stand under the hot water together, being soothed, cleansed of the experience.

Later, while they lay in each other's arms on the bed, she said the men claimed that Miguel had revealed that Sheedy was in possession of the Rabbit Man's papers. They were trying to force her to give them up. 'I was just going to do it, Bill, give them the papers. Then you got back.'

'You should have. Of course you should have.' Sheedy could hardly contain his anger. 'Well, that settles it. I'm going to end this business once and for all. I'm going to get it out in the open with Cruickshank.'

Ignoring the time – it was now 4 a.m. – he rose from the bed and went to the phone. He rang the Englishman's number but was told he was not to be disturbed. His protests were in vain. Sheedy would have to call in the morning. Then he telephoned Inspector Rivas. He was at home too. The *Guardia Civil* had no intention of disturbing their man either. He left a message for him to ring and, frustrated, returned to bed.

MONDAY, APRIL 9

They slept late the following morning and Sheedy, his anger more controlled now, decided to leave his calls to Cruickshank and Inspector Rivas until they had been to Casares. There was a good chance they would know more by then. To get there they drove about six kilometres south of Estapona on the N340 and then turned inland for a further thirteen kilometres. It was not the first time that it seemed to Kate that within a few minutes of leaving the costa they entered a magic door from one century to another. The hills were dotted with peaceful white-washed *cortijo*, still without water supply or electricity. They passed a herd of sheep and goats grazing on the roadside, the shepherd a short man with flat cap and a wooden crook as tall as himself, bright, alert eyes gazing out of a sun-darkened, wizened face. The road began to climb and wind up into the hills and the country became greyer and rockier. Many of the trees were stripped of their bark as high as a man could reach. After wending their way round the edge of a magnificent valley they climbed steeply up another hill and, after a sharp turn to the right, there was Casares, a dramatic-looking white town perched on top of a huge rock, and on top of it the ruins of an old church.

They lunched in El Meson Los Claveles near the town square. Sheedy, who was known to take this forty-five minute detour frequently to sample the restaurant's specialities, warmly greeted the owner Pepe Jose and urged Maria and Kate to share a whole rabbit roasted in garlic.

He waited until they could tuck into a juicy lettuce and tomato salad and a glass of wine before, deliberately low-key and gentle, he said, 'Maria, by coincidence we've come across some information that concerns you.'

The girl's eyes widened. 'Coincidence, Señor Bill?'

'Yes. I have ... or had ... a friend who lived in the hills near Ronda, in fact two friends, the second an officer in the *Guardia Civil*. Recently they both were killed in what appeared to be accidents and in one of the old men's effects we found a photograph.' He handed it to Maria. 'It is you, isn't it?'

'*Si.*' She was astonished. '*Si.* I remember when this was taken, at the fair in Seville, just before I was left at the orphanage. But why did your friend have it?'

'Maria, what do you remember of the uncle who cared for you after your parents died?'

'Not a lot. I was only small, and so much has happened since.'

'Have you ever wanted to find him?'

'No, Señor. I suppose, deep down, I always felt rejected by him, that he didn't want me, that he just passed me on to a gypsy family to rid himself of me. As it happened, the gypsies were good to me, but I wonder whether he cared one way or the other. Anyway, I've adopted the Garcias as my family, just as they have adopted me. But why do you ask?'

Sheedy told her the old man had cared more than she knew. He gave her the letter and she silently read it, by the end with tears in her eyes.

Then she said, 'You say he is dead, Señor?'

'Yes. This is where it gets difficult, Maria. You see it appears the land you now own is the piece of land Sir Brian has been trying to buy. Your uncle was the peasant he had been negotiating with.'

Maria looked at him wide-eyed. 'That is a coincidence as you say. But why difficult?'

'Because,' Sheedy replied gently, 'it makes one wonder, Maria, just how far the coincidence goes?'

'I don't understand.'

'Let me put it to you bluntly. Sir Brian needed that land desperately. Your uncle owned it and wouldn't sell.

Then your uncle had an accident. And Sir Brian began to court you, the new owner. It could, of course, be a coincidence, but . . . '

Maria reacted with anger. 'Señor Bill, Sir Brian is a man of honour. What you are implying is unthinkable. He loves me. And would love me irrespective of all this.'

'You think he had no idea you were related to the old man? That he doesn't know you own the land?'

'I'm certain of it. You say my uncle probably died accidentally. That is what Brian thinks. He told me about it; he said that it was an accident. He said it made life more difficult for him. It is as you say, all a coincidence.' She glared across the table at him. 'I'm angry you should suggest otherwise.'

Kate interrupted. 'But there is also Miguel, Maria.'

'Miguel?'

'Miguel, the policeman. He was your uncle's oldest friend, obviously the man who saved his life during the civil war. He was investigating your uncle's death and he had an accident too. That is another coincidence. Bill and I are journalists; we've learnt to distrust even one coincidence, but two . . . '

Maria rose and stamped her foot, her brown eyes flashing with anger. 'No. No. I will not believe this. Brian is not a criminal . . . a . . . a murderer. This is not possible. You are horrible to suggest it.'

She began to leave the restaurant. Sheedy told Kate to go after her and called to Pepe Jose. Showing him the photograph, he asked, 'Do you know this man, Pepe?'

'*Si*, Señor. He is Diego Rodriguis. He has a small-holding and also hunts. He is the source of many of my *conejo*. Look, I can show you where he is.' He took Sheedy by the arm and led him round the back of the restaurant and up some steps and a winding path to the top of the hill. From near the old church and the small, flower-decked cemetery he pointed out the man's small *cortijo*. It was at the end of a huge valley, towards the coast, perched on one of a number of smaller hills, almost directly under one of a row of big electricity pylons. Pepe Jose showed how it could be reached by driving from Casares towards the Gaucin–Ronda road, and then turning south towards the coast.

At the foot of the hill Sheedy found Kate consoling Maria. They were both sitting on a low white wall by the car, looking over the valley.

'Maria,' said Sheedy, 'Please understand, I also want to believe what you believe. But even if Sir Brian is not involved, I'm positive there's a connection between the deaths and the project. We have to find out what's going on. You could also be in danger. And so could your uncle Diego. In any case, the police are also going to investigate and if we can find an answer that doesn't incriminate Sir Brian that will help him too.'

The Spanish woman looked at him with a mixture of hostility and suspicion and didn't reply.

Sheedy told her they were going to call on her uncle on the way back. He showed her the faded photograph of the two men, the Rabbit Man and the other who Pepe Jose had identified as Diego Rodriguis. 'At least come and see what he has to say.'

It took less than ten minutes to drive there. From the main road they drove between the electricity pylons up a rough lane. At the end was a small white *cortijo* with a brown-red tiled roof, next to it a small corral made of wood. There were two other small huts. Scattered about, scratching in the dirt, were a number of goats and chickens and a small black pig.

They parked the car fifty yards away and walked quietly over, not wishing to disturb the livestock. Sheedy called out, '*Hola.*'

There was no answer. Maria began to step forward but Sheedy, an uncomfortable feeling in the pit of his stomach, took her arm. 'Wait,' he said. 'Wait here.'

He walked up to the curtain of beads that acted as a door, its threads moving slightly in the breeze. 'Is there anyone there?' he called out in Spanish. There was no answer. Gently he pulled the curtains aside.

At first the *cortijo* looked much like that of the Rabbit Man, bare, stone floor, a few pieces of furniture. There was even the same smell of rabbit skins. But there was another smell too and Sheedy, veteran of the holocaust that was Vietnam, recognised it with a sinking heart. You never forgot the smell of death.

The old man's body was lying half-covered by a pile of old skins in the corner of the room. It was naked from the waist up and covered in cigarette burns. Whether he had provided the information his torturers wanted Sheedy could not tell, but even if he had, his reward had been the same as if he had refused. There was a single bullet hole in his forehead.

Sheedy began to back away, then heard a gasp of horror behind him. Standing in the doorway was Maria, her eyes wide, her face losing its colour.

The American moved quickly, took her by the shoulders, wheeled her round, and pushed her outside. She half ran, half stumbled to a nearby tree where she stood shaking, vomiting, then weeping loudly.

Kate tried to put an arm round her but it was shrugged away. Sheedy spoke to her sympathetically but firmly. 'Maria, I want you to go home and pack and drive straight back to the Garcias in Seville.'

The young woman didn't reply.

'This was not an accident, Maria. And three deaths in a row are no longer coincidence. They're all connected and they're all to do with the project and the land.'

'But Brian ... ?' Maria cried out, still weeping.

Sheedy held her by the arms and looked into her eyes. 'Maria, I find it hard to believe Sir Brian would sanction

301

murder. But you must believe that at the very least he's covering up.'

'What are you going to do?'

'About your uncle? I'll have to get the police. But don't forget there is no *evidence* that the project or Cruickshank or his American friends are connected with any of these deaths. That's where someone's been so clever. So no-one is going to be arrested or taken into custody ... unless the police come up with more than we've got at the moment. That's why you're not safe. Until the killing stops you've go to get away from all this.'

Maria sadly nodded and Kate led her gently back to the car. Sheedy went back to the *cortijo* to see if he could find any papers but if they had been there before, they were not now. He looked around for any evidence as to who had been there, but could find nothing useful.

Returning to the car he said to Kate, 'This business has taken a turn for the worse.'

'What do you mean?'

'So far they've made some attempt to make the deaths look like an accident. Now they don't seem to care. That's a significant difference.'

His mind whirling with all the implications, he got in the car and took Maria back to Julio's place and then, asking Kate to take a taxi back to the villa, went to his office, rang Inspector Rivas and told him about Diego Rodriguis. Lastly he rang Hunter in Gibraltar and told him to cancel all the items planned for the next programme.

'We have to stick with this story. We don't have to bother with innuendo. All we need do is spell out the facts, in detail, point by point. We can offer Anglo-Spanish Investors an advance look at the contents and a full opportunity to reply. I'm convinced if we simply tell the story the whole of Andalusia will be demanding a full

302

inquiry,' he said, 'and even if we can't pin the murders on them, we'll make it almost impossible for the municipalities to allow them to develop.'

After his detour on the Gaucin road, Canning had returned to the N340 and driven down to Gibraltar to catch a plane for Tangier. On arrival he took a taxi to the El Minzah hotel and asked for Mr Theodore Jordan.

The tall, bald American came down from his room immediately and, limping more noticeably than Canning remembered him doing before, led the younger man onto the terrace for lunch.

Canning quickly updated him ... on the girl in the photograph and Cruickshank's involvement with her, and on the hunt for the old man's letter and the ownership papers, and his discovery of them at Diego's *cortijo*. He showed them to Jordan. 'We'll have to get our Spanish lawyer to look at the detail. I had hoped they would be incomplete but, in so much as I can understand them it looks as if she's already the legal owner of the land. We're back with the same problem we had with the old man.'

'Do you think Cruickshank can persuade her to sell him the land?'

'I doubt it.'

Jordan put down his fork and looked at him critically. Canning began to feel uncomfortable. 'Look, Mr Jordan, it's just been bad luck, but, in retrospect, killing the old man was a mistake. I'm afraid the reporter Sheedy will convince the girl that Cruickshank had her uncle killed and that by selling him the land she would be vindicating the murder. From what I'm told, I don't think she'll sell. She's been raised by a highly conservative, respectable family and appears to be instilled with a belief, almost an obsession with what she calls honour. This is what attracts her to Cruickshank. Once

303

she becomes disenchanted with him we won't stand a chance.'

Jordan looked at him, expressionless except for a chill in the eyes, one that sent a corresponding chill down Canning's spine. 'Look,' the younger man continued, uncharacteristically rattled, 'there was just no way I could have known that the old man was friends with a reporter on the costa, no way I could have known about the girl. We've been the victims of extraordinary bad luck and coincidence.'

Ignoring the plea for understanding, Jordan asked, 'Will she sell it to us ... not directly, of course, but to one of our American companies, if we choose one that is not obviously connected with us? She could perhaps be persuaded that she would be punishing Cruickshank and avenging her uncle by selling the land to someone else.'

Canning looked sceptical. 'My guess is that she'll now be careful who she sells it to, and if Sheedy keeps in touch with her he'll check on any potential buyer. I don't give much for our chances.'

Jordan turned his thoughts to Sheedy. 'The reporter is a menace. Cruickshank is desperately anxious that we should not attempt to lean on Sheedy in any way. He says that everybody will come down on the case like a ton of bricks if Sheedy is harmed ... and I'm inclined to think he's right.'

Canning reluctantly concurred.

Jordan asked: 'Is it still your view we must have this piece of land?'

'Yes.'

'Why?'

'Three reasons: first, if we don't get it, the access to the site will be via Estapona. If we want to import the ...' He lowered his voice, 'the product ... in considerable quantities it will be extremely dangerous to transport it through the town. It's efficiently policed. But if we get

304

this piece of land and with it a private access road to the valley, we'll have full control over the point of entry. And we can have our own security guards. It will be just like Sotogrande; it too has its own security guards at its own entrance and I doubt if the *Guardia Civil* or the other police ever go near it, figuring the security guards have got it covered.'

'Second, this piece of land will also be a more convenient and discreet entry-point for people going to the casinos or looking for the girls. A lot of our customers will come on impulse, from Marbella and Puerto Banus and even from Fuengirola and Torremolinos; we don't want to put too much time between the impulse and the action. Or make it easier for people to see who comes and goes and when. If they have to enter via Estapona they will have to drive a further ten kilometres south and then through the town; it's bound to have a negative effect on business.'

'Third, a change of plan will involve considerable redesign and delay and additional cost. Also, there's a considerable aesthetic consideration; the land is not in a neat square, it's a valley that winds into the heart of the project.'

'All and all,' he concluded, 'while we can get by without the land, not having it will create all sorts of problems we don't need.'

'So what do you propose?'

Canning suggested there were three options ... at least in theory.

'One, we redesign the project. As I've said, it's possible, but expensive and has the disadvantages I've outlined. Two, we make an extremely generous offer to the girl. But my guess is she'll refuse. Three, we remove the girl. Another accident. There are dangers, of course. Even if it was not traceable to us, the coincidence of another death would be bound to cause an outcry and an investigation of the project, and it would still not make getting the land any easier.'

Jordan weighed up the options. 'If Cruickshank believes we're responsible for harming the girl he'll be out of control. Apart from what he could reveal, we need all the respectability Cruickshank's involvement brings. We need him to get the planning approval for the old man's land and for negotiating with the authorities on a variety of other matters, not least the terms for the race course. How many months do we have before we have to alter the instructions to the construction companies?'

'At least six, maybe even longer. I have persuaded Cruickshank and the architect to accept a construction timetable that concentrates the early activity on the aspects of the project that fit both Cruickshank's project and our variation on it.'

For the first time Jordan smiled at the younger man. 'Yes, you've handled that well.'

His confidence growing, Canning asked, 'But surely it's only a matter of time before we have to reveal to Cruickshank that we have alternative plans?'

'The longer we postpone that, the deeper in he will be.' Jordan paused, thinking. 'Cruickshank will be a problem, but his own position will be extremely difficult. We have him in some trouble. We have tape-recorded proof that he was involved in a cover-up of the old man's murder. And we have a little film of him with a woman in London that he would not be happy to have widely circulated. Also he's going to look a bit of an idiot when people realise how he's been used. My guess is that when he goes, he'll want to go quietly. And with as much face saved as possible.'

For a moment the two men didn't speak, each engrossed in his thoughts. Then it was Jordan who broke the silence. 'Clearly we can't just stage an accident. There's been one too many. He wouldn't believe it.

This must be totally different. I think we'll have to arrange a freak killing. She'll have to be one of a number of victims of a maniac – on an aircraft, or in a crowd.' He considered the problem for a moment. 'I'm told that there's a lot of fervour, sometimes almost uncontrollable passion, around the *Semana Santa* processions in Seville. From what you tell me about them, the Garcia family would normally be in a prominent position there. It should be possible to convince Cruickshank that she's been the victim of a disaster arising out of that, a disaster that could not possibly be related to the project.'

He then spelled out in chilling detail how it could be done. Almost anyone else would have been appalled, but, in Canning, Jordan had the right audience. The younger man listened to the proposal with admiration.

When he had finished, Jordan called for coffee, then added, 'We'll have to bring someone in. You must be seen to be well out of it and I don't want to trust it to someone local who we don't know. While it's being done you can go to Miami and check out the export operation.'

Canning nodded. 'Good thinking.'

The flippancy of the remark irritated Jordan. He looked at the younger man coldly. There could come a time when Canning was more a liability than an asset.

In the meantime, however, business was business, and Jordan spelt out what he would arrange and what Canning should do.

It was four o'clock by the time she got home. Maria was relieved to find the villa empty apart from a maid. She quickly wrote two short notes, one to Julio and Isabella, and one to Cruickshank. Then she hurriedly packed her two cases and, leaving the notes on the table inside the front door, she tossed the cases into the back of her small sports car and, backing with a roar out of the garage, set off for the main road, choosing to drive west to near Gibraltar and then take the Jerez–Seville road rather than drive across-country via Ronda.

As she drove tears rolled down her cheeks. She couldn't bring herself to believe that Brian had caused her uncle to be killed, and also his friend Miguel ... that he had been just wooing her for the land. But she also knew he must at least know about the murders. He had to be covering them up. Bill Sheedy was right about that.

Yet she still believed such dishonourable behaviour wasn't in his nature. Was he being blackmailed for some reason? What kind of pressure was he under? If he was in some trouble, why hadn't he been straight with her? Why hadn't he come and told her? She would have been proud to support him.

Had she put too much value on his honour? She didn't think so. It was what she had respected, and without trust and respect, what else could there be with him?

She drove past the turn-off to La Linea and Gibraltar and, on reaching the outskirts of Algeciras, turned north, off the N430 and began to climb the foothills to the *ruta del toro* – the route of the bulls.

This time Miller felt as if he was at war. Bombs were exploding inside his head causing a blinding flash and terrible pain. One caused him to roll over onto his face and then onto the floor, in the process knocking the empty gin bottle and the alarm clock off the dresser. With a tremendous effort he focused on it. Four o'clock.

Four o'clock! Please God, not four o'clock in the afternoon. He had intended to be back in position by 6.30 in the morning in order to tail Canning. There was no way the American would still be at his apartment at four o'clock in the afternoon.

He crawled to the window and blinked out. The sun hit him between the eyes. The pain was unbearable. He felt as if he had been struck in the head by a cruise missile.

Groaning with both pain and frustration at his failure, he crawled to the shower and soaked his head until a few of the flames were dowsed. He dressed, grabbed what money he had left in the villa after the casino disaster, about 20,000 pesetas in all, and climbed into his car and drove to Nueva Andalucia where he looked at the empty parking spot in dismay. He walked across the road to a telephone booth and rang the yacht and then the villa to check whether Canning was there. He was not.

Miller recalled that the last time he had lost Canning was the night the old policeman had been killed. What was he up to now?

Deeply disturbed, he settled down to wait, every now and then walking to the phone booth to check back with the yacht and villa. It was hot and the war was erupting in his head again.

He desperately wanted a coffee; even more desperately a gin.

But he dare not move. He wanted to keep this assignment, wanted to keep Cruickshank's confidence, and to do that he had to keep tabs on Canning.

He fell asleep. When he woke Canning's car was back in its place. He looked at his watch. It was five o'clock.

He felt so ill he even considered going and asking Canning for a coffee and an aspirin. No doubt the American had seen him sleeping in the car so he wouldn't be breaking his cover. But he couldn't do that; it would be too humiliating. And also, for some reason he didn't in his present state understand, it suited them both not to acknowledge the obvious.

So awash was he in misery and self-pity he almost

missed Canning leaving the building and walking quickly to his car, a small case in each hand.

As a few minutes later he pursued the American on the Ronda road Miller wished he had a faster car.

He also wished he had some idea how far they were going.

He also wished that he was better prepared. Canning's cases had not suggested a short trip.

Ha also wished he could get the chance to ring Cruickshank.

He also wished he could get some food, some coffee.

Above all he wished he could have a gin. Just one gin. A large, cold, neat gin.

For over an hour they climbed until they reached the plateau and Miller saw Canning's car heading towards the lights of Ronda. The American did not stop in the town, however, but took the new by-pass to the Seville road. Miller guessed that this was the destination.

He looked at the petrol gauge. It was half empty. God, he thought, what's wrong with me? Elementary training had taught him to keep the tank filled. To have funds with him – more than the 20,000 pesetas in his pocket. And to be ready for a long journey at short notice.

He reached down and felt the pistol in his inside jacket pocket. At least he had that.

Maria had been on the road for seventy minutes when she reached an extraordinary rock, shaped like a matador's hat. This she knew was the Montera del Torero, the hill of the matador, the beginning of the *ruta del toro*. She drove on past the proud and private bull town of Medina Sidonia and after crossing the Rio Guadalete she diverted into the town of Jerez de la Frontera, driving down pleasing cobbled streets and lanes shaded by orange trees and old and well-preserved buildings, before entering the wide avenue to the huge fairground, where the annual horse fair takes place. She recalled her own appearances there riding beside Juan Garcia, both of them looking aristocratic and handsome on their big black horses.

She recalled, too, her dreams that she and Brian would appear there together, and how impressed she had been by him on horseback the day they had ridden into the hills to visit the site of his project.

As she drove past the fairground and turned east onto the main highway to Seville, paying the toll to drive on the motorway past the fields of grapes that would be used to make Jerez sherry, she prayed that Brian could explain what had happened, that the dream would be kept alive.

She was still praying nearly an hour later when she turned off the main road and drove up to the *hacienda* that was home.

Praying that Brian would share his problems, the truth, with her.

Cruickshank looked at his watch. He had sent the car for her in plenty of time. Where on earth was it? He walked out onto the balcony and looked at the beach. He remembered seeing her for the first time, remembered how striking she had been, and clenched his fists with frustration at the way the joy of her friendship was being marred by the problems over the project.

He thought again of what he would say to her, and how he would tell her the truth, ask for her understanding, involve her in the decision about what to do.

At last he heard the car in the drive and, picking up his jacket, walked impatiently to the front door, only to find the new chauffeur alone on the steps.

'Sir Brian, the señorita, she was not there.'

'Not there? What do you mean, not there?'

'She's gone.'

'Gone!' He went cold. What had happened. Surely Canning . . . no, it couldn't be possible.

'She left a letter, Señor.'

Cruickshank was relieved. If she had left a letter then she had not been taken. There had to be a straightforward explanation. He snatched the envelope from the chauffeur's hand and, walking quickly indoors, tore it open and read the letter with mounting distress.

Dear Brian,

I am sorry to inconvenience you this evening. I have returned to Seville. I have decided that it would be better if we do not see each other any more. Please do not pursue me. My decision is final. Thank you for your kindnesses.
Maria.

It didn't make sense. Something had happened. Damn it . . . Canning! It had to be Canning. Everything else that had gone wrong had been Canning's fault . . . why should this be different?

He snatched up the phone and rang the yacht. Canning wasn't there.

He rang Julio and asked him what he knew.

'I don't know Sir Brian. She left us a note too. To be honest, I assumed you and she had a . . . misunderstanding . . . and that she had gone home for that reason.'

Cruickshank asked for her address and phone number in Seville.

The architect sounded unhappy. 'Well, I don't know . . .'

'Damn it, Julio, get it. I can find it without much trouble. But you'll cost me time. *So get it!*'

The architect disappeared for a moment and came back with the details.

Cruickshank rang off abruptly and then called the Seville number. A Spanish maid answered the phone. Then a man came on the line. 'Sir Brian? This is Juan Garcia. My daughter has telephoned and told us she is coming home. I hope that, if there is a misunderstanding, it can be cleared up, but until she chooses to speak to you I must request that you await her call.'

Cruickshank gripped the phone tightly in his hand. 'Of course I respect your request ... I must ask you, however, to assure Maria of my devotion to her and to tell her that whatever is upsetting her will be put right. Will you do that much for me?'

'Of course, Sir Brian. If explanation is due to you I assure you that you will receive it.'

Cruickshank poured himself a Scotch and went out onto the balcony.

'Maria,' he thought. 'I will do whatever I have to do. But please, please don't leave me.'

For two more hours they drove until they reached Seville. Miller had made a half-hearted attempt to avoid being spotted as he drove behind the American but once more it had proved extremely difficult and he still had the uneasy feeling that his presence was noted and considered of no consequence. Why did Canning not care?

It was after midnight but the city streets were alive with people. Canning seemed unperturbed by the traffic. He drove slowly into the centre, passing the Plaza de España and making his way via the Glorieta de Don Diego and the Avenida del Cid to the Calle San Fernando. He then turned the Porsche into the grounds of the palatial Alfonso XIII, a magnificent old hotel within sight of the cathedral and the Giralda.

Christ, thought Miller, probably the most expensive hotel in town. He would have to get Cruickshank to send up some money in the morning.

He followed Canning into the big car park and, stopping some distance away, watched in the rearview mirror as the American took his cases and went into the hotel. He allowed ten minutes for him to get his room and then walked in and enquired whether there was a room available. Only one – a last minute cancellation – a double at 20,000 pesetas. Miller groaned inwardly but smiled outwardly and accepted.

Unfortunately it wasn't as simple as that. The clerk looked suspiciously at his unshaven, gaunt face and the rumpled suit, sniffed at the gin on his breath, and enquired whether Miller had luggage. Told that he didn't, the clerk then insisted he be paid in advance. Miller had to struggle even harder to appear unperturbed. This would leave him with only a handful of coins. Still what could he do?

He was at least pleased to find his first floor room overlooked the car park. He could see Canning's car and reckoned he could get out to his own within two minutes if necessary. He sat in the window and waited.

As Miller disappeared upwards in the lift, Canning emerged from behind a pillar. Pausing only to request Miller's room number, he smiled to himself and returned to his own room where he unpacked his small case, ordered dinner and a bottle of red Rioja, and settled down for the night.

Miller, he guessed, would have little choice but to stay awake watching for him.

All night.

And that Canning found amusing.

Canning was right. Miller was a frustrated and unhappy man. A prisoner in his expensive room, without money, and unable to contact Cruickshank, who apparently was involved in dealing with some crisis of his own and wouldn't take his call, he sat in the window for three hours watching both the front entrance and Canning's Porsche without reward.

Morosely he picked up the phone to try once more to contact Cruickshank to tell him his fiancée, the love of his life, was in danger of being attacked by a psychopath and that he, Miller, had no idea where or when the move was likely to come. But Cruickshank now wasn't reachable at all. He had been due after having dinner with Maria to take the last plane from Malaga to Madrid to attend a meeting at the headquarters of the project's bankers in the morning and, according to Hobbs, had in fact now left without dinner to catch an earlier flight. He wouldn't be back till at least mid-afternoon tomorrow. Usually there would be a hotel number but, because the meetings had been fixed at the last minute, Cruickshank had said he would organise accommodation himself when he arrived in Madrid. He could, therefore, not be contacted till the morning or until he got in touch.

Miller left instructions that he was to be telephoned urgently at the hotel.

He would, he decided, ring Maria in the morning – if he had not heard from Cruickshank by 10 a.m.

Guessing that Canning was holed up for the night, he turned on the television set, uninterestedly tried all the channels, and then switched it off. He had a shower and lay down on the bed but his head was aching and he still felt restless. Then he noticed for the first time a brown safe-like box in a corner of the room. A refrigerator. A mini-bar!

Miller knew he mustn't drink, but there could be food in there. Peanuts or crisps. He checked the keys provided by the hotel. One of them fitted the lock. He opened it and there he discovered shelf after shelf of bottles. Little bottles. Shiny bottles. Wickedly enticing bottles of alcohol.

Miller hesitated. He could recall no hour in his life when he wanted ... no, *needed* ... a gin as much as he wanted and needed it now. Not since Belfast. Yet he also knew that he had reached a moment of truth. His professionalism was vital for the safety of not just his client, but the girl too.

He hadn't blown it yet.

He was on the scene, on Canning's trail.

He had to stay on the alert, mobilise all of his skill and experience, call on every reserve of energy.

What he didn't need was gin.

Yet what he desperately *did* need was gin.

For several minutes he stood looking at the refrigerator. Then he was struck by a thought. All the bottles were different. There was only one bottle of gin.

One gin. *One tiny bottle.* There was, therefore, no way that one could lead to another.

One gin. It would reduce the pain of the headache. It would help him to think more clearly.

One gin. He quickly removed the bottle, unscrewed the lid, and drained it neat.

Chapter Twelve

TUESDAY, APRIL 10

Miller dreamed there were little men breaking rocks inside his head, pounding at them with sledgehammers, just behind the eyes. The pain was unbearable, and the dust was accumulating in his throat so that he could hardly breathe. Rolling over, he slowly, painfully, lifted his head from the ground and stared about him.

He could see the rocks now. They were scattered all about. Small, round shiny rocks. Like bottles.

He reached out for one, then shrank from the touch. It was a bottle. They were *all* bottles. Small bottles. With a huge effort he picked one up and squinted at it. The label said *Gin*. He picked up another. *Whisky*. A third. *Brandy*. He looked around him. *Vodka. Dubonnet. Sherry*. All bottles. All empty. Miller groaned. The bottles in the mini-bar. He must have drunk the lot.

He crawled to the bathroom and, after being horribly sick, soaked his head under the cold water tap and took some aspirins to combat the splitting headache.

Somehow he succeeded in making himself a cup of

coffee and focusing his mind on what he was doing in Seville. Then, head thumping and hands shaking as he dialled, he tried to telephone Cruickshank. The yacht was unresponsive (probably, he guessed, on instructions from Canning) and Hobbs at the villa couldn't help either. So he rang the *hacienda* only to be told that the Garcias were out for the day, visiting their horse ranch north of the city. The man-servant said that he was not permitted to give the number at the ranch to strangers, so Miller asked him to pass on a message for Maria to ring him urgently.

He slowly dressed and pulled the curtains back just in time to see Canning, a small case in each hand, striding towards his car. Grabbing his own car keys, he raced unsteadily down the stairs and round the front of the hotel to the car park. He could see the Porsche already leaving the hotel grounds.

As he steered his car towards the car park exit he saw ahead of him a pay booth and, blocking his way, a wooden barrier. Having no small change and no time to negotiate with the Spanish attendant in a language he was nowhere near mastering, he took the only course open to him and, lowering his head, accelerated towards the barrier.

The impact reduced it to splinters.

Ignoring the horrified cries of the parking attendant, he swung the car out onto the road and looked desperately for the Porsche.

Fortunately it had taken time for Canning to negotiate his way into the heavy traffic in the Calle San Fernando and Miller was able to catch up. He still had the feeling that Canning knew he was there and didn't care. He even wondered whether the American had slowed outside the hotel to let him catch up. But why would he do that? Surely he couldn't want to be followed?

They turned left almost immediately and half circled the hotel grounds before driving past the *universidad* to the big roundabout at the Glorieta de Don Diego. From there the Porsche accelerated up a series of wide avenues following the signs to Cordoba.

Miller couldn't understand it. *Cordoba*? If Canning had wanted to go to Cordoba, why come to Seville? It made no sense.

They were almost on the outskirts of the city when he realised that there was another series of signs on the same route. *Aeropuerto. The airport*! And within a matter of minutes they were there. Canning carelessly swung into a vacant space in the car park, took his cases from the car and locked up. Miller parked nearby and followed.

From a telephone booth he watched the American go up to the Iberia Airlines desk. He appeared to buy a ticket with a credit card, then, the purchase made, went across to the bar and settled down with a drink and cigarette, always looking straight ahead of him, making surveillance easy. Too easy, Miller thought. But why would Canning want to be seen? He looked at the departure board. The next Iberia flight was to Madrid in an hour's time. He stepped into a telephone booth and, after looking up the number while at the same time keeping a close eye on the American, telephoned the Iberia desk. He watched one of the staff answer the phone. He was telephoning from a Mr Canning's office, he said, just checking that Mr Canning had managed to get a ticket for the Madrid plane. Yes, he was assured, a Mr Canning was confirmed on the list for Madrid. He would be there in good time for his onward flight to Miami.

Miami! Miller was as relieved as he was surprised. His worst fears couldn't be justified if Canning was about to leave the country. Feeling positive for the first time since he arrived in Seville, he wandered over to the newspaper stand and purchased a copy of *El Pais*, both to pass the time and to make it easier for him to stay out of view – just in case Canning was not aware he was there.

But Canning was only too aware of Miller.

Having managed to get a fix on the Englishman in the mirror high above the bar, the American had seized the opportunity provided by Miller's visit to the newspaper stand to look round the bar and catch the eye of a thin-faced, dark-haired man with piercing eyes sitting alone at the other end of the bar. There was the briefest exchange of glances. Contact made, the other man had risen and walked away in the direction of the toilets.

Canning now waited until Miller returned with his newspaper and then stayed on for a further three or four minutes before casually standing up and stretching and then strolling to the toilets himself.

Miller watched him go. It was pointless to follow. He knew where Canning was and if he followed he would undoubtedly be seen – assuming, still, that he hadn't been spotted already.

Had he followed Canning he would have seen the American slip into one of the booths, next to the only one that was already occupied. He would have heard the click of Canning's small case and would have spotted an object wrapped in black canvas material being slipped under the partition between the two booths. He would have heard the toilet flush, and would have seen Canning emerge, look around, then leave with a satisfied smile. And some two minutes later he would have seen the other man emerge and go to the taxi rank, and from there depart for the centre of Seville.

But Miller saw none of this. Instead he took the chance to grab a drink at the bar himself, one gin, he decided, being necessary to still the hammers in his head. Then he waited until the American came back to the bar, until his flight was called, until he actually climbed the steps to the plane, until his plane took off.

He paid for the drink with his very last pesetas. He then drove back into the city centre.

Not far from the Palacio de Justicia his car ran out of petrol.

As he had no money left, he was forced to abandon it and walk back to the hotel, his head aching badly once more, sweat pouring down his back, his legs so weak he could hardly stand up.

He found a back gate to the hotel and slipped in, thus avoiding the mini-crowd of hotel staff, police and passers-by, who were standing around the car park, listening to a near-hysterical attendant describing what had happened to his demolished barrier.

High in the hills north of Seville, Maria and her foster-parents arrived to have coffee before riding out to inspect their herd. This day they would select the horses they would ride at the Seville Fair after Easter and at the Jerez Horse Fair some weeks later.

Maria was handed an 'urgent message' to ring Miller in Seville.

'Oh Brian,' she thought, 'you could at least have come to plead for yourself.'

Petulantly, she screwed up the note and threw it away.

Sheedy lay on the couch in his villa trying to put together a thousand disparate thoughts.

The days after Kate had come to Spain had been happier than any he had known since the years before he went to Vietnam, since the years before Jan became ill. And now it was all such a mess.

How much of it was his own fault?

Perhaps he should have taken Kate's advice and

pressed Miguel to involve the police officially after the Rabbit Man's death. Undoubtedly he should have been more cooperative with them after Miguel's death.

Then there was Felipe. What had happened to him? Sheedy found it hard to believe the boy had run away. If he had been threatened he would have come to him, Sheedy, or to Manuel. Kate had been right about that too; they shouldn't have conned the kid. Now it was possible he had also been killed. If so, he, Sheedy, must share the guilt.

His thoughts moved to Maria's second uncle, Diego. Why hadn't Sheedy considered the threat to him earlier?

And Kate. Even she had been harmed. He remembered the scene last night, her trembling body in his arms as they lay awake together, and he felt his anger return.

Well, he would sort it out now. He would have a talk with Inspector Rivas, see if police pressure could now be applied on Cruickshank and his cohorts.

But what could they discover? It had all been so damned neat. There was no *conclusive* evidence that the so-called accidents were murders, even less evidence of who committed them. There was no evidence that Felipe's disappearance was the result of foul play either.

At least there was no doubt that Diego had been murdered – and tortured. But there was no evidence to link anyone to that crime.

The killers were currently in the clear.

What had been the connection between the deaths of the Rabbit Man, Miguel and Diego, and the attack on Kate?

It had to be the papers from the *cortijo*. The evidence of ownership. They had not found either the letter to Maria or the ownership papers on the Rabbit Man, so they must have traced the letter to Miguel, then to Sheedy (hence their visit to the villa) and then learned

Diego had the crucial documents. Somehow they had been a step ahead of him all the way.

But how had they known Miguel had found papers of importance? Or about Diego?

He thought back. Miguel's note to the office – it had only been seen by Rosa, him and Kate. But Miguel had mentioned his new find when he left his message on the villa answer phone. And Sheedy had telephoned Manuel to tell him they were going to Casares to find Diego.

He thought about those telephone calls. Surely the phone hadn't been bugged. He hadn't even considered it. Yet why not? It was not difficult to do. Not even that unusual; it had happened to him in New York, more than once. He went to the phone and unscrewed the base.

Damn it. There it was.

Christ, he thought, I've been careless.

Still there were questions.

Always questions.

Why was the land so important?

Why had the killers changed their approach, come out in the open with their attack on Kate, their murder of Diego?

And could Cruickshank really be behind all this, sanctioning it?

As he sat trying to put the pieces of the jigsaw together in his mind, Kate came from the bedroom, dressed only in a soft dressing gown of white towel material, her red hair flowing around her pale, tired face. His heart went out to her and he rose and took her in his arms. She kissed his neck and said 'It's OK, Sheedy, I'm OK.'

They were interrupted by a call from Manuel at the office. He read to Sheedy a message from Teddy Gray. 'Am coming today, will arrive about noon. Please be available. Important.'

'I'd bet a million dollars that the key to the mystery is on its way,' Sheedy told Kate. 'Teddy doesn't take holidays and he isn't one for amateur dramatics. If he says it's important, it's important.'

Kate took his hands and looked into his face.

'Bill,' she said, 'will you do something for me? For yourself? And for Maria? Will you go and see Cruickshank? I really don't think he knows about any of this and I really don't believe he would sanction what's happening. The project must be out of his control and if you can help to rescue him you should.'

'I don't see why I should, Kate. Even if he's not directly involved, he and his kind are the cause of this, the reason this country is being invaded by people like Canning.'

'Come on, Bill, for Christ's sake. This country has been invaded for centuries, from the Moors to the Romans ... to you and I for that matter. Cruickshank is a businessman and his project is no different from lots of others all over the world – apart from being bigger and better. But the thing is being attacked by a cancer, and we can help to dig it out.'

Sheedy looked doubtful.

'You want me to go? Kate said defiantly.

He laughed and drew her to him. 'You know better. OK, you're right. I'll ring Cruickshank.'

He rang the yacht. Cruickshank was in Madrid. Unreachable. No-one knew when he would be back.

Sheedy put down the receiver and looked at the phone thoughtfully. 'I don't like it. Cruickshank is always reachable.'

He rang Manuel. 'Get down to Puerto Banus quickly and wait till you see Cruickshank arriving. Get a message to him to ring me immediately, and tell him he must ring from somewhere off the yacht.'

★

Jim Miller was not a happy man.

He had booked into the hotel for a second night and still didn't have the money to pay for it. (Fortunately keeping the room had been easier than getting it in the first place.)

He had lost his car.

He was having to sneak round the hotel to avoid being seen by the car park attendant and asked to explain the demolished barrier.

He still hadn't been able to speak to either his employer or the young Spanish woman, Maria.

He had spent an hour carefully refilling the little bottles, water for gin and vodka, coffee and tea for the darker drinks, and was now worrying whether they looked convincing.

And, after the initial sense of relief, Canning's departure from the country had not ended his feeling of unease. He couldn't imagine why the American had left, and in particular why he had chosen to fly from Seville? Why hadn't he taken a plane from Malaga?

His every instinct told him that Maria was in danger. But from whom?

Despite Canning's departure, he decided he would wait in Seville until he had spoken to Cruickshank.

He wandered down to the beautiful inner courtyard of the old hotel and ordered a black coffee. As he casually stirred it he looked around at the others relaxing in the big leather armchairs. He was just about to return his eyes to the coffee when they rested on a man sitting alone in the far corner of the courtyard. There was something vaguely familiar about him ... especially the piercing eyes, staring out of a distinctively thin face. Miller looked at him closely. But it didn't help. He couldn't place him.

He returned to his room and tried Maria's number once more.

The Garcias had been relaxing over lunch under the verandah of their ranch. Juan, never happier than on horseback in this rugged country and in no hurry to leave, had suggested they could spend more time at the ranch and avoid crossing the city if they went directly to their Seville flat and changed there for the Holy Week processions.

A servant came out of the house with a message for Maria. Miller had phoned the *hacienda* several times, still pressing her to call him at his hotel. This only caused her to feel even more depressed and sad. Why couldn't Cruickshank try to make contact himself? This was not the behaviour of a gentleman, not at all what she would have expected from the man she loved.

'I'm going to have a *siesta*,' she said. And, under the concerned gaze of her guardians, she went to her room where, the second note also torn up and left on the floor by the bed, she wept in her desolation.

Trapped in his hotel room by lack of money, by the need to wait for phone calls from Cruickshank and Maria, and by fear of the security guards, Miller had been dozing and trying to ignore the pounding in his head.

Until he remembered.

The man downstairs with the piercing eyes – he *had* seen him before.

He had noted him in the bar at the airport when Canning was there. Now he was at the same hotel where Canning had stayed.

Of course it could be a coincidence, but there had been too many coincidences in this whole business already.

After all, why had the man been at the airport bar? If he were leaving Seville he would now be on a plane. If he were arriving it was unlikely he would have gone to the bar; he would have wanted to get out of the airport as quickly as possible to head for the city.

Unless he had been waiting to meet someone.

Canning, for instance.

Miller began to think back. What had happened in the bar? He remembered Canning going to the toilet. And he remembered noticing that at that time there was no-one in the bar at all. That meant the other man must have left before Canning. Had he gone to the toilet too? Was it possible that when they were alone Canning had given the man instructions?

Instructions to do what? Kill? He thought about the small case. Had Canning given the man a gun? Had they sent in a new killer – a new Canning? It all made sense. It explained why Canning wasn't worried about having Miller on his tail; he actually *wanted* Miller to see him leave the country. *Miller was his alibi.* As for the new man, he would not have been able to smuggle a gun past airport security; hence the need for Canning to make contact at the airport.

With a new sense of urgency Miller got on the phone. But he still couldn't get a reply from Maria and he still couldn't track down Cruickshank.

Then he remembered the television reporter, Sheedy. He got on to directory enquiries and ten minutes later was talking to the friendly American.

Francisco Benegas could hardly contain himself. It had been three months since the priest and one of the *Confraternity*, the brotherhood, had come to his family's house in the crowded Triana district of Seville and told him that he had been chosen to be one of the penitents in the *Semana Santa* procession. He would share with another boy the honour of carrying the great gold cross from behind the altar of the church and would walk in front of the *paso*, the float containing the church's statue of the Madonna. Francisco at seventeen would be the youngest penitent.

It was the fulfilment of a dream. The last of eight children, he had been born some six years after the others, and had always been his mother's special one. Lithe, with jet-black hair and brown eyes, he had been the only one of the younger children not clothed in pass-me-downs, had been unashamedly favoured, and for as long as he could remember had gone night after night in Holy Week to watch the great processions, holding his mother's hand, and hearing her whisper, 'One day, Francisco, you will carry the Cross.'

On Sundays, long after the other children had mastered the art of evading mass, he had still gone to church with his mother and his sisters and sat gazing in awe at the great gold cross and dreaming that his mother's promise would be kept and that, clad in penitent's garb, he would carry it across the bridge and into the heart of the city, past the dignitaries in the big plaza, and into the great Cathedral itself.

It had become an obsession, shared between mother and boy, and, once Francisco reached an age and developed a strength that made it possible, his mother had applied ceaseless pressure on the priest, inviting him to dinner, feeding him his favourite *rabo de toro* even when she could ill-afford it, assisting with the flowers in the church, helping decorate the float for the procession, and begging him so often that in the end he caved in and persuaded the *Confraternity* to give Francisco preference and thus get the woman off his back.

For days the excited Francisco had talked of little else. His mother had made for him the dark-brown cloak that stretched from head to feet and his father added the pointed black hood with slits for his eyes and mouth.

He had scorned shoes. If he was going to be a penitent

he was going to play the part to the full and walk barefoot the whole way.

Now the moment had come and he proudly joined the others as they assembled at the church in the late afternoon. The senior brothers briefed them once more on the programme. They would take about an hour to parade down the narrow, crowded streets of Triana and over the bridge, the Puente de Isabella 11. They would continue up the Calle de los Reyes
Catolicos into Calle de San Pablo and past the big church, the Santa Maria Magdalena. From there they would begin to veer to their right up the Calle de Rioja until they got to the famous narrow trafficless street, the Calle Sierpes. They would make their way down between its bars and bazaar-like shops until they came to the Plaza San Francisco where they would appear before the city fathers and dignitaries and the huge crowds that would be sitting in stands in a specially-created amphitheatre. After leaving the plaza they would proceed down the wide Avenue de la Constitution to the cathedral, entering by a side door and making their way through the cathedral and back out beside the Giralda into the Plaza de la Virgen de los Reyes where they would be greeted by another huge crowd. From there they would follow a shorter, more direct route alongside the river, back to Triana. All this would take about six and a half hours.

At last, they were on their way. In front walked the priests and church elders, swaying under their heavy gold and red robes, some carrying containers of perfumes and incense, several carrying great crooks embellished with jewels, silver and gold. Behind them came the penitents, carrying crosses or big, white wax candles ready to be lit at dusk. Then came the *paso*, the float carrying the Madonna as Our Lady of Sorrows. The Madonna, lovingly carved from wood, was seated on a throne, surrounded by flowers and sheltered by a velvet canopy, and was bedecked with jewels and lit by candles on silver sticks. Under the float, bearing its weight, hidden by a purple curtain, were some twenty shuffling *costaleros*, porters, their backs bent, unable to see a thing, gasping for breath, and having to rest every few yards and be supplied frequently with drinking water and occasionally be exchanged with someone else to share the burden. Behind the float came a small band of trumpeters and drummers, the latter setting the tempo with a sombre, steady beat.

It was a proud procession that set off from Triana, no-one prouder than Francisco himself.

It was 5 p.m.

At 5 p.m. Cruickshank was just arriving back at Puerto Banus.

He felt as if the day had already gone on forever. He had tried to pay attention at the two Madrid meetings, one financial and one legal, but his thoughts had kept straying to Maria. What was she doing? What was she thinking? What could he do to make things right?

Eventually he couldn't stand the strain any longer and, cutting the second meeting short, he had taken an earlier plane back to Malaga, and from there travelled in the Rolls to the port where he found Manuel waiting at the red and white barrier.

He reacted with impatience to the young Spaniard's request to him to telephone Sheedy and Manuel had virtually to stage a sitdown in front of the car before, using its mobile telephone, he made the call. He listened for less than a minute before asking Manuel to guide him to the villa.

On arrival he found Sheedy with a short, over-weight, balding American, his feet up on the balcony rail.

Judging by the bottles at his feet he was on his third or fourth beer.

Sheedy introduced him as Ted Gray, a crime reporter on *The New York Times*, an old friend and rival. Sheedy appeared to be about to spell out details of Gray's career when Cruickshank cut him short. 'This isn't a social call, Mr Sheedy. If you and your friend have any information of concern to me, I suggest you get on with it.'

Gray looked at Sheedy, raised his eyebrows, and with a shrug began to describe his two-year investigation into the way that organised crime syndicates, especially the Mafia, invested their income in legitimate businesses.

As he listened, Cruickshank's heart sank. In any circumstances Gray's story would have held his un-divided attention, but already he was beginning to see its implications for the project and himself and it was worse than he could possibly have imagined.

Gray explained that the 'laundering' of money from crime was now a big and highly-sophisticated business. Billions of dollars were involved. Whole industries, respectable in every other way, were under-pinned, usually unknowingly, by the profits from drugs, prostitu-tion, protection rackets, illicit gambling. Jordan was at the centre of it, the acknowledged genius at laundering dirty money. So brilliantly was it done, so sound was the façade around Jordan and his range of finance and other companies, that Gray had, after two years' investi-gation, produced little credible evidence to justify the major exposé he hoped to write.

However, Jordan was running out of safe businesses and industries in the United States. He had begun to look for international opportunities to invest his 'client's' money. Outside his American setting he was more visible and more vulnerable and as a result Gray's enquiries were making headway.

The reporter established that the financier had opted

for the Costa del Sol for the laundering of criminal cash but also as a place where additional money could be made. Jordan, it appeared, was no longer content to be the banker, the investor, the middle man. Ten per cent was not enough. He was going into business for himself.

According to Gray, Jordan had decided the Costa del Sol offered all the essentials for a spread of American-style criminal or near-criminal activity. It also had one new ingredient – cocaine, smuggled in from South America, from Bolivia, Colombia, and Peru.

Apart from its cultural and linguistic ties with South America, Spain's proximity to North Africa, its 4,000 miles of coastline with twelve major ports and hundreds of smaller harbours and marinas, and its easy access to and from France and Portugal, made it an ideal 'warehouse' for drugs intended for the whole of Europe.

On the Costa del Sol, marijuana trafficking had been rife for years, and the profits considerable. A kilo of resin purchased in Morocco for 50,000 pesetas was worth 150,000 pesetas if sold a few miles across the Mediterranean in Marbella (600,000 pesetas if smuggled on into the UK). Cocaine smuggling had developed into big business over the past three or four years. While it originated in South America, seventy per cent of it came via Miami. From there, relatively small packages would come by courier on ordinary passenger flights to Madrid, and the big shipments would be sent by sea, sometimes to be unloaded first in North Africa, sometimes to be switched to fishing boats in the Mediterranean in the middle of the night. Billions of pesetas' worth of cocaine was being landed on the Costa del Sol on a regular basis. While the cocaine was destined for every major European city, a considerable proportion of the profit remained on the costa.

Gray told Cruickshank that the Costa del Sol had special attractions for the drug cartel. For instance, nearby Gibraltar's offshore banking facilities enabled funds to be easily transferred to legitimate businesses, and the real estate market on the costa provided unlimited opportunity for this. The big tourist industry would sustain an expansion of gambling. And the many men with plenty of ready money who came to the costa on golfing holidays were the ideal target for a prostitution and possible blackmail racket. There was, too, no shortage of experienced villains who could be employed locally. For a start there were around 100 Britons living on the costa who were wanted in their own country.

Jordan had missed none of this. Instead of just providing his expertise in laundering money to the drug traffickers, he had entered fully into the business himself, importing to Spain and then exporting to countries further north. At least half the money he was now seeking to invest on the costa was his own.

Gray, aware that Cruickshank was looking increasingly agitated, turned to the project. 'Jordan needs a base for his operations. Your project is ideal – for investment of huge sums of drugs-earned money in real estate; for gambling; for drugs and prostitution. Jordan plans to alter it to a Spanish Las Vegas once you have created the physical circumstances. *Just imagine it – a European Las Vegas.* Provided the authorities can be squared, the potential is unlimited. And I'm sorry to tell you, Sir Brian, you were the ideal frontman, respectable, diplomatic and good at handling the Spanish. And vulnerable. Jordan is letting you set the whole thing up. When he's ready he'll take over, put his own plans into effect, and bribe and bully any official or politician who gets in his way.'

'How do you mean, I'm vulnerable?' Cruickshank asked, his face flushing.

Gray looked at him without sympathy. 'Ambitious and vain ... fascinated by money and power. Somebody whose obsession with a dream would make him blind to what was happening. Someone who could be persuaded that ends justified means until he was in too deep to extract himself. These men are clever. If they spot the tiniest weakness, they'll have you.'

Cruickshank, stunned by what he had been told, made no attempt to defend himself. 'Maybe so, but I still don't understand the killing. It wasn't necessary and it endangered their whole plan.'

'I suspect Canning is their Achilles' heel. As you will have discovered he is a brilliant operator but he's a psychopath. My guess is that the killing of the old man *was* an accident in the sense that it was unplanned. The opportunity arose, too good an opportunity to miss, and Canning just took it. To him it was just business and with a bit of luck he would have got away with it. But as for the policeman and Miss Garcia's other uncle, that's been Canning acting as he would in Miami, or New York. He doesn't seem to appreciate the difference between the US and the Costa del Sol. Over there you can wipe out a few people as a matter of efficient business and it virtually goes unnoticed. In Spain it's not so.'

Sheedy joined the discussion. 'The truth is, Sir Brian, that while you may be completely innocent of any ill intent, it's your kind of venture that has led to the costa becoming of increasing interest to crooks. You could say that the killing of the old man was symbolic of the way these modern-day activities are killing the best of the old Spain.'

Cruickshank looked at the end of his tether. 'Mr Sheedy, what can I do to put it right?'

'Expose it now.'

The Englishman nodded and then, suddenly decisive, stood and said, 'I'll do what has to be done, Mr Sheedy. But, first, I must get to Maria. To ensure her safety and

334

to discuss with her what I have to do.'

Sheedy's expression softened. Damn it, he couldn't help liking the man. He offered to drive Cruickshank to Seville, persuading him that his two-seater would negotiate the winding roads and the traffic in Seville more easily than the Rolls.

'In any case, I'm still a reporter, Sir Brian, and this is still my story.'

They left for Seville at 6 p.m.

It took less than an hour to climb to Ronda. Ignoring the new by-pass, Sheedy drove up past the hotel where he remembered with a private smile he had first held Kate's naked body in his arms. After a few kilometres on the Seville road they entered a dramatic mountain pass between steep, rock- and shrub-covered hills. Once over it they were in the midst of rich farming country, fields full of corn, and hills covered with sunflowers. To their left they spotted in the distance Grazalema, clinging to a mountain and surrounded by pine trees. Sheedy pointed it out to Cruickshank as the place where the Rabbit Man had been born.

He looked at the grim-faced financier and, feeling sorry for him, said, 'Look, Sir Brian, do you not think you should tell me all you know?'

Cruickshank looked gratefully at the American. Then, with evident relief, began to talk – about the call from Canning telling him of the death of the Rabbit Man; about his plans to expose the killing; about Jordan's intervention; about his decision to cover up and why he did it; about his belief that all the problems had been overcome . . . until the death of Miguel.

'There is no point in denying it, Mr Sheedy. I should have gone to the police about the Rabbit Man and I didn't. But I genuinely believed that it would achieve little, and that by staying in control I could help the

project to come to fruition in a way satisfactory to everyone.'

'Would you have done the same thing if it had been in
the UK?'

'What do you mean?'

'I mean that when people move onto foreign soil,
places like the Costa del Sol, they play by different rules.
A murdered worker in the UK and you would have been
talking to Scotland Yard within minutes. A dead Spanish
peasant, who cares?'

Cruickshank thought. 'No, I don't necessarily accept
that. My actions were not influenced by the fact he was
Spanish or a peasant. But that one acts differently out of
one's own setting, yes, that's possible. Perhaps I don't
belong here.'

'You don't strike me as the usual kind of Costa del Sol
developer.'

'But that's the point, Mr Sheedy, I didn't want to be.
I wanted the project to be special. The Costa del Sol was
just the place chosen; it could have been anywhere
where the climate and the land was suitable.'

'Exactly. Don't you think developing Spain should be
in the hands of people concerned about Spain rather
than people just building another resort and making
another buck?'

'Well, that's for the planning authorities and the
politicians to decide. If they think this kind of activity is
inappropriate they should say so.'

'Yes? Were they given no incentives?'

'Maybe a few. But they didn't have to accept them. In
any case, there were also incentives for the community –
employment, and more money coming into the area.'

'And you had no idea what kind of man Jordan was?'

Cruickshank shook his head. 'He could not have been
more highly recommended, or by more reputable people.
His finance company in New York doesn't just deal in

criminal money; there are enough respectable names dealing with him to guarantee better references than even I could hope to get. Don't forget your friend Gray has been investigating Jordan for two years and he's still short of evidence.'

Sheedy grinned. 'It'll be ironic if it's this business that brings Jordan down.'

Cruickshank didn't reply. He was thinking of the others, not least himself, who Jordan would take down with him.

Francisco was tiring. He had been walking now for over two hours. Twice he had stubbed his unprotected toes and one was bleeding. He was sweating under the heavy costume and the prickly material was scratching his skin. Also the cross had been heavier than he imagined. But still he would not have changed places with anyone.

The pavements had been crowded in the Triana district as the locals had come out from homes and shops to applaud their own procession, one they wanted to be more splendid than any other. The crowds had become thinner once they crossed the bridge and entered the broad Calle de Los Reyes Catolicos, but were now beginning to build up as they approached the big church, Santa Maria Magdalena, halfway up the Calle San Pablo.

As people pointed to the ornate, gold cross, Francisco raised his head proudly, sorry that the pointed, sinister-looking Ku Klux Klan-style hood hid his face so that they could not know that it was he, Francisco Benegas, the youngest of the brotherhood, who was carrying it.

In particular he looked out for his family. They had promised that before they went to the Plaza San Francisco they would wait on the church steps to see him pass. And there they were, his mother looking as if she would burst with pent-up pride, his father looking ill-at-ease in a suit but breaking into a broad, near-toothless grin as he recognised the slim figure of his son near the front of the procession. Francisco gravely bowed his head in their direction and was rewarded by his mother breaking into tears. For a few moments he forgot his aches and pains; he could have been floating on a cloud for all he was aware of the concrete under his feet.

It was 6.30 p.m.

For a while they drove in silence. The smart motorway outside Ronda had given way to a much rougher country road with potholes and multiple repairs. Soon they reached the Province of Cadiz, crossing the boundary river, the Arroyo Montecordo, and passing the turn to El Gastor, before approaching the dramatic mountain village of Zahara. They could see its cemetery cut into the rock, and an abandoned castle or fort on top.

Now the quality of the road improved once more and Sheedy increased his speed. He asked 'What will you do now? Will you abandon the project, even if you can regain control?'

Cruickshank replied, 'That will depend.'

'On what?'

'On Maria Garcia.'

'Why?'

'This will probably sound pathetic to you, Mr Sheedy, but I couldn't live in Spain without her. She and the project are now merged in my mind. If she doesn't want to marry me after all this, I will withdraw and dismantle the project or sell my interest in it.'

'You really love her?''

'Yes, Mr Sheedy, for the first time in my life I know what it is to really love and be loved. In some ways I wish I hadn't found out, but now I have and I cannot live without it. At least not in Spain.'

Sheedy smiled at the Englishman. 'I understand.'

'Do you?'

'Yes, we're both within a few years of each other and both newly involved with a younger woman. I understand exactly. Of course I had loved before . . . my wife. I never thought I could be so happy with anyone else, but I am.'

'Ah yes, Miss Callaghan?'

'Yes.'

Sheedy looked at the pale face of the man beside him. He looked exhausted and defeated. 'Look, Sir Brian, I know this is no consolation but I feel as responsible for all this as you. If I had left the question of the old man's death alone, it's possible Miguel would still be alive. And Diego. And possibly someone else.' He thought sadly of the vanished Felipe. 'And Kate would not have been assaulted. I thought I could play God and it's caused havoc. We both thought we could play God. You over part of the Costa del Sol. Me as self-appointed policeman. We'll both have a lot to think about when this is over.'

Cruickshank shrugged. He didn't have the strength to console the other for his feelings of guilt, nor did they appear comparable with his own problems. He began to think aloud. He would, he said, fly from Seville to Malaga and make a clean breast of the whole affair to the police and the provincial administrators there.

'You will admit you covered up the death of the Rabbit Man?'

Cruickshank looked at him. 'I suppose I've no choice.'

'No,' said Sheedy, 'none at all.'

'I see. Yes, I suppose it always was inevitable.' He shook his head sadly, only now realising the full implications of his situation. 'That makes my continued involvement in the project equally improbable. It will probably endanger the project itself. And it won't do me much good in the UK either.'

'All because your people could not adapt to the priorities of one old Spanish peasant.'

'Ah well, Mr Sheedy, I've always said that it's not big people who bring big people down. It's little people who are underestimated or taken for granted.'

It was taking longer than planned. The youths carrying the float were finding it hard going and having to rest frequently, and the traffic chaos caused by the assembling crowds led to further unscheduled stops. Processions from a number of districts were converging on the centre, causing their own traffic congestion. The heart of Seville was rapidly becoming a huge, slow-moving mass of people. The police were having to create uniformed human barriers at the junctions between streets, stopping and starting the spectators as they walked to the centre, just as if they were cars being controlled by traffic lights.

Francisco was hungry and glad his mother had insisted on putting a chunk of bread with serrano ham in a pocket sewn on the inside of his cloak. But there was another problem. He was desperate to relieve himself. And it wasn't going to be easy. He was in the middle of a procession in the middle of a crowd and there was a long way to go. He could, of course, just do it under the cloak as he walked, but someone could notice and call out, and Francisco would die rather than suffer that humiliation. He would just have to struggle on. This was all proving a greater penitence than Francisco had expected.

It was 8 p.m.

The clear sky was replaced by smog. Seville lay ahead. They passed huge blocks of commuter workers' flats. The regional command centre of the *Guardia Civil* was about five kilometres from the centre, on the junction with the N4. The road to Malaga and Cordoba was on the right, the one to Cadiz on the left, and Seville straight ahead.

Sheedy swung the car off the road and drove up to the police headquarters. There the two men impatiently waited three or four minutes until directed to a senior officer. Sheedy briefly told him the story. The officer listened impassively until the Garcias were mentioned. Then he sat up and took notice. Clearly it was one thing to be uncaring about the ravings of a couple of manic foreigners, another to overlook a warning that one of Seville's most distinguished families was in danger. His problem was that most of his men were on duty on the streets of Seville coping with the crowds gathered there for the processions. Some were even taking part. Only after he had tried to telephone and got no reply did he put together a group of half a dozen men, telling Sheedy and Cruickshank that the Garcias' *hacienda* was only a few kilometres away on the Jerez road.

It was 8.40 p.m.

Having changed for the evening the Garcias had called on friends who lived in the centre of Seville within sight of the cathedral, and there they waited until it was time to take their place with the Mayor and other city dignitaries on the platform of the Plaza San Francisco.

It was Maria who, thinking of the servants patiently waiting for them at the *hacienda*, proposed they should ring and say they were going directly to the plaza.

Secretly she hoped, too, there would be a message from Brian.

But the number was unobtainable. It was, said the operator, as if the line had been cut. Maria shrugged. Problems with the telephone were not unusual in Spain.

She rejoined her guardians who with their friends

were sharing a bottle of sherry from the Garcias' own small *bodega* in Jerez.

It was 9 p.m.

The procession had been at a standstill for nearly twenty minutes. Another from a church to the west of the city had reached the Calle Sierpes just before the Triana one and the men from Triana were having to wait until it made its way past and then wait another quarter of an hour to allow a suitable gap between processions. Francisco, however, couldn't wait any longer. He whispered to the penitent nearest to him. 'I'm desperate. I'm afraid I'll wet myself.'

'It's no problem,' he was reassured. 'We won't be moving for several minutes. Give me the cross and just slip down that alley there. Maybe somebody will let you into their house.'

Grateful for the minimal encouragement he needed, the youngster exchanged the cross for the other's candle and slipped past the thin line of spectators in the narrow street and into a deserted alley. There were plenty of doors to old houses, their upper storeys over-hanging the alley, but they were all closed. No doubt all their owners were in the Calle Sierpes or the Plaza San Francisco watching the procession.

Francisco saw that one house was little more than a shell, apparently being modernised, and was in the meantime only protected by carelessly-erected boarding. He found a gap and edged himself into the derelict building. Moving quickly to a dark corner he obeyed with unbounded relief the call of nature.

He had just zipped himself up and checked his costume was in order when he heard a sound behind him.

He turned, peering through the slits in his mask, just in time to see a face in the dark, a face briefly illumi-

342

nated by the light from a lamppost in the alley, a thin face with piercing eyes.

In the second that was left of his life he was aware of a flashing object coming at his chest.

Then ... oblivion.

Francisco, his sins confessed, his last mass attended, dressed in penitent's clothes and with bare and bleeding feet, had gone to join his maker.

Dead he was left in the street,
with a dagger in the chest.
Nobody knew who he was.
How the lamppost was shaking!
Mother.
How that little lamppost shook
in the street!

The thin-faced killer couldn't believe his good fortune. He had waited over an hour for his opportunity and the boy's urgent need had provided it. It took but a few minutes for him to slip on the costume, to take the compact repeater rifle Canning had given him out of its black canvas wrapping and hide it under the robes, and to pick up the big candle and join the group who were just ready to move off, down the Calle Sierpes and into the Plaza San Francisco where the mayor and the other dignitaries awaited.

It was getting dark and the candles were now burning brightly. The Madonna glittered in the flickering light, the reflections from its eyes making it seem alive, and as it passed the crowds became silent, looking up in awe, the women's lips moving in silent prayer, and even the most macho of men crossing themselves, briefly humbled by the pageantry and affected by the surge of emotion around them. In front of the float the penitents with their tall wax candles found new energy, new pride from the cries and the applause of the crowd, and behind it, as it neared the square, the trumpets blared into new life. The centre of Seville had become a great living theatre, the night full of unforgettable, magnificent spectacle, as one procession left the plaza for the cathedral and the procession from the Triana district entered.

In the stand at the Calle Sierpes end of the plaza Francisco's mother rose from her chair, eager to see her son. Her eyes ranged the row of penitents, her smile fading as she failed to spot him. She looked more closely, inspecting first one shrouded figure, then another. But he was nowhere to be seen. 'Something's gone wrong,' she cried to her husband, 'our Francisco isn't there.'

'Something's wrong,' she called wildly at the crowd. 'My boy is not there.'

Those around her shrugged their shoulders and looked away. In the emotional atmosphere of *Semana Santa* people sometimes did strange things. No-one would take notice of the cries of one hysterical woman.

It was 9.30 p.m.

Down a road travels
Death, crowned with
withered orange blossoms.
Death sings and sings
a song
with her ancient white guitar,
and sings and sings and sings.

The plane was an hour out of Miami. Jason Canning, who had been dozing for a couple of hours, woke and looked at his watch.

It was 9.35 p.m. Spanish time.

He smiled to himself and, summoning the First Class steward, ordered a glass of champagne.

★

It was time to go. The Garcias walked from their friends' flat down the narrow Calle Granada and behind the grandstand in front of the Ayuntamiento. They climbed up the carpeted steps and, after stopping to shake hands and chat to others on the platform, took their places not far from the Mayor.

To their right a procession was just leaving the plaza on its way to the cathedral. They were just in time to see the Madonna swaying in the candle-light and then disappearing round the corner into the Avenue de la Constitution.

They looked to their left, to the other end of the plaza. From the Calle Sierpes another procession had begun to emerge and stopped, presumably so that the porters could rest. They recognised it as the one from Triana.

It was 9.45 p.m.

Sheedy and Cruickshank were lost in the crowds making their way towards the cathedral.

The last half hour had been a nightmare. It had been getting dark when they arrived at the *hacienda.* The two foreigners, the six police officers, and three servants had stood outside the house while it was explained that the phone had not been working that evening. The servants had guessed that the Garcias would go directly to the *Semana Santa* festivities in Seville.

Sheedy had groaned. 'We'll never find them there. There'll be hundreds of thousands of people on the streets.'

'No, Señor,' he was told, 'you can't miss them. They'll be on the main platform outside the Ayuntamiento in the Plaza San Francisco. You can't miss them.'

Sheedy had looked at Cruickshank and said grimly, 'An assassin couldn't miss them either.'

It had been a relatively short drive because the traffic likely to go to Seville this busy night was already there. They had passed the factories and the worker flats on the outskirts following the signs *Centro Ciudad* until they reached the city's wide tree-lined avenues. There they competed for space on the road with black and yellow taxis and orange buses decorated with Expo 92 posters as the traffic became slower. Eventually they had come to a halt, engulfed in the crowds surging towards the pageantry around the cathedral. It was then that Sheedy and Cruickshank had decided they could get no closer by car and, abandoning it, set out on foot, pushing past the spectators, young couples, whole families, old folk, and tearing at their ties as they began to sweat in the warm evening air.

Taking the Giraldo as their focal point they made their way to the cathedral, two middle-aged foreigners lost in a fervent Spanish crowd.

In other circumstances Cruickshank would have been enraptured by it. '*Let us build a church so great that those who see it completed will say we were mad,*' they said in 1401 when they decided to build it. They then laboured on it for 100 years and the result was the third biggest cathedral in the world after St Peter's and St Paul's. Even in his panic Cruickshank marvelled at its size and spectacular beauty, the dark interior brilliantly illuminated by street lights penetrating the stained glass windows and by the multitude of softly-lit chapels. It was a colossal man-made cavern of antiquity, of treasure, testimony to the power and wealth the Catholic church had wielded in Spain.

And it was packed with people and full of spectacle as one by one the processions of the *Semana Santa* entered by one huge wooden door and made their way between its huge pillars to resurface from the Giralda exit into the triangular Plaza de la Virgen de los Reyes, its beautiful fountain and its orange trees lost in a sea of faces. The two men headed for the far corner of the plaza, the one dominated by El Giralda Meson restaurant, and made their way slowly past the crowds up a narrow one-way street until Sheedy, lost, suggested they cut through the Bario de Santa Cruz, a maze of alleys with white-washed houses and bars, flower pots and plants on the window sills, walls covered in posters for bullfights or the theatre.

But they were becoming even more hopelessly disorientated. Finally Sheedy established from a police-man that they were on the opposite side of the cathedral to their destination, the Plaza San Francisco. They forced their way back, twice halted and literally pinned down by the density of the crowd as another procession made its way by. Eventually they were at the back of the cathedral from where Sheedy spotted the Calle Colon. He called to Cruickshank that this was the one they wanted. They battled up it to the narrow Calle Hernado and from there Sheedy at last spotted the green canopy of the Bar Laredo. Many times he had sat at its pave-ment tables, or behind it, in the old Calle de Manteros, at the tables of the *tapas* bar El Porton. He knew the Bar Laredo was on the edge of the plaza. They had found it. Their struggle with the Seville crowds was over.

It was exactly 10 p.m.

Miller, his face white with fury and frustration, was locked in the manager's office of the Hotel Alfonso VIII, awaiting the arrival of the police. He had been captured earlier by the security guards while following the man with the piercing eyes out of the back door.

His protests that he could pay his bill and for the damage to the car park barrier if he could only contact a Sir Brian Cruickshank had impressed no-one, especially as Cruickshank was unreachable.

As for his claim that another of the hotel guests was a hit man and that he, Miller, should be freed to pursue him, it was the most pathetic story the manager had heard in thirty years in the business.

There were, said the manager, too many conmen attempting to defraud hotels. Miller was going nowhere – except eventually to prison.

Miller, defeated, asked for one last gin.

The procession from the Triana, now five hours from its starting point and at last free of the Calle Sierpes, was crossing the plaza, making its way down a lane between spectators packed into the space between the two grandstands. Sheedy and Cruickshank, having climbed some steps at the back, now emerged on top of the stand looking directly across the plaza to the platform with its three gold-carved chairs occupied by the mayor and two other dignitaries. Around about, behind trestle tables with white table cloths, sipping wine and chatting, were other well known Seville families and officials. Near the centre were the Garcias.

Cruickshank found the scene both impressive and frightening. The nearer he got to Maria the more he felt the danger. He tried to call out but it was hopeless. The brassy trumpets, the pounding drums, and the applause and cries of the crowd were deafening. He and Sheedy were face to face with the Garcias now but for all the chance they had of catching their attention from across the plaza they could have been a million miles away. There were no aisles so they began to fight their way down the rows of chairs, climbing over each one, drawing complaints and being obstructed by annoyed spectators as they progressed towards the front.

Eventually they were there, climbing over the front row of chairs and trying to push into the ranks of the procession itself. A *Guardia Civil* officer intervened, ordering them to go back. Sheedy shouted that they had an urgent message, but the policeman, convinced they were just two tourists seeking a better view, restrained them. Sheedy, desperate now, tried to break loose and was immediately pinioned by two more officers. Cruickshank took the chance to slip away and, pushing his way between the priests in their heavily-ornate gowns, got to the other side and began to climb towards the platform.

In her place near the mayor, Maria, pale and sad, had been looking into the plaza with unseeing eyes but now even she was becoming moved by the magic of the night, the fervour of the crowds and the special enthusiasm of the Triana procession. As she began to look intently for the first time she saw at her feet two columns of penitents in dark pointed cone-like hoods, their faces covered except for slits for mouths and eyes. Her eyes on the glittering procession, she did not see Cruickshank climbing the stairs to her left and running down the row towards her, impatiently stumbling over the feet of the other dignitaries on the dais.

One penitent she noticed was different from the others. Instead of looking straight ahead, he was staring at the platform. Directly, she felt, at her.

In the flickering light of his candle she could see his eyes staring through the slits in the hood. Glinting, piercing eyes.

He was, *he definitely was looking at her.*

She saw his cloak rustle. It was as if he was pointing towards her.

Then she heard a familiar voice. Brian's! *It was Brian's!* She looked up, her heart leaping with hope and joy. He had come. To explain. To reassure. It was going to be all right.

Then he was leaning towards her.

He was speaking but his words were drowned by a series of loud banging noises. Fireworks perhaps.

She heard a woman screaming and was half aware of people falling forward across a trestle table near to her.

There was pandemonium. People were climbing over the seats and shouting. She saw several people covered in blood.

It was all happening so quickly and Maria couldn't understand any of it.

For a moment a gap opened in front of her and she saw the American, Sheedy, wrestling a penitent to the ground and calling on a *Guardia Civil* officer to hold him. Why was he doing that? Didn't he understand this was a religious procession?

Then she saw only Cruickshank, now standing over her, between her and the procession, his face full of love, then shock, as with a shudder, as if struck from behind, he began to fall, to fall towards her as she opened her arms to embrace him.

Then she became aware of more blood, blood on Cruickshank's shirt, blood on his hands.

'Brian, Brian . . . what's happening?' she cried.

He saw her white dress, the shape, the beautiful shape of her breasts, the place where he so desperately wanted to bury his head. He reached for her. There were red marks on the dress now. He heard her call his name. He felt her hands, pulling his head down, and then he was there, home, falling into the softness of her, he could hear her heart beating even as his own slowed to a stop.

'I've come home Maria,' he said ' . . . in time, Maria . . . just in time . . . it's the last, Maria . . . the last of the 10,000 deaths.'

From the upstairs window of a building overlooking the plaza, a tall, bald, distinguished-looking American watched the scene impassively.

Then he limped over to a telephone in the corner of the room and made two calls.

350

The first was to book a taxi to take him to the airport.

The second was to a number in New York.

'I want a meeting in the morning,' he told the man who answered. 'The Costa del Sol deal hasn't worked out. We'll have to change our plan.'

'Do you want me to circulate any papers?' he was asked.

He paused for a moment, then said 'Yes. Tell them to read the other file . . . the one on the Costa Brava.'

Epilogue

It was spring of the following year and with spring came flowers, every day adding fresh colour to the hidden valley until it was ablaze with blue and purple, crimson and scarlet, yellow and gold. The orange and lemon trees around the abandoned *cortijo* were heavily pregnant with fruit, the now plentiful rabbits plump in the long grass.

The two riders, man and woman, paused at the top of the hill and looked down at the peaceful scene below. Then, holding tightly to the reins, they carefully guided their horses down the rocky track to the foot of the valley and round the ravine to the *cortijo*. On reaching it they dismounted, the woman choosing to rest under the trees while the man went inside alone.

Little had changed, except there were a few missing items including the old rifles, no doubt taken by passing hunters who knew from the *sierra* grapevine that their owner would never return. He tore down the curtain from over the door to let in the air and pulled down the decaying rabbit skins from the rafters and tossed them out of the back window ready for burning, together with the old bedding and bits of clothing. Then he took an aerosol from a bag on the back of his horse and, re-entering the *cortijo*, he energetically dowsed it in an air-cleansing spray.

He left it to recover from this initial assault and the two sat on the grass and ate fresh bread, *serrano* ham and a salad of lettuce and fresh Andalusian tomatoes. They drank from a *bota* of dry white wine. Then they lay in the grass under a lemon tree and dozed for an hour or so.

Later, escaping the afternoon sun, they both went back into the *cortijo* and swept and dusted and cleaned. While the man collected cones and pieces of wood from under the pines near one wall of the valley, and water from a spring near the ravine, the woman laid out blankets and sleeping bags on the floor and prepared the food they would cook that night under the stars.

In the early evening the man took from his saddle bag two small urns. On one was etched the name *Miguel*, on the other *Pepe* ... El Conejero. Taking one each, they walked slowly and silently across the grass until they stood in the centre of the valley. There they let the breeze catch and sprinkle the two Spaniards' ashes across the land they had loved.

Later, much later, sated with barbecued chicken and hot garlic bread and wine, they lit a fire and, naked and shiny in its glow, they made love on top of the soft bedding, rolling over and over as first one, then the other, set the pace and rekindled the passion of an act that in its intensity seemed to transcend their own desires, as if they were determined to inject human warmth back into the bare walls, the stony floor, and the tiled roof of the *cortijo* itself.

When, eventually, they lay in their separate sleeping bags, the woman spoke.

'I'm glad we came.'

'So am I. You know, I once felt sorry for the Rabbit Man, because he lived alone in these mountains. But he wasn't alone at all. There was life all about him. And beauty. And peace. Thank God there's little chance we'll do to this place what we've all done to the Costa del Sol.'

'It's funny,' she said, 'to think it all began in this valley. If Canning had not thrown that stone the company would probably have got that land in the end, the Rabbit Man would still be alive ... and Miguel ... and Felipe ... and Diego. And Cruickshank would be married to Maria. Do you think he acted on impulse, that in a way it did all happen by accident, or did he come to the valley intending to kill the old man?'

'Who knows? But I keep remembering what Cruickshank said ... that it's not big men who bring other big men down, it's the little men they under-estimate, who they take for granted, who they arrogantly assume to be of no consequence.'

'Maybe Canning, and Cruickshank too, assumed the Rabbit Man had no friends, no-one who would care.'

'Well,' he said, 'maybe there were only two who really missed him ... but two were enough.'

She leaned over and kissed him. He buried his face in her hair and, with the fire still crackling and flickering in the hearth, they began to fall asleep.

The valley was silent now. And still.

And then, out in the moonlight, by the ravine, there was a movement.

It was a rabbit, resting on its hindlegs, its nose twitching with curiosity at the horses grazing near the old building.

A contented rabbit.

Well fed.

Safe.

Or was it?

Back indoors, Bill, reaching out to touch her hair,

354

now aflame with gold in the firelight, said to Kate: 'Tomorrow I'll catch you a rabbit for supper.'

'Oh God,' she giggled sleepily, 'it's the return of the Rabbit Man. Poor little *conejo*. El Conejero is back.'

Out by the ravine, as if it had heard and understood, the rabbit became tense, sprang onto all four legs, and disappeared into the night.

All Sphere Books are available at your bookshop or newsagent, or can be ordered from the following address: Sphere Books, Cash Sales Department, P.O. Box 11, Falmouth, Cornwall TR10 9EN.

Please send cheque or postal order (no currency), and allow 60p for postage and packing for the first book plus 25p for the second book and 15p for each additional book ordered up to a maximum charge of £1.90 in U.K.

B.F.P.O. customers please allow 60p for the first book, 25p for the second book plus 15p per copy for the next 7 books, thereafter 9p per book.

Overseas customers, including Eire, please allow £1.25 for postage and packing for the first book, 75p for the second book and 28p for each subsequent title ordered.